Dreams for the End of Summer

a novel by

Preston Pairo

This is a work of fiction. Any resemblances to actual persons (living or dead), events, or locales is entirely coincidental.

All rights reserved. No portion of this book may be reproduced, copied, performed, or otherwise duplicated without the express written consent of the publisher.

ISBN: 9798844343490

For Moira, as always.

Author's Note

A benefit of digital publishing is the opportunity to keep making books better based upon reader comments. From minor errors that may have slipped by the copy editor to descriptions that could be clearer (or more creative), there is always room for improvement. Your comments are welcomed by email at pres@prestonpairo.com.

September

Hurricane Dominic made landfall just after midnight, causing a powerful tidal wave that surged across the narrowest span of the barrier island, carrying off power lines, houses, cars, and anyone who may have stayed behind after a mandatory evacuation was ordered.

☐

1.

Four months earlier.

"Goodbye, Ms. Tyler! Have a wonderful summer!"

"Watch where you're going, Charlotte!"

The fourth grader tended to look one way while running the other, and countless falls and a scary collision with a tree had failed to break her habit. But that sunny afternoon—the last day of school—Charlotte managed her way without incident, maneuvering through fellow students wildly crisscrossing the sidewalk.

"Fifteen times thirty-nine, Ms. Tyler," pig-tailed Jenny McGaw shouted, racing by.

"Five-hundred, eighty-five," Megan called after her, needing mere seconds to see the answer in her head. "Divided by fifteen," she challenged as the little girl reached her bus.

At the top step, Jenny paused and went into "calculation face"—eyes squeezed shut behind her funky cat-eye glasses, lips pursed as though tasting something bitter—then, bright as a starburst, announced, "Thirty-nine."

"Correct!"

It was a game they'd started back in November when Megan was a volunteer math tutor before Karen Krantz's illness left the school in need of a full-time replacement and Alice asked Megan to fill the position.

To think she'd hesitated about taking the teaching job. The months had passed so quickly and been so rewarding

Megan had actually hoped that summer—her favorite season—would wait just a little longer. But it was here.

Along the small school's front driveway, bus doors were closing, students inside laughing as they settled into their seats. Corrine Taub did a quick curtsey in front of Megan, then hugged her and whispered secretively, "I'm sorry Ms. Krantz got sick, but I'm glad you took over."

Megan kissed the top of the little girl's head. "Have a great summer."

"Will you be here in September?"

"We'll see."

"Just say yes," Corrine encouraged, "and you will be. And if it turns out you're not, that doesn't make it a fib. It's just trying to picture what you want to happen. Like you tell us to do."

"Mm."

"So you'll be here in September? You can picture it?"

Megan nodded. "Yes."

"Good." Corrine clapped, then hurried off to one of the small vans that transported kids who lived farthest away, some traveling as long as an hour to Villa James.

The private school, grades kindergarten through five, was considered exclusive but by no means excluding. Its students were a diverse group, not just culturally and financially, but academically.

Admission standards were as puzzling as the universe itself, which frustrated the hell out of those wealthy parents who couldn't seem to buy their children's way in. Megan wasn't privy to the school's inner workings, but however Alice selected students, Megan couldn't imagine a wider mix of kids getting along so well.

As the buses pulled off, Megan remained at the sidewalk and waved. Wearing khaki slacks and a striped cotton blouse with the sleeves rolled up, she looked ready to take her class on another trek through the woods—something they'd done many times and in all sorts of weather. Megan didn't get teary until the last of them had been driven away.

3

As Megan dabbed her eyes with her sleeve, Maury Gibson fanned open a precisely folded handkerchief from the breast pocket of his blazer and offered it with a friendly chuckle. "Oh, heavens, the stink of their sweaty little bodies is still in the air, and she misses them already."

Megan laughed. She wore little make-up so there wasn't any mascara or eye shadow to smudge Maury's fine handkerchief, just a salty tear or two.

With the children gone, the rolling hillside fell quiet except for the breeze.

Villa James occupied 30 unspoiled acres less than an hour north of Baltimore. In nobler times, the area had been hunt country, a pristine blend of open fields, streams, and hardwood forest.

The draping arms of a willow tree cast shade upon the pond where Megan had ice-skated with her young students during a long cold snap in February. They'd held hands and formed a chain, the sound of their skates etching across solid ice.

That little circle of placid water reminded Megan of the pond near the house where she'd grown up in Southern Virginia, the place she'd been the afternoon her aunt came to tell her that her father had died. That was 19 years ago, when she was 15. Nineteen years since her father last told her, No one loves me like you, Meggy. And I don't think anyone will ever love you as much as I do … but I sure hope one day they do."

#

Megan dove into the cool water and began swimming laps in the indoor pool where Villa James' swim team hosted regional events.

She usually swam before the start of the school day or after any evening activities were completed. But that afternoon, with most everyone gone, she had the pool to herself in the middle of the day.

John, the handyman who kept the physical plant running, had given Megan a key to the building and shown her how to test the water and balance the chemicals. She considered it more than a fair barter: swimming in exchange for a little maintenance.

Back in high school, she'd been on a swim team and won a few races, the ribbons for which remained in a box, unpacked since she went away to college. Since then, other than lounging on vacation and teaching her stepdaughter to swim, Megan hadn't spent much time in a pool until last fall. At Villa James, she'd begun swimming again—at least an hour a day.

With her dark-brown hair tucked into a swimmer's cap, she glided easily through the water in a one-piece Speedo. Sometimes she did flip turns, other times a casual standing turn with her head and shoulders out of the water.

The pool was enclosed in an aged greenhouse-like structure. Whenever the wind galloped across the hills, the building's glass panes rattled as if about to come apart. John always assured there was no cause to worry: "Nothing's going anywhere," he'd say.

Megan was almost finished her swim when she noticed Alice Martinelli, the school's director, sitting alone in the second row of wooden bleacher seats.

Hands folded in the lap of her plain black skirt, 58-year-old Alice looked very much like a dutiful older mother waiting for her daughter to finish practice. "I know I've told you before, but I don't think I've ever seen a more beautiful swimmer." For a pixie-sized woman, Alice's voice brimmed with confidence.

Megan smiled as she pulled herself out of the water. Removing her cap and goggles, she picked her towel off the pool coping and began drying her hair.

Alice asked, "How does it feel to have survived your first year back teaching?"

"I still can't believe it's over."

"And before you know it, it will be September and we'll start all over again."

5

Megan didn't want to think about September.

"Have you decided if you're going to the beach?" Alice asked.

Megan nodded. "I'm going down tonight."

"Good for you. For the summer?"

"We'll see... I hope so."

"And Stewart?" Alice asked of Megan's husband.

"He says he'll be back when he can," Megan answered, still drying her hair. "Weekends here and there, I guess."

"He's busy in Scottsdale."

Megan nodded.

"And wants you there with him."

Megan nodded again, having shared with Alice how the possibility of moving to Arizona for Stewart's job had come to dominate her life—which not that long ago had seemed so comfortable and settled. But that had been an illusion, she realized—her illusion. Changes had been happening all around her, she just hadn't wanted to see them.

2.

It was night time when Megan drove onto the Chesapeake Bay Bridge. With the windows down to the Volvo, sea air flowed through the five-year-old sedan like a summer spice.

There was little traffic on the eastbound span. Ships' lights on the bay's dark waters looked like fallen stars, with a massive freighter appearing as an entire constellation.

Until now, most all her trips to the beach had been as a family: Megan, Stewart, and Cassie. Tonight, she was alone— as she'd been for most of the past nine months with Stewart in Scottsdale for work and Cassie away at her first year of college.

Spending so much time by herself sometimes felt like growing up as an only child in rural Virginia. As if somehow the last ten years with Stewart were merely a dream and she was the same as she'd been that day Cassie first entered her classroom as a sad third-grader trying to adjust to a world without her mother.

Megan had felt an instant connection with the little girl. Cassie had seemed so vulnerable, as if awaiting whatever the dark hands of fate were going to deal next after taking her mother.

Stewart, Cassie's father, had presented a similar anxiety, his expression knotted with concern at that first parent/teacher conference. He'd arrived fifteen minutes early and paced outside Megan's classroom while she'd finished with parents who, talking about their third child, were well settled into the routine.

Stewart had listened intently to everything Megan said and took notes, so careful not to miss a word he didn't realize it was all Megan could do to keep from telling him she thought his daughter was perfect. She'd described Cassie as smart, delightful, respectful, and kind, but did not admit Cassie was her favorite, because teachers were not supposed to say such things. Or confess how she sometimes touched Cassie on the head and brushed her hair from her eyes. Or admit how when Cassie once fell in the hall and cried, how she'd picked her up and held her in her arms—and that when Cassie clung to her it made Megan feel as if her heart melted.

Stewart hadn't heard Megan's compliments because he was yet to recover from the shock of losing his wife and finding himself a single parent to a young daughter. He later told Megan the time after his wife died was like walking a tightrope, always trying to look straight ahead to keep from falling into the depths of despair. That he'd been certain he would never be a good enough parent for Cassie. And he would certainly never fall in love again. But then he'd met Megan.

#

On the other side of the bay, the landscape made a dramatic change. The way Spanish moss draping from oaks in Savannah gave visual clues of a more languid lifestyle, Maryland's Eastern Shore offered impressions of halcyon days. The land was low and flat, as if too tired to raise from its slumber, choosing instead to dangle its grassy toes in lapping waters that wove among sprawling farms and small towns.

For fifty miles, the spool of two-lane highway ambled south before banking east to the Atlantic Ocean, where, after another forty minutes of darkness, the familiar glowing skyline of Ocean City welcomed Megan's arrival.

The beach town's Ferris Wheel lit the southern tip of the six-mile-long barrier island, while golden lights from low- and mid-rise hotels, condos, and cottages stretched north to the spikes of high-rise towers built in a frantic '70's building boom.

Once across that final bridge and on the island, Megan sensed her core relax, not appreciating she'd been holding herself a little tensely during the drive down.

Their summer place was a modest one-bedroom condo in Ocean Vista, an older, well-maintained building directly on the beach.

Getting out of the car, Megan heard waves breaking across the dunes. Otherwise, it was quiet, but that would quickly change once vacation season started.

Megan's only luggage was the weekend bag slung over her shoulder. Whatever other clothes she needed were already in the bedroom closet upstairs.

The elevator made a familiar clanking noise, rising slowly to the top—fifth floor—of the 45-unit building.

Inside their condo, Megan turned on lights and opened the electric panel, switching on circuits for the water heater, refrigerator, stove, and laundry room, then adjusting the thermostat—the reverse process of closing the family house in Hunt Valley four hours ago, although at home she'd also set the alarm system and emptied the refrigerator.

The condo's kitchen, dining, and living rooms were open to one another, the only separation being a peninsula with two stools between the kitchen and living room. The décor was "functional-beachy"—Megan's term for what a decorator would label "outdated"—primarily in muted shades of tan, pale orange, and sage. There was low-pile carpet in the living and dining rooms. The kitchen floor was porcelain tile. The wooden cabinets were painted white—the same color as the appliances. The counter was Formica.

Other than the sofa bed and microwave, the condo looked much the same as the summer they bought it. But it was comfortable and practical and had stood up well to the sandy feet and wet bathing suits of Cassie and her friends.

Megan hadn't been here since February—a short trip with her best friend, Jillian, who'd flown in from Ohio. It had been a girls' weekend, like when they were college roommates, never having gone to those crowded places full of bad Spring Break decisions, but cabins in the mountains or B&B's near state parks.

At the end of that weekend, when Stewart had called from Scottsdale to ask what they'd done and Megan told him, "Nothing," Stewart laughed. "Well you had to have done something." Mostly, she and Jillian had talked and watched movies and made fun of people on TV shows looking to buy houses, imagining how plastered you'd get playing a drinking game if you had to do a shot every time someone said, open concept or stainless-steel appliances or family and friends. She and Jillian had also bundled up for long walks on the beach— although no running because Jillian had never been a fan of working out. But none of that had reached the level of what Stewart considered "doing something."

Now, months later, Megan opened the sliding door and went out onto the balcony.

The moon hung over the ocean, casting enough light to reflect the white breakwater of waves coming ashore to an empty beach.

The day she and Stewart first saw this place they hadn't been looking to buy a second home, but they'd been curious. They'd been inside other units for sale the summer before. But something about this place had felt right.

Cassie, only eleven at the time, had thought so too, standing at the sliding doors, her nose just about to the glass, gazing at the ocean.

Megan had cuddled behind her while Stewart talked with the real estate woman. "What do you think?" she'd asked Cassie.

"Oh, Mommy, I love it," Cassie had replied somewhat breathlessly. Eleven had been one of her more dramatic ages as she'd continued to come out of her shell, becoming more confident every month it seemed. "Let's stay here and never leave."

"Never?"

10

"No—never."

"What about to get something to eat? Would we go out to eat?"

"There's a kitchen," Cassie had replied, enchanted by the ocean view.

"We'd still have to go out for groceries."

"Daddy will get the groceries. And we'll stay here."

"And what will we do inside here all day?"

"Not inside. Out there." Cassie had pointed to the ocean. "We'll swim with the dolphins."

That day, peering between balcony railings, Megan had spotted more dolphins than she'd ever seen before—or any time since—swimming in the sea.

An hour later, she and Stewart had signed the contract for the condo, and they'd spent much of every summer here since. Together, as a family. But they did not feel like that family anymore.

#

An hour later, Megan was getting ready for bed when Stewart texted: *R U @ the beach?*

She took a breath before replying—hesitant about Stewart's response now that she was actually here—that she hadn't changed her mind at the last minute and decided to join him in Scottsdale. She typed: *Yes.*

When Stewart texted back: *Me, too*, Megan felt her spirits lift, hoping this was one of his surprises—Stewart loved surprises—and that he'd flown back to be with her. Then she saw the picture on her phone. Stewart was at the beach, but not this beach. Stewart was over 3,000 miles away, in Southern California.

He texted: *Just formalized the offer on Talbot-Glen. They'll be crazy not to accept.*

Megan did not remember who—or what—Talbot-Glen was. There was so much business talk the last few years. She texted: *Congratulations*, then thought to add two exclamation points. Because whatever Talbot-Glen was, Stewart really wanted it. And when Stewart wanted something, he worked hard to get it. The man once shattered by the death of his first wife had found a new confidence and determination in the years since marrying Megan.

And become a much different man.

3.

At 75, William Clary was comfortable in his habits. After taking care throughout most of his career not to fall into predictable patterns, he considered his daily routines as luxuries.

Although retired for years, Bill still got up every morning—God willing—at dawn and fixed himself coffee "by hand," spooning fresh grounds into a paper filter and pouring in water heated by his mother's kettle.

Weather permitting—meaning a temperature of at least 50, rain was okay—he'd take his coffee and newspaper outside. Although he made efficient use of an iPad, he still had the newspaper delivered, a continuing practice despite numerous squabbles with the paper's billing department about missed and late deliveries and long hold times to talk to a real person whenever he needed to suspend his subscription because he was going to be away.

The house where Bill and his wife lived in Annapolis and this oceanfront townhouse at the beach both had partially covered balconies that kept him out of wet weather. That sunny morning, there was no need for cover, save the Washington Nationals' baseball cap he put on his head of thinning hair at the instructions of his good friend, the dermatologist, who had already carved half a dozen "evil" spots from Bill's head and arms.

In a cushioned chair facing the ocean, Bill drank his coffee and read the news, trying not to become aggravated by decisions of policymakers he no longer had even the most remote chance to influence, save a sharp letter to the editor or email to a former colleague still on the job.

After a while, he diverted his concerns over geopolitical wrangling by watching nature—both winged and finned, four-legged and upright. Today, there was little in the way of "wildlife" to see. Save a few early morning walkers, the beach was empty.

After a rather grey Maryland winter, Bill was eager for summer. His wife, Mary Jane, who still enjoyed working as an interior designer, was in Charleston, overseeing an ambitious restoration of a historic home on Broad Street. His wife's absence had left Bill alone for three days now, soaking up the tranquility before the upcoming Memorial Day weekend, when the "zoo"—as he often referred to it—would open for the season.

Shortly before 9:00, Bill observed the arrival of the Surf Patrol lifeguard, a young blond-headed guy with his own rituals.

Outfitted in red OCSP sweats, the lean guard jogged onto the beach with a worn canvas bag and life buoy slung over his shoulder. Taking hold of the guard stand he'd moved back to the dune line last evening, he tipped the five-foot wooden structure onto his back and drug it effortlessly across 50 yards of soft sand to where overnight's high tide left a dark watermark.

With his stand positioned, the guard wedged a tipped end of his orange buoy into the sand, looping its strap precisely in place so he'd be able to grab it on the run. Satisfied, he climbed the ladder rungs of his stand with the effortlessness of a cat, then stood and scanned the ocean.

Bill Clary didn't need his binoculars to know the young guy was smiling.

Half an hour later, the girl arrived. At least Bill first thought she was a girl, judging from her confident stride toward the ocean in a blue Speedo. Her hair tied back in a simple ponytail, she entered the cool water without hesitation and dove into the first wave that broke in front of her. She swam freestyle out to deep water, almost 75 yards from shore, then turned and swam parallel to the beach.

The lifeguard stood, watching her.

Bill Clary did the same, using his binoculars now—not the Zeiss Victory HT's his wife bought him for his 70th birthday, but a long-range pair like the army issued him in Vietnam over 50 years ago, when he'd been a fresh-faced West Virginia kid just out of Yale, learning firsthand how big and complex the world was.

He focused on the swimmer, her steady pace sliding through the water, breathing on every fourth or fifth reach of her right arm. She passed in front of Bill's townhouse and continued to the next block.

The lifeguard gave two short whistle bursts and snapped his signal flags, alerting his fellow guard, who, because it was still the off-season, was two blocks away.

Bill deciphered quick semaphore sent from guard to guard: three letters, *WOF*—Watch Out For.

The second guard, also standing now, saw the lone swimmer coming his way, and signaled back what the local guards used to indicate a question—which was the same signal the blond guard flagged back in reply. Neither of them knew who she was.

Now three of them were watching: the two lifeguards and Bill Clary, who was also keeping time on his Rolex Presidential. A few blocks later, a third guard was alerted. Then a fourth.

Half an hour and almost three-quarters of a mile from where she entered the water, the girl swam ashore and started walking back along the beach. Her gait was easy, the stroll of someone lost in thought as she looked out to sea. She breathed deeply but didn't appear tired or cold. To the contrary, Bill thought she probably could have swum back if she wanted.

It was when she came closer that he realized she wasn't as young as he'd first thought. How old, though, he wasn't sure. He had such a damned hard time figuring age anymore. She was old enough to be married though—he could see her

15

wedding band. If detailing her on a surveillance report, he'd have estimated her to be 30.

When she passed in front of Bill's balcony, he was tempted to call out to her—applaud her efforts—but had the feeling his words might interrupt whatever she was thinking about. Maybe she wouldn't even hear him—a suspicion that proved true when the girl—the young woman—walked behind the blond-haired lifeguard who, still standing, spoke to her and she didn't react.

#

"Want a job?"

Megan heard the words, but it didn't register that the surf patrol guard was talking to her until he repeated it louder, cupping his hands and calling to her back:

"Want a job?"

She turned and saw him atop his stand.

He said, "You're a kickass swimmer."

Megan shaded a hand over her eyes but couldn't make out his features for the glare of the sky—other than he was tall and lean.

"I'm serious about the job," he said. "You swim better than half the crew I'll end up with this summer."

"Thanks." Megan continued toward her building with small backwards steps. "Maybe next year." She wasn't sure what she meant by that, preoccupied with thoughts that had kept her up most of the night.

"You change your mind," the guard said, "I'm here."

#

On her fifth-floor balcony, showered after her ocean swim, Megan ate a toasted open-face English Muffin spread with peanut butter and jelly, sipped a mug of English Breakfast tea, and contemplated the ocean. She'd spent countless hours in that water, but never swum as she had this morning.

The thought of not being able to see bottom in the ocean had always been a little intimidating. As had the possibility of a face-first meeting with a long-tenacle jellyfish or spotting the ominous fin of a shark—even the little sand sharks that were supposed to be harmless and more afraid of her than she was of them. (Did anyone tell the sharks that?)

But swimming the ocean had been in her mind the past few weeks because their condo didn't have a pool. If she wanted to keep up her daily swim, she'd either have to join a health club and share lanes with other people or get over her hesitation about going out beyond the waves.

So last night, kept awake by an uneasiness that shone like a spotlight behind her closed eyes, she'd visualized herself in the ocean. Pushed back fears of what else might be out there. And told herself not to flinch from the water being cold. To just dive in, let the chill momentarily take her breath, get out past the wave break, and swim. Get into that hypnotizing rhythm that helped her believe everything wasn't as bad as it seemed: that last month's argument with Stewart—one of those rare, heated exchanges in their marriage—had merely caught them both at a time when they were tired and stressed and had spent too much time apart.

Until that night, she and Stewart had agreed on most everything, at least the important matters. So they'd never had to compromise, not really. They'd gotten the big issue out of the way before they ever married: that they wouldn't have children of their own.

Stewart had a vasectomy after his late wife's difficult pregnancy with Cassie. And before Cassie, his wife Caroline had lost two babies to miscarriages. Stewart could have had the procedure reversed, but they worried adding a baby to their new family might complicate the progress Cassie had made since Megan came into their lives—first as Cassie's teacher, then as Stewart's "friend" they called it when dating, then as Stewart's wife.

Last month, increasingly frustrated how their natural inclination to be on the same page about most everything had abandoned them, Stewart hadn't understood Megan not wanting something that was so important to him. It was all about moving to Scottsdale, which to Stewart was opportunity, but for Megan was upheaval. She was happy the way things were, and it hurt that Stewart didn't feel the same. That he wanted more.

What were they to do? The answer, at times, seemed obvious. They should move. It was Stewart's career, after all. His business. He had always been their source of income—a very comfortable income. Stewart's late wife hadn't worked but been a stay-at-home mom for Cassie. When Stewart had asked Megan if she'd be comfortable with that same arrangement, she'd left her teaching job the year they were married. Maybe that had been the wrong choice. Maybe it had been the easy choice.

It made Megan feel selfish and spoiled to resist moving because Stewart had merged his small Maryland engineering firm with a larger company in Arizona—and in the process been given a position of authority, an impressive sum of cash, a sizeable raise, and a benefits package his own smaller firm could have never afforded.

And yet here she was at the beach in Maryland—not in Scottsdale—when there was no reason for her to stay other than she liked it here. She couldn't even use Cassie as an excuse.

Just finishing her freshman year at George Washington in nearby DC, Cassie didn't need her anymore. Or didn't need her very often. And even if that wasn't entirely true, it certainly felt that way, especially in the middle of sleepless nights—of which Megan had experienced many over the past nine months.

4.

The following morning, Bill Clary was on his balcony with his coffee and newspaper when the lifeguard arrived and proceeded through his start-of-the-day routine: dragging his stand from the dunes, setting it closer to the ocean, positioning his life buoy.

Ten minutes later, the young woman in the blue one-piece came out of the condo building next door and went directly into the ocean, diving through waves that were larger today, the sea having turned choppy overnight.

As she'd done yesterday, the woman swam beyond the breakers, then aimed her course south, only today she was fighting a current that had her swimming harder, and after only 400 yards or so she angled for shore.

Bill assumed she was giving up, but once in waist-deep water, the woman took long strides, using her arms to help propel her onto the beach, where she broke into a hard sprint.

She didn't look as natural running as she did swimming but covered the distance back to the lifeguard's stand without stopping, where she pulled up and checked her watch (which she hadn't worn yesterday), then spoke to the guard who'd been watching her the entire time.

#

"I don't want a job…" Megan inhaled deeply, winded from running. "…I just wanted to see if I could do it." She drew

19

another breath, gestured to the ocean. "Four-hundred-meter swim in under ten minutes. I took a little more than eight." Her thighs burned from exertion. She hadn't run in months—a chilly 5K with Cassie and some of her former lacrosse teammates. "Three-hundred-yard sand sprint in less than sixty-five seconds. I did four-hundred in sixty." Another deep breath, then said: "I checked the testing requirements on the surf patrol website."

Atop his stand, the guard smiled—an honest, pleasant expression that reflected his demeanor. Everything about him—lanky frame, straw-blond hair, suntanned skin (and it was only May)—radiated the ease of summertime.

"Assuming I measured the distances right," Megan added.

"What's your name?"

His question surprised her, although she didn't know why. Maybe because she hadn't expected to talk to him. But he'd watched her run and she was pleased she'd bested the testing times by what seemed like a significant margin.

Or maybe she was surprised he was older than she assumed. She hadn't gotten that good a look at him yesterday and figured he'd be 19 or in his early twenties—like most of the other guards she'd seen over the years. But he looked in his mid-twenties and could have been even older behind that boyish face.

When she finally told him her name, she wondered if it actually took as long to respond as it felt.

He said, "I'm Pip." Still smiling.

"Pip?"

He nodded without explaining the nickname—what Megan assumed was a nickname—then told her, "You know there's more requirements than the swim and the run." He settled into a sitting position with his legs dangling over the side of his stand.

"I saw. I just wanted to know if I could do that part."

"Can you move a 150-pound person fifty yards?"

"Like I said, I'm not looking for a job."

"I'm just wondering if you can do it."

Megan shrugged. "Maybe."

"You should apply—even if you don't want the job." Pip brushed one bare foot over the other, knocking off sand. His red sweatpants were faded, the hems frayed from lots of summers in the sun. "It's actually kind of a thing. We probably had twenty people take the test two weeks ago who had no intention of spending their summer on a chair."

"On a chair? Is that what you call it? I thought it was surf rescue technician." Quoting the Surf Patrol website.

He laughed. "Leftover offspring of political correctness."

"Did you make that up?"

Pip shook his head. "A friend of mine calls it that."

She crossed her arms over the front of her wet one-piece, starting to cool down from her swim and sprint.

Pip pulled a towel from his canvas bag and tossed it to her. Megan caught it but offered it right back.

"It's clean," he assured.

"I know." The scent of laundry detergent was fresh on the soft fabric. "I don't mind being cold." She neatly refolded the towel and handed it up to him.

He considered her a moment, his smile never fading. He nodded toward her building. "You staying here?"

"We have a place on the fifth floor."

"You stay the whole summer?"

"Usually. Me anyway. My husband's back and forth. Our daughter—who knows. She's in college now and the beach doesn't seem to hold the same charm for her."

"That's too bad … for her."

For me, too, Megan thought but didn't say—didn't want to be one of those people who manage to force a poor-me reference into every conversation. "How long have you been a lifeguard?" she asked, no sooner saying that than she realized it probably gave away she was curious about his age.

Maybe he was used to that because his expression changed. And while he didn't actually wince, he hesitated as if about to make a confession, then held up both hands with all his fingers and thumbs extended.

"Ten years?" Megan interpreted.

His smile returned. "Safe to say the beach still holds the same charm for me."

Ten years? That would make him—what—at least 27? "Is ten years some kind of record?" Megan made it sound like a good thing. And why couldn't it be?

Pip laughed. "I'd be afraid to ask."

"Why?"

"Well..." He smiled. "...you know..."

But she didn't—and didn't ask because it didn't matter. Wasn't really her business anyway. "Is this your beach this summer?"

"Yep."

"Good..." She couldn't think of anything else to say. "Then I guess I'll see you tomorrow ... Pip." She thought it might feel funny calling him that, but it didn't.

"See you tomorrow, Megan."

Taking two backward steps, she said, "I like your name."

He said, "I like yours, too."

5.

At noon—lunch break, Megan assumed—Pip whistled to the guards stationed on each side of him, snapped of a series of flag signals, then, canvas bag in hand, jumped off his stand, snagged his life buoy, and trotted to the head of the side street at the north end of Megan's building.

His gait was natural and effortless. Even joyous, Megan thought.

Hopping into an aged Jeep Wrangler with its top already down, Pip grabbed a set of keys from beneath the front seat and started the engine. Backing down the street, he made driving seem athletic, as if called upon he'd be able to spin that four-wheel-drive vehicle through a series of dizzying maneuvers.

Megan had been watching Pip from her balcony in between emails and phone calls, most of which were preparing for the elementary and middle school students she'd tutor online this summer.

Throughout the morning, she'd wondered what Pip thought about as he watched the ocean. He made it seem almost Zen-like. Maybe he enjoyed the calm. Or maybe he couldn't wait until his days were busy reuniting parents and lost children, warning swimmers who went out too far beyond the waves and pulling unsuspecting people from rip tides.

Megan was about to take her laptop inside when she got a text from Cassie: *How's the beach?*

Wonderful, Megan sent back.

Cassie replied: *As if I had to ask.*

Tops on the long list of what Megan disliked about texting—and emails for that matter—was the lack of tone of voice: how words tapped by the writer in a light-hearted, perhaps even loving context could have the opposite impact on the reader. And all the emojis in the world didn't help if that cartoon smile was hiding a real-life eye roll. As if I had to ask could have been Cassie appreciating Megan's love of the beach, or snarky reference about how Megan would think being here was wonderful regardless of the circumstances—the way she didn't mind the crowds that had begun to annoy Cassie and Stewart the past couple summers.

Cassie sent another text: *Just talked to S.* "S" meant Stewart, like "M" was short for Megan, not Mom. When Cassie was 16, she'd stopped calling them Mom and Dad and started using their first names—following a trend of her friends.

Stewart never seemed to mind—and had even been amused—while Megan found it hurtful and wondered if Stewart's ready adjustment to the change had been because having Cassie refer to her as Mom had begun as a sensitive issue.

The first time Cassie called Megan "Mom" was months before she and Stewart were married, and it made Stewart uneasy. He'd worried Cassie was forgetting her real mother, who Stewart had dearly loved and never truly recovered from losing.

Megan respected that, much the way she understood how when she and Stewart first started going out it took him months to admit his feelings for her. Even then he'd been guilty about it. Stewart's mother—who Megan had adored—had slowly managed to steer him in the right direction, assuring her son the marriage vow was, 'Til death do us part, and that he'd lived up to his end of that bargain with Caroline.

But there was no such vow for children, forever linked to their "real" parents by birth. And part of Stewart seemed to need his late wife to always be Cassie's mom, whether or not Megan loved Cassie, or Cassie loved Megan (who still remembered how warm it made her feel that first time Cassie called her mom).

Now—and for the past couple years—Megan was no longer Mom, just M. And all the logic in the world didn't diminish the chill that put in her heart, even though Cassie still said she loved her. But "love" could be an easy word to throw about. "Mom" carried meaning.

The rest of Cassie's texts went on to divulge a series of secrets: That S—also known as Stewart/formerly known as Dad—was going to "put the push on" for Megan to spend Memorial Day weekend with him in Scottsdale. However, S had a ton going on at work and while it would be great for Megan to be with him in Scottsdale, he didn't really expect her to make a weekend trip on such short notice. (If true, this was a marked difference of thinking for Stewart from last month's argument, or perhaps Cassie mentioning this was her way of trying to prevent a replay of that unsettling exchange.)

What S was really hoping—again according to Cassie—was for M to be with him for the Fourth of July. *On 7/4,* Cassie texted, *S is going to be in Newport Coast, CA. You cannot let S know I told U! And pretend to be surprised, Cassie emphasized. But CA could be bigger than Scottsdale.*

Per Cassie, if the "CA deal" Stewart's new company was working on went through, Stewart would be working there, not in Scottsdale—which would mean the Arizona move that had been on the horizon for almost a year now would be no more. And it wouldn't be living just anywhere in CA, but Near the beach! Cassie texted. Already seen pics of houses. So beautiful! Warm weather every day!! Sunsets over the Pacific!!! And then, Cassie's final digital thought for the day: *LUCKY YOU!!!*

Their text exchange ended, Megan found herself wondering if this "secret information" may actually have been daughter doing father's bidding: trying to make the move from Maryland more enticing. If so, maybe Stewart making that effort (even through Cassie) was a good thing.

There hadn't been any finesse last year when Stewart announced his company's merger required him to be in Scottsdale, which made moving there a given—failing to consider how attached Megan was to their life in Maryland.

Since then, however, there was more to it. Now, with Stewart spending so much time away, and Cassie off at school, Megan's deeper worry wasn't about moving but that she and Stewart might be falling out of love.

Being with Stewart used to feel so natural and easy. They'd seemed so alike. And while she accepted that love changed, how did you work at love? Should you have to? Wasn't love more like art or beauty—something that existed organically and wasn't constructed?

She hadn't changed. She was older of course, but still liked the same things, to do the same things. Or was that stagnation? Sometimes she thought maybe Stewart's changes were more natural. Maybe she was the problem and owed it to him, to them, to change with him, grow with him.

And if that was the case, it wasn't going to happen here. It was going to happen wherever business took Stewart. Which meant this could end up being her last summer at this wonderful beach.

6.

The Thursday before Memorial Day weekend, Megan crossed the dunes onto the beach as she had for each of the past eight mornings, ready to swim even though there was an unseasonable chill in the air.

Pip and three other guards were talking alongside his stand, all outfitted in red Surf Patrol gear. When he called her over, Megan wasn't sure what he wanted. They'd spoken a few times over the past week, but rarely more than a quick, "Nice swim," or "How's it going?" Sometimes they'd just waved.

"Everybody..." Pip said as Megan approached, "this is Megan. Megan—this is Will..."

Young Will shook Megan's hand like she was one of the guys, putting a quick pump to it. He was a slender 17-year-old, about equal to Megan's five-seven height, with a thick mop of black hair and the keyed-up energy of a coiled spring.

"These two," Pip continued, "are Adrian and Art—usually joined at the hip."

"Hey, Meg," Adrian greeted.

Megan had seen them on their separate stands over the past few days as Surf Patrol staffing had increased for the start of the season. Art was one block north of Pip and Adrian at the block beyond that.

Adrian looked like a lot of girls Cassie played lacrosse with—a certain smart confidence about her Megan liked. Even before Pip introduced her as part of a couple, Megan could tell Art was smitten with her.

Art was a good-looking guy with a touch of worry tugging at his eyes that gave the impression he was trying his best to keep up with Adrian so she wouldn't slip away. Megan figured Adrian knew that—and probably liked it.

"Okay," Pip said, "we ready?"

Will said, "Let's do it, boss."

The group began shedding their sweats, tossing them to the beach. The guys stripped down to Speedos; Adrian to a red bra top and boy-short bottoms.

"All set, Megan?" Pip asked. It looked like he and his crew were joining her in the ocean today—or was it the other way around?

Trotting toward the water, she asked Pip, "So that's you: boss?"

"I guess."

"Where's your suit and tie?"

"Don't own either." Pip strode into the ocean, dove into a wave.

Megan was right behind him, bracing against the sharp chill of the water.

The five of them swam out through choppy surf. Angling south, Will took the lead, with Adrian and Art twenty yards behind him, and Pip and Megan another ten yards back until Megan pushed herself.

Once she and Pip moved up alongside the boyfriend/girlfriend pair, Pip called out, "Let's catch the kid," and the four of them pulled even harder, Pip barking, "Coming after you Will."

The final quarter mile—chasing Will—almost wore Megan out.

Pip sprint-swam close enough to grab Will's ankle, laughing as he pulled him backwards and took over a lead Will couldn't catch.

But even Pip was breathing hard as they reached their mile mark and tread water in place. "Good swim," he said.

Megan tried to conceal she was the most out of breath.

After a minute, Adrian pointed. "Hey, guys, look—dolphins."

Coming toward them, the animals' sleek grey backs gracefully broke the surface, appearing and disappearing. They shifted course to avoid their human visitors, but still passed near enough to reveal smiling faces.

"Just a pair," Adrian said.

Megan thought that was unusual. She'd seen dolphins dozens of times during their family summers at the beach and they were usually in pods of at least a half-dozen.

"Very cool," Will admired.

Pip was quiet, watching.

Adrian said, "It's going to be one of those special summers. I can tell already. Things are going to happen you can never explain."

7.

Suddenly it felt like summer, with the weather and calendar welcoming Megan's favorite season in unison, the calendar by turning the page to Memorial Day weekend and the temperature rising into the low 80's.

By noon Friday, cars streamed onto the island across the 62nd Street bridge. By sundown, turning onto Ocean Highway required a wait, as did checking out at grocery stores or getting a table for dinner.

For the first time in her marriage, Megan would be spending this holiday weekend apart from Stewart and Cassie.

Tomorrow morning, Cassie was heading to Lake Anna with some of her former lacrosse teammates, but just for one night. Monday, she'd be back to the analytics firm in Northern Virginia where she'd snagged a prestigious internship.

As for Stewart—and as Cassie had foretold days ago—his invitation for Megan to join him in Scottsdale for the weekend included the caveat that he understood if she wanted to pass, so she did, and he seemed fine with her decision.

Stewart said the Talbot-Glen offer had been made public and his new company was using the holiday weekend for a retreat to soothe employees still adjusting from the merger with his firm that the latest round of changes would be positive. He said they didn't want key personnel to get uneasy and look to leave, so his original Baltimore staff was being flown to Scottsdale—by private jet, no less—to let them know they weren't being left behind.

Stewart hadn't mentioned anything to Megan about spending the Fourth of July in California. Maybe that surprise was for another day.

Friday night, instead of another evening with HGTV, Netflix, or a book, Megan drove to the boardwalk, a picture postcard location of wonderful summer memories.

Practically empty just nights ago, the beachfront walkway was now a sensory blur, crowded with tourists like bees at an elaborate neon hive, bustling in and out of tacky gift and souvenir shops, eateries, bars, and noisy arcades. The smell of candy, fried food, and crab spice mixed with the salty, humid air.

The excitement of the start of summer seemed to crackle everywhere, but sparked most intensely among younger teens, all seemingly on their way somewhere, to meet someone, and hoping no one's parents found out what was really going on.

Wearing a comfortable t-shirt, shorts, and hiking sandals, Megan made her way toward the inlet, enjoying the familiar sights. She didn't carry a handbag, having picked up the practice of Cassie and her friends to put her license, a credit card and a couple bucks, phone, and keys in her pockets.

She got a slice of pizza and a soda, which she ate on a bench facing the beach. Watching high school kids play volleyball, she thought about Cassie at that age: 14-years-old, trying out for her high school lacrosse team in a t-shirt that had FEARLESS imprinted across the front (in case her style of play didn't make that clear).

Cassie looked like her late mother but was competitive like her father. And while she might help an opponent up after she knocked them down, she'd never say she was sorry. Megan had never quite gotten used to that—but did her best not to cringe or feel self-conscious when it happened. The first time she'd talked with Cassie about being more sensitive in her approach to sports, she got a protesting, "You mean girly," in reply. That Cassie had been offered athletic as well as academic scholarships seemed to reward all that aggressiveness.

Her pizza eaten, Megan continued toward the end of the boardwalk. At a favorite arcade, her preferred skeeball lane was available, so she put in a quarter and rolled a game, scoring a nifty 310—a tally worthy of a photo she texted to Cassie with the caption: *Think you can beat that?* Which was not so much a challenge as thinly veiled invitation, hopeful they'd have some time together this summer.

From the arcade, Megan went inside the building of kiddy rides, where the noise produced by loud machinery, blaring carnival music, and yelling grade-schoolers bounced off low ceilings at near ear-splitting levels. Dodge-'em cars, a mini merry-go-round, little fire engines, boats, and planes—each with their own blaring musical accompaniment—spirited small passengers on circular routes.

The place always made Megan smile, figuring it's what the world would look like if designed by young children. Stewart used to shout to her over the chaotic din: "How can you stand it in here?" Stewart was used to a quiet house.

Back on the boardwalk, hawkers promised stuffed animals for high scores at a variety of games as a cacophony of sirens, whistles, bells, and gleeful cries made it seem as if someone was always winning something.

A neon arch marked the entrance to a small amusement park Megan hadn't been to since Cassie lost interest in rides a few years ago. A nostalgic relic from the 1950's—and tiny by modern standards—the park still drew crowds like the rickety thrills wheeled into county fairs. There weren't any multi-million-dollar roller coasters, just the chance to hop on older rides like stepping back in time.

Banzai Bobsled—painted in the style of Japanese anime favored by one of Cassie's middle-school "boyfriends"— whipped riders in sled-like cars around a short, swerving track while music blared over a crude sound system, and a DJ announced: "Do you want to go faasssster?" The riders, in unison, shrieked: "Yesss!"

"Then let's go faasssster!"

The DJ, Megan was surprised to see, was Pip, who was also the ride's operator. Seated inside a cramped metal shack with a Plexiglas window, Pip sped up the ride, boosted the music, and tempted: "Do you want to go even faasssster!"

"Yessss!"

"Backwards?"

Cries of feigned protest mixed with delight as the bobsleds braked to a slow stop, then started up again in reverse.

As though just remembering, Pip announced, "That's right, you want to go faasssster!" He accelerated the ride until the entire mechanism screeched madly.

Megan watched for a few minutes and was about to leave when Pip spotted her and waved.

She smiled and waved back.

He motioned her to join him, so she made her way around riders waiting in line.

"Come on in!" Pip called over the music.

She considered his tiny workspace, barely the size of a broom closet. "Is there room?"

"Plenty."

Megan climbed a trio of squishy wood steps and squeezed inside, standing shoulder to shoulder, hip to hip. The smell of motor oil and warm metal rose from the ride's underbelly.

"You like my night gig?" he asked loudly.

"Sure." She nodded in case he couldn't hear.

Pip switched on his microphone, broadcasting through bass-heavy speakers: "Not fast enough? Let's go faaassster!" He offered Megan the long handle that controlled the ride. "Want to do it?"

"I don't think so."

"Come on." He placed her hand on the vibrating control knob. "Just shift up a slot," he instructed. "But first, you've got to say it." He held the microphone toward her. "Ready?"

Megan shook her head.

"It's really fun..." Pip switched on the mic.

Megan figured what the hell—and gave the line her own twist: "Do ... you ... want to goooo ...... faster!"

The riders screamed.

Megan shifted gears and the bobsleds flew by the booth in reverse, shaking the floor on which she stood. The music blared and the riders screamed. Wanting to go faster.

\#

"So where you from?" His job at the amusement park finished for the night, Pip walked alongside Megan on the boardwalk. Both heading to their cars.

She said, "I grew up down in Virginia but live in Hunt Valley now. About halfway between the city and Pennsylvania line."

"I know where you're talking about—although I don't really know the area. I'm from Severna Park."

She liked the firm but gentle quality of his voice. The unhurried pace of his words.

"What do you in Hunt Valley?"

"Teacher," she answered, keeping it simple.

"What grade?"

"Elementary kids—mostly math."

At just before ten o'clock, the boardwalk was no longer crowded, and away from the amusement rides and asking if everyone wanted to go faster, it was quiet. Megan could hear the soft sound of Pip's flip-flops against creosote-stained planks.

"And your daughter?" he asked. "The one you said the beach no longer holds any charm for. She back home?"

"No. In DC"

"DC... I met an older guy the other day—in the townhouses next to you—who called it Rome, DC He seems like bit of a politico—in a non-crazy way."

Megan noticed a slight chip on one of Pip's white teeth— his right canine—and wondered how he got that.

Walking slowly, hands in the pockets of worn jeans, he asked, "So what's your daughter doing in DC?"

"An internship. She's on summer break from GW."

"So she's one of these types that makes the rest of us feel like underachievers."

"I don't know about that."

"She smart?" Pip wondered.

"Yes."

"And what's her name?"

"Cassie."

"Cassie… So does Cassie get the smart genes from you or dad?"

"She's all dad," Megan said.

"I doubt that."

Megan didn't usually tell people Cassie was her stepdaughter—basically because she didn't think of her that way. Some people might ask—or figure it out—picking up the age difference more readily now that Cassie was older, and Stewart was getting some grey at his temples. Stewart was nine years older than Megan—43 to her 34—which meant Megan had been 16 when Cassie was born.

"And where's dad while daughter's in DC?"

"Today, Scottsdale. Tomorrow, maybe California."

"Not as impressive as DC, but it's probably going to be once you tell me what dad does."

"He's a structural engineer."

"There you go." Pip smiled, looking across the moonlit beach as if ingrained to keep check on the ocean.

"How about you? How did you get here from Severna Park?"

"Hitchhiked a couple times when I was 15. I've always loved it here. Something special about this beach. It's why I went to college in Salisbury." Referring to the state college a half-hour drive from Ocean City. "I actually thought about being a teacher."

"Really?"

"Then my uncle said I only wanted to do that so I could have summers off and told me to grow up. So I let him change my mind and switched to business. And there wasn't a second of joy in it. I even spent a summer taking graduate courses because he wanted me to go to Wharton, like him. What a ruined summer that was. I only got down here weekends, and it just about killed me leaving every Sunday night. Every time I turned onto the bridge I wanted to bail—let the car go on without me."

"I take it you didn't go to Wharton."

Pip shook his head.

"And uncle?"

"He still sends Christmas cards. He's a good guy. I just think he felt obligated to take my dad's place."

"Why? What happened to your father?" Megan hoped that wasn't too personal to ask.

"He died when I was twelve." Saying that, Pip seemed much younger, and very innocent, as though part of him was still the age when he lost his dad.

"I'm sorry," Megan consoled.

"Kind of hard to believe I've spent so much more of my life now without him than with him."

Megan understood. "My dad died when I was in high school. It was pretty terrible for a long time afterward."

"Yes, it is," Pip agreed.

"My mom's dead too now, too," Megan added. "For six years. They were both older when they had me, but it still felt way too young to be without a mom or dad. At least they both went fast."

"People always say that," Pip considered. "Not wanting to linger when their time comes."

"I know … I guess it seems better."

"My dad went about as quick as you can. There's the saying about going like you get hit by lightning. That literally happened to him. He worked for the power company and was out after a storm trying to get service back up and was killed by lightning."

"Oh, no. Pip..." Megan touched his arm. "That's terrible."

"It still doesn't seem real—like it didn't actually happen. You know? I still think about all I missed with him."

"I know."

"I'll just be doing something simple, just going through my day, and think how nice it would be to call him and say what I'm doing." He was looking toward the ocean again.

They continued on in silence until she pointed to the side street just ahead. "My car's up here." Wishing there were a few more blocks to go because she enjoyed talking with him.

They turned off the boardwalk, where beech trees lined the sidewalk in front of older wooden buildings, mostly small apartments but a few individual houses. Muted conversations carried out opened windows.

Megan dug her keys from her pocket.

"This you?" Pip assumed.

"It is."

"She swims and parallel parks." Pip checked the even distance of the Volvo's wheels from the curb. "Nice job, too."

Megan fobbed open her door. "You need a ride?"

"I'm just back a couple blocks." He pointed toward the inlet, having walked out of his way to see her to her car.

She opened the door, but didn't get in. Thinking it would be nice to go somewhere they could sit and talk some more, maybe have coffee or ice cream, but she didn't want to give him the wrong impression.

Pip smiled. "Glad I saw you."

"Me, too."

"Good." He nodded. "So I'll see you tomorrow."

"See you tomorrow."

8.

Saturday afternoon, lots of people were on the beach, but few were in the water. The sunshine was warm, but the ocean had turned inhospitable. The water was chilly and unsettled, sloshing back and forth—what complaining surfers called "slop," because not even the usual modest mid-Atlantic waves were forming.

Single-engine planes flew low over the ocean, pulling advertising banners for sunscreen, restaurant specials, and bands playing at local bars. Lulu, the beach stand girl, stayed busy setting up umbrellas and chairs she rented by the day or the week. Folks strolled by, their varieties of shapes and sizes from remind-me-to-never-eat-cupcakes-again to the cut-and-buff beautiful.

From a beach chair, Megan watched Pip and his fellow guards flash semaphore signals, the surf patrol still using that very "analog" system of communication. A pair of handheld red flags represented different letters of the alphabet depending upon incremental shifts of arm position. Being a form of code, semaphore was essentially mathematics, which came easily to Megan. Once she picked up the basic pattern, it was just a matter of practice to keep up with how quickly Pip snapped from one letter-position to the next to discern the content.

"So when Will flags P and goes into the ocean," Megan asked Pip, "it means he's going out there to pee."

"Yep." Pip smiled, leaning over the side of his stand. "Lack of options," he explained in case she objected to the practice.

"Do all guards do that?"

"Not just guards—everybody pees in the ocean."

"Really...?" She considered his all-inclusive theory. "So if the Queen of England had ever been out there...?"

"The Queen of England in Ocean City?"

"You never know."

"Well, if she'd here and she had to go..."

"Huh..." Megan waved to Lulu, trudging by with a pair of folding chairs: "Hey, Lu—do you pee in the ocean?"

"Every day."

"Told you," Pip said.

"Yes, you did." Megan gestured toward her own beach chair. "I think I'm going back to my book."

"Thanks again for lunch," Pip said.

Megan had brought subs from the little grocery store across the street for all four of the guards she'd swum with again that morning: Pip, Will, Adrian, and Art. And also Lulu, who Megan rented chairs and an umbrella from for the season.

By late afternoon, when shadows cast by Megan's building extended toward the ocean, Lulu began "closing the beach" as she referred to it, collecting her rental gear. A stout girl, she could carry three umbrellas on her shoulder and as many chairs in the opposite hand. She came for Megan's stuff last, but instead of taking it away plopped down on a chair. "Phew. Out of shape." Lulu removed her Wayfarers and wiped the back of her hand across her eyes. She favored bikinis in primary colors—today was Kermit-the-Frog green.

Megan patted the top of Lulu's thigh. "I'm glad you're here. I've missed you."

"Missed you, too." The girl squeezed Megan's hand, then slid her sunglasses back on and scanned the beach. "I can't believe Cassie's missing this." Lulu and Cassie had become friendly—not necessarily friends—three summers ago and stayed in touch over the winter. "Guess she's really getting super serious. The day I posted this new tattoo..." Lulu pointed to an arrowhead on her left calf. "...Cass put something up about having dinner at Charlie Palmer's."

"Who's he?" Megan didn't recognize the name.

"Not sure it's he. Maybe it is. Some DC hotspot. I didn't know that either until I Googled it and saw it on some Washingtonian Magazine top-this-or-that list."

"Tell me it's not a bar," Megan hoped.

"Super-high-end restaurant I think."

Megan wondered who Cassie had gone with.

Lulu picked up the book Megan was reading. "Not very good?"

"What's that?"

Lulu checked Megan's bookmark. "This is what—thirty pages? All day? You usually burn through these."

"Just enjoying it being summer."

"I get that." Lulu set the book back on Megan's blanket.

After a minute, Megan asked Lulu how long she'd known Pip.

"I dunno. Four years? He's kind of an icon. And super nice. Really sweet. Most days, you watch, he'll have a dozen chickadoodles stop by."

"Did you two ever go out?"

"Nooo. That'd be like being with my older brother—if I had a really good-looking older brother."

"I was trying to figure how old he is." Megan considered him sitting atop his stand. "He told me he's been a guard for ten years."

"I think he's like twenty-six. Twenty-seven maybe." Lulu boosted herself up. "I'll find out." Starting toward Pip's stand.

"Lulu. Wait. Don't."

"Oh, relax. I won't tell him you asked—not that he'd care." Lulu crossed the sand, her gait somewhat of a sexy plod. She was back in two minutes. "Twenty-eight. What else do you want to know about him?"

"Nothing, you nut," Megan laughed.

"Good. Because I'm tired. And I need a beer."

"You're not twenty-one."

"I am according to my new ID."

"Lulu..."

40

"Don't worry, mom, I won't get caught. Now—beach is closed." She nudged Megan with her bare foot. "So up off my chair."

#

That night, Megan returned to the boardwalk and walked to the inlet, strolling beneath the neon arch to the amusement park. Because there was more she wanted to know about Pip than his age.

Only someone else was running the bobsled ride. The first two people Megan asked about Pip—both young summer workers with East European accents—didn't know him, but said they'd just started last night and didn't know many co-workers. An older mechanic said Pip only filled in when they were short, or to cover for friends who wanted to take a night off. "He could be back tomorrow," the man said, "or in three weeks."

Megan thanked him and returned to her car.

On the way back to her condo, she drove up and down a few bayside streets where college kids with seasonal jobs piled into small apartments to share expenses.

At most any of the older stick-built apartment houses—two units on each floor—there would often be mismatched furniture, maybe a thread-bare sofa, outside on the front balcony. Laundry would be drying on a line, music would be playing, beer bottles clanking, and everyone would be laughing.

Megan had often wondered what it would be like to spend a summer that way.

9.

"There they go," Bill Clary announced to his wife.

Back from her decorating job in Charleston, Mary Jane Clary sat with her husband in a shaded section of their deck, overlooking the beach.

Mary Jane was a petite redhead, still energetic at 74, with a keen eye for design and distaste for politics, the latter trait probably having saved their marriage by keeping Bill from becoming too obsessed with world affairs (regardless of that having been part of his job)—or at least keeping him from being too obsessed about it around her. Anytime he might forget his wife's strong feelings on the subject or think she would surely be interested in the latest debacle coming out of Rome, DC, Mary Jane would tell him, "Can that and stick it on the shelf," a saying adopted from growing up on her family farm on Maryland's Eastern Shore.

Always in search of safe subjects to provide conversation, Bill found observations of others—provided he wasn't too judgmental—of interest to his beloved wife.

When Bill said, "There they go," Mary Jane knew he was talking about the group of surf patrol guards that had been ocean swimming every morning. At least four of them were guards. Mary Jane and Bill weren't sure how the fifth swimmer, a woman who came out of the Ocean Vista next door, fit with the others except she was an excellent swimmer.

Mary Jane picked up her own binoculars as the five swimmers headed out beyond the breakers.

Overnight, the white caps and chop had disappeared. Sunlight glistened off blue water as waves formed nicely, providing surfers with decent rides since daybreak.

"She's not one of their mothers," Mary Jane surmised, watching the woman in the blue one-piece.

"You don't know that," Bill countered, perhaps a bit too sharply.

To which Mary Jane rebuked, "I'm telling you, Captain…" Emphasizing his one-time field rank in the Army as if reminding she was his wife, not one of his soldiers. "…she is not one of their mothers."

"I agree with you, but we don't know that."

"Fine. How about a bet then?"

"I'm saying, I agree with you, it's just not something we can prove at this point."

It was the sort of conversation couples who have been married a long time can make sound like an argument when it's really not.

#

Pip changed their swim every day, not letting them know how long or hard they'd go or even when it was over until he called an end. And it wasn't just swimming. Also jogging and sand sprinting. Sometimes he led them in and out of the ocean multiple times. Even when they walked, they might be called upon to run at any moment. Today, they took turns dragging one another fifty yards across the beach.

Adrian positioned Megan on her back, grasped beneath her armpits and pulled, digging in with her legs as much as using her arms and lower back, surprising Megan with her strength.

When they changed positions, Pip coached Megan how to get into position, and before telling her, "Go," told her, "Think light." Megan didn't know what that meant until she tried to move Adrian—who couldn't have weighed more than 120—and could barely budge her.

"Think of her as being light," Pip said. "That she's a bag of feathers."

"You're kidding, right?" Megan responded.

"Try it. And push like hell with your legs."

Megan grunted and pulled—arms, legs, and back—and got Adrian moving.

"Think light," Pip encouraged.

Megan grunted louder, tugging Adrian ten yards, twenty. Muscles in her legs burning. Arms straining. Breathing hard. She was on the verge of letting Adrian go but kept going until Pip said, "Good."

Even though it wasn't. Megan had been counting in her head—knowing the time within which the Surf Patrol test required its candidates to move a 150-pound person over soft sand. She'd blown that deadline before getting Adrian ten yards.

"It gets easier," Pip said.

Megan remained on the sand where she'd dropped onto her butt.

Adrian, already on her feet, offered a hand to help Megan up.

Pip started them off again—jogging, not running, which Megan felt was for her benefit.

Alongside Megan, Adrian encouraged, "Push-ups and squats. I'll text you a link to some drills." A nice way of telling Megan she needed to get stronger.

And maybe also younger, Megan thought to herself.

#

"Damn if she's not a tough one," Bill Clary said to his wife.

The husband and wife "binocular team" were watching the guards when the woman swimmer pulled the younger "girl guard"—as Bill called her—across the sand, a maneuver similar to one of the basic training exercises he'd been through before shipping out to Southeast Asia after college.

"And you say the crew leader's name is Pip?" Mary Jane asked.

"That's what he told me. Said he's been a guard here for ten years."

"I imagine there's some story behind that."

"I imagine you're right."

"Well," Mary Jane admonished, setting down her binoculars, "don't make a nuisance of yourself finding out." Getting up to go inside, she asked, "Does he always swim alongside the one in the blue suit?"

Bill thought before answering. "You know, I think he does."

"You mean you don't know for sure?"

Bill chuckled. "Is that anyway to talk coming up on our fiftieth anniversary."

She kissed the top of his head. "You've got ten months of forty-nine to keep me happy through first."

"Darling, you make that easy."

In the townhouse next door, the screen door banged opened, and a West Highland terrier dashed out, scampering down the steps and onto the beach. "There goes Houdini," Bill laughed, spotting the dog. "Escaped again. He'll be to Delaware before they come home and realize he's gone," Bill said of their summer neighbors.

#

Pip accepted the plastic container and fork Megan reached up to his stand. "This is really nice, but you don't have to do this. Not that we don't appreciate it."

For the second day in a row, Megan brought lunch to the guards and Lulu. Today it was homemade pasta salad made from fresh ingredients she'd bought at a farmer's stand after their swim.

45

"Another thing to know about guards," Pip continued, "other than that peeing-in-the-ocean business, is we never turn down food."

"Happy to do it. I used to make lunch all the time for Cassie and her friends." She left out how spending an hour or two tutoring math students online every couple days instead of full-time teaching was leaving her with too much idle time.

Insulated bag over her shoulder, Megan walked up the beach and delivered lunch to Art, who said, "Man this looks good," and dove in with such ferociousness the plastic container looked in peril of being consumed along with the pasta.

A block farther north, Adrian appreciated, "You're spoiling us." The girl definitely had that same confidence as Cassie and her lacrosse teammates, but without the aggressive swagger. Perhaps that was a difference between being a lifeguard and playing competitive sports.

Heading south to Will's stand, Megan walked by Pip, who was being charmed by two—what did Lulu call them: chickadoodles? Girls in small bikinis in their late teens who tried to act older than their age, asking Pip what clubs he went to. Megan didn't hear his answer, but he was nice to them—the way he seemed to be to everyone. Never impatient or dismissive. The Chamber of Commerce definition of hospitable.

The next block down, Will hopped off his stand seeing Megan coming. The youngest of the group, he was also the most restless, seemingly always in motion. Megan had seen him do waist twists and stretches atop his stand, and figured he'd probably burn off the calories of lunch by the time she was back to her beach chair.

"Looks really good," he said, popping the plastic lid with sandy hands, not caring how bits of the beach ended up in his food.

Megan gave him a napkin, imagining Will's parents had spent a great deal of time following after him with a vacuum cleaner.

Eating, Will said, "You really kill it swimming."

"Thanks." Megan hoped Pip—or Adrian—hadn't told him to say that. The thought was sweet, but she'd rather be told to get her ass in gear—although she wouldn't have reacted well to that growing up. Maybe some of Cassie had worn off on her.

#

The next morning, Pip added push-ups to their routine. Counting them off, he watched Megan, and as soon as he saw her struggling had them stop. But Megan kept going, counting out loud. Straining, she made it to 15. The rest of them could probably do 50.

Arms like rubber, Megan stood, brushing sand off her palms.

Adrian smacked her on the butt. "Nice one."

Pip started them on a 100-yard sand sprint. Megan was last to reach the finish line, but not as far behind as she used to be.

10.

It was unusual for Stewart to call in the middle of the day. If Megan heard from him during work hours (including weekends), it was typically a text. Phone calls were generally at night—two or three times a week—the most recent had been the day before last: a conversation cut short when Stewart, still at the office at 8:30 p.m. Scottsdale time, received an email he'd been waiting for.

The timing of Stewart's call caused Megan to wonder if something was wrong, but she could tell from his tone of voice all was well even before he filled her in on what had been going on at work: the Talbot-Glen deal progressing better than expected.

Sitting on the balcony, talking with Stewart, Megan watched the ocean, the beach, and Pip.

She and Stewart spoke about Cassie—who neither had heard from in days. They agreed she seemed even more involved with her internship than her first year of college, a period of time when Cassie's phone calls home had dropped from every few days to irregular to pretty much only when she wanted something she figured she'd have a better chance of getting by voice than text.

Megan mentioned picking up a new student to tutor online, and that she'd seen some of their fellow condo owners and might get together for lunch with the women in the building who went out as a group a few times every summer.

She said she was still swimming in the ocean but hadn't yet told Stewart about doing that with the lifeguards. Not that it was a secret, she just didn't want to give him the opportunity to seem disinterested. When she'd taken up swimming again last fall at Villa James, the most he'd ever said was one of those standard acknowledgments of marital indifference: "sounds like fun" or "good for you." And when she'd first mentioned swimming in the ocean last week, he'd said, "I bet it's cold," then changed the subject.

Sometimes Stewart's reactions could make it seem as if it mattered no more what she did with her days than the laundry detergent she used. As if her life, unlike his and Cassie's, had no trajectory, but was merely varying shades of idleness.

At the same time, Megan was mindful Stewart may have had similar thoughts about her reaction to his daily routine. She picked up his impatience when she didn't follow his explanation of a business deal, or she forgot the importance of one of the corporate officers (or whatever they were called) at the new company in Scottsdale. Stewart's small firm in Baltimore had never needed a titled-employee structure: there had been Stewart and everyone else who worked for him, all of whom Megan had gotten to know—along with their partners or plus-ones—at various company functions over the years.

Or maybe none of those interpretations were accurate. Maybe being apart from Stewart for prolonged periods of time were causing her mind to play tricks on her. Maybe everything really was fine. Different, but fine. Sometimes it was easier to believe that than others—to dodge those checklists of insecurities that awakened her in the middle night and wouldn't wash away until she was swimming in the ocean.

Ten minutes into Stewart's call, their conversation began to lose momentum when he mentioned, "I'm heading back out to Newport Coast tomorrow. And if all goes as it should I'll be there until the fourth." Meaning July 4th. "How about meeting me there?" He made the offer sound very, very casual—as if mindful of emotional landmines.

Having been briefed of this possible invitation by Cassie days ago, Megan was prepared, and quickly responded: "Sounds fun."

"Really? Fantastic. I'll have Anna book your flight and call you with the details." Anna was Stewart's long-time assistant. "Maybe you'll come out a couple days ahead of time?" Stewart was being casual again, more tiptoeing.

They didn't used to be that way.

Megan hesitated just briefly, then: "Sure."

"And afterward...?"

The question triggered a reflex in Megan's mind: trying to figure how she could leave California after the fourth and get back to the beach as soon as possible. She needed to stop doing that.

Megan agreed to stay in California for a week and immediately regretted that—it would be cutting short what might be her last summer here by seven precious days. After Stewart ended their call, she actually began to feel sick about it when she saw Pip sprint into the ocean on a save.

#

A middle-aged couple on a flimsy raft had drifted beyond the waves and couldn't get back in.

Megan was amazed how quickly Pip swam out to them.

He had them hold onto his life buoy along with their raft. Treading water alongside them, he seemed to chat easily, maybe making sure they were okay, or giving instructions. After a minute or so, the couple nodded, and Pip pulled them toward the beach.

By the time they reached shallow water, most of the onlookers who'd collected along the shore had returned to their beach chairs or blankets. Will and Art, who'd been ready to assist Pip, returned to their stands.

The life raft couple shook Pip's hand, their postures a mix of thanks and embarrassment.

It had been a "routine" save, folks used to the safe borders of a swimming pool losing track of how deep the water was and getting caught in the current of an outgoing tide, which tended to induce panic, especially in poor swimmers. Spotting those situations and resolving them quickly was what kept the save routine.

Two hours later, Pip was dragging his stand back to the dunes for the night when Megan crossed the path in the sea grass to meet him.

Pip smiled at her. That ever-present smile.

Megan asked, "When's the next surf patrol test?"

"So you do want to see if you can do it."

"No," Megan replied, "I want the job."

If this ended up being her last summer here, she was going out in style.

11.

Megan's swims with the guards became more intense, preparing her for the next surf patrol test, yet to be scheduled sometime in July.

Five mornings into that new routine, the weather lost its springtime innocence. Ominous, grey clouds moved low across the sky. The ocean was dashed with white caps. Waves rose tall and heavy, spraying foam off their tops as they curled and crashed like explosions of watery glass. Other than the four surf patrol guards and Megan, the beach was deserted.

"It's really kicked up out there," Megan called over the roar of wind and waves.

"You ready for this?" Pip asked.

Megan refused to admit she was afraid.

Will sprang up and down on his toes, eager to hit the water.

Pip gave instructions: "Here's what we're going to do: you guys swim south." Pointing Will, Art, and Adrian in that direction. "Put in your distance. I'm going to show Megan how to get out of a riptide."

Starting for the ocean, Adrian brushed close to Megan and offered a happy smile. "Have fun."

The three guards entered the wild ocean side by side, diving through a rising wave like a trio of spears.

Still on the beach, Pip slung his buoy's leash around Megan's shoulder and secured her grip on the handle. "Hold on until you get to the breakers. You go under a wave, you let it go—let the line run out behind you. You'll feel the wave jerk the buoy." He gave the leash a stiff pull as an example. "Like that."

Megan steadied her balance against Pip's tug on the leash.

"Waves this size," Pip directed, "you've got to swim under them. Really kick. Or they'll slam you and you'll be exhausted getting out there."

Megan flinched when an exceptionally large wave crashed with a tremendous boom.

"Once we're past the break, there's gonna be one kick-ass current." He made sure she was looking at him. "Let the buoy float behind you while you're swimming. You need a break, pull it in, hug it under your arms, and float 'til you catch your breath. Okay?" He smiled as if they were about to start off on an adventure.

Megan's heart pounded with anticipation. She nodded, pushing away hair that blew in her face. She followed Pip into the ocean—no sooner in up to her thighs than she felt the power of the current.

They went under a wave and the white water threw the buoy behind her until the leash ran out and there was that hard, snapping pull on her shoulder, just like Pip said.

When Megan surfaced, Pip was twenty-five yards ahead of her. He'd swum a long way underwater and was now rising up the face of a building wave that was about to crash on top of her. "Swim, swim!" he called out before disappearing over the other side of the breaker.

Megan took a deep breath and dove, kicking. Her shoulder jerked back when the buoy was wrenched into the surge, but she kept going, staying under as long as she could.

When she came up, Pip was still fifteen yards away.

"Swim to me fast as you can."

Megan propelled herself forward and reached where he was treading water. They were beyond the wave break and in a crosscurrent, which she didn't recognize until Pip pointed toward the beach: they were already well north of where they'd gone in, almost to Art's stand.

53

Pip had Megan clutch the buoy under her arms. "We're going to let it pull us out. When it eases, we'll swim north, with the current, until we find a spot where we can angle into shore. Okay?"

Breathing hard, Megan nodded.

"Hold onto the buoy," he said, "and I'll hold onto you." He got behind Megan, wrapped his arms around her waist and pulled her securely against him. "Rip tide coming up." He wasn't winded at all. "You see it? The color of the water's slightly paler. And look to the beach: no waves in this section. Because all the water's pulling back out through a break in the sand bar. All water—including the ocean—looks for the path of least resistance."

The rip was powerful, like a river within the sea, and took them fifty yards farther out to deep water. The beach suddenly seemed far away.

Pip said, "I've got you."

Megan wasn't afraid.

"Riptides account for two-thirds of our saves. You never swim against one this strong. Okay?" Pip squeezed his arms around her to prompt a response.

Megan nodded. "Okay."

They drifted in the wild ocean without speaking. Pip holding her.

"And now it's over," he said.

Megan realized she'd closed her eyes. She opened them now.

"You feel it?" Pip asked. "We're through the rip. It just ends. It always ends. I'm going to let you go." When she didn't respond, he said: "Okay? I'm going to let you go and we're going to swim in."

"Okay."

"It's going to take a little while. So pace yourself." He made it sound like fun.

"Okay."

Maybe he didn't hear her because he didn't let go. He kept her firmly in his arms, holding her against him, floating. "Okay?" he asked.

"Yes."

He let go and they swam for shore.

Megan wasn't scared by the waves or the riptide. All she thought about—swimming to the beach and for the rest of the day and all through that night—was how it felt being in Pip's arms.

She kept telling herself it was nothing. Nothing had happened. Nothing was going to happen. He'd just held on to her to make certain she was safe. That was all. Telling herself that over and over as she counted the hours until morning when she'd see him again.

12.

Overnight, the weather worsened. A squall darkened the morning sky. Streaks of rain slashed the white-capped sea.

When a bolt of lightning crackled and hit the ocean directly in front of Megan's building, she jumped back from her balcony door and gasped when her entire building shook from the powerful rumble of thunder that followed.

Then she saw Pip: a glimmer of bright-yellow rain slicker scrambling out from behind the blue storage box where Lulu locked her umbrellas and chairs. She couldn't believe he was out in this storm.

Megan grabbed a rain jacket, threw it on over the t-shirt and Cassie's lacrosse shorts she'd slept in, and sprinted out the door. She ran barefooted along the open walkway toward the stairs, bypassing the elevator in case the power went out.

Inside the stairwell, rain pounded the roof as she hurried down five flights. At ground level, she yanked open the door and stepped out into the rain, feet splashing into water gushing from a downspout. "Pip!" Calling through the storm. "Pip!"

He trotted out from beneath a townhouse deck across the side street, beach bag and buoy slung over his shoulder.

Megan waved anxiously. "Hurry. The lightning."

"Man, did you see that!"

They retreated under cover of the garage, both of them drenched.

"What were you doing out there!"

"Watching the ocean." Pip pulled down the hood of his slicker, shedding rainwater.

"Aren't you afraid of lightning?"

"No."

"But your father...?"

"He wasn't afraid of lightning. He thought it was beautiful."

There was a majesty to storms Megan appreciated—the uncontrolled power of nature. Even now, it created a sense of solitude, as if the storm had sequestered them from the rest of the world. Megan didn't see any other people. Didn't hear any traffic on the highway. Didn't see or hear anyone or anything at all. As if there was only the rain. And Pip.

She asked, "Do you have to stay out here?"

"No."

"Have you had breakfast?"

#

Megan slid open the bottom drawer to the single dresser she shared with Stewart, looking for dry clothes Pip could change into. She unfolded a sweatshirt Stewart hadn't worn in years. Finding pants long enough for Pip's height proved more challenging. She grabbed a pair of faded jeans and khaki shorts to give him the choice.

Pip was in the bathroom with the door open, drying his hair with a towel. Shirtless. Rain pants slung low on his hips.

Megan felt herself blush. Even though she'd seen him in nothing but Speedos, this felt forbidden. This was undressing, which made the leanness of his body seem raw, drawing her eyes from the breadth of his shoulders to the taper of his hips.

"Sweatshirt." She tossed it to him.

He caught it. "Thanks."

"Pants or shorts?" She held one in each hand.

"Shorts work."

She handed them to him and became conscious of still wearing what she'd slept in, that the softness of her top—damp at the collar from where rain had gotten inside her jacket—

revealed she wasn't wearing anything beneath it. "I'm going to change."

"Okay."

Megan retreated to the bedroom. Closed the door. Pulled off her t-shirt and put on a pale cotton blouse and black tights.

In the dining room, dry and wearing Stewart's clothes, Pip looked at the row of framed family photographs on the floating picture ledge. "This is Cassie," he assumed.

Taken by a newspaper photographer during a lacrosse game, the image captured Cassie taking a shot on goal, stick drawn back at three-quarter angle, readying to be whipped forward. A brutal grimace on her face. Muscles of her arms and legs taut.

Megan said, "It's from the championship last spring."

"I take it she scored."

"She did." Megan spoke plainly. "That goal and six others. She set a state record for goals in a championship game." She opened the refrigerator. "How does an omelet sound?"

"An omelet sounds great. But that was most understated mom-boasting I've ever heard."

Megan took out a carton of eggs. "The picture's not my favorite."

Pip moved on to the next photo: one of those professional portraits that seemed standard in every place at the beach: Megan, Stewart, and Cassie three summers ago, each wearing a white shirt and white pants, sitting on the sand at sunset against a background of dunes and sea grass.

Looking at a different picture, Pip asked, "This your mom?"

"Stewart's."

"Really?"

"I know. People often mistook us for mother and daughter. Freud could have had a field day."

Pip slowly moved along the rest of the pictures then came over to sit on a stool at the peninsula as Megan chopped mushrooms, cheese, and an elongated sweet pepper. "So why don't you like that picture of Cassie?"

Megan didn't answer at first, then, taking a breath, said: "Because ten seconds later, that shot Cassie took hit the helmet of the other team's goalie. And the sound was like a car accident—this awful explosion. The poor girl dropped like a rag doll." Megan closed her eyes and shuddered. "I can still hear the girl's mother screaming when she ran out onto the field. I can't imagine how that felt—seeing her daughter like that—it looked like she was dead…"

Megan released a deep breath and opened her eyes. She stared at the vegetables she'd started dicing. "It was very scary. For what seemed forever the girl didn't move at all. And her mother kept shrieking. She finally came to, and they took her to the hospital. And I assumed after something like that they'd call the game off. But they didn't. The ambulance was hardly off the field when they started playing again. I couldn't believe it. I was still shaking when Cassie came out of the face-off with the ball, charged down field, and fired another shot that seemed even harder than the one that just hurt that girl. The other team's replacement goalie ducked. I got so lightheaded I thought I was going to pass out. Meanwhile, some of the fathers from our school—mothers, too—started high-fiving, saying the game was as good as over. Stewart was in his glory. And I was mortified. Stewart told me I didn't understand sports because I'd never played. But that had nothing to do with it."

Megan remained in a stare. "I'd been watching Cassie play lacrosse since she was six. And once she got to high school, I don't know, something changed, and she was suddenly much more aggressive than most of the other girls. But that day, I don't know if it was playing for the state championship for a second year in a row, or that long string of undefeated games, or because it was going to be her last high school game, but there was a ruthlessness to her—as though nothing was going to get in the way of what she wanted."

Pip said, "You liked it better when she wore butterfly bathing suits." Referring to another picture on the ledge, taken the first summer they had this condo: Cassie holding Megan's hand as a wave lapped at their ankles.

"I did," Megan admitted. "It went by too fast. It got away from me."

"Time does that," Pip agreed. Even when he wasn't smiling, it felt as if he was—his eyes seeming soulful and bright at the same time.

Megan fixed their omelets and toast—Pip liked jelly on his bread—and they ate at the dining room table. Megan sat at one end and Pip sat at her elbow, so they both had a view of the storm through the sliding glass doors.

It continued to rain hard, but the thunder and lightning stopped. Pip said if it didn't clear by noon, he'd have the rest of the day off. But he expected the storm to pass by then.

As they ate, Megan asked about his nickname, which he said was just a shortened version of his surname: Pippinger. His first name was Blake, which Megan thought sounded far too formal, and Pip said his mother told him was a family name, but later admitted was from a prime-time soap opera she used to watch.

Megan asked where he lived, and he told her he shared a little house on the bay with two friends. The place belonged to Pip's aunt, who'd once lived there year-round with her second husband. After her husband died, she'd told Pip he could have the attic bedroom if he wanted—rent-free—so he took it. Last year his aunt moved to Pittsburgh to be with her sister. "She said it was because I was never going to get married if it looked like I still lived with my mother," Pip laughed.

"She obviously never saw all the girls who stop by your stand... You know they're flirting?" Megan teased. "All those girls. Chickadoodles, Lulu calls them."

Pip laughed. "It's just..."

"What? It's just what?" Megan nudged his arm.

"I don't know. What do I say?"

Megan picked up their plates and carried them to the kitchen. "You can't say you don't like it."

"I don't know." He leaned back, stretching his legs beneath the table.

"Do you ever take them home?" She rinsed the plates. "Any of these chickadoodles?"

He started to respond, stopped.

"Yes...?" Megan encouraged, only because while he seemed uncomfortable, he was smiling.

Pip said, "When I was a kid—like Will—yeah. It was a good way to meet girls."

"I bet it was." Megan put the plates in the dishwasher. "Is there anyone now? Are you any closer to making your aunt happy? I take it she wants to see you get married."

"I don't think she really cares about that," Pip said from the table. "I think it was just an excuse why she wanted to move other than admitting she hadn't been feeling that great and wanted to be with her sister."

"I see..." Megan returned to the table and sat down, angling her chair toward the balcony, legs outstretched alongside Pip's.

They fell quiet, looking at the rain still coming down hard, screening their view of the ocean.

A whisper of anticipation increased Megan's pulse just breaths before Pip placed his hand on her forearm, resting it there.

Electricity different than lightning coursed through her as she continued looking straight ahead. She moved her hand to his, letting their fingers entwine. The sort of moment she'd imagined in glimpses over the past two weeks but always cast aside, never wanting the idea to take hold, to admit the temptation. And now: what was she doing? How could this be happening?

He asked, "Do you want to sit on the sofa?"

Megan nodded.

Holding hands, they moved to the couch, where Pip settled Megan onto his lap.

That he had on her husband's clothes shot around in her mind like a ricochet, but Megan didn't care.

Pip put his arms around her. His kiss blossomed across her lips with a sweetness that made her gasp, which his tongue took as invitation to enter her mouth.

As his hand slipped inside her untucked shirt, she anticipated his touch sliding up to her breasts—to discover whether her bra snapped in the front or the back. She wasn't going to say no. As wrong as it was.

He whispered, "I fell in love with you the first time I saw you."

#

Two hours later, sunlight broke through the parting clouds. Pip was back on his guard stand. People came out onto the beach. And Megan was packing a suitcase.

13.

"They're one short today," Bill Clary reported to his wife, binoculars focused on the lifeguards headed into the ocean for their pre-work swim.

Mary Jane came to the screen door, having long ago given up reminding her husband he might want to check her proximity before saying something he expected her to hear.

"The one who wears the blue bathing suit," Bill said.

"What about her?"

"She's not with them this morning." Bill watched the guards dive through waves that remained large after yesterday's storm. "You ever ask Marjorie if she knows who she is."

"I told you yesterday: Marjorie and Frank aren't down yet." Referring to their friends who had a place in the Ocean Vista next door.

"Well if you told me, I forgot or didn't hear you."

Mary Jane stood alongside her husband. "Maybe she's got better sense than to go out there in that. Look at those waves."

"Heard them pounding all night." Bill lowered his binoculars, letting them hang around his neck. "They're late getting started today. They waited for her. Pip even went into the building. Looking for her I figure."

"And maybe she told them, you're all are nuts, I'm not going out in that today."

"She was out there the other morning. Way the hell out with Pip in a riptide."

"And maybe she's not doing that again."

"I don't think that's it."

"So what is it, Captain?" Mary Jane asked, used to
indulging how her husband was often more interested in people
from a distance—people he would never get to know—than
many of their own friends. Given his former profession, it was
a natural hobby. But if he ever got to the point of suspecting
some grand conspiracy, she'd put an end to it. "What do you
think's going on with the girl in the blue bathing suit?"

Bill grinned, knowing she was teasing him a little—the way
she said, girl in the blue bathing suit, making it sound like a title
to one of the old Travis McGee novels he used to read. He
said, "I'll keep you posted, General." Believing the key to a
good and lasting marriage was being clear about the chain of
command.

#

During yesterday's storm, they'd kissed on the sofa for a long
time—Megan and Pip—and would have done more had Pip
not eased back and gently held her face, looking at her as if to
say, Not here, not yet. And she'd understood. Just as he
seemed to understand he needed to leave. Because the rain had
stopped, and people were going to start coming outside.
People who might see him leave her condo.

Megan asked Pip not to tell any of the other guards,
although, thinking about it later, she suspected Adrian might
already think something was going on between them, the way
the girl had told her to "have fun" when Pip took her out to
experience the riptide. At the time, Megan thought Adrian had
been trying to ease her anxiety about being in a dangerous
current, but thinking about it now, her expression may have
implied something else. And don't tell Lulu, Megan made Pip
promise, because Lulu knows Cassie.

That fast, it had all begun to feel so complicated and made
her guilty. How had she let it happen? She assumed because
of too much time away from Stewart, who she'd been always
completely faithful to, any thoughts of other men no more than

idle curiosity, the way she would have wondered what it might be like to climb Mt. Everest. So she'd called Stewart and asked if he'd like her to come out to California early. How about now? Pleasantly surprised by Megan's request, Stewart had Anna, his assistant, book Megan a flight and arrange a car for the three-hour drive to the airport.

Megan had checked into the BWI Marriott last night, had dinner in her room, a sleepless night, then taken a shuttle to the airport by 9:00 a.m. this morning for an 11:00 flight, first class to Orange County, where another car—a limo this time—picked her up.

Twenty-four hours after Pip's last kiss Megan was in Southern California.

14.

As the limousine crested Newport Coast Drive, the Pacific Ocean didn't just appear on the horizon, it consumed it. Viewed from the steep hillside, the sea was enormous, flawless, smooth, and silvery blue, dashed with sailboats playing catch with the summer breeze.

The inland landscape was no less spectacular. Splendid homes with Spanish-tile roofs terraced down to winding Pacific Coast Highway. Sleek, exotic cars—some looking straight off a racetrack—sped past, engines winding out with perfect horsepower-pitch, oblivious to speed limits and possible dangers of curves in the road.

Proceeding down the hill, the limo turned beneath formidable twin arches of rose-hued stone trellised with flowering vines. Inside a gated 50-acre enclave of palms and evergreens, impressive Mediterranean-style villas were arranged along small cul-de-sacs. Every villa had an iron entrance gate, front courtyard, and privacy walls climbing with bougainvillea.

A trio of women—all impossibly slender, blond, and tanned—jogged the sun-dappled sidewalk in designer athletic wear.

The limo eased into the driveway of a two-story villa that had a view of blue ocean and even bluer sky so splendid it seemed as if painted. Megan was about to ask if this was the correct address—she'd assumed she'd be driven to a hotel—when the home's massive front doors opened, and Stewart strode outside to greet her.

Megan's handsome husband extended his arms as if taking possession of the hillside, smiling. "Isn't it fantastic."

There wasn't time for more than a quick hug and kiss. Stewart wanted to show Megan inside the house: the impressive foyer with its sweeping open staircase, dark-stained moldings, and wide banisters. High ceilings, butterscotch-beige walls, and pale marble floors throughout. A large open living room with a fireplace and pair of oversized sofas piled with soft pillows led to a comfortable dining room with a mission-style table for twelve. A spacious kitchen offered marble countertops, commercial gas stove, Sub-zero fridge, walk-in pantry, and more cabinets than Megan could imagine filling. Every room had dazzling window views of the Pacific.

"Like it so far?"

Stewart didn't need an answer, but Megan replied anyway. "It's beautiful." She was pushing through the lack of sleep that had her feeling this trip was a mistake. Yesterday, the thrill and excitement of being with Pip was overcome by panic about what she'd done. She couldn't be with him. What was it going to be, an affair? She'd needed to get away from the temptation.

"If you don't like the furniture, we can change it." The soles of Stewart's cap toe oxfords echoed off the high ceiling as he led Megan back through the foyer and past her suitcase which sat just inside the door. Wearing a starched dress shirt and well-fitting slacks, Stewart started up the marble stairs to the second floor, three steps ahead of her. "There are other houses. But this one seems like us."

Stewart's tour would have been more enjoyable if Megan didn't so desperately want to peel out of her slouchy airplane garb—wide-leg pants and t-shirt—and try to get some sleep. She'd figured on doing that before Stewart finished work for the day—what she'd estimated would be hours from now given his usual schedule. Instead, he was showing her five large bedrooms on the upper level.

The house kept going on and on. The same beige walls, tall ceilings, and marble floors in the second-floor hallway, but carpet in the bedrooms, four of which had king beds with the fourth set up as a home office. The main bedroom had a view not just of the ocean but the home's private pool and spa.

Stewart opened the bedroom door to a small balcony and stepped outside, announcing, "We have a visitor from the east."

At first Megan thought he was talking to her, then she saw someone in a chaise by the pool wearing a yellow two-piece.

"Hey, M!" Cassie waved. "Welcome to California!"

#

"When did you get here!" Hugging Cassie, part of Megan still melted with that same intensity as when Cassie was a lost little girl in Megan's classroom a decade ago.

"Last night. S pulled out all the stops once you said you were coming. Got me on a flight out of Dulles."

Stewart stood to the side, proud of making these arrangements. "We tried getting you on the same flight…"

The two women were equal in height at five-seven, with shoulder-length hair in similar shades of silky brown. Neither wore make-up. Both slender, Cassie had avoided adding pounds by sticking to the sports-performance diet that had been her regimen since 10th grade. Cassie also had the stronger legs from all the running, while Megan's shoulders had become more defined from swimming.

"I've missed you," Megan sighed happily.

"Missed you, too."

Megan didn't want to let Cassie go, but her daughter was easing away—there was a time limit, wasn't there, for how long an independent young woman would remain in an embrace with a parent. Which to Megan felt like rejection, although she knew she was being overly sensitive, still stung by an incident last fall, when Cassie—back from college for the weekend—went to a party with some former lacrosse teammates and came home drunk.

If Stewart hadn't been away when it happened, maybe it would have gone differently, maybe he would have cushioned Megan's reaction. And not as much about the drinking—although that was bad enough—as how that drunkenness had been a sign of Cassie not just getting older but having less in common with Megan, who had never been much for alcohol or drugs. Mainly, though, was what Cassie had said.

That awful night, Megan had been in the living room with a fire in the fireplace, reading while waiting for Cassie. Thinking they'd sit together for a while and talk, because Cassie hadn't been home in five weeks—the longest stretch Megan had been away from her.

The car—an Uber—had pulled in the driveway around 1:00 a.m., bringing Cassie home. Coming up to the house, Cassie dropped her keys, muttered, "Shit," and was on her hands and knees looking for them, illuminated by the Uber driver's headlights when Megan came outside. "Effing keys," Cassie had sworn moments before violently throwing up into the bushes, pitching forward, groaning when it was all out, wiping her mouth with the sleeve of her hoodie, then struggling to her feet.

Megan assumed Cassie had eaten some nasty food until the girl tumbled over onto the lawn and started laughing. "Oh, God, M, I am so drunk." No shame to it at all.

Megan had been so shocked and disappointed and sad she'd wanted to cry.

She'd helped Cassie inside, too upset to talk, just getting her upstairs and into bed. Cassie had laughed sourly, "Oh, no, the silent treatment. I'm in big trouble. Big trouble." Then, as Megan had turned off the light in Cassie's room and moved into the hallway to close the door, Cassie had muttered after her, "You're not my mother you know."

Those words had pierced Megan like a dagger. Cassie never said anything like that before, not even during her impetuous early teens.

The following day, there were apologies from Cassie, a long discussion, and promises never to do that again—all taking place late in the afternoon by the time the girl could finally get out of bed. Absent from that exchange, however, had been any reference to Cassie having told Megan she wasn't her mother, an accusation which, by that time, had replayed in Megan's head hundreds of times, bringing out tears she'd managed to suppress the night before.

Maybe Cassie didn't remember. Megan didn't bring it up, not then and never since. Not to Cassie or to Stewart, from whom Megan had kept the entire incident a secret. Because what was the point? Why get into more emotional upheaval by reliving it and possibly making it worse?

And what could Stewart have said to undo what had happened? Especially since he'd become much more in sync with his daughter than Megan, who was sentimental about the sweetness of Cassie's youth ebbing away. Stewart, in his calm, confident way, would have likely blamed his daughter's drunken words on alcohol and provided assurance—as he had when Cassie started referring to them as "M and S" instead of "Mom and Dad"—how much Cassie loved her and thought of her as her mother.

Megan had never even mentioned the matter to Jillian, her best friend, other than to say Cassie had come home drunk. Which Jillian hadn't thought was a big deal and wrote off as part of being that age.

So Megan tried to pretend that whole night never happened. But even now, happily reunited with Cassie at a beautiful house overlooking the Pacific Ocean, Megan heard echoes of those horrible words from that cold night: You're not my mother.

Then, just behind that memory, a much sweeter refrain played back: I fell in love with you the first time I saw you. Pip had told her that just yesterday—words which Megan also needed to pretend never happened.

15.

They sat poolside in the sun, a family reunion, catching up the way they did now with Stewart working primarily in Scottsdale and Cassie in DC, having sailed through her freshman year with a 4.0 and landing a coveted summer internship.

Stewart, much as always, talked about work, but it was a different dialogue since his much smaller company had merged with Dunhill Infrastructure, a conglomerate aggressively buying up engineering firms in North America, with aspirations to go worldwide. Instead of handling everything his own firm had been involved with—from HR to bidding to performance—Stewart had quickly become one of Scott Dunhill's trusted inner-circle and now led a team that evaluated target companies to see if they were worthy of being added to Dunhill's growing stable of engineering talent.

Stewart's confidence—tested thirteen years ago by the sudden death of his first wife—had never been stronger. And he liked the money.

Stewart had grown up in a lower middle-class family, the youngest of five. His father had been a supervisor at a tire plant in a small Maryland town at the base of the Appalachian Mountains. It had been a good job, but finances were always tight.

In high school, Stewart was a football standout—a starting quarterback his junior and senior years—but he'd been even better at math, which got him a partial scholarship to nearby Frostburg. In college, when he wasn't studying, he was working. Manual labor, then an entry position at a tunneling company. When he graduated, he had offers from three different engineering firms and took the one in Baltimore—a job no longer involved with tunnels but commercial buildings, the city going through a bit of a renaissance at the time.

Stewart's first wife, Caroline—Cassie's mother—died just a year after Stewart started his own business. When Megan met him, Tyler Engineering consisted only of Stewart and three employees. When he merged with Dunhill last year, Stewart had 17 people on his payroll and jobs up and down the east coast, including lucrative federal government contracts.

Megan had gotten to know most of Stewart's employees—spending time with them at various company outings and parties over the years—but the new Dunhill people he spoke about were a blur, names she couldn't associate with a face because she was yet to meet them. Cassie had the roster down pat, though. Maybe she paid closer attention. Cassie liked the business end of what Stewart did while Megan more enjoyed seeing projects come to life and appreciated the mathematical calculations involved.

At. GW, Cassie was a business major with a concentration in analytics—decision modeling, programing, data mining. An entirely different application of math than Megan had grown up loving, and one that felt soulless. But Cassie thrived in that world, especially when it came to how it made money, which she was good at spending. If Megan had to guess, she'd say Cassie's yellow two-piece with its asymmetrical cutouts probably cost $250, and Cassie would think it was worth it. Then again, she'd grown up with an indulgent father.

Stewart had come a long way from that three-bedroom bungalow with one tight bathroom and strict orders that the thermostat never be dialed above 62 no matter how high the snow drifted outside. He no longer wore Jos. Banks clearance suits as during the days when Megan met him, having moved up to full price at Nordstrom. And since the Dunhill merger, he'd bought half a dozen luxurious dress shirts at Neiman Marcus, one of which he had on now: a mini blue gingham fabric worn open at the collar. Megan thought he looked very

California-modern in that shirt, with his sun-tanned skin, smooth-shaved face, and precisely trimmed brown hair set off by flecks of grey at his temples. A handsome, successful man.

Seated alongside her husband, Megan rested her hand on his arm out of habit. When it was her turn in their family discussion, she talked about the students she was tutoring online. She didn't mention swimming in the ocean and couldn't imagine Stewart and Cassie's reaction if she said she was thinking about joining the surf patrol as a guard—or what did they call it online: surf rescue technician?

Stewart hadn't wanted her to take the teaching job at Villa James—telling her they didn't need the money. He hadn't understood why she'd wanted to make that commitment when she could come and go as she pleased as a volunteer. In retrospect, Megan suspected the heart of that disagreement was that Dunhill wanted Stewart in Arizona full-time and Stewart hadn't wanted to break that news to her, knowing she wouldn't want to leave Maryland.

When Megan told Stewart and Cassie about the 4th-grader she was tutoring who used the UK term and called it "maths", Cassie said she was going British and using that plural from now on.

Their family time was interrupted by a voice coming from the side of the house.

Someone asking for "Ms. Tyler," preceded the arrival of two fit-looking women in matching uniforms—loose fitting white shirts and pants—both carrying plush towels over their arms.

Cassie clapped. "Yes! Massage time. Come on, M."

As their daughter rounded the pool to greet the masseurs, Megan looked at her husband, who did like setting up these surprises. "How much is all this costing?"

He gave her a kiss and said, "I'm going back to the office. See you at dinner."

#

The mother-daughter poolside "traveler's detox" massage was just the amazing start.

Megan lay on her back, draped by a luxurious towel, as the woman with beautiful dark hair and tireless hands plied every last bit of tension from her neck and shoulders.

"You have a strong back," the woman said softly, her voice interrupting the quiet.

Megan thought to say something about swimming but her will to do much more then enjoy the moment faded away.

On a portable massage table alongside her, Cassie murmured repeated praises of, "Oh, my God this is fantastic." She laid face down, towel covering the bump of her backside, as the masseuse dug her hands into her strong thighs.

These were the moments Megan missed most: being with Cassie, who had become such a powerful part of her life so fast. She would have never thought love at first sight could apply to someone else's child, but it had.

Megan closed her eyes, letting the masseuse hypnotically roll her head side to side, lulling her into a pleasant buzz that began to drift toward sleep when the sound of sliding doors alerted the arrival of a third woman—this one younger, wearing a three-quarter-sleeve chef's coat and fanning a tablecloth over the wrought iron table.

"Lunch," Cassie announced pleasantly.

What was this costing? Megan wondered again. And how had Stewart set it up so fast? Anna, she imagined, his assistant. But still... After months of putting off joining him in Scottsdale—wanting to finish out the school year, but also—and mainly—not wanting to leave their home, their life in Maryland—she'd only asked 24 hours ago if Stewart would want her to come out now.

Maybe he saw this as his opportunity and was making the most of it. As if to propose: how could she not love it here? Their new life: Cassie and Megan, post-massage, slipping into matching robes, sitting in the partial shade of the cedar-post pergola. A personal chef serving endive-watercress salads with sliced avocado on chilled plates. Thin-sliced chicken breast on multi-grain bread with bean sprouts, wasabi mayonnaise, and paper-thin slivers of dried dates. A small side of quinoa/parsley salad.

After lunch, they dipped in the pool. Megan and Cassie side by side, elbows on the coping, legs extended in front of them, kicking idly in the silky water. Overlooking rooftops of red tile that stepped down the hill to the ocean.

Megan asked, "I wonder if there are dolphins?" Thinking about that first day in their condo in Ocean City, Cassie with her nose to the glass balcony door.

Cassie said, "I bet there are."

Megan's memory from years ago blended into one much more recent: being in the ocean with the guards, with Pip, when Adrian spotted the pair of dolphins swimming nearby. She pushed that thought away. Took a deep breath, let it out. Closed her eyes. The urge to sleep was pulling at her, but she couldn't imagine that happening. Too many thoughts in her head, bubbling to the surface now that the massage and lunch were over. But she also didn't want to lose precious time with Cassie. "Tell me more about your internship," she asked, interested because it was important to Cassie, so it needed to be important to her.

"I might quit."

"What?" Megan hoped that came out as surprise, not hopefulness they might get the chance to spend the summer together after all.

"I might quit. And come out here. I mean Scottsdale's nice ... but ASU?" She made a face, nose and mouth pinching as if a rotted smell soured the air. "Here, though? Stanford. It's a poke up the coast, but doable. Plus, I mean, Stanford. All the tech up there."

"Really? You'd transfer?"

"You and S are going to be here." Cassie made it sound decided. "What's to think about? Otherwise it's five hours in a plane, and that's going to get old fast."

75

The already-conflicting emotions swirling inside Megan sped their rotation. "Is this really where dad's going to be, though?" Megan asked. "Is any of this final?"

"Probably. Talbot-Glen is a major acquisition for Dunhill." Cassie talked about business with her father's confidence. "It's a mega company—like ten times what S's was. I mean they called that a merger, but Dunhill really bought S's company. Merger just sounds more democratic. Talbot-Glen's more of a true merger. Although Dunhill would have control."

Megan marveled how Cassie could have that insight, imagining it the product of late-night emails and texts with Stewart. "You love GW, though."

"Yeah… And I could love Stanford, too. Maybe more. It would probably be a year from now, though. I doubt I could transfer by fall. Which would mean either a gap year or I stay at GW one more year and do the five-hour flight thing. And a gap year doesn't feel right."

"And you could get into Stanford? I mean I'm sure you could."

"If it's close, I'll tell them I'll play lacrosse. I'd still have three years of eligibility by my junior year. I might have lost a step just playing club, but I could get it back." Out of high school, Cassie had turned down lacrosse scholarships to concentrate on academics, which had come with its own offers.

"This's a lot to think about."

"Is it, though?" Cassie asked. "Look at this place. This's amazing."

"But it's like vacation, Cass. And we just got here. And whatever this place is, it's beautiful but a resort isn't real life."

Cassie laughed. "M—this isn't a resort. This is a house. This is where you'd live. The house, the furniture, it's for sale. The chef and massage people aren't included but everything else is. All you have to tell S is you like it, and it's yours."

Before Megan could digest that possibility, Cassie, checking her phone, determined, "Okay, M, time for shopping."

"Shopping? I'm feeling jetlag catching up with me."

"There's Red Bull in the limo. Plus, there's no way you packed the right clothes."

Megan's style choices were often a source of good-natured ribbing from her fashionable daughter. "You haven't seen what I packed," Megan defended with a smile.

"No—but I've seen where we're going for dinner."

16.

The limo that carried Megan from the airport was waiting in front of the house. Cassie piled into the spacious back as if practiced at being driven in style. Megan slid in alongside her daughter and wondered if there really was Red Bull in the car fridge. But she might not need it. She felt a second—or was it third?—wind kick in, being with Cassie as the limo steered down the hill toward Pacific Coast Highway.

Megan had been to LA and San Francisco—one trip accompanying Stewart on business and the other a family vacation when Cassie was in middle school—but this Southern California coastline was new to her.

"I feel like I need more eyes to take this in," she commented. Leaning forward for a better view out the side window, Megan felt like a tourist.

Expensive homes that covered the rocky hillside looked as if built since the 90's, while all the houses, small apartment buildings, and businesses that lined the highway and spilled onto the beach were a blend of old, new, and rehabbed.

Megan found all the oceanfront shopping centers unusual, locations that would have been reserved for homes or hotels back in Maryland. Maybe that was because California had coastline to spare.

Still, humanity's footprint seemed endless, with paved and striped parking lots stamped atop cliffs that offered switchback paths down to public beaches. As one small town washed almost imperceptibly into the next, the streets and sidewalks were a kaleidoscope of shoppers and beachgoers. Surfers peddled bikes with boards under their arm. Valets hustled cars. Everyone with something in their hand it seemed—bags, coffee, their phone—moving and talking and eating and spending, as if managing a mere singular task would have been underachieving.

Fifteen minutes from the house, the limo pulled to the curb. There were no available parking spaces but a convenient open loading zone in front of a small boutique, a storefront with red awnings that shaded the late afternoon sun.

When the driver opened the rear door, Megan briefly felt conspicuousness, but a limo was nothing here. A quick inventory along the street—Bentley, Porsche, Maserati Ghibli, another Porsche, Tesla, Mercedes Maybach-S, yet another Porsche—quickly put the rather standard limo at its bottom rung of the pecking order. Not to mention, within drone's eye view was an Aston Martin DBR1 bought at auction for $2.25 million.

At the shop's entrance, Cassie pushed a doorbell. Seconds later, a lock freed and Cassie led the way inside, where the air was cool and lightly scented with lavender. An oversized handmade Persian rug lay atop restored Formica floors with swirls of red and grey against a white background. Instead of racks of clothing, vintage mannequins in glamorous dresses and suits lined the walls.

There were no other customers, just a tall blond woman who rose from behind an antique desk and strode toward them with effortless runway posture. "You must be Cassie and Megan." She extended a long slender arm. "I'm Dahn-yahl." That was how she pronounced it anyway. Megan had no idea how that might be spelled. Danielle, maybe.

"That's us." Unintimidated by the woman's height or beauty or make-up, or that she looked red-carpet dazzling, Cassie shook hands as if greeting the opposing lacrosse team's captain.

Megan loved when Cassie did things like that.

"I have some beautiful items selected for you."

"Great. We're all yours."

Megan again found herself wondering how all this had been arranged. Whatever this was, exactly. Were they here by appointment?

At the back of the shop, Danielle lifted garment bags from clothes hanging on a moveable metal rack and put them in two spacious dressing rooms: one for Megan, the other for Cassie. "Some of these are by Bohdana. She's very new. Very hot. One of the young designers coming out of eastern Europe. Ready wear, but still stunning."

As Megan considered which outfit to try first, she looked for price tags. There were none.

Cassie whispered, "Try to pretend you're not at TJ Maxx."

"Got it," Megan replied.

#

They spent an hour with Danielle, trying on clothes, most of which fit surprisingly well, which Megan knew Stewart likely had a hand in arranging. Stewart knew her sizes, committing those details to memory early in their relationship. He also knew her taste in clothes, that she preferred more conservative styles, classic tailored looks, but in bold or contrasting colors and patterns. More rich blues and browns, not so much pastel yellow or orange, which she didn't like against her cooler skin tones. She rarely had to return a birthday or Christmas present from Stewart if it was clothing.

After Danielle's shop, they stopped for coffee at a matchbox-sized place that roasted special blends of Ethiopian beans. Megan needed the caffeine boost. They sat outside on the two-table front patio in the shade of an umbrella. Cassie sipped coffee she drank black. Megan liked cream and two sugars.

"It's like the boardwalk," Megan said of all the people going by, the blond-to-brunette ratio unusually high.

"Mm. With money."

Cassie was likely right about that. No one seemed to be wearing cheap clothes. Even outfits that were supposed to look worn were more likely from a pricey vintage shop than the back of the closet. Shoes were the giveaway—lots of expensive footwear. And high-priced watches and jewelry. All very showy.

Sitting back, Megan stifled a yawn.

"Keeping you up?" Cassie asked.

Megan raised her coffee and drank. No way was she losing time with Cassie to sleep. Moments like this, she dismissed her concerns about them growing apart. Just because they weren't together as often—and Cassie was getting older—didn't mean they weren't still close.

After coffee, the limo drove them back up the hill but continued past the turn to the house and pulled into a small shopping plaza lined with palm trees.

Megan asked Cassie, "And this is?"

"Blowouts."

Out of the limo, Cassie linked arms with Megan, and they entered the salon: mother and daughter. And Megan kept telling herself she was forgetting all about Pip.

17.

Bill and Mary Jane Clary walked barefooted in moonlight along the beach. In their 70's, they still held hands. Bill felt a residual warmth on his face from spending more time in the sun today than usual.

It was a pleasant night for Ocean City, Maryland in mid-June, a time when temperatures could vary as if each day might choose between being spring, summer, or fall.

Music playing loudly from a condominium balcony across the dunes drew Bill's ire. "Barbarians are coming," he sighed.

Because the summer crowds got larger and louder every year, they'd talked about selling their townhouse and had looked at a few places in Rehoboth, half an hour north in quieter and tax-friendly Delaware, but they hadn't found any place that would make the effort and expense worth it. Besides, Bill was just as likely to find something to complain about there, not to mention how one positive aspect of getting older was losing some auditory capacity, which meant the "barbarians" were becoming harder to hear.

In front of the Ocean Vista, Bill looked to the fifth floor. Through curious snooping, he'd determined the unit where the woman in the blue bathing suit had been staying. "Dark up there," he said.

"The mystery continues," Mary Jane replied, aware of what he was referring to.

"Pip must've looked up that way a dozen times today. And the chubby little girl from the beach stand—she glanced up there once or twice herself, then did something on her phone. Text it looked like."

He'd told her bits of that earlier, but Mary Jane didn't say anything because with Bill it often wasn't so much him repeating himself as "reviewing" a set of circumstances he was mulling over, yet to find an answer. "You think they were looking for the woman who's been swimming with them," Mary Jane confirmed. "Who wasn't there this morning."

"I think they're wondering where she is."

"And this interests you why…?"

Bill chuckled. "There's just something about when those two are together—Pip and the woman in the blue bathing suit, as you call her. Makes me smile."

"Then I hope she comes back soon. I like it when you smile." She tugged his hand so he'd lean down the little bit it took for her to be able to kiss his cheek.

#

As the sun slipped into the Pacific and waves crashed onto the beach down the rugged hill, Megan and Cassie emerged from the limo in their new clothes, fitted hours ago at the boutique in Laguna. Megan wore a butter-soft suede military-style jacket with a high waist and soft lapels over a white silk blouse with a matching stitched-in scarf, worn untucked over black slacks with wide legs that pushed the limits of current styles. The look was much more progressive than Megan preferred, and influenced by Cassie, who wore a pale-blue pullover top with a swooping shirttail and skin-tight denim pants patterned in a mosaic of white and dark blue.

Mother and daughter, both in high heels and little make-up, strode arm-in-arm along a torch-lit path, passing a monolithic slab of black rock into which was carved the restaurant's name, C.

The exterior of the modern building was stone, wood, lava rock, and glass—a futuristic architect's vision of Hawaii. A cantilevered deck—teak over steel beams—appeared suspended in mid-air like a high-dive over the edge of the rocky cliff to the ocean below.

C's front doors opened to a dark, intimate interior from which swelled the sounds of laughter and happy conversation, expensive silver touching fine china, and ice cubes kissing crystal. Hints of botanicals and whiffs of cigar smoke from the deck smelled foreign and exotic.

A table for twenty was set along a west-facing window. A beautiful woman in a backless dress sat beside a handsome grey-haired man, thirty years her senior. Another beautiful woman—much younger than the first—looked like someone Megan had seen in a movie not long ago. Every seat was taken except for two. And there was Stewart, seated next to Scott Dunhill, at the center of the table.

So much for an intimate family dinner, Megan thought. Not all her husband's surprises were good ones.

Stewart stood when he saw them approach. "My girls," he said, and everyone turned and looked, and smiled. Stewart drew Megan close and put his arm around her.

For a moment or two, she felt as though she didn't know him.

#

"We were beginning to think you didn't like us." Scott Dunhill, head of the company that bore his name, shook Megan's hand. "So we decided to move the company out here in hopes of bringing you out of hiding."

Dunhill looked very much un-Newport Beach, inches short of six-feet and rangy cowboy thin, with short salt-and-pepper hair, sharp eyes, and deep sun-etched creases in his face. His hands were rugged as though he spent hours a day mending barbed-wire fences.

Megan managed to appear relaxed and at ease, a trait first acquired at parent-teacher conferences, then through hundreds of business functions attended with Stewart. It had been over a year since she'd last endured one of these, but her skill at corporate small talk quickly resurfaced. "I thought you were all in Scottsdale. This is a surprise."

"Well," Dunhill drawled, "if things go well…" He left that sentence unfinished and gestured to the table. "Let's sit down."

Everyone else had retaken their seats. Cassie joined the younger cadre at the end of the table—three men and one woman in their late twenties/early thirties—one of whom Cassie seemed to know. That group had been quickly introduced at a distance to Megan as lawyers from LCW and "belonged" to the good-looking grey-haired man, Holden Lassiter, who Megan first met last fall. Lassiter was the L in LCW—Dunhill's attorneys.

Megan, somehow, ended up seated between Stewart and Dunhill. The company's aggressive leader reached for his glass—scotch/rocks—and took the hearty swallow of a man raised on drinking shots, doing that almost as if daring anyone to tell him it wasn't the couth way to partake a $25 cocktail.

"You know," Dunhill said, speaking to Megan as if they'd known one another for years, not merely having met at an expensive steak dinner in Baltimore last year. "The first ten things I had your husband do, he did nine. The tenth he told me shouldn't be done. We argued about that for two days before I went ahead and did it, and it was a mistake that cost the company a million dollars." Dunhill raised his glass toward Megan's husband. "We haven't argued about anything since, have we, Stewart?"

"Not once," Stewart acknowledged confidently. He sat turned toward Megan with his elbow cocked on the padded back of his chair.

Around the table, conversation carried on with an easy mixture of levity and seriousness.

Dunhill said, "Your husband's a good man, Megan. And I'm glad you're here. Sometimes wives don't understand business. All the sacrifices. And I guess I shouldn't just say wives, because we've got plenty married women working for us whose husbands don't understand all the time they spend at the office. And all the travel. The sacrifice is more than most people can muster."

"It works for us," Megan said, knowing what to say. "I'm a homebody and Stewart loves what he does."

Dunhill laughed and asked Stewart, "How come none of my wives felt that way? I could've saved a bank's worth of alimony."

Megan had noticed last year that Dunhill didn't wear a wedding band and wondered if there was a Mrs. Dunhill somewhere—apparently there had been a few.

Seriously, Dunhill asked, "Megan, do you think you could be happy living out here?"

"I understand it's very sunny," she replied. "And the ocean, well, let's see," she glanced at the window over her shoulder, "oh, well look, it's getting dark, but I'm pretty sure it's right there. Of course, I just got here, so I don't know about the shopping..."

Dunhill grinned at Stewart. "I think your wife's making fun of me."

Not that far from Hollywood, Megan assumed the role she'd flown 3,000 miles to rejuvenate: Stewart's wife, in Stewart's new world.

Jackie Mack, the woman seated beside Holden Lassiter, was introduced as the person handling Dunhill Infrastructure's west coast public relations. Seated with her legs crossed sexily, Jackie smiled friendly and engaging, and extended a slender arm to shake Megan's hand. The slit up the side of Jackie's dress exposed legs as perfect as Megan had ever seen—almost as perfect as the cleavage revealed by a low-cut neckline. Up close, though, the threads of time skilled plastic surgery better concealed at a distance were more visible, and Megan recalculated Jackie as being in her mid-40's.

The girl Megan thought she recognized was an actress, Cara Moore, the lead in an indie film that had won honors at Sundance. Fluttering Megan a wave and singsong "Helloooo," young Cara wore lots of funky necklaces over a designer t-shirt that didn't quite reach the waist of her short skirt. Her knee-high boots had spike heels and were the color of a glossy banana.

Next to Cara was Alex Farrell, head of Farrell-Cruise Investing. Trendily unshaven for three days, thick black hair slicked back, Alex was 35 trying to be 25, and wore a black sports coat over a black dress shirt left unbuttoned at the collar.

Megan didn't get the chance to meet the LCW lawyers Cassie was sitting with by the time dinner was served, and during the meal—with Stewart switching places with her to discuss business with Dunhill—Megan found herself pulled into the eel-slippery conversation of Alex Farrell's group of young investment bankers. All slickly dressed, sporting thick gold watches and more jewelry than Megan was used to seeing on men, the "Ibbies" (as the bankers called themselves) talked over one another about obscene salaries, "points on deals," cars with six-figure price tags, and Maui real estate.

By the time desert orders were taken, Megan was desperate to escape, and slipped onto the deck for a breath of air. More than jetlag, she was feeling numb from all the unfamiliar people and surroundings.

Looking down at the dark ocean, hearing waves break against the rocks, Megan tried to clear her head and find a comforting place for her thoughts to cling. It didn't take long for images of Pip to appear from where she couldn't keep them suppressed.

"Homesick already?" a voice asked.

Megan hadn't heard the man come up behind her.

"Your timing couldn't be more perfect. Being here." Holden Lassiter patted Megan's hand where she gripped the iron railing—a strictly paternal gesture that reminded her of her father. "This is all coming in line quicker than anticipated." The lawyer's broad shoulders filled a classic-cut suit that wouldn't make the cover of GQ but would never go out of style. "If it comes up, the reason you've stayed in Maryland is you don't like being more than a short drive from Cassie. And leave it at that."

Although the statement was true, Megan wasn't sure why Lassiter was bringing it up, or how he knew. She'd met him once—last year at the meeting in Lassiter's DC office when papers were signed about Stewart's company becoming a part of Dunhill Infrastructure.

As though prepping a witness for trial, Lassiter continued: "Dunhill's got two daughters. He's bad with wives, but good with his girls. So he can understand you wanting to be near Cassie. At the same time, Dunhill's contemplating grooming Stewart to be his successor. Which is what a lot of people want to see, and the reason your husband's company was bought in the first place. But it's going to hang Dunhill up if he think's Stewart's got a wife to worry about. Stewart doesn't think that's an issue." Lassiter angled to look at Megan, his frame blocking the view of anyone who might be able to see her from inside the restaurant. "Is it an issue?"

The conversation made Megan uncomfortable, but she delivered the necessary answer: "No, of course not."

"Good." Lassiter smiled—the sort of man with the unyielding determination to found a country. "Shall we go back inside?"

Megan nodded and fell in step alongside the veteran attorney, who delivered a final instruction: "And this conversation was just between you and I."

18.

"I'm afraid I've been terrible company tonight," Scott Dunhill apologized to Megan.

After dinner, everyone stood outside to await their cars.

"I've monopolized your husband," Dunhill continued, "but it's his own damned fault." Dunhill grabbed Stewart's arm as though taking the reins of a thoroughbred about to run its most important race. "Sometimes I think he knows my own company better than I do. If I'd had someone like him all along, there's no telling where I'd be now."

A garnet-red Lamborghini prowled slowly along the entrance drive, engine idling powerfully as it stopped at the curb.

"Alexxx!" one of the Ibbies proclaimed.

The sleek car's gull-wing doors eased opened, and an impressed valet got out.

"Alexxx the man!"

Farrell grinned, his arm around actress Cara Moore's bare midriff.

A yellow Ferrari came out next, and one of the other Ibbies handed the valet a tip.

Dunhill admired the cars. "Stewart, you think we're in the wrong business?"

"No I don't."

"Me neither," Dunhill chuckled, then called, "Hey, Farrell," getting the lead banker's attention. "Don't kill yourself with that thing before we close our deal."

Farrell grinned. "You talking about the car or Cara?"

"Smart ass," Dunhill laughed.

Megan noticed Holden Lassiter standing away from everyone else with one of his older associates, who looked like an Olympic skier. Lassiter looked to be giving instructions the other lawyer took in with the sobriety of a soldier.

Alex Farrell, at the door to his Lamborghini, called back to the others, "You guys coming? Mr. Scott?" Farrell asked. "Mr. Stew?" he asked Stewart.

"We celebrate after deals close," Dunhill remarked, one of those comments it was hard to tell how much was kidding and how much was criticism.

"Misses Stew?" Farrell asked Megan.

"Come on, Mom," Cassie encouraged, waving Megan toward the Saab convertible she was about to get into with the young lawyer she'd sat alongside during dinner. "How often do you get invited to a party at a movie star's house?"

#

Megan was glad to have the top down to the Saab. The cool night air helped keep her awake. Having slept less than four of the past 24 hours, her eyes felt heavy, and her thinking was fuzzy.

Along Pacific Coast Highway, the colors of lit shops and restaurants seemed painted from neon watercolors. Up in the hills, houselights twinkled from rocky ledges overlooking the ocean.

Alex Farrell's Lamborghini had raced out of sight miles ago, chased through traffic by his banker buddy in the yellow Ferrari.

By comparison, the young lawyer drove the Saab like a grandmother. In his late twenties, Conner Vance was boyishly handsome and had the easy confidence of someone raised with privileges and a legacy. He kept the car at or under the speed limit and slowed when approaching yellow lights instead of speeding through them.

"You are planning on getting us there tonight," Cassie teased when they stopped for yet another traffic signal.

"He's doing that for me," Megan suggested from the back seat. "He doesn't realize how your father drives."

"You mean Alejandro Del Speedo," Cassie said, referring to the name she'd invented for Stewart when she was 12, having created a storybook for him to tell the story of a make-believe race car driver. "You, on the other hand," Cassie told Conner, "would be Pico Di Slow-go."

Conner laughed good-naturedly. When his phone directed a right turn onto an upcoming ramp, he steered casually around a circular exit onto a short bridge that crossed over PCH and aimed them toward Balboa.

The little beach town was crowded with traffic and pedestrians and gave the impression of very much wanting to be young and hip. Beyond a tree-lined main avenue of older retail stores and shops, the area turned residential with uncoordinated styles of homes built closely together on narrow lots. Aged, salt-sprayed bungalows with peeling paint sat alongside newer architectural marvels of glass, brick, and stone.

On a side street near the beach, a section of curb was marked by orange cones and manned by parking valets.

Cassie unbuckled her seat belt before Conner stopped the car. "This is going to be so great." As soon as a valet opened her door, Cassie was out on the curb, impatiently gesturing for Conner and Megan to pick up the pace. "Come on Pico, let's go-go. You, too, Mom."

Conner laughed and asked Megan, "Is it exhausting being her mother?"

#

The party at Cara Moore's beach house was like walking into a movie.

The house was a visually jarring multi-level structure of teal-tinted glass which, lit from inside, looked like a massive aquarium with people inside instead of fish. The flat roof and second-level balcony railing pitched parallel fifteen-degree slopes, while a crow's-nest balcony rail angled fifteen degrees in the opposite direction. Optically, it was somewhat dizzying, as though everything inside the house should be sliding one way or the other even though the floors were level.

The front patio was packed with revelers dancing, drinking, and yelling to be heard over music played by a seizure-tempo band up on the crow's nest.

Jackie Mack, in her sexy-slit dress, stood between two muscular bouncers at the patio gate. Seeing Cassie, Conner, and Megan, she waved over the party din. "Thought you got lost."

Cassie pointed at Conner. "Pico Di Slow-go."

Following Jackie through the cavorting bodies, Megan smelled a wicked combination of beer, marijuana, and perfume. "It's like Halloween in July."

"Or Mardi Gras on acid," Conner replied.

At least half the hundred-plus crowd was legitimately show-business beautiful, and the more beautiful the body, the more of it showed. Shirtless guys with defined arms and rippled abs wore pants tight and low. Girls went for halter tops, string bikinis, and the occasional thong.

Inside, the smell of marijuana was stronger, surviving a gentle cross breeze that circulated through opened windows. Megan was reminded of the Three Dog Night song that had been an oldie by the time she'd heard it in high school: Mamma Told Me Not to Come had been a favorite of a boy she'd gone out with a few times.

Here, though, there weren't any wasted teenagers draped over sofas and passed out on the floor. Like the group outside, these were beautiful people in one of the most beautiful areas of the most beautiful state.

Making a path between bodies, Jackie Mack raised her arm, alternately waving and snapping her fingers to get someone's attention, calling, "Sonny. Sonny."

Sonny was a short, barrel-chested man with the heaviest gold watch Megan had ever seen. A weightlifter at 55, his head and face were shaved smooth except for a pencil-thin moustache. Shorter than Megan and Jackie in their heels, Sonny was confident and relaxed.

"Sonny does development deals," Jackie announced to Megan over the party noise, "and we've been working on a web channel joint venture, running out lots of different ideas. One that keeps popping to the top is something we've given the working title, Hard Change. It's a reality show. Every episode will follow a woman experiencing a major life change. Nothing heavy. Not someone going through chemo, anything like that. Something positive, uplifting—dealing with change in a pro-active manner. And I was telling Stewart about this over lunch the other day, and he said maybe you'd be interested."

"Me?"

"Being featured on the show. Your daughter's off to school. Your husband's had a major career change. The show would be how you react to that. How you deal with it. How you feel about it."

"Who'd want to watch me pack up one house and unpack at another?" Megan suppressed offense that Stewart had been talking about their family with some woman she didn't know. Maybe she was just tired.

"A little of that could be interesting," Jackie pitched. "What you decide to keep, what you leave. What memories certain items rekindle. But there would be more than that. Changes you might not even think are that significant. Stewart told me all the years you've been together he's never known you to swim in the ocean. But a couple weeks ago, you did, right? That's not a coincidence. And that's what the show's about."

Images of Pip pushed into Megan's thoughts.

Sonny said, "A year from now you could be on the cover of a dozen national magazines." He shook Megan's hand and walked off into the crowd.

Jackie draped her arm around Megan's shoulder. "Let's get you a drink. Have you ever had a ginseng zipper?"

\#

Megan found Cassie and Conner among those dancing on the second-floor balcony. Cassie was barefooted, having cast off the heels Danielle had selected to accessorize the tight pants.

Just overhead in the crow's nest, the band blared what sounded like a storm siren, but Conner spun Cassie gracefully as though doing a free-spirited interpretation of a formal dance step.

As coordinated as Cassie had always been at sports, she'd never looked comfortable dancing until now. It was beautiful to watch.

Cassie waved. "Mom!"

Conner twirled Cassie and released her, then surprised Megan by securing her confidently in his arms.

Megan, who considered herself no better than a wedding dancer, followed Conner's firm lead.

His arms and hips foretold his next move as he counted quietly through his smile, "One, two, three. One, two, three." Providing cadence as an added clue. "One, two, three. It's a waltz."

Megan marveled how Conner had deciphered rhythmic sense out of the band's audible chaos.

After a few minutes, Conner turned Megan into the arms of a gorgeous young guy with sideburns and tattered jeans.

In a foreign accent Megan didn't recognize, the young guy asked her name. Maybe it was the lack of sleep, or maybe she'd picked up a contact buzz from all the marijuana being smoked, or maybe there was something more potent than ginseng in the drink Jackie Mack had ordered for her, but for some reason Megan said her name was Starburst.

He said, "Like the candy."

After the young guy, Megan danced with a girl in a red t-shirt, plaid schoolgirl skirt, and one-inch heels. Notably taller than Megan, she rested her hands on Megan's shoulders and in a German accent, said, "You have a beautiful mouth. You should be a lipstick model." Then she stepped back, clasped her hands over her head, and twirled so her skirt fanned out to reveal slim, long legs. And with that, she walked away.

Beginning to feel light-headed, Megan found her way to the railing for support, and watched Cassie and Conner dance.

Cassie looked so happy, throwing her head back, laughing. A very different Cassie. But still Cassie—very much still Cassie—just the Cassie who was never coming home again.

#

Megan kept falling asleep in the back of the Saab. The cool air no longer kept her eyes open as Conner drove with the top down.

Cassie was wide awake in the passenger seat, elbow resting out the opened window, hair blowing. She wore stylish sunglasses Jackie Mack had handed out at the party by the boxful.

The glasses were Damon V's—another Jackie Mack client—and retailed for $500 a pair.

Cassie seemed more familiar with Conner than someone she had just met that evening. Megan had lost them for an hour at the party and found them coming back from the dark beach, the two of them casually bumping shoulder to shoulder as if whatever had happened out there had been fun.

"What's this music?" Megan asked of classical piano playing on the car's sound system.

"This is Conner," Cassie said, turning up the volume, "when he was seventeen."

95

"It's beautiful."

"Conner was accepted to Juilliard."

"Didn't go, though," he said.

"What happened?" Megan wondered.

"Dad said I could play the piano on weekends."

"That's too bad."

"That's what I thought," the young lawyer mused.

Cassie turned around in the front seat. "We're going for breakfast food. You want to come?" It was not really an invitation, but politeness—Cassie's tone subtly suggesting behind words to the contrary it was time for her mother to gracefully exit this very odd evening.

Megan obliged. "I'm asleep on my feet."

Cassie laughed. "You're not even on your feet, M!"

"Exactly." Megan was tired. And disoriented. She curled up in the backseat against the chilly night air, listened to the sweet piano music. And thought about Pip kissing her.

19.

"When would we move?" Megan asked.

Stewart joined Megan in the big bed she'd never slept in. The two of them alone in the spacious bedroom of the impressive house she'd never seen until that afternoon, in a place she knew nothing about. "October, probably." Stewart didn't need to think before answering. "We could be settled by Christmas that way."

And there it was. After months of skating around the issue, the idea was firmly on the table. No longer a wait-and-see.

Christmas in California. What would that feel like with sunshine and palm trees? Without first having watched the leaves change colors in the fall, and seeing the first snowflakes swirl in the cold, crisp sky.

"Make sense…?" Stewart laid alongside her in bed, not touching, both of them on their backs as reflections of swimming pool lights twinkled across the ceiling. "…as a timetable?"

"I think so," Megan replied, a lie she believed she'd need to make true.

It wasn't as though she'd be leaving a host of close friends in Maryland. Jillian was in Ohio now. The other women she'd been most friendly with had been mothers of kids Cassie went to school with, and she'd already begun to lose touch with them over the past year. "Cassie mentioned something about transferring to Stanford."

"I think that would be a good fit for her." Stewart spoke as though he and Cassie had already discussed the idea.

"But not this fall," Megan added. "Next year."

"Something might happen in the next sixty days if we get it in motion." Stewart's confidence and positivity were the result of achievement. He'd survived losing his first wife. Gotten through being a single parent until he and Megan married. Started his own business and made such a success of it he was now, according to Holden Lassiter, being considered to lead the company he'd sold to—something Stewart hadn't yet mentioned. Maybe he thought divulging that possibility would make it seem he was pressuring her to make this move instead of waiting for a situation where she'd want to do it.

"Do you like this house?" he asked.

"Yes." Maybe that was another lie. Megan didn't know. She was more interested in the feel of a home than its finishes. All the square footage, crown molding, and top-end appliances meant nothing if it didn't feel like home.

Their house in Hunt Valley had been an easy choice. Megan had known the neighborhood, admiring its established tree-lined streets and brick homes before she and Stewart married. They'd only looked at three other houses before making an offer on where they now lived—what would soon be where they used to live.

The condo at the beach had been an equally quick decision, falling in love with the comfortable one-bedroom place and signing papers the same afternoon. Nothing at all like some of the clients Megan's friend Jillian complained about, couples who'd tour a hundred houses, wanting everything to be perfect, including the price.

"Cassie not back?" Megan guessed. She'd been in bed for an hour now, having come in the front door to find Stewart working on the sofa, looking up from his laptop but not closing it, which had been Megan's clue he was in middle of something requiring concentration. When he'd asked if she had fun tonight, she'd said yes but she was sleepy and going to bed—having known Stewart would be too distracted by whatever he was doing to talk—although he would have set work aside if she'd needed him to.

It was the way their marriage worked. Their time together at home was often engaged in different pursuits: Stewart almost always with work, Megan reading, solving or creating math puzzles, taking care of the house, or streaming something online, much of which she used to do with Cassie.

"She's still out," Stewart said of their daughter, then a few moments later asked, "What's his name? Conner?"

"Yeah."

"Seems like a decent guy."

"He does," Megan agreed, knowing that meant nothing, really, how he seemed. Thinking how much older he was than Cassie but not mentioning that because Stewart was as confident about Cassie as he was himself. Often assuring Megan that Cassie could "handle herself."

Could she, though, really? In every situation? Would Stewart maintain that opinion if he knew about Cassie coming home drunk last fall and telling Megan she wasn't her mother. Cassie had been drinking again tonight—and was still out after three in the morning. Maybe having breakfast. But maybe doing who knew what. Megan tried to tell herself not to worry.

A few hours later, she remained awake as the room began to brighten with daylight. From bed, she looked outside and saw the sun was not where it was supposed to be, rising over land instead of the ocean. This was going to take a lot of getting used to.

20.

"I didn't hear her come in." Megan was in the kitchen, getting her brain in sync with the dials of a commercial-grade coffee machine that probably cost more than her first car out of college.

Stewart shrugged. "I didn't either."

Cassie was outside on a chaise, texting in her bathing suit. Thin lines of steam rose off heated pool water and drifted into cool morning air.

"You want breakfast?" Megan asked Stewart. "I could fix just about anything you want. The refrigerator's stocked." Which she hadn't noticed yesterday.

"Just coffee." Like daughter like father, Stewart was also on his phone, scrolling through emails. It was just after seven but three hours earlier back east where the workday was already in full swing.

Stewart had showered and dressed for work: another expensive-looking new shirt and trousers.

Going on a couple hours sleep was nothing new to him. Megan had watched Stewart work around the clock more times than she could remember. That used to concern her, worrying about its effect on his health or that he might miss an important calculation, but she'd never seen that happen.

She was tempted to ask where he bought the new clothes but there was a lot she seemed not to know, and the source of his wardrobe, like the cost of the rich-smelling coffee in a burlap sack imprinted with fancy fair-trade-promises, seemed trivial by comparison. Measuring ground coffee beans into the machine, she decided to start with the most critical question: "How sure is all this? California?" Hoping that sounded as casual as she believed she needed to approach the issue.

"What do you mean?"

"Moving here." She got instant hot water flowing into the elaborate machine. "This other company becoming part of Dunhill—is that the right way to phrase it?" She didn't have a firm grasp on the business terminology.

"Merger—yeah." Stewart looked up from his phone. "It's not final, but the move is. This location is a link to expanding into Asia, so we're opening an office here with or without Talbot-Glen. On the off chance that deal falls through, this's still where we'll be."

By "we" Megan wasn't sure if Stewart meant the two of them or Stewart and Dunhill. She assumed the former. "Okay... I just don't want to move if we might have to undo it."

"I understand."

A slight tension tightened their respective postures, each careful not to let their words or tone of voice tip the conversation to the point where Stewart became impatient, or Megan looked for alternatives that might somehow keep them home in Maryland—which she'd told herself throughout the night she needed to forget about. It was why she was here, after all, wasn't it? To commit to the move.

"If this house isn't right," Stewart proposed, "or you see another one you like better, say the word."

"Okay." Megan smiled through an uneasy quiver in the pit of her stomach, caused by the thought of losing everything that had become home.

Cassie came in from the pool looking very much awake— as adept at pulling all-nighters as her father. "Ah, yes. Coffee!"

"Do you want breakfast?"

"No—not hungry." Back on her phone, she sat at a bar stool at the kitchen island—a piece of hard modern furniture that, like most of the decor, seemed intended for staging, not living in.

"That's a cute suit," Megan complimented. Cassie's bikini showed a little less ass cheek than yesterday's cutaway.

"Thanks, M."

"And you're not looking bad yourself," Megan told Stewart, thinking that might inspire him to mention where he was getting his new clothes.

Instead, Stewart sighed and muttered, "Ah, shit," at something on his phone. "Can you put my coffee in something to go? I've got to get into the office and deal with this."

Megan opened double doors to what turned out to be more of a small storeroom than a pantry. "Wow." Walls were lined with full shelves of cans and boxes and packages. Expensive and custom labels. At least six different brands of sparkling water. "I'm sure there's something in here somewhere. How long it takes me to find it…" She stepped inside. "It's like Penzey's," she said of the spice assortment. There was also an entire shelf of specialty baking goods. And packages of dried exotic mushrooms. "Cass, have you seen this?"

"Holy hell!" Cassie laughed, finding Megan on her knees, opening a plastic bag. "Look at all this."

"I've got Styrofoam cups," Megan announced. "No lids. I could make you a souffle, but I don't think I can get you coffee to go."

"I'll get something on the way," Stewart replied.

"I've got something in my stuff from the plane," Cassie remembered. "I'll rinse it out—you can use that."

"Still looking," Megan updated.

"Really. I'll get something on the way."

"All right," Megan surrendered. "Be like that." Then thought to ask: "How are you getting to work? Is there a car?"

"Yeah. In the garage." Stewart was heading in that direction Megan assumed from how his voice trailed away. "Two cars actually."

Yesterday they were taken around by limo. Today there were two cars. How was all this happening? Megan wondered.

"You want to go out," Stewart advised, "keys are on the driver's seat. See you girls tonight. Have fun today."

"Assuming I ever find my way out of here," Megan called from the pantry.

"You're a smart girl. You'll figure it out."

Still on her knees, looking up across the stocked shelves, Megan sighed, "This place is crazy." It was a moment of happiness because they felt like a family again. Even just for a few minutes, which sometimes was all it took, enough to confirm their separate lives still orbited back together.

21.

Megan jogged through the neighborhood's impressive entranceway, waving to the uniformed guard at the gatehouse she imagined would become familiar if they ended up in this house. Wearing running shorts over her blue one-piece swimsuit, phone banded to her arm, she started down the wide sidewalk along Newport Coast Drive.

The footway was separated from the road by a knee-high hedge of spiny evergreens she didn't recognize. The plants appeared healthy and tolerant of dry spells, mulched with pale-colored pebbles across which darted the occasional small lizard.

Ahead, the sparkling-blue ocean was visible for miles to the horizon. But for the proximity of water, the air was unusually dry, an impression that became stronger once she crossed busy six-lane PCH at a traffic light and trotted into Crystal Cove State Park.

Away from landscapers and sprinkler systems, the terrain was treeless and near desert dry. Squat cacti grew amidst grey rocks and smaller rose-colored stones, and the scent of dried sage mingled sweetly with salty sea air.

The beach park's parking lot was half full. Families carted gear from SUV's. Wetsuited surfers unstrapped boards from roof racks. Kids Cassie's age stood around listening to music, some smoking cigarettes. Most of the vehicles looked newer and upper end, but there were still some beaters in there along with a couple classics: a 1965 Mustang convertible and a Woodie station wagon.

A macadam trail along the edge of a craggy 50-foot drop to the beach led from one end of the park to the other—a distance of about seven miles according to a map posted at a ranger's hut where Megan took a brief water break.

Back up to pace, following the trail, Megan admired the view. Cassie had stayed back at the house by the pool, plugged into her earbuds, doing something for her internship she said, but ten minutes earlier Megan had seen her taking a full-length bikini selfie, and when Megan had asked if that was for Conner, Cassie rolled her eyes.

Once down to the beach, Megan pulled off her running shoes and socks and ran barefooted along the water's edge, weaving her way around other people.

She'd never been on a coastline like this, which felt foreign to her. The beach seemed like a flimsy ribbon between the massive ocean and formidable cliff, and felt oddly claustrophobic and threatening, as though at any moment a huge wave could sweep ashore and send her crashing into the rocks. Shadows in the ocean she first thought were caused by scattered clouds were actually large clumps of seaweed that when drawn into the face of a rising wave looked like Halloween witches.

She didn't like it.

#

Where RU?

Megan was sitting on the sand in warm sunshine, arms wrapped around knees pulled up toward her chest. She checked her phone.

The text was from Jillian.

The beach, Megan replied.

I figured! Assuming Megan meant Ocean City.

Not that beach. Megan snapped a picture of an outcropping of large black boulders that jutted into the sea like a stone jetty, her frame capturing some of the surfers she'd been watching ride perilously close to those rocks. And sent that along with a map link.

After Jillian had time to absorb that: *OMG! Beautiful! Vaca?*

Megan took a breath. *No. We're moving here.*

Her phone rang seconds later. Jillian. No hello, but: "What is going on?"

Megan was happy to hear her friend's voice. "I know." She tried to sound positive, talking over the waves and seagull squawk.

"You're moving to California?" Jillian asked with disbelief. "What happened to Scottsdale?"

Megan provided the shortened version: that it was a Stewart surprise, how the new company he was with was expanding. Editing out any reference to Pip. Although Jillian was Megan's one confidante, Megan had not mentioned Pip other than as one of the surf patrol guards she'd been swimming with. Keeping secret about them kissing on the sofa, with his hand inside her shirt. She was still unsure how she'd let that happen, other than it had been a temptation that caught her at a wrong moment. No matter how wonderful it felt. Or how much she missed him. Because it was really the idea of him she missed, making him some kind of fantasy he couldn't be. And to Pip, what could she have possibly been other than a casual opportunity? Sex at the beach—they even named a cocktail after that didn't they? Which was why she'd left. Because she couldn't chance letting that happen again. Or admit it had happened at all.

"You don't sound thrilled," Jillian deciphered.

"Probably because I'm going on no sleep." Megan also wasn't really thinking about what she'd been saying, rambling on about the house, the too-modern décor, the massive pantry, the party last night in Balboa, Cassie possibly transferring to Stanford.

"And Cassie's there?"

"Another Stewart surprise."

"And you two are good?"

"Cassie? I think so."

"Okay..." Jillian didn't seem convinced. "Well that's a plus. So how long's she there for? How long are you there for?"

"I don't know. You know... a little while—that I'll be here. I don't know. This's all happening fast. I think I caught Stewart a little off guard. But I felt like we needed to be together and said I could come out now—thinking it would be Arizona. And he seemed happy I wanted to do that after all we've been through about moving. And here we are. Here I am."

Jillian fell silent.

"You could come out," Megan offered her unmarried friend. "I miss you."

"Oh, I miss you, too. I wish I could. But work is a bit of a bear at the moment." After a decade riding the financial gold rushes and droughts of the housing market as a real estate agent, Jillian had accepted a job with a national builder and been promoted to the company's home office. That meant a move to Columbus, but also full health insurance and a 401(k). Only three weeks of vacation though.

Jillian described a new development her company was starting outside Charlotte. When Megan asked about Andy, someone Jillian had been to dinner with a few times, the reply was an unremarkable, "Enh."

"Is that the conversation or the sex?"

"Still no sex. Which I think might be pushing my luck. I'm thinking he's due a little something, but I can't get inspired. I hope I'm not pre-menopausal."

Jillian always managed to make Megan smile.

They talked a while longer. The latest on Jillian's sister and mother. Jillian's car issues. The weather. After they disconnected, Megan watched the surfers then pulled off her shorts, stuck her phone inside her shoes with her socks, and asked the two mothers with small children on the sand behind her if they'd mind watching her stuff. When they said yes,

Megan went into the ocean, drove through a chilly wave, and swam.

22.

"Missing your fifth this morning."

"What's that?" Pip looked over the side of his guard stand, not having seen the man approach.

Bill Clary shaded his eyes against the bright sky even with the brim of a Washington Nationals cap offering some protection. "I like to watch your group swim," Bill explained. "You were a man short today. Four instead of five."

"Yeah—we were. Do you know Megan?"

"Is that her name?"

"Our 'man short,'" Pip replied, using Bill's term. "Lives up there." Pip pointed over his shoulder toward Megan's building.

"I'm down there." Bill gestured toward his townhouse a block south.

"Yep. I remember. Rome DC," Pip smiled, recalling Bill's political reference.

"That's me." Bill held his dock shoes in his hand, wearing a casual short-sleeve shirt that buttoned down the front and khaki multi-pocket shorts Mary Jane referred to as his old man beachwear, saying all he needed was a metal detector. "And you're Pip."

"Yes, sir."

"Well I hope you get your fifth back. She looks a little older than the rest of you but seems like she's giving you a run for your money. I like that. Keep you youngsters in your place."

"I hope she comes back too." Pip kept his smile, but his eyes gave him away.

Returning to his townhouse, climbing the steps to the deck, Bill found Mary Jane waiting for him.

"What've you been up to?"

Bill grinned the way he did when he was right about something. "Girl in the blue bathing suit's named Megan. She's gone off and Pip's heartsick."

"The boy told you that?" Mary Jane doubted.

"Doesn't have to tell me. I can see it in him."

23.

Megan felt like she might be able to sleep. But she was hungrier than she was tired, standing in the kitchen in her bathing suit that had mostly dried during the half-mile walk back up the hill. Her skin was slightly sticky from evaporated salt water, her damp hair beginning to feel like a hardened shell, tied back in a ponytail that had held through her swim.

"Hey, Cass," she called, not knowing where her daughter was. "Cass!" Louder. "Cass!" If all else fails, text. Still nothing.

Megan went upstairs to the large back corner bedroom which didn't seem like it should be referred to as Cassie's room yet.

Still in her bathing suit, Cassie sat at the grey elm-wood desk with metal legs. A large window offered a view of the pool and brilliant horizon of ocean, but the girl was occupied by her laptop, fingers dashing across the keyboard.

"Hey, Cass!" When she didn't respond, Megan rapped loudly on the opened door, assuming Cassie had in earbuds they used to tease weren't so much noise-cancelling as parent-blocking. "Cass!"

She turned and popped out one of her earpieces. "Hey, M. You swim?" Seeing Megan's hair. "How was it?"

"Cold. And there were patches of slimy seaweed. And surfers shouting at one another about cutting off their lines. But once I got out beyond that … pretty good."

"Cool."

"Have you eaten?"

"Some rice cakes."

"You want to find somewhere for us to get lunch? I'm going to take a shower."

"Lunch is a plan." Cassie reached for her phone.

But the plan never happened.

After a quick shower, Megan laid down for what she thought would be a couple minutes and didn't awaken for hours—the most she'd slept since Pip's kiss.

#

"Hey party girl," Cassie teased when Megan came outside.

Megan dropped onto the chaise alongside her daughter. "Sorry," she apologized for sleeping through lunch.

"No biggie." Cassie shut her laptop. "I had lots to do anyway."

"Did you get something to eat?"

"Had some Thai food delivered. Some left in the fridge for you. Was pretty good."

Wearing a plain t-shirt and athletic shorts, Megan squinted against late afternoon sunshine and looked at the similar houses built on each side of them, and hundreds more that terraced down toward the beach like oversized steps. She was yet to hear or see any neighbors. "Do you like it here?" she asked Cassie.

"Sure."

"It's different."

"Well, yeah." As though Megan had just stated the obvious.

"I mean, I know, not like India-different. Or even Europe-different."

"SoCal…" Cassie half sang.

"Right…" After a few quiet moments, Megan suddenly sat up. "Oh, hell. I missed Trenton."

"You mean Maths?" Cassie asked, referring to the young boy Megan tutored online in calculus. "I took care of it. Your iPad pinged and there was this little guy looking all studious. I told him you had to reschedule."

"I can't believe I slept through that."

"That kid's really funny. It was like a police interrogation. He had about a thousand questions for me. Who was I? He didn't know you had a daughter. He said I didn't look like you. I don't know what he was thinking," Cassie laughed. "I guess maybe you'd been abducted, and I was in on it. He wanted to know where you were—I said California. He asked why you were here. Was it vacation? Did you have other kids besides me. Then how come not. He wanted to know my name. How old was I? Where did I go to school? Was I any good at maths? Was I better at it than him? I put him in his place about that. Don't worry, I was nice about it. And my being good at maths is probably what saved him from calling the FBI to report you missing."

Megan smiled and patted Cassie's leg. "Thanks."

"Kid does seem really smart for his age," Cassie appreciated.

"He is."

"Does he go to Villa James?"

"No. Home schooled."

"Parents whack jobs?" Cassie had a low opinion of home schooling.

"They don't like the public school system where they live and can't afford private school."

"Where's this?"

"A little town on the Eastern Shore. His grandparents are sick, and Trenton's folks take care of them. I think they have a small farm."

Cassie put her finger to her head as if it was a gun and made the sound of a weapon being fired.

"Dad and I both grew up in places like that."

"Yeah—and got the hell out." When Megan's stomach growled, Cassie laughed. "Eat already. Thai food."

"Have you heard from dad? Any idea what we're doing about dinner?"

"No."

Megan hoped it would be just the three of them tonight. It had been a couple months since they'd had dinner as a family, when Cassie last came home for a weekend during one of what had become Stewart's less frequent and shorter trips back to Maryland.

"We should look at other houses, don't you think?" Megan asked.

"You don't like this place?"

Megan was careful with her words, knowing they'd probably be relayed to Stewart. At the same time, she wanted to feel out Cassie's reaction as a preview of how Stewart might respond, because daughter and father thought alike. "It don't not like it. But maybe we'd like someplace else more. Where we went last night was nice."

"Balboa? I've gotta think that's really pricey. That close to the beach? This O.C. out here—Orange County—a lot different from our O.C., M." Referring to Ocean City, Maryland.

"I'm not talking about a place like that actress' house. Malibu—anything like that." Megan didn't know about Malibu other than the name and its upscale reputation. "When I started teaching, before I bought my condo, I rented an apartment for a year until I got to know the area. And I'm glad I did, because some places that seemed nice at first turned out not to be."

"I don't see S wanting to rent."

"No..." Megan agreed. Stewart was very investment minded. Any improvements they'd made to their Hunt Valley home always included consideration as to how it would affect resale, as if Stewart had been planning for the day they'd move, even before Dunhill came into the picture.

"But, sure, yeah, look at other places. That'd be pretty fun. If you think you can stay awake," Cassie kidded. "I'll text Jackie Mack. Get her to line up some places we can look at."

Jackie Mack: the woman from last night with the cleavage and slit up the side of dress. And Cassie had her contact information? "She's a real estate agent?" Megan asked.

"Branding specialist," Cassie specified. "But—yeah—she has a real estate license. She's the one who set up this place for S." Cassie's text was no sooner sent than her phone pinged with a reply. "Jackie," Cassie identified. "Says we can start tomorrow."

24.

They began to feel more like a family again, all under the same roof at night, at the same dinner table, talking about their day, laughing, comparing Newport Coast to other places they'd been.

Stewart worked his usual long hours—out the door early every morning with coffee Megan brewed in the elaborate coffee machine (which she'd become an expert at using). Stewart drove to the office in a new Mercedes roadster convertible, leaving an Audi A6 in the garage for Megan—both cars leased by Dunhill Infrastructure as a part of Stewart's upgraded compensation package.

Megan swam the chilly Pacific after breakfast, becoming a familiar sight to surfers. She got used to peeling off the seaweed she swam through and called the occasional hello to playful sea lions who kept their distance.

Cassie did her internship online, often up as early as her father to accommodate the time difference with the east coast. She found a gym she liked and drove there in the Audi during what was lunch hour back east, returning to the house 'for lunch with Megan, who arranged her tutoring sessions for the time Cassie was at the gym.

Mother and daughter typically ate outside by the pool, weather permitting—which, so far, it had—high protein meals Megan fixed as if in training, which Megan felt she was, swimming longer, doing sand sprints, and jogging back up the hill from the beach.

After lunch, it was house-looking time, at first being shown around by Jackie Mack in her Range Rover with the custom opalescent paint job, then it was just Megan and Cassie once they became more familiar with the area, usually getting back to the house—what they referred to more often as "home"—before traffic crawled for extended rush hours, which wasn't that different from DC, really.

And it wasn't just house hunting. Megan and Cassie checked out shopping centers and malls, and bought clothes to supplement having only packed enough to stay for days not weeks. They investigated grocery stores: Whole Foods was still pricey; Ralph's was the established area chain; Von's and Pavillions turned out to be owned by Albertson's (which used that name in Scottsdale and owned Safeway back east); but there was also Megan's favorite, Trader Joe's, in a strip center that overlooked the ocean.

They explored as far north as Long Beach, went out onto Balboa, down to Dana Point, and even considered inland towns to get a sense of neighborhoods away from the ocean—Irvine, Mission Viejo, Santa Ana—usually with the same result: a mutual shrug or pinched expression and shake of the head. Not that there weren't lovely houses in wonderful areas, but once Megan and Cassie began to confuse which house they'd seen where they considered maybe where they already were was the best choice.

They even toured a few homes nearby but didn't like them as much.

"I told Stewart this is a wonderful opportunity," Jackie Mack said of the house they'd been in for almost three weeks now, explaining how it was owned by a "foreign investor" who'd bought it from blueprints and was yet to ever set foot inside, having arranged for Jackie to furnish and rent it for the past fifteen years, then renovate it over the winter before putting it on the market.

"So is this a decision?" Stewart asked over dinner after their daily house report.

It was the second week of July. Just the three of them in a little neighborhood seafood place that served amazing sesame-crusted ahi over baby arugula.

Megan looked at Cassie, who she'd spent more time with than any other three-week span in recent years—probably back to before Cassie had her license, when Megan used to drive her and her friends everywhere.

"I'm good with it," Cassie said.

"I think I am, too," Megan added.

"Fantastic." Stewart raised his craft beer as a toast. "To California."

Megan lifted her green tea. Cassie reached for her sparkling water.

Megan added: "And to Stanford coming through with Cassie's transfer."

"It's going to happen," Stewart assured, having made contact with a Cardinal alumni who all but guaranteed success. "I'll text Jackie and have her prepare the papers."

Megan started to tell him not to bother Jackie at dinnertime, that it could wait until morning. Which she would have made sound like she was being considerate but was actually hesitation. Because every day, behind the smiles and laughter and sense they were on an extended vacation where they all just happened to be doing work, Megan hoped for a turn of events, some change, that would put them back in Maryland. Where there were still two months of summer left.

But she didn't stop Stewart from sending that text. Tomorrow they would sign papers to buy the house. Which would start the timetable she and Stewart had been discussing about selling their home in Hunt Valley and the condo in Ocean City. Stewart had been pushing the idea they could do it all from here—hire movers to pack up the house and condo— probably because he worried if Megan went back there might be complications, that Megan might not want to leave.

They were still keeping thoughts private from one another, trying to make their way through change without conflict. Megan had been doing her best to ignore quivers of nervousness that often invaded her stomach. Whenever thoughts of Pip came to mind, she pretended the time she'd spent with him happened a long time ago—before she met Stewart. Or happened to someone else. Or happened in a dream.

But more than that, she tried to pretend that the three of them—Cassie, Stewart, and her—hadn't changed over the past nine months. That living apart hadn't made them each more independent.

After almost a month together, it still felt strange being in the same bed with Stewart. Sexually, she experienced a peculiar detachment. Stewart had always been reserved in bed, interested certainly, but never insatiable, which when they first met Megan thought may have had to do with her being Cassie's teacher, or that Stewart's wife had only died within the past year, and he was still grieving. Or maybe it had to do with the low dose of medication Stewart took to control borderline genetic high blood pressure. But over the years she came to understand that was just the way Stewart was, and she was fine with that. While he may not have been impassioned, he was kind in bed, giving, just not, as Jillian once described one of her own boyfriends: a man who "wore his cock on his sleeve."

As for Cassie, Megan couldn't pinpoint why exactly, but she felt Cassie was hiding something from her. That Cassie was involved with something or maybe someone—maybe Conner the lawyer, who Cassie said had flown back to DC weeks ago. Or maybe, Megan rationalized, she was transferring her own secret—her own guilt—onto Cassie. Because Megan did feel guilty about what she'd done with Pip. She tried to rationalize that what happened on the sofa had not really gone that far, but that didn't play. If Stewart had gone "that far" with another woman, she would have been hurt. But she had never been unfaithful to Stewart—never even been tempted—which made the entire experience with Pip more dreamlike. And definitely difficult to understand. Not just what had happened, but how.

She kept trying to put that all out of her mind, telling herself Pip had likely forgotten all about her by now. That he'd probably been with a different admiring chickadoodle—as Lulu the beach stand girl called them—every week. But Pip continued to swim into her thoughts. Memories of his smile. How he held her when they drifted in the riptide. The caress of his hands. The sweetness of his kiss. All of which caused her to ache with an empty feeling that she would never again feel the way she'd felt with him.

25.

Jackie Mack came to the house with contracts her buyer had already signed. Stewart and Megan added their signatures. Cassie let out a happy whoop and gave Megan the sort of jostling congratulatory hug she used to share with her lacrosse teammates. "We're Californians now, M!"

Megan smiled through a strange numbness. Stewart grinned. Jackie Mack explained the escrow process—how house buying was different in California than most other states. Megan half paid attention. She wanted to swim, and as soon as Jackie Mack collected the paperwork and sported off in her shiny Range Rover, Megan jogged down to the beach. She no longer took her phone or bothered with a towel.

She went into the ocean and swam hard through the waves. Once beyond the swells, instead of swimming north, she went in the opposite direction for the first time. She kicked and pulled through the cold water until her arms and legs ached and she had to breathe on every stretch of her left arm. She felt strong so she kept going. Not watching how far from the beach she'd angled. Or how close to the rocky point.

When she saw the big black boulders just ahead—waves crashing into them—she wasn't afraid. Because the sea lion who popped up in front of her, his smooth water-slicked head glistening in sunshine, looked right at her, smiled, and winked and nodded toward shore. Then slipped back under the surface and swam away. At least that's what she thought she saw. She had salt water in her eyes. But the sleek animal had been right there, hadn't he?

Treading water, Megan looked toward the crowded beach, the strip of sand rising in and out of her view as waves rose and tumbled over, sweeping surfers along watery curls.

Less than a hundred yards inland from the water's edge, nestled near the base of the hard rock cliff, she spotted a collection of colorful little cottages that looked like a shantytown.

Megan swam in, catching a wave she bodysurfed, following the break the way she'd watched a young boy do it last week. She strode out of the ocean into warm sunshine and the happy noise of families enjoying the seaside.

Retying her wet ponytail, she crossed the sand, making her way around beach blankets and children darting with the reckless abandon of summer fun, briefly touching one little girl's blond head as she skimmed by.

There were more cottages than she'd seen from the ocean, three rows of them. Those closest to the sea were painted brightly, while the second and third rows back against the weedy hillside looked forlorn in disrepair.

A sign designated the area as a restoration project—a sliver of time being revived. The oceanfront enclave, originally built in the 1950's, included about two dozen separate dwellings, each of its own unique, crude design. The largest was perhaps 20 feet long. A few had crooked chimneys or little porches. Sandy footpaths connected each home to the beach.

Like tree houses, the original shacks' sagging roofs and porches had been constructed of mismatched materials, as if utilizing what had been left over from other jobs or salvaged for cheap. Even in their prime, few of these places likely included a single level board or true right angle.

The restored cottages, however, looked perfect and were currently occupied by vacationers who lounged on sandy yards and draped towels across porch railings to dry in the sun.

Megan admired how the renovations managed to keep the original "hodgepodge" feel. Each restored beach home was now a structurally-sound replica of its original, honest perhaps to what some paying guests might consider a fault: there was no air conditioning.

Megan strolled among the beach village, peeking through smudged windows into the empty cottages waiting to be restored.

She sat on the drooping porch of an empty shack, its coarse boards prickling the backs of her legs. Watching the ocean, she thought of living here, in another time, another life—with Pip.

Six days later, she was on a plane.

26.

It was easy for Megan to attribute her decision to fate, as if happenings over the past week had not been mere chance or coincidence, but indications true as a compass pointing north. As if life was pre-determined, free of intentions, or desires, or guilt.

The day she'd discovered the cottages, Megan had jogged back up the hill and was about to ask Cassie what they should do for lunch when she noticed a text on her phone.

It was Lulu, the beach stand girl: *Got your # from someone in your building. Hope it's OK to text. Everything OK? Everyone misses you.*

Megan sat on the end of the bed and wondered—as she often did—what they were all doing right now. It would be mid-afternoon back home. Lulu would be in a bold-color bikini, scanning the beach through her Wayfarers, keeping track of her rented chairs. Young Will would be doing waist twists or somehow otherwise burning off all that energy. Art and Adrian would be flashing semaphore, perhaps messaging about a lost child or passing along intel on a band playing somewhere that night. And Pip … Pip would be on his stand, smiling, talking to tourists or his chickadoodle fans.

It was all Megan could do not to call Lulu and ask her to aim her phone along the beach so she could see for herself. Instead, she texted Lulu that she was in California, with Stewart and Cassie. She started to send more—that they were moving to Southern California and had signed a contract to buy a house that very morning—but she deleted all that before sending.

Instead, she texted she'd been swimming in the ocean every day. And today she saw a sea lion. And no, it wasn't scary like a land lion.

Writing that, she'd stopped and checked the time of Lulu's text. And estimated it had come within moments of the sea lion winking at her. That had been the first sign.

#

The second sign came the following evening. Megan and Cassie were at their now-favorite neighborhood restaurant— more ahi tuna over mesclun—when Stewart texted he wouldn't be able to join them. He was still at the office—far from the first time that had happened over the past ten years, so Megan and Cassie ate without him.

By midnight, Stewart still hadn't come home. No more calls or texts. Megan knew not to contact him, so she checked with Cassie, who said she hadn't heard from him either but wasn't concerned. "You know S and work." As if that explained anything.

It wasn't until almost 2:00 a.m. that Megan was awakened by the sound of the garage door opening to accept the new Mercedes. Stewart came upstairs into the bedroom and Megan sensed his tension through the darkness.

Marital history clued her there wasn't anything she could say when Stewart was in one of these moods. Even a pleasant hello could spark a sharp reply, as if she was part of whatever problem he was dealing with.

She waited until he was brushing his teeth, then went into the bathroom and lightly caressed his back as he leaned over the sink.

He said, "Sorry I missed dinner."

"That's okay."

He'd tell her whatever was going on if he felt like talking. Otherwise, she might never know. Megan got back into bed and waited.

Stewart settled alongside her without speaking.

When he was like this, Megan felt powerless and excluded. But accepted it as part of his personality, a pitfall that undercut all that was wonderful about him. A career that allowed them to buy a house like this—as with their home back in Maryland—involved more costs than the mortgage, especially when you came from next to nothing. When family money hadn't propped you up in life and you'd had to work extremely hard for what others were given.

Neither of them slept that night and Stewart was out of bed before sunrise. Getting dressed, he snapped buttons of one of his expensive new shirts as if girding for battle. He said, "Could be another long day."

"Let me know whatever you need."

Stewart nodded and was gone, footfall hard on the stairs. The quiet rumble of the garage door powering open followed by the Mercedes pulling out as the sky remained black.

It was Cassie who learned what was going on: the company Dunhill had come to California to buy was "playing games," trying to up the purchase price and keep more of their principals in top positions.

Megan assumed Stewart had told Cassie—he always discussed business more with Cassie than her—but it was actually Conner Vance, the young lawyer from LCW, who gave Cassie the news.

The following day, Stewart assured Megan, "It doesn't change anything." A statement Megan believed was meant to keep her from asking if they'd still be moving or if they should try to get out of the contract for the house.

She pretended to accept his simple promise, at the same time concealing hope this turn of events might put them back in Maryland even though, in her heart, she knew there was no going back. That people couldn't be turned back any more than time.

Over the next few days, an awkward uncertainty filled the house. It no longer seemed to Megan as if they were on an extended vacation, but that they'd been swept from their foundation and left grasping for safety.

Stewart flew to Scottsdale for an emergency board meeting and didn't return that same night as planned, calling to say he'd need to stay a few more days. Cassie picked up added insight from Conner, who said the "Dunhill team" of LCW lawyers from DC had flown by private jet to Phoenix to file a lawsuit in federal court. "They're going to smash Talbot-Glen into submission," Cassie claimed, speaking with the brazen confidence she'd carried through two undefeated seasons as her lacrosse team's captain.

That same night, Cassie started dropping hints about going back east for her internship, saying she felt excluded from interesting projects because she was working remotely. And Megan thought how the digital age could provide so many conveniences and contradictions—in one breath extolling the virtues of working from home and in the next blacklisting its pitfalls. But she didn't question Cassie's motives—whether she really wanted to get back to her internship or if Conner or someone else Cassie wasn't telling Megan about was waiting for her. Nor did she seek updates about Cassie's possible transfer to Stanford. Because when Cassie wanted, she could paint responses like a lizard camouflaging into its new background.

Two days later, Cassie told Megan she was returning to DC, probably for the rest of the summer. She'd already booked a flight for the following morning.

That was the third sign.

#

The fourth sign came the afternoon after Megan drove Cassie to LAX.

Cassie never cried going away, not leaving her parents, not parting with friends and teammates when graduating high school. Megan usually got teary-eyed enough for both of them.

From the airport, Megan drove back to the house through aggressive traffic, then jogged down to the beach and dove into the water, swimming toward the rocks and coming ashore at the old cottages.

She sat on the tilted porch of the empty two-room shack she liked the best and watched the ocean, imagining what it might have been like to live there sixty years ago. Imagining what she would have been like. Long hair to her waist, styled with braids and wooden beads. Wearing a handsewn hippie dress with a low neckline, imprinted with geometric shapes in pastel shades of pink, yellow and lime. No underwear, but a bikini underneath, so she could peel the dress over her head and slide into the sea anytime she wanted. And no shoes—she would have been barefooted all the time.

There would be a little girl playing on the beach with her friends. Making sandcastles. Laughing. Her little girl. With long hair that was wavy like Megan's, but blond like her father. Like Pip. Images that seemed so real it was if she could touch them.

But that fantasy was not the fourth sign—that was another text from a number Megan didn't know: *OCSP test in 4 weeks. You ready?* Pip.

27.

Two days after Cassie flew back to DC, Megan was on a plane, rising into the blue midday sky out of John Wayne International Airport.

With Cassie gone, the new house had begun to feel like a cave. Megan had spent most of the past 48 hours on the beach, staying until the sun settled into the sea, when she'd head back up the hill to fix herself dinner, alone.

Stewart remained in Scottsdale, their conversations over the past week having been brief and strained. Dunhill's merger with Talbot-Glen not only remained contentious (and maybe Megan was imagining it) but seemed as though much more was at risk than Stewart was revealing.

Pip had not sent any more texts. Nor had she—though she'd started a few only to delete them.

Now, on the plane, looking out the window, she wondered if Pip remembered how when they were last together he'd told her he fell in love with her the first time he saw her. She discounted his having said that—perhaps he'd felt the need to justify kissing her and easing his hand inside her shirt. She'd been an opportunity. It was the beach. Moments like that happened.

Megan again reminded herself he'd probably been with other women—girls—while she'd been gone. Dozens perhaps. The beach…

In her thoughts of Pip, he was a fantasy. And she would keep him emotionally catalogued to that limit. As much as she looked forward to seeing him again, she was not going to cheat on Stewart. And in the off-chance Pip might think of her that way, she would make clear that couldn't happen.

What Megan did want was to become one of his surf patrol crew, to experience being with him in that way but no more. To do that until the end of summer, then she'd fly back to California or Scottsdale or wherever Stewart was, hopefully with fond memories of Pip and Will and Adrian and Art and Lulu, and a summer at the beach. And she would have accomplished a challenge. At least that's what she told herself...

#

When Megan's flight landed in Denver for a scheduled layover, she remained in her seat and switched on her phone. There were no texts or voice mails from Cassie or Stewart. She considered sending something to them—nothing to say really, just let them know where she was and that she was thinking about them.

But to Stewart, she would probably be an interruption. If he replied quickly, it would likely be meaningless rhetoric. And if he didn't reply for hours, it would make her feel unimportant. It would be the same with Cassie. No matter how Megan tried to consider it less emotionally, when hours—or sometimes days—passed before Cassie responded to her texts or calls, it hurt. So, instead, Megan texted Jillian, who she hadn't heard from in a few days.

Jillian responded in minutes. She was swamped at the office but needed to know: Is it still happening? Meaning was Megan still moving to Southern California?

Megan replied: *Yes.*

There was a long pause before Jillian responded: *Maybe it will be okay.*

Megan started to reply, Maybe, but deleted that and sent: *Yes.* As though there wasn't any other option.

To be continued, Jillian texted, then headed off to a meeting.

Megan set her phone on her lap and looked out the window.

A belt loader pulled alongside the plane, its crew setting about the tiresome task of unloading baggage. At least it was a beautiful day, blue skies and mountains.

Megan had never been to Denver, and it seemed a missed opportunity to merely view it through a pane of polycarbonate. She wondered if any passengers on these layovers ever got off the plane instead of flying on to wherever their ticket was sending them. She imagined it was something Pip might do.

She picked up her phone and sent him a text: *It's Megan. Flying home. Swim tomorrow morning?*

His response came in two minutes. *Great. Yes. See you then!!!*

Megan set down her phone and looked out the window. Contemplating the mountains, a pleasant warmth quivered inside her, swelled by memories of Pip's touch and the anticipation of seeing him again. She'd gone away because her feelings for him frightened her. The attraction had been wonderful, but the momentary loss of inhibition and reason unsettling. Like nothing she'd ever experienced. But she understood it now. It was still a bit conflicting and layered with guilt, but nothing to be afraid of. And she again reminded herself she was likely making way, way too much of it. He wasn't in love with her. And she wasn't in love with him. It was just the idea of someone like him, the thought of a different life. Because even though the life she had now with Stewart and Cassie had been wonderful, was still wonderful, it was changing. But it would still be wonderful. She just wasn't sure how.

Megan looked at Pip's text again. And was still looking at it minutes later when the pilot came on the intercom with an announcement.

28.

Delayed in Denver, Megan texted Stewart and Cassie. *Waiting for 23 passengers from a flight coming late from Sacramento. Probably going to miss my plane to Salisbury. Might rent a car. Miss you.*

Within five minutes, Megan got a response, not from Cassie or Stewart, but Anna, Stewart's assistant: *What's your flight info? Let me see what I can do.*

Megan replied: *I'm fine. Just a short delay.*

Are you going to miss a connection?

Maybe. It's OK.

I'll check for different flights.

Really, it's OK.

Do you need a hotel? Car? Car service?

Maybe a car. But I can take care of it. Thanks.

Sure?

Yes, Megan replied, then texted: *How are things going?*

Fine.

Megan imagined "fine" was Anna glossing over the truth, judging from her phone calls with Stewart over the past week. Anna had been with Stewart from the early days when his company had a staff of three. She was friendly with Megan but didn't share secrets. Anna was loyal to Stewart.

Last year, when Stewart began spending more time in Scottsdale, Anna moved into a rented house in Paradise Valley. Megan wasn't privy to details—if there was financial compensation for Anna to make the move from Baltimore or if Dunhill Infrastructure was picking up her lease—but whatever the terms, Anna was where Stewart needed her.

Megan wondered if Anna had always responded to situations in tandem with Stewart or if she'd picked up his personality. A few years older than Stewart, Anna had been working as a paralegal with thoughts of law school when Stewart hired her. She'd never married and had come to company parties with three different men, and whenever Megan asked what happened to the last guy, Anna would report without rancor that she'd moved on. She had a daughter who was now in her mid-twenties, a software engineer in Seattle, so maybe, Megan thought, being in Arizona put Anna closer to her only child. Then again, thinking that way may have been Megan downplaying the idea that Anna might have been more loyal to Stewart than she was—at least to his career.

Ending their exchange, Anna texted: *Anything you need let me know.*

Will do. Thanks.

Megan put away her phone as other passengers grumbled about the delay. The plane was less than half full and the seats alongside her were unoccupied, which made it better.

Seat reclined, comfortable in the same wide leg pants and t-shirt she'd flown west in weeks ago, Megan closed her eyes even though she wasn't tired. She'd slept well last night. Alone in the big house, she'd felt safe, just lonely, still not knowing any neighbors, not knowing anyone really. But she'd found comfort that she was going home, and now was glad Stewart wasn't with her.

If he'd been beside her now—well, he wouldn't be beside her, he'd be bearing down on someone in a supervisory capacity, wanting to know exactly when the plane was going to take off or making demands for a different flight or compensation. He'd be on his phone, rallying Anna to join the battle. While Stewart's determination could be appealing, overplayed it was embarrassing. Quite a few evenings had been ruined by Stewart's reaction to poor service in a restaurant or a hotel room with a view he considered unacceptable. And Cassie had grown up to be the same way.

Two hours passed before the Sacramento passengers began to board Megan's flight to Baltimore. She was definitely going to miss her "puddle jumper" from BWI to Salisbury, having planned to Uber the final half hour to Ocean City.

She texted Cassie and Stewart when the plane was about to take off from Denver but didn't provide further details. She wasn't sure what she was going to do once she landed in Maryland but didn't want Stewart to task Anna with helping her. Depending on how she felt when she got there, she'd either rent a car and drive two hours to the beach or spend the night in a hotel and drive or fly tomorrow.

As the flight attendant announced the cabin doors were being closed and cellphones had to be turned off, Megan texted Pip: *Just now leaving Denver. Might not be there tomorrow morning after all.*

As she was about to power off her phone, Pip replied: *I guess I can wait another day.*

Without hearing his tone of voice, she didn't know if he was being sweet or sarcastic. If it had been Cassie, she would have assumed sarcastic.

None of the late-boarding passengers took either of the seats alongside her, so once in the air, Megan raised the arm rests and sat sideways, stretching her legs. Halfway to the east coast, she ate a protein bar she'd packed in her carryon.

By the time the plane banked north and began its descent to BWI, the sky was darkening with nightfall. Coming in over the Chesapeake Bay, the waterway's twin bridges were visible in the distance.

It was nice to be home, even if she wasn't all the way there yet.

Once at the gate, Megan remained seated so other passengers could deplane ahead of her, some hurrying to connecting flights. Her ten-seat-propeller plane to Salisbury—the last scheduled flight of the day on a small regional airline—had departed an hour ago.

Travel weary, but not really tired, she decided to rent a car, figuring she could drive to the beach before midnight.

The airport was uncrowded and familiar. Megan took her time going into the terminal, carry bag over her shoulder. She hadn't checked any luggage so she continued through baggage claim, heading for the exit where a bus would take her to the rental car area.

At the sliding exit doors, wearing a red hoodie, cut-off sweat shorts, and flip flops, his blond hair uncombed, was Pip.

Megan stopped, waiting for the image of him to evaporate as if he wasn't real. And then he smiled.

As though carried on a wave, Megan rushed to him and was in his arms, her feet coming off the ground as he hugged her. He smelled of the outdoors and the ocean. And whether his lips actually tasted salty from the sea or she imagined it, she couldn't tell. Didn't care.

"I missed you so much."

Megan thought she'd spoken those words, but it was Pip saying that.

He brushed her hair from her face. "I thought I'd never see you again."

Megan felt as though drawn outside herself, light and weightless with joy, swelling with opposing sensations of freedom and capture. Clutching him as though knowing as soon as they separated from this embrace, complications would start pushing them apart.

29.

Outside, it was warm and humid, so unlike cool California nights. Her arm around Pip, Megan leaned her head against his shoulder and played with his sweatshirt's frayed drawstring, the back of her hand brushing against the surf patrol initials, large block OCSP letters cracked and partially peeled away with wear across his chest.

They followed a covered walkway to the garage where Pip's aged Jeep sat with the top down. The passenger door made a loud squeak as he opened it for her. As Megan slid onto the worn seat, the soles of her espadrilles settled into threadbare spots on floor mats dusted with beach sand.

Pip hopped in and leaned over to kiss her.

The airport hadn't been crowded but someone she knew could have seen them. Someone could see them now. She cared but felt powerless to stop kissing him. Didn't want to stop.

She'd been telling herself she wasn't in love with him, couldn't be in love with him. And he wouldn't be in love with her. But she'd been wrong about all of it. Hadn't she?

"This doesn't feel real," she whispered between kisses. "And I don't want it to be a dream."

"It's not a dream. You're awake."

"Promise?"

"Yes."

"Are we going to the beach?"

"Yes."

"I can't wait."

Pip started the Jeep and its engine burst loudly to life.

When he shifted into gear, Megan was reminded how he'd operated the amusement ride at the end of the boardwalk—does everyone want to go faster! She gripped the roll bar as they started down the ramp to the exit.

Pip paid the parking fee with a crumpled bill pulled from his pocket.

The attendant smiled, "Drive safe, cutie."

He steered into travel lanes out of the airport, the Jeep bouncing over every seam in the roadway. Megan let her hair blow free.

Pip held her hand as he drove, taking his other hand off the steering wheel and reaching across his body to shift gears. They spoke over balmy night air rushing around them.

"How did you know where I'd be?" Megan asked him.

"You texted you were delayed in Denver. That narrowed the possibilities."

"You should have said something. You could have driven all this way for nothing."

"I didn't want to give you the chance to say no." He gently squeezed her hand. "I'm glad you're back."

"Me, too."

"Are you okay with the top down?"

"Yes—fine." She looked at him and took a deep satisfying breath. "I'm fine." She thought about explaining why she'd gone away without saying goodbye but wasn't sure how to be that honest with him yet—if he'd even want her to be that honest.

Pip merged onto the highway, steering to the fast lane, accelerating over the limit but not by much. "How was California?"

"Awful." Megan had no trouble being honest about that, the first accurate comment she'd said aloud about Newport Coast—even to Jillian—as if being that blunt would have admitted to herself how unlikely it seemed she could ever be happy there.

"Really?" Pip seemed surprised.

"It's crowded. The ocean was cold. And it felt like everyone wants to be in the movies. Or just be famous. And rich, of course. Everyone looked like they wanted to be rich. The whole laidback vibe is put on. It feels like…" She searched for the word. "…a hustle. Nothing seems genuine."

"Not what I'd expect. But I've never been."

"There was one place—these old cottages on the beach. From the sixties. I did like it there."

"So it wasn't all bad."

"No. But those places made me think of you. And made me wish you were with me."

"I would have come."

She nodded. Still holding his hand. Loving the feel of east-coast summer air on her skin.

Pip asked if she was hungry.

"A little. But I don't want to stop yet."

"Okay."

"Tell me about everyone," Megan said.

Pip talked about the guards she'd swum with—all the saves they'd made so far in what had been a busy summer. Lots of riptides.

"Is Art still swooning over Adrian like a little puppy dog?"

Pip laughed. "I guess. But don't let her coolness fool you. She's possessive as hell when someone else flirts with Art."

"He has chickadoodle followers, too, then. And how's Lulu?"

"Good."

"And how are you?"

"Now? Now—I'm good now. And you?"

"I'm good too. I'm really good."

Pip drove with the same relaxed ease as he swam. His motions seemed smooth and effortless.

In half an hour, they crossed the Chesapeake Bay on the eastbound of twin bridges that, to Megan, was the gateway to the beach, even though the ocean was still two hours away. Once east of the bay, the landscape and mood became quieter, darker.

Late on a weeknight, there were few other cars. The highway, divided by stands of tall pines, seemed to glide through long straight stretches of farm and woodlands. Traffic lights were visible from miles away, hanging over intersections that led to tiny places the names of which Megan had read on road signs over the years but knew nothing about.

It felt like months to Megan since she'd last been in darkness. In California, there were so many lights. So many people. Too many.

When they passed a small roadside motel, Megan imagined going inside and getting into bed with Pip. If he'd ask, she'd say yes. At least she thought she would. Although she wasn't sure how this could be happening, how she could feel this way. She didn't really know him. But she dismissed that fact as not just irrelevant, but not a fact at all. Because what mattered was how she felt about him. How she felt being with him. Which was a way she'd never felt with anyone. Maybe that should have scared her. But it didn't.

Still an hour from the beach, Pip turned off the highway in Cambridge—the middle of three small water towns that were Megan's countdown to the beach.

Half a mile down a side road that didn't look like it led anywhere, a burger shack sat on a gravel lot. It was a local's place run by a guy named Butch who'd been a surf patrol guard when Pip was starting out.

At the walk-up counter, Megan leaned into Pip, who had his arm around her. With only fifteen minutes until closing time, they were the only customers.

Megan noticed a security camera mounted to blue-painted rafters and imagined they were being recorded but didn't care. She could never remember being so reckless. As if being with Pip made everything else—everyone else—fade into the background.

As she contemplated an eight-item chalkboard menu, Pip said, "Shrimp burgers are amazing."

"Sounds good."

A cook in a white-t-shirt, who was also the order-taker and would be the clean-up crew—Butch's was often a one-person operation—ducked into view at a screened opening. "Hey, Pip. What's going on, man?"

"Usual stuff, Donnie. How about you?"

"Like that. Another day. You coming back from a concert?"

"No. Just out. Butch been alright?"

"Freaking and pretending not to. Baby panic," Donnie grinned.

"Yeah—I heard. I've been meaning to call him. Kinsey okay?"

"Better than Butch, which ain't saying much. Calls herself The Wobbler. She is huuuge, but don't say that so she can hear you. That kid comes out big as Butch you're gonna hear her scream all the way at the beach." Donnie glanced at Megan and nodded a bit awkwardly when their eyes met.

Megan considered maybe there was some guy code not to say anything about a girl he didn't know.

"Get us two shrimp burgers?" Pip asked.

"Yup—sure thing." Donnie turned toward the flattop that along with a fryer were the shack's only means of cooking. "Drinks?"

"Lemonade?" Pip suggested to Megan.

"Yeah. Anything."

"Lemonades, Donnie," Pip relayed.

"You got it," came the cook's reply.

Megan and Pip sat at a gnarled picnic table, each straddling the same side of a homemade bench, facing one another, knees touching, lit by a mosquito-repelling bulb mounted to the side of the wooden shack.

Pip leaned closer and kissed her. Softly. Once. Twice. Again. A soft, sweet mouth. When she parted her lips, his tongue eased into her mouth. They smiled between kisses. Kissed again.

Megan found herself aroused and comforted at the same time. How wonderful, she thought.

When their food was ready, they ate at the table.

"This is really good," Megan said of the shrimp burger. What she'd expected to be more like a crab cake was actually a thin juicy hamburger with hunks of sweet shrimp, dusted with Old Bay and served on a butter-toasted bun with a Worcestershire aioli. The lemonade was fresh-squeezed and not too sugary. "So Butch's wife is having a baby?"

"She is."

"And he's nervous?" Megan guessed from Pip's brief conversation with Donnie.

"Kind of ironic, I guess, because Butch is a big guy. Fearless. And a real good swimmer. He'd go out in any kind of surf. To think of him being nervous about a little baby…?" Pip weighed that possibility. "But I guess that happens. Right…? Were you nervous?"

Megan hesitated, not quite nodding, her head rolling slightly side to side as she considered how to answer. "I wasn't nervous, no. But that's because I've never been pregnant. Cassie is my stepdaughter. Her mother died when she was little, and Cassie was a student in the elementary school class I was teaching. That's how I met her father. My husband, Stewart." Saying their names at that moment, they felt like strangers to Megan—people from her past who'd drifted away like clouds. For what was almost a year now, she'd spent more time apart from Stewart than with him—and the separation from Cassie had been even harder.

"Oh—sorry," Pip apologized. "That was too personal. I didn't know."

"No, of course. How could you? How could you know? I don't usually mention it—about Cassie. Hardly ever, in fact, because I think of her as my daughter. And it's not personal … for you. It's not. You can ask me anything you want."

"Okay. Well, the same goes for you. Ask me anything. Anytime. Anywhere."

"Okay."

He waited with warm expectation. "So ... is there anything you want to ask me?"

She shook her head. "No. You?"

"Maybe in a little while..."

"Okay."

Donnie came around from the back of the shack, heading to the dumpster with a trash bag. Seeing Pip and Megan watching him, he called over: "Raccoons'll probably get this before the garbage men."

"Good burgers, Donnie," Pip complimented, holding up what was left of his.

Donnie gave a thumbs-up and continued with his chore.

"Quiet here," Megan appreciated.

Beyond Butch's shack, no lights were visible through the trees—no other businesses or houses. And not a single car had driven past. Frogs chirping nearby and the occasional distant rumble of a tractor trailer out on the highway were the only sounds.

Pip said, "I like quiet."

"Me, too. But I also like the ocean."

"It's a different kind of quiet."

They took their time finishing their burgers. Pip carried their trash to the dumpster and then they were back on the road.

An hour later, passing through another stand of pines, the golden lights of the Ocean City skyline spread across the horizon and reflected off Assawoman Bay.

Megan breathed in the salty air. It felt so good to be back.

Across the Route 90 bridge, stopped at the traffic light waiting to turn onto Coastal Highway, Pip was still holding Megan's hand. He said, "Okay ... here comes my question."

Before he could say more, she said, "The answer is yes."

30.

Pip parked his Jeep in the reserved surf patrol spot on the side street at the north end of Megan's building.

Unlike on the empty highway driving across the Eastern Shore to get here, there had been a lot of cars on Ocean Highway. It was almost midnight, but the beach town was active. Lots of vacationers stayed up late. Voices came from different directions and music played somewhere.

Megan said, "Let's use the stairs."

Pip nodded in agreement, but a slight tension ran between them—not with one another, but as unspoken acknowledgment there were people who knew her—and who knew Pip—in this resort, in this building—who also knew Stewart and Cassie.

And while that realization triggered the risk of being found out and also jostled morality, it did not instill doubt in Megan. It did, however, invoke caution. She had never done anything like this before. Never been unfaithful to Stewart or to any man she'd dated before him, or the boys she'd gone out with growing up. This was so entirely out of character she could not explain it any more than she could deny it.

Against the sound of the surf pounding ashore on the other side of the dunes, they crossed the side street and entered the enclosed stairwell, doing that to prevent the chance of being seen together in the elevator. Megan opened the heavy door and went in first, with Pip close behind. They agilely ascended the concrete steps, neither of them at all short of breath as they reached the fifth floor and stepped out, exposed now along the open walkway, passing doors to other condos.

Megan withdrew her keys from her bag. Her hand was steady as she unlocked the deadbolt, then the knob lock.

Pip held the screen door as Megan stepped inside, then followed her, shifting positions so she could reach back and close the door. Lock it.

No lights were on. The air was warm and stale from Megan having turned off the air-conditioning when she'd left.

She dropped her bag and put her arms around him.

He moved her hair to the side and kissed her neck over and over as his hands caressed her body through her clothes. When he tugged at the hem of her blouse Megan lifted her arms so he could take it off. Kissing her, he slid down the straps of her bra, then its soft cups, caressing her breasts.

Megan felt him getting hard against her. "I want to take a shower."

"Okay."

"With you."

In the dark, Megan eased from his embrace and with her bra below her breasts found the thermostat and turned on the air-conditioning. Then went into the bathroom and switched on a nightlight, turned on the shower.

With Pip watching in the doorframe, she undid the snap of her bra. Kicked off her shoes and came back against him. Pulled off his sweatshirt. His t-shirt. And felt his firm chest, his lean stomach. She undid his belt.

It was not, at that moment, just about the sex. It wasn't that kind of desire. She wanted to be naked against him. In his arms. To be desired by him—yes—but also to be held. She wanted that closeness.

She pushed down her pants and panties, took them off. Sticking her hand under the shower to test the water temperature, she watched Pip undress, slipping his thumbs inside the waistband of his pants and underwear, taking them down together. He was hard for her.

They stepped into the shower, under warm water as steam began to fill the small room. Megan leaned against the tile wall so Pip could press against her, his hands low at her waist. They kissed again, hungrier than before. Megan slipped her touch between their bodies, caressing him as his kisses moved down her neck, onto her shoulder.

He lathered his hands with a bar of soap and spread handfuls of suds from her throat to her breasts, onto her stomach, around her waist, along her hips and ass, down her thighs.

Megan turned for him to wash her back, and when she was slick with soap from her shoulders to her hips, he rubbed against her from behind, his erection sliding over her lower back as he drew aside her hair and kissed her neck. Then slid his hand around her hip and pressed between her legs.

Megan moaned quietly.

He whispered, "I don't have a condom."

Megan cleared her head enough to count the days since her last period, then asked, "Have you been with anyone else?"

"Not since February."

She believed him. Perhaps because it was the answer she wanted to hear. But she trusted him. "Okay," she sighed. "We're okay."

"Sure?"

"Yeah." Tilting forward at the waist, forearms flat against the wall, shower spray all around her. "Yeah." Thinking—yes, do it right here. Unable to remember the last time sex had felt this urgent. This good.

#

In bed with Pip, Megan lay on her side with him against her from behind, his arm around her. Both of them naked, clean from the shower, and warm from the glow of orgasm—two, actually, for her: the first standing in the shower, the second here, with Pip on top of her, in the bed where she last slept

145

with Stewart almost a year ago. A bedroom that, in Stewart's absence, had come to feel like hers—no longer theirs. The way the entire condominium seemed like a place where she stayed by herself. As if absence had not necessarily erased history, but rearranged it, the way the tide coming onto the beach smoothed footprints in the sand.

"I'm falling asleep," Megan whispered dreamily.

"Mm." He nuzzled the back of her neck. Sighed contentedly. "Sweet dreams."

"You, too."

Briefly, Megan wondered if she should text Stewart or Cassie—those two strangers—to let them know where she was. Maybe they had texted her. Her phone remained in her bag in the hall where she'd dropped it coming inside. Tomorrow, she decided—she'd text them tomorrow. Maybe that was a mistake, but right now, all she wanted was this.

31.

Early the next morning, the sky was still pink with sunrise when Megan and Pip followed the sandy path through sea grass across the dunes, finding the beach so empty it added to the illusion the world was their own. Side by side, they dove into the ocean, just the two of them, and swam beyond the breakers. The water was warmer than when Megan left last month and far more pleasant than the Pacific.

Alongside Pip, she felt buoyant and fast.

Going on six hours sleep and a pair of protein bars and spoonful of peanut butter each, they swam three blocks before angling for shore, getting just inside the break line when a swell rose behind them, a beautiful wave forming.

"Catch it, catch it," Megan called, paddling along the face of the swell as it began to roll over. Pip was right with her, both of them catching the wave. Megan let out a whoop that blended into the crash of the water, thrilling on the ride.

On the sand, Pip scrambled upright, encouraging, "Let's go, let's go." Grinning for her to run with him.

Bare feet kicking up sand, they found a quick pace that, half a block from his guard stand, became a sprint.

"Nice," he exhaled, breathing deeply when they stopped. "You've gotten faster. That was 400 meters in less than ten minutes in the water. Actually, 800 meters in less than twenty minutes. And 300 meters in less than 65 seconds on the beach."

Winded but feeling strong, hands on her hips, Megan nodded and smiled—when what she really wanted to do was put her arms around him. Even with the sun still low on the morning horizon and no one else close by on the beach, there were balconies and windows, someone might see them.

#

"There's been a development." Awake for hours ahead of his wife, Bill Clary had already fixed himself fried eggs, toast, and coffee for breakfast, completed two crossword puzzles, and suppressed outrage at numerous newspaper articles.

"Good morning to you, too." Not yet fully awake, Mary Jane poured herself a coffee.

Bill said, "The woman formerly known as the woman in the blue bathing suit is back."

"Is she now?"

Bill's use of the phrase, *the woman formerly known as*, was because he had discovered more about Megan than her name—the result of idle curiosity and being retired without any meaningful hobbies. It hadn't taken much sleuthing, actually. A neighbor had a friend in the Ocean Vista who didn't know Megan other than to say hello, but knew her husband, Stewart, and that they had a daughter, Cassie, who was a high school sports star.

A Google search of Cassie Tyler had produced dozens of web pages about the girl's lacrosse accomplishments, including one writer's opinion that her "style of attack on offense is wonderfully merciless." That line had been written before the championship game when one of Cassie's shots on goal struck the opposing goaltender's helmet with such velocity that it knocked the girl unconscious. A short feature article on high school athletes of the year reported Cassie had turned down lacrosse scholarships but accepted an academic ride to George Washington, where, through other channels, Bill confirmed the girl had just completed her freshman year with a 4.0.

A search of Stewart Tyler, meanwhile, had brought up pages about Stewart's Baltimore-based engineering firm, including its recent merger with Dunhill Infrastructure, a company currently embroiled in nasty federal litigation in Phoenix involving its attempted acquisition of another company, Talbot-Glen.

"She and Pip," Bill relayed to Mary Jane, "came out on the beach around seven-thirty. Swam like hell a few blocks south." From a chair by the balcony door, Bill pointed left because Mary Jane was a talented designer but lacked what Bill considered basic navigational skills, such as compass directions, remembering highway numbers, or being able to estimate miles or kilometers—Mary Jane often warning him, as to the latter, that if he referred to them as "clicks" one more time she was going to click him in the ass. "Then they raced back this way on foot. And I'm telling you, Pip was ahead of her, but not by much. Woman can run like hell," Bill chuckled. "Might be where the daughter gets her athletic ability. She's out there now," Bill pointed. "Got an umbrella from the chunky girl and a couple chairs. Been back out in the ocean a couple more times and bodysurfs like Carl used to," Bill said, referring to an army buddy from his Southeast Asia days. "Head out of the water, puts her arm in front like a forward rudder. Carl used to call that Hawaii style."

"Well, there's that mystery solved then," Mary Jane determined, Bill having provided tidbits of his detective work about the woman he'd insisted on referring to as "missing" when Mary Jane assumed she had just left the beach to go back to wherever she lived. But Bill had been adamant there was more to it. A story behind it, he liked to say.

"No, no," Bill chuckled, "you're not waiting for the best part."

Standing at the kitchen counter, Mary Jane drank her first welcomed sip of coffee.

"The best part..." Bill paused dramatically. "...what you're missing ... is the love affair."

"Love affair?" Mary Jane scoffed. "No one says that anymore."

"Add that then to what's wrong with the world," Bill replied. "And I know I'm right. You watch. Love affair—call it what you like. Doesn't change what it is."

Mary Jane came over, her interest tickled now. "Give me those," she said of his Zeiss binoculars on the coffee table.

"Get your own," he teased, first pretending to block her way, then handing over the powerful lenses. "Down there just behind Pip's stand," he directed. "Sitting on the beach chair in that blue bathing suit."

"I see her."

"Now … watch anytime Pip turns toward her, says something. You look at that smile on his face. See how easy he laughs."

"Oh, lordy," Mary Jane remarked not a minute later.

"It just happened, didn't it? Pip looked over at her. You saw it?"

Mary Jane's tone was a mix of pity and amusement as she kept the binoculars focused on Megan and Pip. "And she's married, isn't she?"

"Uh-huh," Bill replied with great satisfaction. "Told you there was a story behind it."

#

Megan couldn't remember a more glorious day on the beach. Sunshine, blue sky, an easy breeze, warm temperatures, and perfect small waves.

"I'm going back in the water," she told Pip, pushing out of the beach chair Lulu had set up for her along with an umbrella, near Pip's stand.

Over the past two hours, she'd already been in the ocean three times, riding waves, something she'd never done until watching bodysurfers in California—what she now considered the only positive thing to have come out of that trip.

"Remind that little kid on the raft not to drift out any further," Pip asked.

Megan smiled and gave him a half salute. "Do you do that?" she asked of the military gesture. "You are a lieutenant." Having just found out this morning the surf patrol had ranks.

"No," Pip laughed. "We don't do that."

"Too bad. I kind of like how it feels."

She went into the ocean, weaving her way around small children and parents milling about in shallow water. At the peak of vacation season, the beach was crowded. For the next six weeks, traffic would snarl the highway, lines would be long at grocery stores and restaurants, and seagulls flying overhead would look down and see more towels, chairs, and beach umbrellas than sand.

Megan dove into a wave and swam out to the little red-headed boy Pip had been watching. He was paddling idly on a cheap grocery-store surf mat—the kind that would buckle in half and maybe split apart if he tried to ride a wave on it.

"Hey," Megan greeted, coming alongside him.

"Hi." The boy, chin resting on the front end of his mat, lifted his hand to give a little wave. Megan guessed he was eight or nine.

"It's a little deep here," she told him. "See?" She planted her feet to show the water level at her shoulders. "Are you a good swimmer?"

"I don't know. I got this." He gave the raft a little squeeze.

"But if you fell off, could you swim to shore?"

He shrugged, looking over the side of his mat into the water. "Where's the fish?"

"They're around."

"I don't see 'em."

"It's not really that kind of water."

"Yeah." He seemed disappointed.

"Not very good for seeing things. It's not that clear. Which sometimes I'm glad about."

"How come?"

"How come?" she echoed, looking around, wondering where his parents were. The nearest adults were 50 yards away.

"How come you're glad about not being able to see what's in the water?" He seemed puzzled.

"Well, um, sometimes because I guess I don't want to see what's there. Because even if it probably won't hurt me, it might scare me."

"Like a ghost?" he wondered.

"Maybe … maybe like a ghost."

"I believe in ghosts, but I haven't ever seen one. I think they're there, but they're hard to see. And it would probably be scary. Unless there are good ghosts—but I'm not sure about that. They could be good. Right? I mean why do things like that have to be scary and bad?"

"Those are good questions," Megan considered.

"Yeah…" He returned his attention to the water, looking for fish.

Megan looked along with him.

"There!" he said after a moment, then laughed. "No, those are your feet."

She wiggled her toes. "How about if we go in where it isn't so deep?"

Ten minutes later, with red-headed Charlie digging for sand crabs, Megan returned to her beach chair.

Pip leaned over toward her. "Congratulations. Your first save. How was it?"

She shaded her eyes, looking up at him. "Philosophical."

"Interesting take," he nodded. "You look really good in that suit, by the way."

"You're okay yourself."

"Thanks."

Pip said, "I've been thinking about another question I may have for you." Picking up on a thread of conversation begun last night.

"What's for lunch?" Megan guessed.

"I was hoping you were just going to say, yes."

"I probably will. What's the question?" She loved talking with him, loved being with him. Loved every word they exchanged, how effortless it felt. How simple and satisfying.

152

Loved looking at him. Loved the way he looked at her. It made her feel as if peering through a unique lens that blurred everything in her vision that wasn't him. There were hundreds of people close enough by to throw a frisbee to, yet they all seemed to fade, their movements and conversations blending into the background.

Pip said, "I'll save it for later. Because now you've got me thinking about lunch."

#

Megan crossed the highway on foot, having slipped shorts over her one-piece and buckled on hiking sandals.

She went into Greenies, a small stand-alone grocery store/sub shop that had been on Coastal Highway for almost 70 years, since this end of the beach town was little more than dunes and sea grass and the occasional cottage. Originally a gas station, the flat-roofed concrete building had been retrofitted over the decades, although never with the aid of an architect or meaningful budget.

Holes, originally cut through the wall for a single plug-in air-conditioner in the sixties, followed by two more in the seventies, had since been patched over, making way for the current ductless system that still struggled on hot days to keep employees and customers from sweating.

Original wood slat floors continued to warp and bow from the humid salt air despite the persistent onslaught of fresh nails and screws and were a toe-stubbing hazard. Upgraded electrical lines were run inside conduit left exposed and attached to the walls with whatever fasteners the electrician happened to have in his pocket. Metal dry goods shelves were old and cockeyed, while tired refrigerator cases ran on aged compressors jerry-rigged by the ingenuity and patience of older repairmen who'd been around long enough not to abandon hope.

Waiting in line, Megan picked up one of the resort's free newspapers, the one that used to feature a tastefully-posed-but-still-bikini-clad girl on the cover but had switched to more politically-sensitive pictures—kids building sandcastles, families playing putt-putt, a couple on a jet-ski. Vacation or not, people still got offended.

Megan skimmed the section that listed live entertainment. Ever since Donnie had said something to Pip last night at the burger shack, wondering if she and Pip had been to a concert, Megan wondered what he'd been talking about. She saw the list of bands playing at various bars and outdoor venues, but they were all local. Nothing that would have taken them as far west as Cambridge. She'd ask Pip.

Her number called, Megan ordered six subs, having brushed up on her semaphore to read orders flagged by Will and Art. Lulu's request had been the least specific, the beach stand girl telling Megan, "Just get me something sloppy." Megan hoped a cheesesteak—extra cheese—met those requirements.

The subs prepared and bagged, Megan paid with her credit card, the one in her name only that emailed monthly statements to her, not Stewart, and that she paid from her own bank account. It was a practice carried over from before they were married.

There wasn't a substantial sum in her account, but more now than last summer, with her Villa James paychecks having been direct deposited—the last one going in the Friday after the final day of school.

Throughout their marriage, Megan always had some money of her own: her pay from her old teaching job and some savings, including a nice chunk from the equity in the condo she'd sold after marrying Stewart, along with some dividends and interest from a modest investment account established with the small inheritance she'd received when her mother died. She mainly used that money to buy presents for Stewart, not wanting him to be paying for his own gifts from the household account he funded with his salary and used to pay all their bills, including whatever she charged to their joint credit cards.

While using her credit card meant Megan was buying lunch for everyone at Greenies, not Stewart, it also kept secret what she was doing. Not that Stewart was one to question what she bought, and a $40 charge from an Ocean City grocery store was hardly a red flag. So maybe it was guilt she was yet to feel about sleeping with Pip last night. Or spending time with him today. And wanting to spend more time with him again tonight. And tomorrow. And the next day. And the next.

She hadn't gotten any calls or texts from Stewart or Cassie, which helped prolong the fantasy that being with Pip was as simple and carefree as it felt. She was going to enjoy that while it lasted—anticipating the luxury would endure longer than the next 45 minutes.

#

Adrian insisted on paying for her own lunch. The dark-haired college junior came down off her guard stand, unfolding bills she'd pulled from her surf patrol bag.

"Really, it's okay," Megan said again. "My treat."

"No." Adrian was curt, almost cold, which took Megan by surprise. Maybe she was having a bad day. "How much?"

"I think six bucks. Just give me the five," Megan said, seeing a bill of that denomination in the girl's hand.

"Here's six." Adrian handed Megan the money and started to clamber back up her stand.

"You okay?" Megan asked. It was the first she'd seen Adrian in weeks, and it felt as if more had changed than her haircut—shorter now and styled with more body.

Adrian paused, one hand on the ladder rung of her stand, the other holding the bag with her sub. Looking straight ahead, not at Megan, she said, "You were in California?"

"Yes."

"With your family? With your husband?" She looked at Megan now, her expression hard, accusing.

Megan felt a whiplash of shame but pushed it away. "Yes."

"I thought you were separated."

Megan wasn't sure where Adrian got that idea. She'd never talked to her about that—never talked to her about anything.

"Pip was really sad when you left. He didn't know where you'd gone. Or why. Or if you were coming back. He was sad the whole time. Until today."

Megan wanted to tell Adrian everything but didn't know how to start because she didn't understand it herself—not really. She only knew how it felt. At the same time, she didn't want to admit anything to Adrian. Because so far—at least as far as Megan knew—the girl didn't know what was going on between her and Pip. Adrian may have had her suspicious— that look she gave Megan weeks ago, telling her to have fun when Pip said he was taking her out in the ocean to learn about rip currents—but Adrian didn't know. Not unless Pip had told her—and Megan didn't think he had.

Adrian said, "He's not like most guys, Megan. He's … it's like he's from a different, I don't know, era, world even. Someplace better than here. He's really sensitive. He hurts easily. And you hurt him."

Megan said nothing. But nodded. And turned and walked away.

32.

"This is so good," Lulu chewed, steak sub juice running down her arm. "Thank you again."

"Thanks for the chairs." Megan ducked under the pair of beach umbrellas Lulu tilted against one another, creating a blue canvas roof for her wall-less office.

"I'm just glad you're back. We were worried about you. Here—sit." Lulu nudged an empty chair with her foot. "Have your lunch."

"I should have let you know I was going away. I'm sorry. The trip came up suddenly." Megan sat but didn't feel very much like eating. The two-block walk from Adrian's stand had served to lessen the sting of the girl's words but left her uneasy. Now, looking at Pip down by the water's edge, his tanned back and blond hair, she felt such a deep wanting ache she had to close her eyes. She didn't know what she was going to do. Maybe she needed to end this right now, with Pip. How could it possibly go well? What was she thinking? Obviously, she wasn't. She was feeling.

Lulu tapped Megan's arm. "Hey, you with us?"

"Yeah." Megan blinked. After a moment, she asked Lulu, "Were Adrian and Pip ever a couple?"

"What?"

Megan regretted having asked. "Never mind. It's none of my business. I just wondered. I got kind of a vibe from Adrian just now."

"Oh, forget—don't pay any attention to her," Lulu advised brusquely. "What'd she say?"

157

"Nothing. She just seemed kind of cold. And I got the feeling maybe she thinks I'm an intruder."

"What? No. Ignore her. I mean, don't ignore her, but don't—just don't worry about her. She's like a faucet. Hot and cold," Lulu rattled off. "One day she's your best friend, the next day she's offended by something you've done that's going to unravel the universe. Last summer, she got into a shouting match with two women because they were excited over some magazine article about Farrow and Ball announcing a new line of paint colors. Do you know Farrow and Ball?"

"No."

"Well I didn't either, but apparently it's some fancy company that makes fancy paint for houses, and wallpaper and shit, and that these women were so into that at that particular second teed Adrian off and she went nutso. She yelled at the women how people in half the world don't have drinkable water and all these two cared about was painting their dining rooms some color that would make their friends envious. She got suspended from the surf patrol for a week—cause she was working when it happened. They'd have probably fired her if not for Pip. But that was just him being Pip, not because he and Adrian were a thing. He was just standing up for one of his guards. You screw up, he'll do the same for you. I think it's pretty cool, by the way, you doing the guard test." Lulu nodded appreciatively. "I can see you up there like that." She gestured to Pip on his stand. "Blow your whistle at people being idiots. Go out there in a rip tide to pull people in." Lulu returned to what remained of her cheesesteak, offering a final bit of advice while eating: "Don't worry about Adrian."

#

At ten minutes to three, Megan was in her condo, having showered and changed into a clean t-shirt and shorts. Hair tied back, she sat at the dining room table with her iPad, waiting for her afternoon student to sign on.

158

Her phone chimed. It was Stewart. She froze momentarily seeing his name on her screen. It was an unusual time for him to call—what would be almost noon in Scottsdale. Typically, if they were going to talk—not just text—it was at night. She considered letting the call go to voice mail, not having given necessary thought to whatever lies she might need to tell him today. But she answered. "Hi."

"Hey." He sounded like he was walking, his tone serious—what Megan thought of as his "at-work" voice.

"Everything okay?" she asked.

"Leaving the courthouse."

"That doesn't sound like a good place to be. At least you're leaving."

"Yeah."

Talking to him, she felt less anxious than she'd anticipated. "Is this about Talbot-Glen?" She'd heard Stewart mention that company enough to remember it. "Why you're in court?"

"A chambers conference, actually. So not really court. And yeah, it's about Talbot-Glen." He no longer sounded enthused saying the name. "We're going to win. Their game-playing, their greed is going to backfire on them. But it's taking so goddamned long. But anyway … you got back alright last night? I didn't hear from you, so I assumed everything went okay."

"Yeah. Fine."

"Good. So where are you? The beach?"

"Yes."

"I'm glad you got there."

She hoped he wouldn't ask how she'd gotten from BWI to the beach. Maybe he'd forgotten the delay in Denver had caused her to miss her connection, or he'd just assumed she'd gotten another flight.

"Weather nice?" he asked.

"It is. Beautiful. I swam and had lunch. Now I'm waiting for a student to sign on."

"Hot as hell here. A hundred-fifteen."

"That is hot."

"Hold on a sec, I'm at the car. Let me get in and get the AC on."

"Okay." She heard the chirp of a car being unlocked. "You still have the big Mercedes?"

Dunhill had leased a top-of-the-line SUV for Stewart when he'd started working in Arizona, not knowing he preferred sedans, a benefit that had been rectified in California.

"Yeah, and right now I'm glad I do, the AC is fantastic."

The small talk that used to be comforting caused Megan to experience an intense sadness. She'd fallen in love with someone else and Stewart didn't know. Had no way to know—no reason to suspect it any more than she had reason to think it possible. And beyond that...beyond that... She couldn't bring herself to admit what else she was feeling. Didn't want it to be true. Stewart was a nice and kind man, intelligent and driven and successful. But... But... She put her hand over her eyes and rubbed the bridge of her nose.

"Okay," Stewart said over the sound of the Mercedes' engine starting. "Sorry about that. Thank God for covered parking." Then: "Another sec..." Megan heard him say: "I'll meet you there. Be right behind you." He came back on the line. "That's Gruder. He's point on the litigation. A specialist in injunctions. I think you met him at dinner the night you flew out. Tall guy."

"I think so, yes. Very Nordic."

"That's him. He's sharp."

"Good he's on your side then."

Stewart asked, "Have you talked to Jillian?"

"Not recently, no."

"We talked about seeing if she could recommend someone to list the house with," he reminded. "Get that sold."

"Right. Yes." Megan fought to keep her voice steady. "I'll call her tonight."

"And the condo. And if she doesn't know anyone, I'm okay using one of those agents that has their face plastered all over everything. It's the same everywhere, I guess. There's a couple names out here I already feel like I've seen a thousand times."

"I don't—I'm not sure Jillian would know anyone here anyway, at the beach. But I'll ask." Megan pictured standing at the balcony door with Cassie that first day, looking out at dolphins in the ocean. And all the summers since. Teenage Cassie and her friends piled on the sofa bed and futons on the floor, as many as five girls sleeping there one weekend, after which Stewart had a larger hot water heater installed. Those memories suddenly seemed much more distant than just a few years ago because they weren't going to be repeated.

Stewart said, "Maybe find someone who'll do it for less than five percent. Both places should sell fast. Any papers I need to sign just have them email me."

"Okay."

"Great. All right. I'll talk to you soon. Love you."

"Love you, too."

The same ending as hundreds of their other conversations over the years—yet different in one very profound way.

#

Megan sat on the sand back near the dunes, where a rectangle of shade cast by her building extended toward the ocean. Lulu had finished for the day and collected her rental chairs and umbrellas, storing them in the big wooden locker at the head of the street.

The beach was almost empty, most of the sun worshippers having retreated to condos and hotel rooms, getting ready for the evening, maybe going out for dinner, hitting the boardwalk, doing rides at amusement parks. A trio of high school boys had plenty open space to throw a football. A father and son feathered a kite in the gentle breeze. Surfers—five guys, one girl—waited near the water's edge with boards under their arms, watching waves. Only a handful of people remained in the ocean, but surfing wasn't allowed until after five.

Pip stood atop his stand, sweatshirt pulled on, whistle in his mouth, still keeping an eye on the ocean but also watching the time. One of the surfers said something to him that made him laugh. A few minutes later, Pip whistled in Will's direction while flapping semaphore flags one across the other in front of his body, then turned and repeated that signal north toward Art, who relayed the signal to Adrian while Will sent the "day's end" notice south. It was five o'clock—quitting time.

Pip jumped off his stand, a catlike dismount. Picking up his life buoy and bag, sliding their straps over his shoulder, he moved behind his guard stand, tipped the heavy wooden structure onto his back, and was dragging it on two legs toward the dunes when he saw Megan and smiled. "Didn't see you come back down," he called over to her.

"Just got here a few minutes ago."

He settled his stand near the dunes and trotted over. "Your student smarter than he was yesterday at this time?"

Megan looked up at him. "She. And, yes, I think so."

He offered his hand when she started to get up. She took it and let him help her rise to her feet. Brushing the back of her shorts, she wondered what they looked like to anyone in her building who happened to be watching. Did they appear as intimate as she felt?

"Here's my question," he began, renewing that thread of conversation.

"My answer's yes."

"Sure you don't want to hear the question?"

"Does it have to do with being with you?"

"It does."

"Then I'll stick with yes." Because of all the questions and doubts running through her mind over the past hour—the past month—what she was most certain about was wanting to be with him.

"Ride with me?"

"Yes."

They started across the sand, side by side, not holding hands but very much looking like they should have been—

162

shoulders leaning toward one another, an ease to their stride, walking in unison as if already becoming one person.

"Your place?" she guessed of where they were going.

"That okay?"

"Yes."

"You need anything from upstairs?"

"No." She'd put on a dry one-piece bathing suit under her t-shirt and shorts, on the chance she might get back in the ocean, but she'd ended up sitting and thinking instead. At the same time, she had her condo keys, license, credit card, a few dollars, and her phone in her pockets. Having hoped for this invitation.

Home less than 24 hours and she already wasn't being as careful as she should have been.

33.

Less than a ten-minute drive from Megan's condo, the little clapboard cottage with yellow siding and sea-blue shutters sat on the calm shores of the bay at the narrowest point of the island, a place where a quick walk could cover the distance to the ocean.

The little home had survived half a century atop six short pilings, its main floor three feet above sea level. There wasn't any front lawn, but a spread of crushed shells, which made grass-cutting unnecessary and parking easy.

Pip pulled his Jeep alongside two other vehicles: a critically old BMW and a white Sprinter van. The van had ladders secured to a roof rack and a plain logo painted on the side for Big B's Handyman Services.

A simple set of steps led to a shallow, covered front porch, where a screen door tapped against its frame, pushed by the breeze. Double windows on each side of the door were open, as was a single window up on the attic floor. The sound of woman singing opera carried out from inside.

"They're usually gone by now," Pip said, his arm around Megan.

Although the yellow cottage was a short block off the island's main highway, the penetration of bay waters limited nearby development to a small strip shopping center out on the road and a dozen homes. Nine of those residences were new townhomes directly behind the shopping center. The backwoods-style shack to the right of Pip's place was boarded over and stapled with sun-brittle NO TRESPASSING signs.

The house to Pip's left, beautifully remodeled, appeared vacant, and had a for-sale sign in the yard and a realtor's lockbox on the front door.

As they stepped onto the porch, the aria grew louder.

Pip opened the screen. "Kell? Ben?"

Inside, the floorboards were the home's original planks, sanded and refinished countless times to what was now a worn, smooth patina. Steps led to an upstairs attic bedroom. To Megan's left was a short hallway and two closed doors. To her right was an uncluttered living room with a sofa and two cushioned armchairs that looked comfortable and well-worn, the sort of furnishings that didn't object to sandy feet and wet bathing suits. All the walls were painted the same warm white.

The aria played from speakers mounted beside a flat-screen TV that, small by home theater standards, dominated the narrow wall space between opened windows. Megan knew little about opera, but the woman's voice was so loving and melodic it made her want to close her eyes and dream.

"Vision of delight," a young man's baritone voice proclaimed.

At first Megan thought those words were from the opera, then realized someone had entered the living room from the kitchen.

About Pip's age, Kelly Holcomb stood a few inches shorter and had a full head of silky, black hair he combed straight back. His round belly was the result of an occasionally unrestrained appetite. His soft oval face sparkled with cheer. "Megan," he greeted, as though she could be no one else. Wearing checkered cook's pants and a crisp chef's tunic, he dried his hands with a clean towel. "Even more beautiful than imagined." He actually kissed her hand.

"This is Kelly," Pip introduced, his arm still around Megan's waist. "And he was born a bullshitter," Pip discounted genially.

"Born a gentleman," Kelly corrected, "in an age of oafs. But I am ultimately not to be trusted in the company of beautiful women, nor them in mine, so..." He headed back to the kitchen, voice raising to be heard over the opera. "...to ease your worries, I'm out of here in minutes. Die Zitrone is, no surprise, again on the fritz, so I am at the mercy of Irish dishwashers for tonight's transportation. And while they are charming and hard-working, they are not especially good with time." Pip's roommate came back through the living room without his towel. "Apparently the hands of the Irish clock proceed around the dial more *slooowly* than those here in the heartland of democracy that runs the world—albeit in the style of a bullying older brother who welcomes actual dissent with bombs the size of railroad cars. But..." He breathed in and let it out. "...I digress. And again remind myself all is cured with a good meal and better glass of wine."

"You're a chef," Megan said, having liked him on sight.

"A cook," he said simply and with great satisfaction. "I am a cook."

"A great cook," Pip said.

Megan said, "I love to cook, too."

"Then one night we shall dazzle them with our skills." He bowed toward Megan, then looked at Pip. "A brief bit of housekeeping if I may. The casserole in the fridge is for Big Ben. I would have made more if I'd known you were coming home. Frankly when you left for the airport yesterday, I didn't expect you for weeks, if ever."

"It's okay."

"Please remind Ben that cast iron does not go in the microwave, even at low. It goes on the stove, medium flame, to bring the temperature up slowly." Kelly lifted his hands as if gently allowing an invisible object to rise. "You'd think, coming from a family of masons, he'd have a better understanding of metals."

"I'll tell him. Where is he?"

"Sleeping." Kelly turned off the music.

"He working tonight?"

"Supposedly, but if not, text me. I'll tell him I need him at the restaurant. You'll have the place to yourselves until at least three—later if luck strikes. And if I do come home, I'll do my best to do so moderately sober and on tiptoes."

The sound of tires crunching over oyster shells out front preceded the quick tap of a car horn.

"Ah…" Kelly raised a finger along with an eyebrow of surprise. "The Irish have arrived with amazing promptness." He backed toward the front door, offering a grand wave as though projecting to the back row of the balcony. "*Adiós, amantes jovenes.* It means, goodbye young lovers—I think. The guys in the kitchen are trying to teach me, but they're not exactly Rosetta Stone."

"It's a lovely sentiment," Megan replied.

"Last night, a kid from Honduras told me if I was in their country, I could be king. Alas, some theories are best left untested."

"Have a good night, Kell. Cook up a storm."

Sincerely, he offered, "And you two have a wonderful night."

As Kelly headed out the door, Megan's senses peaked in anticipation of being here with Pip, sleeping with him in his bed. And for one of the first times in her life, she was looking forward to being somewhere that would be new to her.

34.

"What an amazing view."

Exiting the cottage by the back door from the kitchen, Megan and Pip walked arm-in-arm across the small sandy yard toward the bay, their presence alerting sea terns that fluttered out of cattails at the water's edge.

The bay was smooth and sparkled reflections of the sun, which hung low in the mid-summer sky, just above forest treetops two miles across the water.

"How long have you lived here?" Megan asked.

"Five years."

"Year 'round?" She wondered what it would be like when the air was cold and the town's streets barely traveled. "You spend the winter?"

"Last year I did."

"What did you do off-season?"

"I worked part-time for the surf patrol. Mostly administrative stuff." His words came slowly, as though dividing his attention between the thought needed for conversation and the pleasure of experiencing this view with Megan close alongside him. "I did some recruiting and interviewing new guards. After storms, I checked beach erosion. I swam."

"In the ocean?"

"With a wet suit."

"Brrr."

"In February, I went to a seminar in Key West. That was pretty cool. I'd never been there."

"Did you like it?"

"I was glad to come home."

She knew how he felt. Snuggled against him, she let her gaze and thoughts drift. After a few quiet moments, she asked, "What about this coming winter?"

"It depends on Aunt Nan, I guess."

"Who's Aunt Nan?"

"My aunt—my mom's sister. She owns the house—sort of. She can do with it what she wants while she's alive—and right now that means renting to us. But as soon as she passes on, the house goes to her late husband's children. He had kids from a first marriage, and Aunt Nan's pretty positive they'll sell once she's gone. The guy who bought that old place next door," Pip gestured to the boarded-over shack, "wants this so he can tear both places down and put up some huge thing."

"Is your aunt in bad health?"

"She doesn't really talk about it. But spring before last, she had a bout of pneumonia that nearly killed her."

Megan considered asking if he'd thought about looking for someplace else to live, but instead hugged her other arm around him and settled her face against his shoulder. "I hope Aunt Nan lives forever."

"Me, too. And not just because of this house, but because she's really sweet. I lived here with her the summer after her husband died. I rented the upstairs—the converted attic—it's where I still am. Lots of nights playing gin rummy. And she could really cook. Between her and now Kelly, I've gotten spoiled."

"How did you meet Kelly?"

"We grew up together. We were friends since second grade when Kelly's family moved away our junior year of high school. We kept in touch a little but drifted apart, which seems to happen a lot. Then, out of the blue, three summers ago, I came home and there's a car out front I didn't recognize and there's Kelly in the kitchen, cooking dinner for the two other guys who were my roommates then. I remember thinking, is it really him? How'd he get here? Turns out he'd gotten married, she'd gotten pregnant, but lost the baby and she left him for some guy at work. He said he'd needed to get out of Ohio and just started driving. He called my old house number and my mom told him where I was. He said he didn't have anywhere else to go. He's been here since."

"That's so sad," Megan said. "Losing a baby. I can't imagine."

"I don't think he's gotten over it. Some days I can tell he's been crying."

"So sad," Megan repeated, holding him.

#

As the early evening sky became painted with the pastel shades of sunset, Pip made a pyramid of driftwood, charcoal, and mesquite atop the sand and lit it with a single match. When the flame quieted and embers glowed, Pip placed a grate over the fire and cooked cheeseburgers they ate on toasted rolls, sitting side by side on a chaise pad set on the sand, facing the bay. They drank red wine from a small Western Maryland vineyard Kelly had discovered, its rich woodsy undertones significantly outclassing their plastic cups.

"Compliments to the grill man," Megan offered as they ate.

Frogs singing in the marsh harmonized with a reggae band playing somewhere south along the bay. An occasional boat passed in the distance, its lights shooting long reflections across the water.

They talked about where they'd each grown up, finding similarities in their respective small towns, though Pip had been much closer to a big city, Baltimore, while Megan had been almost three hours from Richmond.

Last night, on the ride from the airport with the Jeep's top down, they'd mostly enjoyed the quiet and just being back together, but Pip had mentioned it being a busy rescue summer so far. They talked more about that now, how the number of saves were up and that they'd been dealing with more rip currents than any of his ten previous seasons.

Megan also picked up on one of their first conversations and asked what kind of teacher he'd thought about being before his uncle persuaded him to switch majors. Pip said he'd considered biology or chemistry. He asked if she'd always been interested in math.

"I have. My dad liked math. We used to do my math homework together, then one night he said I was smarter than he was, and he couldn't help me anymore. I remember feeling really proud about that. So then I'd help him. We balanced his checkbook together. Only we wouldn't use paper and pencil. I did it in my head."

Pip slightly furrowed his brow. "How do you mean?"

"Give me five numbers."

He did, and she quickly recited a single number in return.

"What's that?" he asked.

"Those five added together."

He smiled but looked doubtful.

Megan said, "But that was too easy. Give me bigger numbers." Finished eating, she playfully shifted positions, going on all fours so she was over him, looking in his eyes.

Pip rattled off five random numbers, the smallest being 155, the largest 101,237.

Never breaking eye contact, Megan quickly responded with a single number.

He laughed. "I have no way of knowing if that's right."

She reached for his phone, nearby on a towel, and handed it to him. Her own phone was back inside the house. Pip needed to be available to the surf patrol around the clock. Megan didn't want to hear if her phone rang or chimed with a text. "Five more numbers," she said. "Add them up as you say them."

He did, and Megan's answer matched the calculation on his phone. "That," he said, "is amazing. How do you do that?"

"I see the numbers in my head. I used to go on hardware store runs with my dad and he'd give me the price of each item he was buying as it was being rung up and he'd ask the clerk not to give the total until I had a couple seconds to add them together. I can also do the sales tax—which on those last five numbers you gave me is 12,040—assuming you're in Maryland at six percent."

Pip laughed, "That is scary smart."

"Thanks."

Then he added, "Almost as scary as how in love with you I am."

"I love you too. And it is a little scary."

#

Hot water splashed off Pip's back and sprayed the shower's deep-blue tiles and opaque glass door before streaking down like rain.

The shower was small, built into a corner of the attic bathroom, where the ceiling angle followed the pitch of the roof.

Pip gently rubbed a bar of soap in his hands, creating a lather that smelled sweet of honey and cream. His soapy fingers moved slowly behind Megan's neck and down her arms. When he got to her hands, he softly rubbed each of her fingers.

Once she was covered with suds, he moved back so the warm spray rinsed her off, and watched the slick lather disappear as though the water was undressing her.

They left the bathroom without completely drying off, their footprints leaving damp outlines on painted floorboards on the way to Pip's bed. Other than the bathroom and a closet, the entire attic space was open and sparsely furnished—a single nightstand and table lamp, a dresser, an old rolltop desk, and the queen bed with a simple headboard. None of the pieces matched, other than being made of wood and stained a dark-cherry and had the feel of having been picked up cheaply—

maybe even for free—when a landlord decided to redo a rental property.

The window on the far side of Pip's bed was open, and without curtains offered a view of the starlit bay.

Megan pulled back the sheet and slid longways across the mattress. She rolled onto her back and Pip settled on top of her. They looked into one another's eyes, watching the soft changes in their expressions as they kissed.

As Pip eased inside her, slowly, all the way, Megan gasped, then softly bit her lip, feeling him hold still there.

"This is so nice," he whispered, kissing her a long while before he started to move.

#

What Bill Clary missed the most about being young was not the energy, the physical strength, the quickness of mind, being free of a roster of "maintenance" prescriptions, or the optimism, but sleep. Ironic. How the sleep that used to come so easily, hours he used to cut short by staying out late and getting up early, now eluded him.

He'd read books about sleep patterns and how they changed in the elderly—a demographic classification into which he had fallen with far less kicking and screaming that he'd envisioned in mid-life. Frankly, he'd never imagined making it this long. In many situations, decades ago, he'd estimated the odds were against even making it out of Southeast Asia. But here he was, in his 70's, at two o'clock in the morning, looking at the dark bedroom ceiling, again.

Mary Jane shifted positions alongside him. She was a better sleeper than he was, but still nothing like they were 40 years ago, when they could both snore through bright sunlight streaming into the room. Now, a seagull squawking out over the ocean could awaken him.

He said, "She makes me think of Penny." Maybe he shouldn't have said that, but he'd been thinking it for weeks and it had gotten to point, like worrisome thoughts did, he had to say it out loud.

Mary Jane didn't reply.

"Not looks-wise," Bill said. "Penny would have been shorter. Had hair like yours. But..." His voice tailed off and he fell quiet before finishing his thought: "I don't really know why."

Mary Jane rolled onto her back and reached for his hand and held it. She knew he was talking about the woman in the blue bathing suit—Megan, her name was.

"Sorry," he apologized.

"It's all right," Mary Jane whispered softly. "Just go back to sleep."

"Probably best." He nodded and closed his eyes.

35.

Megan and Pip awakened with the sunrise.

Looking out the bedroom window with Megan in his arms, Pip said, "I'd been hoping for rain."

"Do you ever call in sick?"

He made a cute face of denial. "That would be cheating."

She looked around the bedroom for the first time in daylight, confirming it was as uncluttered as it had appeared last night in the dark. It was a pleasant space. The natural color of the rugged wood floors was especially handsome, but the sparse furnishings and absence of personal items made it seem a little lonely. There weren't any photographs. The walls were bare save a retro Endless Summer poster in Day-Glo colors in a black frame without glass and a large calendar tacked above the closed roll-top desk. There weren't any papers, or books, or family memorabilia.

On the bedstand table was a kitschy Hawaiian lamp that had a painted hula girl on the base who seemed to be winking at them. "This's cute," Megan said, touching yellow fringe that dangled from the bamboo shade.

Pip got out of bed and pulled on a pair of shorts. "It used to play ukulele music. I bought it at a flea market because the tune reminded me of a song my father's best friend used to play." Pip opened the desk and his laptop to check the morning surf patrol briefing. He remained standing and leaned forward, scrolling through page views. "Surfers will be happy—going to have some waves today. Sun, mid-eighties, humidity's going up a little."

Megan got out of bed naked and stood alongside Pip. "Looks like a workday. Do you eat breakfast?"

#

Megan took a carton of eggs from the refrigerator and a loaf of French bread from a metal tole-painted box. Having confirmed they were alone in the house, she wore one of Pip's beach-patrol hoodies as a dress.

The high-end gas stove was the small kitchen's only appliance upgrade, and likely cost ten times more than the old fridge, dishwasher, and daisy-yellow metal cabinets. Megan guessed the stove had arrived as a result of Kelly becoming resident cook.

The plates were likely also a Kelly-addition: a matched set of a discontinued Mikasa pattern Megan recognized from the Rehoboth outlet stores.

Standing at the kitchen window, the view of the bay drew her into a wonderful stare. "The old cottages on the beach in California..."

Pip was wiping the counter, clearing a place for them to eat.

"...I'd go there and think about you. And picture living there and watching you out in the ocean."

Pip hugged her from behind. "When you were gone, I watched the sunset every night. And tried to imagine throwing a life buoy around the sun, and that as it tracked across the sky, I'd be pulled along behind it, and I'd look down and find you— and bring you back."

Megan leaned against him. "I think you did."

An hour later, their breakfast eaten, Pip pulled his Jeep into his reserved spot at the north end of Megan's building. They trotted across the dunes onto the nearly empty beach, stripped down to their swimsuits, and dove into the ocean to swim south for three blocks.

Jogging back, they were almost to Pip's stand when Megan noticed a man standing on one of the townhouse decks. Wearing a baseball cap, the man waved, seemingly at them—there wasn't anyone else on the beach.

"Is that for us?" she asked Pip, who turned and squinted the waving man into focus, then waved back.

"That's Rome DC," Pip told Megan. "That's what he calls Washington. Older guy. He comes over and chats sometimes."

Megan remembered Pip mentioning that. She smiled and waved back, too. Then looked straight ahead, and for the first time, seeing her condo—the place she'd always looked forward to being, where she always felt she was most herself—loomed with a sense of foreboding.

Neither Stewart nor Cassie had called or texted last night. She'd anxiously checked her phone—left turned off overnight—before leaving Pip's cottage. She glanced at it again now, retrieving it from the pocket of her shorts she'd left on the sand. Still no calls. But that was only a temporary reprieve.

"You okay?" Pip asked.

She nodded.

"It's okay," he understood. "I get it." Suspecting why she'd checked her phone.

She started to touch his arm but stopped because they were in public view. "If I could just snap my fingers…"

Pip smiled and did just that. "That'll be our signal then. You snap your fingers and I'll be there. And we'll go."

She nodded. "Okay." Wishing it could be that simple, and for a brief second thinking it could be. Then she went upstairs, where being back in her condo filled her with memories and promises and commitments unwilling to let her go.

36.

"I don't love him enough to move to California." Sitting at her dining room table, her iPad open, Megan put her hands over her face, fingertips resting against her closed eyes. "I'm not sure I love him anymore … at all. And I don't know how that happened."

Alice Martinelli, on Megan's iPad screen, waited for Megan to say more. Villa James' petite headmistress was seated near a window that overlooked a much different coastline, her brief summer break being enjoyed in a friend's guesthouse somewhere near Narragansett, Rhode Island.

Megan hadn't known who else to talk to. She'd thought about Jillian, but their friendship didn't feel as tight now with Jillian in a different state. Meanwhile, she'd grown close to Alice over the school year, sharing all the changes happening in her life with Stewart and Cassie. But never opening up like this.

Megan said, "I went out to California for a couple weeks, and the whole time I was there, I realize now I was pretending, going along, because that's what I feel like my life has become—trying to be content with the way things are when I don't want them to be that way."

"Let me see your face," Alice asked softly, having requested they do this as a video call and not merely by voice when Megan first phoned.

Megan slowly revealed her troubled expression, easing her hands aside and folding them in her lap. Sitting back, she looked beyond her screen to the cloudless sky and glimmering ocean.

Alice said, "You need to explain your feelings to Stewart."

Megan shook her head. "I've tried. He knows I don't want to move. He has to."

"Does he? I'm just asking, because I'm not sure you've ever told me that you specifically said to Stewart: Honey, I don't want to move. But maybe you have."

"I … I don't… Alice, I'm so tired of it. Really. I'm tired of talking about it. Thinking about it. For almost a year now. He never said, from the beginning, we might need to move. He just … kind of eased it out there … you know … a suggestion here and there … when I think now—all along—I think he knew. And the only reason to do that was because he knew I didn't want to move. And now it's too late. And I'm being told my being there with him is important to his moving up in this new company. That somehow I'm getting pulled into corporate … I don't know what you even call it."

"Who told you this? That you need to be there?"

"A lawyer that's handling—"

"A lawyer? When did lawyers get involved?"

Megan recounted the conversation from her first night in California, when Holden Lassister found her on the restaurant terrace and stressed how important it was for Stewart's continued advancement with Dunhill Infrastructure that she be in California with him.

"That strikes me as an odd thing to say," Alice said.

"It's what he told me."

Alice waited to see if Megan would add more. When she didn't, she repeated the kind advice she'd offered in past conversations. "All marriages go through periods like this."

"I don't think I love him anymore, Alice." Megan still wasn't looking at her screen but at the ocean. Thinking about Pip. Wanting to be with him. "I don't. The other day it just hit me. And it took my breath away. And I'm sad about it. But I don't think it's new. I think I stopped loving him months ago and didn't want to admit it. And I don't … this is terrible to say, Alice … I can barely bring myself to say it, but I have to tell someone…" She began to cry.

"Okay. Take a breath. Take a breath."

Megan wiped the back of her hand across her eyes. "I think I've lost Cassie."

"Oh, Megan, no, no. Stop."

"It's never been the same since that night she said I wasn't her mother."

"Megan—really—stop. She was drunk."

"But she still said it. And it ripped my heart out." Megan clutched for air as tears streamed down her cheeks. "And it's had me thinking that all this time, all this time, I don't know if she ever loved me. If she ever thought of me as her mother. Or I was just someone that got her through a terrible time in her life. And I did the same for Stewart. And now they're through that and they don't need me. They've moved on. Cassie hardly calls. Stewart only cares about his career. And I've been alone most of the past, almost a year now, and … and … and now … now I've fallen in love with someone else. And all I want is to be with him. That's all I want."

"Okay. Megan. Okay. Take a minute. Just relax. Just relax," Alice coached. "Come on. Look at me. Please, look at me."

Megan took time to steady her breathing, saying more than once: "I just want to be with him." She hadn't planned on telling Alice about Pip—it just came out. "When I'm with him, it feels like the rest of the world has gone to sleep. He isn't distracted by work. Isn't looking at his phone. He's just with me. Stewart isn't like that. He's never been like that. And he's kind…." Talking about Pip again. "…not competitive. He doesn't expect the world to treat him a certain way—or demand it. He's patient. And I just want to be with him. I just want to be with him. But I don't want anyone to get hurt, and I don't know how to keep that from happening."

Alice waited until Megan stopped crying, then proceeded firmly. "You may—just may—be confusing fantasy and reality. I'm not judging you. But I have to ask: how long have you known this new man?" When Megan didn't answer, Alice gently prodded, "Not long?"

Megan shook her head.

"So not someone from your past you've reconnected with. Not some social media reunion?"

Megan shook her head again.

"So not someone you've had time to get to know very well."

"I feel like I do," Megan replied, recognizing the defensiveness of her response. "I've never felt this way about anyone. I didn't know it was even possible."

"Love changes over time," Alice believed. "You can't compare feelings you've had for Stewart over a period of years to the flash of excitement of someone new. Who's to say how you'll feel about this new man in ten weeks, let alone ten years. Regardless of how strongly you feel for him now. It might not last. And to complicate what you're going through—and I'm sure you've thought about this, you're a smart woman, Megan—but complicating this is that your circumstances don't provide you the luxury of figuring out if these new feelings are sincere. If they're real, or just a response to what's been an emotionally stressful time for you. You need to be very, very careful."

37.

"You're quiet this afternoon." Leaning over the side of his stand, Pip talked above the crash of the waves, which had been larger than normal all day. "Everything okay?"

Megan sat back on one of Lulu's chairs. In full sun with the umbrella angled to the side, she was getting tanned from all the time on the beach. "Just enjoying the day." Which was true. Her tears had ended hours ago, and her eyes were no longer red, although she'd put on aviator sunglasses just in case.

Her conversation with Alice had been emotional but felt like it had done some good to actually say aloud what had been weaving around in her thoughts.

"Come home with me again tonight?" Pip asked. "Kelly has the night off. He's cooking."

Megan didn't hesitate. "Yes."

"Great." Pip turned back toward the ocean.

The beach was crowded, but fewer people were in the water today, discouraged by the rough waves. The usual entertaining parade of swim-suited vacationers walked by, the ocean splashing around their ankles. Little kids dug in the sand with plastic shovels—some content to excavate holes while others built elaborate castles with motes and spires of trees made by letting wet sand slide through their fingertips into abstract sculptures.

The sudden blare of Pip's whistle startled Megan, followed by the thump of his feet landing in sand as he jumped down, grabbed his buoy, and sprinted into the ocean.

People got to their feet to see what was happening, some moving toward the ocean for a closer look. A rescue was always cause for curiosity. A show with the surf patrol guard as center of attention.

Megan stood on the first rung of Pip's stand and spotted a cheap inflatable boat beyond the wave break and what looked like a young teenager leaning over the side, reaching toward someone in the water, arms flailing.

Pip was already halfway to them as Will came running up from the south and Art legged it down from the opposite direction—procedure being that they would each now cover half of Pip's beach while Pip was in the ocean and go in to assist Pip if necessary.

Pip closed to within twenty yards of the two kids when the one still in the raft, trying to reach her struggling friend, unbalanced the raft and tipped it over. Seeing that, Art crashed into the ocean, not as smooth as Pip getting through the waves but he was fast.

In deep water, Pip slid his buoy across the surface, keeping hold of its leash end. The girl who'd just fallen in clutched hold of it as Pip swam behind her friend. He secured his arm around the second girl, positioning her face-up on top of him as he tread water on his back. The girl coughed and flailed in panic until Pip calmed her.

By the time Will reached them moments later, the situation was seemingly in hand, but Megan had been reading in training materials how saves remained cause for proper practices until everyone was back on the beach. Fear could cause someone to struggle even after imminent danger was over.

"Those things are a menace," Art told Megan, having run all the way to Pip's stand. He was talking about the discount store life raft Pip was pulling behind him, giving it lower priority to the girl he swam back to shore.

Will brought the second girl in alongside Pip, both guards talking to the girls, trying to reassure them, pausing briefly until there was a break in the waves that let them safely reach the beach.

Once they were all out of the water, one girl hugged Will, then she and her friend started down the beach, dragging the raft behind them. A story to tell once they were back in school in six weeks, Megan figured.

Half a dozen people offered Pip and Will congratulations or thanks, a high-five or two.

"You good?" Art asked Pip when he returned to his stand, dripping wet and smiling.

"Yep."

"All right. Nice one." Art set off at a trot back toward his stand, whistling an all-clear to Adrian, who stood watching, hands on hips, farther up the beach.

"That was nice," Megan said. "I didn't even notice them out there."

Pip positioned his buoy upright in the sand the way he liked it, the end dug in, the leash looped just so. "They'd been drifting up for blocks. The one who can't swim has the worst sunburn. Poor kid looks like she's been in a crab pot." He climbed two rungs of his stand and stopped, reading Megan's expression. "If you were working, you'd have seen them. You'd have gotten out there just as fast and pulled them in."

"You sure about that?"

"Not a doubt."

38.

"To our new roommate." Kelly raised his wine glass and toasted Megan.

"Is that what I am?" Megan enjoyed the sound of it, a description resulting from her having arrived at the cottage an hour ago, getting out of Pip's Jeep with a small travel bag—hardly enough to move in, but a change of clothes or two and some toiletries.

On the sandy yard behind the cottage, places for five were set at a folding table Kelly used for occasional catering jobs. The tablecloth matched the glowing color of the sun, which dipped toward the horizon across the bay.

"May you stay forever." Kelly touched his glass to Megan's, then Pip's.

The humid breeze blew a lock of Kelly's hair onto his forehead as he turned to the young girl seated across from Megan. Less serious, he offered, "And to Big Ben's latest..." He paused, having forgotten her name already.

"Donna," she smiled, not at all offended, a brown-eyed college girl with curled, highlighted hair. Her make-up and halter dress expected much after-dinner barhopping. "Have there been that many?" she kidded Ben.

Kelly interjected firmly, "My client will take the fifth."

They all laughed.

Kelly raised his glass again. "Donna, we will love you until..." He looked questioningly between Ben and Donna. "...Sunday?"

Donna smiled at Ben, who grinned happily. She asked, "Are you ready for that kind of commitment?"

"Absolutamente," he confirmed, sounding romantic in the language still spoken at his family gatherings. He kissed Donna, both of them summer-happy and carefree.

Born Benvenuto Serio, Big Ben, as Pip and Kelly referred to him, was good-looking in a classic Roman way, with dark-cinnamon eyes and wavy, jet-black hair. He was not tall, but inches shorter than Megan, so perhaps his nickname was because he was muscled like a laborer, his shoulders and arms filling a black t-shirt.

Kelly set down his glass and prepared to serve. "And now, dinner."

"Wait." Ben stood so abruptly his folding chair toppled onto the sand behind him.

As everyone laughed, Kelly sighed, "Yes, your grace..."

Ben righted his chair, planting its legs firmly in the sand. He raised his wine glass to the southeastern sky. "To Tropical Storm Anita. Most recently tracked 1,050 miles east of San Juan."

Megan looked questioningly at Pip, who nodded as though this was normal.

"Ah, yes," Kelly joined in. He wore a starched white shirt with colorful mismatched cufflinks, and chef's pants. "To Tropical Storm Anita." His glass scanned the sky like a sextant seeking direction. "May she find her way to our shores just enough to loosen some roof boards so Ben has work."

"Just keep the ocean safe," Pip added.

With that amendment, everyone sipped the wonderful red wine uncorked as fitting accompaniment to their meal: mushroom-zucchini lasagne and a salad of baby greens with a basil-infused vinaigrette.

Megan felt as if this place, this time, and Pip, had been waiting her entire life for her.

Around the table, conversation came easily and sparkled with laughter. There was an uncomplicated honesty to all that was said. There wasn't any pretense or agenda—none of the braggadocio or critical innuendo of the wine parties or dinners she and Stewart attended.

After dinner, Ben and Donna headed off on a club run.

When Kelly began to clear the table, Megan offered to help, but he shooed her off. "My pleasure," he insisted, carrying plates into the house.

With the sun minutes from disappearing for another day, candles on the table seemed to flicker more brightly. Bay waters moved through the sea grass, lapping against the shore.

When Pip shifted closer to Megan, she leaned against him and watched Kelly go into the house. "He is sad, isn't he?" she asked Pip. "You can see it in his eyes no matter how happy the rest of him tries to be."

"I used to think he was coming out of it. He'd meet someone, they'd seem like they were getting along. Then it would end. I'd ask him what happened, and he'd just say, 'She wasn't Laura.' He's convinced she was the only one for him, but he wasn't the one for her. So now, anyone else will be gone by Sunday."

"What's that mean? He said that in his toast to Donna: Love her until Sunday."

"Sunday's a euphemism. Lots of people come into town for the weekend—get here on Friday and leave on Sunday. Others stay Saturday to Saturday. Or for the season. Eventually, though … they go home."

Maybe Pip was seeking her assurance. Megan wasn't sure and wanted to say something, but the right words didn't come. Thoughts turned over in her mind—imposed upon by the memory of her exchanges with Adrian and Alice over the past two days. Both women, in essence, giving warnings, although Alice had been more understanding. Megan wondered if Pip had been hurt before. Maybe that was what had caused Adrian to act the way she had—not jealousy. But how do you ask someone about that?

#

Two hours later, in Pip's upstairs bathroom with the door closed, Megan tapped a text to Stewart. She figured he'd still be at the office—it was just after seven in Scottsdale, assuming he hadn't gone back to California or travelled to another job.

Crashing, she texted. *Been getting up early and swimming a lot.* Then she added: *Everything fine here.* Then: *Waiting to hear from Jillian.* Texting that although she hadn't yet asked her realtor friend about an agent recommendation for selling their home and the condo. She closed with: *Hope all's good with you. Maybe talk tomorrow. XO.*

Texts sent, she brushed her teeth. And waited.

Her phone pinged with a message after five minutes. Stewart: *Busy. New project in San Diego. Might be a fun place to see together one weekend.*

Megan responded: *Congrats.* Because she was happy for him. Those feelings for him hadn't changed. It was love that had gone.

#

"Would you rather go out somewhere?" Megan asked Pip, making that offer even though she'd already changed into the t-shirt and athletic shorts she'd sleep in.

It was a pleasant temperature in Pip's bedroom, with the windows open and salt air drifting in.

He smiled and shook his head.

"You sure?" she wanted to confirm. "I don't want to be…"

Still smiling, he lifted her t-shirt.

"I see..." Megan raised her arms so he could take off her top. Then shook out her hair as he began to caress her breasts. "So that's the way it's going to be," she laughed quietly.

He kissed the side of her neck. Got his hand under the curve of her ass and lifted her. Megan wrapped her legs around him as he carried her the short distance to bed, eased her down and laid on top of her. Kissing her some more, he said, "There's nowhere else I'd rather be."

"Mm…"

"You okay staying in?"

"Mm-hm," she sighed. The rhythm of how he touched her was so pleasant and warm. Unhurried yet urgent. A whirlwind of sensations she'd never experienced.

#

Later, in bed together with the lights out and windows still open, not quite to the point of drifting off, Megan half whispered, "You don't have a TV."

"Downstairs." Pip sounded closer to sleep than she did. He shifted positions but kept his arm across her back. "Something you want to watch?"

"No. Just—I hadn't noticed before."

"We can use my laptop."

"I don't want to watch anything. It's just … I don't know … I like it. No TV."

"Okay…" He kissed her and smiled—such a pleasant smile, as if nothing in the world could ever go wrong.

In the quiet of the night, the afterglow of sex fading, Megan's mind stirred with what felt like a thousand questions she wanted to ask him—some serious, others completely frivolous.

What did he think about her being seven years older than he was? That when she married Stewart, Pip would have only been 17. Sometimes that seemed like a significant age difference to her, other times not so much, if at all. Or was that because she was nine years younger than Stewart? And was it that age difference that had caught up with them, changed their perspectives as to what was important. Did that lie ahead for her and Pip?

She thought about her father at the age she was now, within a couple years of suddenly dying. Pip's own father had probably been about her age when he was killed by lightning. Were those family tragedies part of why this felt so vital? Was being robbed of a parent at a young age what made it seem more urgent for them to have this time together? Or was it because Megan's father had so often told her how much he loved her and how he wished for her to find someone else who would love her as much as he did—someone Megan always assumed her father meant would be her husband. But she never felt Stewart loved her as much as her father had—but she hadn't expected it, really. Imagining no one else would ever love her that intensely. And while it was too early to be sure (wasn't it?) it felt like Pip did love her every bit as much. Maybe more. Which she wanted to tell him, but what if she was wrong?

The small worry did lurk in the back of her mind that, despite her strong feelings, maybe this was just a sexual relationship. And not just for him. Maybe for her. Maybe what she thought was love was a smokescreen of justification. Maybe Stewart and Cassie having been out of the house for prolonged periods of time—leaving her on her own in a big house—had brought on loneliness and wanting. She didn't think that was the case. But it also wasn't something she yet knew how to talk about with Pip.

Two months ago she hadn't even met him. And while the past 48 hours had been wonderful, it was just 48 hours. How was that possible? How could this be happening so quickly? How was she even in bed with him already? How could it seem this right this soon?

She'd dated Stewart for over a month before they'd shared a tentative kiss. But Stewart had been a widower, still mourning the death of his wife. Besides which, it was Cassie who Megan had fallen in love with first. She didn't develop feelings for Stewart until months later. But even at that point, Cassie had been Megan's priority as much as she'd been Stewart's main focus.

From the beginning, theirs had never been a lustful relationship—Megan and Stewart. The first times they'd had sex, Megan could tell Stewart felt guilty, as if he'd darkened the memory of his late wife. Megan had understood that. Her own mother had often said she would never be with another man after Megan's father died—and she never was. She had also never been happy again.

Before Stewart and since Megan's first serious boyfriend when she was a senior in high school, she had only been with three other guys. Two in college that were more curiosity than the barest hint of love. And one six-month relationship that began on a blind date when she'd just started teaching and ended three months later when he got a job offer out of state. And none of them made Megan feel the way she did with Pip.

But she wasn't sure how to tell him that because maybe he didn't feel the same way. And at least for the time being, if that was the case, if all the right things he was saying were only because he knew it was what she wanted to hear, she wanted to linger in that fantasy. She wanted to feel as loved as he made it seem.

39.

Early the next morning, when Megan and Pip crossed the dunes onto the beach, the other three guards were waiting at Pip's stand. Megan tensed seeing Adrian, who she hadn't had contact with since their unpleasant exchange days earlier and wondered if Adrian had marshalled Art and Will's support to stage some kind of confrontation, like an intervention, looking to drive a wedge between Megan and Pip.

Only Will called a cheerful, "What's happening you two?" as he bounced in place, warming up.

Pip offered a happy, "Morning everybody," as if expecting them to be there. When they began stripping off sweats, Pip said to Megan, "Guard test's in ten days. The real training begins today."

"Thanks for the warning," she teased him, but felt up to the challenge.

They went into the ocean as a group and quickly made their way through the waves then swam south. They put in a strong 3/4 mile before coming ashore to return north on foot at a fast jog that intensified to sprints on Pip's call. Megan trailed the group, but not by much, and at one point pulled alongside Adrian and between deep breaths confided to the girl, "I heard what you said the other day."

By nature, Megan was not confrontational, and looked for opportunity to remove tension from a situation. She wanted Adrian to know she cared about Pip without divulging the extent of her relationship with him—not that it was any of Adrian's business, but Megan respected the girl's concern for

Pip and didn't want her as an adversary, especially if they were going to end up working together.

Adrian nodded but responded with a somewhat rigid, "We'll see," before pulling ahead of Megan on the final 200-yard run to Will's stand. Not exactly the reaction Megan had hoped for. But when they spent the next 20 minutes working on Megan's technique at pulling dead weight across the sand—Megan practicing on all three of the younger guards—Adrian offered encouragement. And when they were finished, with Megan plopped down on the sand, breathing hard, Adrian told her, "You're getting stronger," before she started off up the beach with Art.

"You are getting stronger," Pip complimented, offering his hand to help Megan up.

With the others out of earshot, she said, "Must be all the sex," then playfully swatted away his hand and got to her feet without help.

"In that case," he laughed, "I look forward to being as much help as possible."

As Megan brushed sand off the back of her suit, she heard a man's cheerful encouragement: "Good job! Keep those young ones in line."

Bill Clary waved to them from his balcony.

"I'm trying," Megan called in reply. She asked Pip if he knew the man's name.

"No."

"Maybe we should ask."

"Sure. He's nice enough. Go ahead," Pip suggested. "I gotta get up the beach. Almost nine."

Legs burning from sprints and practicing shoulder pulls on the other guards, Megan trotted toward the beachfront townhouses, where Bill Clary leaned his elbows on his balcony railing, standing a single flight of painted wood steps above the beach.

Dressed neatly in multi-pocket shorts and a short-sleeve shirt that buttoned down the front, he gave the impression of someone who stayed active but didn't look ready for the golf course or country club. He wore a baseball cap and a gold watch she imagined was a Rolex.

"You spying on us?" She smiled up at him, hands on her hips.

"If I was spying, you wouldn't notice," he kidded, his voice slightly gravely, with a drawl that might be country. "Just enjoying watching you keep those young ones in line."

"I don't know about that."

"You're one helluva swimmer," he complimented. The lively twinkle in his eye and knowing grin made it seem as if he was sharing a secret.

"Good enough to be a lifeguard you think?"

"Every bit."

"We'll find out in soon enough. I'm going to swim the surf patrol test."

"Congratulations."

"I haven't done it yet."

"Oh, I think you have."

"No, really." She thought he'd misheard her. "The test is in ten days."

"But you've already done the work. Which means the outcome is a mere formality."

"Let's hope so."

He appeared to study her, not trying to sneak a look at the snug lines of her bathing suit the way many men would but looking into her eyes. "Where'd you go? You don't mind my asking."

"When's that?"

"You were here last month—I saw you out there swimming. Caught my eye out there all by yourself. Then you joined up with this crowd." He gestured up the beach. "Pip and them. Then I didn't see you for a few weeks."

"Oh." Coming from someone else, the observation might have made her uncomfortable, but this man—she still didn't know his name—seemed very genuine and it was easy to imagine him waking early every morning and sitting on his balcony, watching the day go by. "I'm Megan, by the way."

"Bill Clary," he responded.

"Nice to meet you, Mr. Clary."

"It's Bill—and likewise."

"Where I went was out to California."

"Have a good time?"

"No."

He smiled at her honesty. "Glad you're back?"

"Very much so."

"Good—me too."

A small dog barked behind a closed door nearby. "Yours?" Megan asked of the barker.

Bill shook his head. "Houdini. Next store."

Megan peered through the balcony railings and saw a furry white face pushing back a curtain to look outside.

"Escape artist. He'll bust free any minute now. Run like hell on wheels for the ocean. Pip and the young boy out there've pulled him out twice already this summer. I don't know how he does it. But people over there leave him by himself. Not too bright—the people, not the dog."

"Hi, Houdini." Megan waved.

The dog barked a couple more times, then disappeared behind the curtain.

"Thanks for saying hello," Bill said. "Means a lot. Stop by anytime. Introduce you to my wife, Mary Jane, next time. She's in Charleston for a few days." He drew his elbows off the railing and stood upright.

Megan asked, "Do you miss her when she's gone?"

"Every minute."

"Can't you go with her?" she wondered.

"Could. But I don't. I'd get in her way. And I like it here. So I stay. Here in summer. Annapolis in the winter."

"Have you been married a long time? Don't mind that I asked that, do you?" she inquired, paraphrasing him.

"Fifty years next spring—'less she kills me first."

"Wow." Megan was impressed. "Congratulations."

"All I've got to do now is figure out an anniversary present for her."

"What does she like?"

"She's easy to please, which is probably why we've been married so long." He lowered his voice slightly, furthering the impression he was sharing a secret: "She came to the marriage with low expectations, hitching up to an old boy from West Virginia."

Megan laughed. "I doubt that."

"What would you want for an anniversary present?"

"For fifty years? I don't know." Megan thought a moment. "Fifty good years?"

"Every one of them."

"Then I'd want fifty more."

"By God," he chuckled, "that's a good answer. I think that's what I'll get her. But maybe include a gift slip in case it's not what she's after. Thanks again for the hello. Don't keep your fellow waiting."

Megan turned and saw Pip remained where she'd left him. He waved again. Pivoting back to Bill, she said, "Oh, he's not..." Her voice trailed off because she couldn't finish the sentence—couldn't lie to him.

Bill gave a little nod and told her, "Be strong, girl. Life's short. It'll surprise you how fast fifty years goes by."

40.

Megan ate lunch alone on her condo balcony—peanut butter and jelly on grain bread she'd toasted out of the freezer. Since coming back from California, she hadn't been to the grocery store.

Pip's lunch had been unexpectedly delivered in Tupperware by a friendly woman a few years older than Megan—something the woman apparently did whenever she "whipped up" some pasta salad. And Pip had been happy to have it. Megan didn't blame him. It looked good.

Making her impromptu meal visit to Pip, the woman had recognized Megan from the building but hadn't said anything at first, just smiled, although she did seem to take note of Megan sitting unusually close to Pip's stand. The guards usually kept a ten-foot clearance around their station. It wasn't until after the woman and Pip chatted a few minutes that the woman's memory seemed to bring back who Megan was. Even then she hadn't been sure, peering under Megan's umbrella and asking, "Megan, isn't it? Fifth floor?"

"Hi. Yes."

Their conversation had run the usual course for people who have known one another for years but never formed any bond, sharing updates on children and spouses, and a few comments about maintenance issues in the building the woman thought were important that Megan considered superficial.

For a few minutes after the woman left, Megan worried about rumors starting in her building: What's the Tyler woman doing sitting down there next to Pip's stand? Then put it out of her mind the way she'd been doing since Lulu first set her up in that spot, wanting to be near Pip more than she worried what people might think. Not that they weren't being careful. Although anyone up at eight in the morning would see them get out of Pip's Jeep and cross the dunes together. And see them leaving in the afternoon. But they weren't showing any public signs of affection, as difficult as that was to resist.

Megan wanted to be back down on the beach with Pip now but had two students that afternoon and after that—and more importantly—was expecting a call from Stewart. Half an hour ago she'd texted asking if he had time to talk about selling the house and condo. He'd responded promptly: In meetings until 4. Call when I'm finished?

Megan hoped between now and then she didn't lose her nerve.

#

When Stewart's call came in early, Megan took a deep breath and picked up her phone. "Hi," she greeted. "This still a good time?" Half expecting he'd tell her something had come up and their conversation would have to wait until tonight.

"Yep—perfect. I'm on the way to the airport to fly to San Diego and meet Scott for a dinner meeting, then I'll drive up to Newport Coast."

"Be careful."

"Always. I'm taking a car service to the airport. In fact, I'm in the back of a Lincoln Navigator as we speak. It's about the size of my bedroom growing up, and thankfully I don't have to share it with my brother."

Hearing Stewart's voice made Megan doubt herself. He sounded to be in a good mood, and she was about to spoil that. "I've been going over some things," Megan began, "and been thinking ... how would you feel about not selling this condo?"

Silence.

Not unexpected. Stewart knew sometimes his first reaction—albeit an honest one—might not be the best option in terms of marital harmony. Which Megan appreciated. But that silence could still be damning, as if making clear he was restraining words she wouldn't want to hear.

"I like it here," Megan said. "And can't imagine having to walk out of it one day—one day soon—and never be here again. I know it doesn't mean anything to you anymore. Or Cassie. You two have outgrown it. But I love it. And I'd always like to know it's here. That I could come here even if just for part of the summer."

"Okay…" Stewart offered hesitantly, sounding like it wasn't okay at all, but Stewart—to his credit, Megan thought—didn't dismiss the idea outright. He may have been—probably was—crafting arguments to show her it was impractical and expensive, but she was ready to deal with that. "…all right…" He continued. "… um … okay … well … you're catching me off guard."

"I know."

"I thought we were getting on the same page…" He started to sound stern, but quickly corrected. "…but that's okay…" Again, obviously it wasn't. "Let's um… What are you thinking exactly?" That wasn't an accusation, but a polite question. "It's a long flight from California for an Ocean City weekend here and there."

"I was thinking more like a month or so at a time, in the summer."

"A month…? All right." He exhaled. "Well, we could rent a really nice place for a month for a lot less than it'll cost to carry the condo. I mean mortgage, taxes, condo fees…"

Megan pictured him sitting in the oversized SUV's comfortable seats, eyes closed, calculating the costs. "I'll pay it," she said determinedly. "I'll cover the costs. I'll keep working. I don't want to go back to not working anyway. I liked Villa James. And we always talked about me working again when Cassie moved out."

"We talked about that a little bit … a long time ago."

Clearly their recollections differed. They also used to imagine how Stewart would continue to run his own company until he retired, when he'd turn it over to some trusted employees. And that they'd travel—some, but not much, because Megan didn't have that kind of wanderlust. She was a homebody. And now, here they were, way off that course. Way, way off.

Stewart said, "You don't have to work anymore."

"I want to. I don't have anything to do without Cassie around. And I missed it. And whatever it is, I'll use my paycheck for keeping this condo."

Silence.

"And if it doesn't work out," Megan interjected, "we can sell it later. Maybe it will even appreciate between now and then."

"What about Hunt Valley?" he asked of their main house.

"We go ahead and sell that."

A hesitation, but then: "Okay. Well, let's see how the numbers work out. I'll talk to Jackie Mack when I get back to Newport Coast tomorrow—actually, maybe I'll try to reach her now. See what it does to the new mortgage approval if we don't sell Ocean City. I was assuming we'd have that equity as part of the down payment."

"Another bit of news," Megan said, "I'm going to take the surf patrol test in ten days."

"You're doing what?"

"The surf patrol has a test—swimming, running, simulated rescues. They call it a pre-employment physical skills test," she quoted from the website. "And I'm going to do it." Megan hadn't planned on telling Stewart that yet—it just came out. And she felt better for it. If she'd been stronger, she would have told him she didn't love him anymore. And how sorry she was about that. But that conversation needed to be in person.

"That's crazy. But it's also fantastic. Good for you. Sounds like something Cass would do! Sometimes I think she's more like you than me. Have you told her yet?" Which wasn't at all the response Megan expected from him.

41.

In the middle of the night, as lightning flashed against the skylights and windows, and the thunder of an approaching storm rumbled in the distance, Megan laid alongside Pip but thought about Stewart—how he'd sounded enthused about her taking the surf patrol test and hadn't applied subtle pressure about when she'd be returning to California. Which made her wonder: if he'd been like that over the past few months, would she have been attracted to Pip? Was love like that? Did it require a steady flow of water, like a river, least it run low or dry and seek a new source? If Stewart hadn't sold his business and gone to Scottsdale, would that have saved them?

Megan didn't think falling in love with Pip happened because of need. She hadn't been looking. Being with Pip was just one of many factors that made her honest with herself about her feelings for Stewart, who had become so consumed with his work that there weren't enough hours in the day for a career like that and the sort of marriage Megan wanted.

She didn't cast herself as one of those spending wives—a life of spas, lunches, and girl-cations with friends in financially-comfortable marriages; pulling out credit cards for whatever she wanted, running up charges that would magically be paid when a bill she'd never see arrived in her husband's inbox. She didn't want a life merely shared over the dinner table or in a restaurant or at opposite ends of the sofa streaming a bad movie. And while she didn't need adventure, she wanted a friend she was in love with. Someone who liked being outdoors, and long drives, and watching sunsets; not talking about business or new things to buy but the colors in the sky and how warm the water was or the different birds nesting in the trees. And someone to play with their children—most of all, she wanted that.

#

The days passed with an almost magical ease. Megan arranged her calls with Stewart to a predictable schedule: ten o'clock at night, when she'd find someplace private to text or talk.

Stewart typically steered the conversations. Dunhill's takeover of Talbot-Glen, complicated and mired in litigation, was showing promises of resolution. Megan didn't follow details about proxy voting and special board meetings but responded with what she hoped was the correct amount of enthusiasm at the proper moments.

Stewart said he'd "worked something out"—his words—so they could keep the Ocean City condo. When Megan reiterated her offer to cover the condo expenses, he said, "We'll see." She didn't press the issue. It would all change by the end of summer any way.

Getting their home in Hunt Valley listed for sale moved to the top of Stewart's marital-to-do list. Megan's real estate friend, Jillian, recommended someone at her former brokerage and the woman promptly emailed Megan and Stewart an introductory package that included her impressive resume and a hefty boilerplate list of strategies to get top-dollar for their house—bullet points that included renovations and staging, none of which Stewart was interested in, telling Megan maybe the Realtor would change her opinion once she actually saw the interior of their home.

Over the same period of time, Cassie made one of her reappearances, all via text, and claimed she might come to the beach to watch Megan do the lifeguard test.

By quarter after ten at night, Megan would turn off her phone. Pip never asked about Stewart or Cassie, as if furthering the fantasy they were already a couple and Stewart was an ex-husband she'd managed to stay on good terms with.

Megan's afternoons were split between tutoring her students online and lounging on the beach, most of that time spent alongside Pip's stand but sometimes she'd sit back near the dunes with Lulu. And when Lulu made her end-of-the-day rounds to "close the beach," Megan often helped collect her rental wares, lugging chairs, umbrellas, and boogie boards.

At night, Megan and Pip no longer stayed in. One evening, they drove half an hour to Rehoboth for dinner, not the expensive French restaurant Stewart liked, but the place across the tree-lined side street that was little more than a glorified food truck with a wooden deck strung with colorful lights—a setting Megan used to overlook from the window table of that French bistro and wish she was there, having a casual dinner in shorts, t-shirt, and sandals.

After dinner, Megan and Pip held hands and strolled to the boardwalk, where they sat close together on a bench and people-watched and kissed, as though crossing a state line into Delaware had bettered their odds of not being seen in public by anyone Megan knew.

Another night, they met Big Ben and Donna at a bar in Dewey, another Delaware beach town, and checked out a ska band Ben wanted to see. It was hot inside, and the music was sultry. Megan got sticky dancing with Pip, then they went out to the back parking lot and kissed passionately up against Pip's Jeep beneath a starlit sky.

The following night they did some grocery shopping, again crossing the state line into Delaware. They put their arms around one another and laughed and teased the way couples did in that early stage of love when even picking out cereal could be a fun discovery about the other person.

In the morning, they swam with Will, Art, and Adrian. And Megan kept getting stronger.

The morning that tropical storm Anita stalled offshore, churning the ocean, they swam against a strong current and were only able to cover half their usual distance before coming on shore. Sprinting, Megan finished ahead of Will, who was slowed by a long night out.

When Megan successfully shoulder-pulled Adrian the distance required by the surf patrol test, Bill Clary hollered a congratulatory, "Atta girl!" from his balcony.

Megan no sooner waved back than Bill bellowed, "Houdini's done it again!" and Megan spotted the little Westie bounding across the dunes, paws airborne, making a beeline for the ocean.

Will moaned, "Not again. You kidding me."

Pip cut off the terrier's line to the water only to have the dog dart to the side, avoiding him and eluding Adrian's lunging grasp seconds later.

"You've got to sweet talk 'im," Art laughed, bent over at the waist, fingers waggling. "Here puppy. Here fella. Here, fella, fella."

Pip scrambled for a better angle. "Don't let him go in the water! He's nuts for the ocean."

"More like just nuts," Will complained, turned completely around when the dog swerved past him.

Megan sprinted to the water's edge and positioned herself to play "goalie." She was in ready position, knees bent, but instead of trying to keep the dog from getting by her, let Houdini splash into the ocean, then used the change in terrain to her advantage, swooping in behind the dog when the water took away his maneuverability. She gathered him in her arms before he got into the pull of the current.

"Nice catch!" Pip congratulated, rubbing the dog's wet head and telling him, "You gotta cut that out fellah."

With Megan holding him against her chest, the dog laid back, panting and seeming perfectly content, his brown eyes glistening in the sunshine. "Let's take you home, Houdini." She half expected the Westie to squirm and try to jump free, but he remained willingly in her arms as she carried him onto the dunes.

"Houdini's met his match now," Bill guffawed from his deck. "Bring him over here, Megan. Nobody home next door to watch him anyway."

Megan assumed the short red-haired woman now alongside Bill was his wife.

"Houdini, you been a bad dog again?" the woman laughed. "I'll get some towels." She went inside as Megan climbed the steps onto the Clary's deck.

"See, that's what experience does," Bill winked. "Youngsters out there falling all over themselves. You knew where to be."

"I grew up with dogs."

"You want to take that one home with you, we won't tell. Idiots over there probably won't figure he's gone for a week."

"They're not that bad," his redhead wife said of their neighbors, coming outside with an armful of plush bath towels.

"Not if you like big and dumb," Bill countered, then chuckled, "don't answer that."

Megan handed the dog to the woman, who said, "I'm Mary Jane." Nodding toward Bill. "He'll think to introduce me ten minutes after you leave." Getting a whiff of ocean water matting the dog's fur, Mary Jane made a face. "Phew. Someone needs a bath."

Bill objected, "Don't back up the drain with all that dog hair."

"Calling the groomer," she retorted quickly.

"On a Friday?"

Mary Jane stopped making baby noises to the dog long enough to shoot Bill a quick: "They'll be here."

"Wouldn't believe how much of my pension goes toward dogs I don't own," Bill complained with a grin to Megan, who had become their audience.

Mary Jane rolled her eyes. "Pension? I got my own money."

"Has since day one," Bill laughed, telling Megan, "Her mother gave her two dollars to keep in her garter we went out on dates. In case I abandoned her somewhere."

"My God," Mary Jane moaned. "Like I ever wore a garter." Adjusting her hold of Houdini, she offered her hand to Megan. "Happy to meet you. You're making his summer."

Megan felt herself blush, thinking Mary Jane was talking about Pip, then understood she was referring to Bill. "Nice to meet you, too. Your husband said the other day you'll be married for fifty years next spring."

"I don't kill him first," Mary Jane warned, taking Houdini inside.

Bill winked again. "What'd I tell you?"

Megan smiled.

Bill said, "Congratulations on your first save by the way."

"The dog? I'm not sure that counts."

"Sure it does."

"Thanks." She nodded and angled her shoulders toward the beach, preparing to turn to leave. "I'll guess I'll see you later."

"Hope so." Bill nodded toward Pip, who stood with Will next to the younger guard's stand. "Don't keep that fellah waiting."

"Right." Megan went down wooden steps and jogged to Pip. Without thinking, she put her arm around him, then realized what she'd done and pulled away, making a sheepish face.

Will grinned. "I thought so."

"Keep a secret?" Megan asked him.

"Better than you," Will laughed, starting up his stand. Then pointed to his wrist where a watch would have been had he worn one, telling Pip, "You got five minutes, Lieutenant."

"Right."

It was almost 9:00.

Pip and Megan sprinted to Pip's stand.

Will hollered after them, "Let's try and get through the day without too much excitement, okay? Nice, restful, easy day at the beach."

Five hours later, all four guards were in the water on multiple saves. The current they'd swum against calmed when the tide went out but left a series of strong hidden rips.

Megan stood on the second rung of Pip's stand, watching Pip and Will power swim to a couple struggling in the ocean, while a block north Art and Adrian were in deep water on separate rescues. Moments later, a man she'd noticed earlier went under one wave, then the wave behind that, and another after that, taking longer and longer to surface between each tumbling breaker. When he came up flailing his arms, waving toward the beach in distress, Megan went out to get him.

42.

Megan swam hard, 75 yards out when she felt the strong pull of the same riptide that had hold of the man struggling to keep his head above water.

As she closed in on him, she saw his pale face. He looked middle-aged, eyes wide with panic. His weakening calls were choked back as he gulped salty water.

Megan swam along the pull of the rip, lifting her head on every other catch of her left arm to keep sight of him. She was within ten feet when he went under.

Taking a deep draw of air into her lungs, she kicked down after him, blindly spreading her arms, feeling for him. When her hand brushed his shoulder, the man clutched wildly and wrapped Megan in a panicked bear hug that pinned her arms against her sides.

She squirmed and kicked her legs, but that only made him clutch hold more desperately. He was taking her down with him.

Megan focused on the position of their bodies. He was behind her, arms around her, fingers digging into her sides. She found the thumb of his right hand, and with all her strength pried it from her torso and yanked it back.

His scream of pain gurgled underwater, but his grip loosened enough for her to wriggle free.

She clawed her way to the surface, took in a fast gulp of air and dove back under. Reaching out in dark-green water, she found the man's arms, secured him in a save hold, and brought him up.

He broke the surface coughing violently, arms whirling.

Megan kept hold of him. "I've got you! You're all right!" She used a calm, firm voice.

The ocean splashed his face and he flailed, afraid he was going under again.

"I've got you. Just relax. Relax. Stop trying to swim. I've got you." Her legs worked hard, scissor-kicking to keep them both afloat. "You're okay. I'm going to hold you, and we're going to glide a little bit—let you catch your breath. Then I'll take you in."

Gradually, his overweight body became slack, and Megan coaxed him to float alongside her.

His breathing eased and he looked at her for the first time, their faces inches apart. He had green eyes and hadn't shaved in days.

"You're okay," Megan repeated. She could feel his heart pounding hard against his chest.

He nodded. He believed her now. "I thought I was a better swimmer."

"It's okay." Megan felt the rip current weakening. "Let me do the work, and we'll be on the sand in a couple minutes." She began a strong side crawl toward shore.

They were half a block north of where she'd gone into the water. A small crowd watched from the beach as Pip swam hard toward them, coming up to Megan, his expression stitched with concern as he positioned his buoy where the man could take hold of it.

Megan said, "We're good."

The man seemed reluctant to let go of Megan until she assured him he was safe. Once they were in four feet of water, she asked if he was okay to walk in.

He was unsteady but nodded. "I think so."

In a scene Megan had witnessed dozens of times over the years, but never from this perspective, spectators on the beach clapped and cheered her rescue, then slowly dispersed.

She stayed with the man she'd brought in as he bent over at the waist, his legs quivering. She rubbed her hand across his back, asking if he was having any chest pains.

He took a deep breath and shook his head. "I'm okay. Thanks." After a few moments, he straightened and shook Megan's hand. "Thanks so much."

"No problem."

Pip flagged an all-clear to Art and Adrian.

From the opposite direction, Will slowed to a jog coming up alongside them. Just out of the ocean from his own save, he asked Megan, "You pull that guy?"

"Yeah." It was an incredible feeling.

"Well, how 'bout you." Will grabbed her hand and swung it back and forth a few times before letting go. "Nice going."

As the three of them headed back down the beach, Megan and Pip had their arms around one another.

Will chuckled, "I'm the one supposed to be keeping the secret?"

#

Megan couldn't remember the last time she was this happy.

Life felt so fresh. And fulfilling. And loving—most of all, loving. This beach. This summer. These people. Strangers just weeks ago who now felt like family. Pip and the other guards and Lulu—and, okay, Adrian was still a bit of a rough spot, but every family had someone who wasn't the easiest to get along with. And being with Pip and Kelly and Ben at night at Aunt Nan's cottage on the bay. Even Aunt Nan seemed like family, although Megan had never met her, only seen old photos of her with Pip, playing gin rummy.

"To your first rescue," Kelly toasted Megan that night at dinner.

Her "cottage family" sat on two old comforters spread across the backyard, overlooking the bay while burgers cooked on a pit grill.

"Congratulations," Ben joined in, still accompanied by Donna who had stayed longer than a weekend after all.

Megan happily thanked them and sipped her wine. She moved closer to Pip, who was unusually quiet, leaning back on his elbows, legs outstretched. "You okay?" she asked.

"Fine. Worn out, I think." He smiled, but his expression lacked its trademark sparkle.

"Bullshit," Kelly called, gesturing with his wine glass toward Pip. Telling Megan: "He does this. These little dips. Nothing compared to my spells of desperation, but everything's relative."

Pip's broad shoulders offered a shrug of admission, as if confirming his childhood friend's theory.

Kelly continued, "Let me guess—in fact, let me state— he's thinking he wasn't careful enough today. All these saves. He should have kept people out of the ocean. He should have seen the danger. Predicted it. Crystal-balled it."

Megan nuzzled her face to Pip's. "Is this true?"

He gave a small nod and another joyless smile.

Kelly advised, "It passes."

"Does this help?" Megan asked, kissing Pip's cheek. She didn't want her happiness, the thrill she felt from bringing that man in out of the ocean today, to be at Pip's expense, to be because he thought he made a mistake. At the same time, lingering more in Megan's thoughts—those brutally honest glimpses of concern the light of day often pushed aside—was whether Pip was waiting for her—even expecting her—to tell him she was leaving her husband. That perhaps Pip had been hoping, every night when she talked or texted with Stewart, she would emerge from the bedroom or bathroom or wherever she afforded herself some privacy and say she'd told Stewart their marriage was over, and she was leaving him. Or was Pip dreading her saying that? Maybe deep inside he didn't want any more than what they already had.

Maybe this was enough for him. Maybe he only wanted her to stay—what was the reference Kelly made the other night—until Sunday? That reference to the end of a vacation, which could be the end of a week or a season—the end of summer. She didn't believe that, though—didn't want to believe that. So she returned to the moment, these new friends, the beauty of the setting sun brushing clouds with shades of purple and deep orange.

She remained snuggled against Pip until Kelly served burgers and salads on old, mismatched flea market plates full of chips and scratches. As they ate, conversation was lively, although Pip remained quiet. Kelly met Megan's eyes a couple times and shook his head, an expression she interpreted to mean not to worry, one time even mouthing to her, "He's fine. Really."

"You sure?" she replied silently, hoping Kelly was a good lip-reader.

He gave a wave of dismissal, then picked a marshmallow from the bag alongside him—a simple dessert item in waiting—and tossed it lightly at Pip, hitting him on the forehead. "Oi, you're spoiling the sunset."

Pip managed a half smile. "Sorry."

"I know you are—she doesn't know you that well, yet. Tell her."

Pip set aside his plate and met Megan's eyes. "Sorry. I love you."

"I love you too." She kissed him and whispered, "Snap your fingers and we'll leave."

He shook his head, whispered back. "That's your signal. I'm ready any time."

After dinner, Megan and Pip were alone at the cottage, still outside on the sandy backyard. Pip removed the grate from the sand pit and added larger logs, so the low cooking flames became a small blaze that crackled and sent sparks and whiffs of smoke into the dark-blue sky. Music from a cover band at a bar half a mile down the bay drifted to them between calls of night birds and frogs.

Each time a new song began they'd try to name its title and artist. Pip was surprisingly good with music from the 70's.

"My mom's playlist," he explained. "Once she found out about Sirius, I don't think she ever left that channel."

Megan's parents hadn't been music lovers. There hadn't been any albums or CD's in her house growing up and the only music Megan owned had been songs she downloaded.

At 10:15, without needing to tell Pip why, Megan said she was going into the house for a couple minutes. He nodded.

Megan started a text to Stewart as she crossed the yard, the sand cooler now between her bare toes. She waited until she'd opened the screen door and was inside before sending the short message, telling Stewart she hoped he'd had a good day and she was going to turn off her phone if she didn't hear from him in a couple minutes. She almost added that she was going to bed. Very fortuitous that she didn't.

Two minutes later, her phone rang. Seeing Stewart's name on her screen made Megan's stomach drop. She didn't want to talk to him tonight and considered not answering, letting the phone ring four times. One more ring and it would go to voice mail. Instead, she answered. "Hi."

"Hey." Stewart was very upbeat. "Where are you?"

Megan hoped she was wrong, but the way he said it, something in his tone of voice, an inflection Megan picked up because she'd known him a long time, seized her with panic. Her mind raced, whirling with a slight dizziness. A lie came to her that she didn't have enough time to reason whether it could work or not. She had a split second to make a decision. She said, "I'm on the beach. Taking a walk." Still hoping her suspicion was wrong—it wasn't.

43.

Life sometimes seemed as if little more than a series of choices. Some were obvious, almost banal and short-term: whether to take a raincoat, the wrong option which would do little more than leave you wet or waiting for a passing shower to stop. Some decisions were more long-range and marked by reminders of responsibility: such as whether to instruct HR take out a few extra dollars per paycheck and put it toward retirement or have a little more in your digital pocket for Starbucks.

Other choices had to be made so quickly they were more like reactions: whether to hit the brakes when a car ran a red light in front of you or try to steer around it, either of which might avoid a deadly collision, or might not. The only way to know the outcome was to select one, after which the consequences of the unchosen choice would forever remain unknown, subject only to conjecture.

Megan hurried out of the cottage and ran barefooted across the sandy yard toward Pip. Calling his name, her voice was tense and urgent.

He immediately got to his feet, calm but alert, the way he responded when someone was in trouble in the ocean.

"He's here. He's back." Megan's words ran together, not wanting it to be true but needing Pip to understand. "Stewart. My husband. I just talked to him. He's back. He's in the condo." Megan raked a hand through her hair. She felt jittery. Trapped. Looking for an escape. "I told him I was on the beach—taking a walk. I have to go."

"Okay." Pip gave a hard nod.

"Can you drive me?" Stepping back toward the house, urging him to follow her, still trying to calculate how to keep from being found out. "Just down a couple blocks."

Pip's cottage was less than a mile from her condo, and across the highway—a little farther than she'd walk if out for a stroll this time of night.

He said, "I'll get my keys."

They went inside, the screen door banging shut behind them. Pip strode up the stairs two at a time.

Megan waited anxiously by the front door. "Damn, damn, damn." She'd already put her keys, license, and credit card in her shorts pocket—glad she'd adopted Cassie's practice of doing that instead of carrying a handbag, which would seem odd to have with her on the beach.

She pictured Stewart already out looking for her. When he'd said he'd meet her and asked where she was, she'd replied with what she hoped worked—another lie—trying to figure how far away she should be and what landmark was there, a place she thought made sense that was about fifteen blocks from their condo. That was a long walk but not unheard of for her. Stewart had said he'd drive up to get her and she'd said quickly—too quickly?—she wanted to keep walking. "It's too nice a night." And he'd accepted that.

"Pip!" Megan called upstairs, feeling he was taking too long. She was going to get caught.

"Right here." He hustled down the steps and read her panic. "It's okay. Come on." He held open the front door and trotted with her to the Jeep, stood alongside her as she got in, the vehicle's top still down. He slid behind the wheel, started the engine, and drove sharply in reverse, tires spinning over crushed shells.

Megan bounced her leg, ran her hand through her hair again. Felt her heart racing. Her hands were cold. Imagining Stewart's reaction if he found out where she'd been. Outrage, but perhaps even deeper, hurt. Pain.

216

Pip turned onto the highway, accelerating into a break between cars just coming off the light a block away. "Say where," he told Megan.

"Two more blocks. No. Three." But when a signal turned red in front of them, she didn't want to wait and said, "Here, here!" and Pip made the earlier turn.

The Jeep swayed as they crossed northbound lanes, aiming down the side street. Megan clutched the seat with one hand, the rollbar with the other.

Where paved road ended at the dunes, Pip braked to a stop and Megan jumped out. "I'm going to tell him. But not this way. He doesn't deserve it to end like this."

Pip nodded tightly. "Okay."

Megan turned and set off at a sprint, feet digging into soft sand.

Just over the crest of the dunes, silhouetted against the moonlit ocean, she saw a lifeguard stand and she stopped, realizing what this looked like. Not what it felt like to her, but how it must seem to Pip. That she was running away from him.

She turned and ran back to where he'd dropped her off. He was gone.

44.

Megan saw the approaching beam of a flashlight waving back and forth across the quiet beach and knew it was Stewart. Even though ample ambient light reached the sand from low-rise condo buildings and townhouses, Stewart would bring a flashlight, not so much out of caution but the option to reveal more clearly what starlight might not give up.

Five blocks from where Pip dropped her off, Megan walked briskly. Her phone was awake in her hand. She'd started three texts to Pip only to delete them. Nothing seemed sufficient. She blamed herself for not being more honest with him—not about her love for him, but the duty she felt she owed Stewart. That as tempting as it was to snap her fingers and run off, that was more fantasy than reality. So, she'd put off that discussion, in part because she thought they had time to get to it, but mainly because she didn't want to spoil the pleasure they'd found together—which was another fantasy. A selfish fantasy. The thrill of new love tugging her from the obligations of a love that had faded with time and changes of circumstances, and, in comparison, never felt as strong as it was with Pip.

As small waves rolled over and spread like silk onto the shore, the beam from Stewart's flashlight grew brighter, closer.

Megan had calmed somewhat, but her hands remained clammy, and her breathing felt tight in her throat and chest. The knots in her stomach quivered. She began to rehearse how to greet Stewart, as though having lost all sense of how act naturally with him.

When only a couple hundred yards separated them, Megan's phone pinged with a text. She hoped it was Pip, that he would have a solution out of this emotional maze. But it was Stewart:

Where RU! As if he'd been stalking across miles of arid desert.

She texted: *CU*, tapping that response so quickly it felt automatic after all, as though a decade of marriage had trained her to that reaction.

Receiving her reply, Stewart raised his flashlight and swept it side to side as Megan aimed her phone toward him. Giving up her location extinguished any fantasy that some wild quirk of fate would sweep her off her feet and send her back into Pip's arms.

Stewart began to take shape. Thirty yards away, he waved and called, "There you are!" He sounded happy, not at all suspicious. But why would he be? Megan had never given him any cause for that.

The distance between them closed.

Stewart wore expensive-looking trousers, another of his new dress shirts, and a pair of sandals he kept in the closet of their condo he'd probably figured on never putting on again. "This is quite the hike," he said, pleasant, but it still came across as a mild complaint. "How far did you go?"

"I lost count."

They hugged, not passionately but familiarly, as if time had smoothed their edges and worn them together. There was no display of longing to suggest the days they'd been apart.

Briefly in Stewart's arms, the thick feel of him felt foreign to Megan. He was broader than Pip, not as tall and more dense, heavier. She broke from that embrace, worrying perhaps she smelled like Pip before realizing even if she did, Stewart would likely assume the aroma was the ocean air.

"You been doing this every night?" he asked.

"Not every night. Sometimes."

Stewart seemed at ease, but that was a relative mood because he was prone to ambition, not relaxation. Megan associated his pleasant demeanor with an achievement at work—the lull between one success before moving on to the next. Those were the situations for which Stewart reserved his smile.

They faced one another at a slight angle, the night breeze pushing Megan's hair across her face until she drew it back. She wondered if he noticed she hadn't tied a ponytail the way she would have had she truly been out for a walk.

"What brings you home?" she asked, making herself sound pleased by his surprise appearance.

Stewart kept the flashlight on, holding that instead of Megan's hand. "I flew back with Lassiter and a few of the other lawyers to take care of some business in his office." He paused for effect, as if that statement was a cliffhanger that would hold her in suspense—always forgetting she wasn't like Cassie. "Talbot-Glen caved." He swelled with victory. "They're ours now. And the pricks who got greedy and tried to drive up the price got voted out."

"Congratulations." Megan thought she made that sound genuine.

Stewart spoke over the waves, the ocean little more than background to him, as though he was the dominant force. "Once the transaction closes—we're looking at mid-October— Scott's having me head up the new west coast division. But beyond that," Stewart paused briefly again for effect, "Lassiter confided the board of directors is talking about me as Dunhill's successor—and maybe sooner than later. Lassiter says there's growing unease among the board with Dunhill's reckless style. Frankly, I'm not sure how I feel about that. Scott's been really good with me. But he can be a wild card. I can see where the board would be more comfortable with a steadier hand running things. The sort of person it takes to start a company isn't always the best to keep it going."

Megan had no doubt Stewart envisioned himself taking Scott Dunhill's place and when it happened, however it happened, Stewart would reason the ends had justified the means. That competitive streak—that hard ambition—ran through Stewart's DNA and connected him with Cassie, with whom Megan assumed he'd already shared this latest news.

Walking, talking, Stewart dominated the conversation. His point of view had always been prevalent because his days determined their family's standing in the world, their projection. Cassie's achievements—her development—were second. Megan was third, and she responded as she typically did, impressed by his triumphs, and in a sense, subservient—an audience, support staff.

That night, it was to her advantage. Stewart was so focused on himself he didn't notice signs that might have made another husband suspicious. How once back in the condo, Megan changed the pillowcases, putting the one Pip had slept on in the wash in case any of his blond hairs remained. That the carpet hadn't been vacuumed. That the air-conditioning was set higher than usual. That there was hardly any food in the refrigerator. Clues that, to Megan, made it so obvious she'd been away, been with Pip, but to Stewart meant nothing, because he didn't know her habits when she was alone, and maybe assumed she liked the temperature warmer and didn't need a full refrigerator to feed herself.

Still, she braced herself for that one circumstance that would trigger Stewart's suspicion and prepared to confess she'd met someone else. Prepared to apologize, tell him it wasn't intentional, that she hadn't been looking to fall in love with someone else, it had just happened. She'd take the blame, not try to put it on Stewart for being away so much for work. Not ask him if he didn't feel they'd grown apart.

When Megan said she was tired, Stewart didn't comment it was before she usually went to bed. When she asked if he wanted her to fix him something to eat before she took a shower, he thanked her, but said no, already settled with his laptop at the dining room table.

Turning on the shower, Megan felt relieved to be in a different room. She needed to think and hoped Stewart didn't want sex, not expecting he would, but dreading the possibility.

As strange as it might seem, sex with Stewart would feel as if she was being unfaithful to Pip.

Emotionally, she felt committed to Pip, even though, as warm water sprayed over her, she had no idea what she would she have done if Pip had still been there when she ran back across the dunes to where he'd dropped her off. Would she have jumped into his Jeep? Would she have snapped her fingers?

Was he really ready to leave this place with her, this beach they both loved? And if they really did leave, where would they go? Didn't they need a plan? She'd need to divorce Stewart, didn't she? Thoughts of lawyers and courtrooms gripped her stomach with nausea. When her legs went weak and the bathroom began to wobble in her vision, she grabbed the towel bar to steady herself. She drew in deep breaths, pleading with her emotions to find a calm place to land and let her get through the night. Let the sun come up. Let her be back on the beach, back in the ocean, with Pip.

Suddenly, like a wave rolling over and crashing down, she was struck by the dark thought it would never happen. She would never be able to leave Stewart. She would never be with Pip. She saw herself on a plane, flying back to California. Back to that house with a view of the ocean that faced in the opposite direction of where she really wanted to be and who she wanted to be with.

"No, no, no," she whispered. "Please no."

45.

Sleep was impossible. Megan laid on her side, eyes open in the dark, facing away from the door so her back would be to Stewart when he came to bed.

Outside, passing beneath her bedroom windows, a family with young children was getting home late, happily comparing putt-putt scores—someone had won a free game.

Megan thought of all the nights here with Cassie—wonderful memories of their summers as a family. How she'd fallen in love with Cassie first, then Stewart, initially feeling like an outsider who wanted to be accepted into their hearts then made her way there. Only now she felt on the outside again while father and daughter enjoyed an indelible bond that didn't include her.

Or had she let that happen? Had she stopped working at being in love with them both, let the changes in their wants and needs slip away? Had she let them go instead of trying to stay connected and following along? She couldn't have gone to college with Cassie—the girl needed to find her independence, didn't she? But nothing had kept her from following Stewart to Scottsdale other than her own choices. It was that same driving force of the emotional merry-go-round she'd been struggling with for a year now—and no closer to the answer. Again considering there may not be an explanation other than it was the way life—and love—responded to time, changing in subtle degrees, like the sun moving across the sky until eventually it set and gave way to the night.

It pained her heart to imagine never seeing Stewart or Cassie again, but at the same time she felt as if that had already happened. That the man she'd married wasn't the man on the other side of the bedroom door, coming down the hall into the bathroom, beginning his familiar routine getting ready for bed.

Stewart quietly opened the bedroom door and eased inside, always careful not to waken her if she went to bed before him or stayed in bed if he woke early—always having been thoughtful in that way, and in many other ways. He had made their lives comfortable and secure. Perhaps not passionate, but he was loving in a very solid way—that's how she thought of him. Solid. And dependable.

When he got into bed, she felt horribly guilty. Stewart didn't deserve a wife who cheated on him. Lying alongside him, as Stewart shifted positions a few times, his breathing slowly becoming calm and steady, sliding toward sleep, Megan felt anxious, anticipating the conflict ahead, the hurt feelings. She couldn't imagine being able to bear it, but the thought of not being with Pip seemed worse and made her feel like she was falling, twirling downward in an endless spiral. How could she have fallen in love with someone new that hard and fast?

Minutes peeled slowly off the clock on her nightstand. She forced herself to remain still until she thought Stewart was asleep, then slid the sheet down her shoulders—a test to see if that subtle shift of positions caused him to stir. Hearing his breathing remain deep, she eased out of bed, padded lightly to the door, slowly turned the knob, and tiptoed into the hall, leaving the door slightly ajar behind her.

Starting toward the bathroom in the dark, she was drawn to the sliding glass door and moonlight reflecting across the ocean. She unlatched the handle lock and quietly opened the door just enough to step across the threshold into the warm, salty air, remaining near the door as if making an escape, moving from one hiding place to another.

She glanced back inside to see if Stewart might have gotten out of bed, wondering what was keeping her awake. She didn't want to be drawn into that conversation yet. She needed more time to think.

Listening to the gentle cascade of waves breaking onto shore, she took a series of deep breaths and moved toward the balcony railing, wanting to see more of the ocean.

Down on the beach, Pip's guard stand wasn't by the dunes where he left it every night. Someone had dragged it closer to the ocean—kids she imagined, or maybe whoever was sitting atop it now. At least she assumed it was a person she saw silhouetted atop the stand against cresting waves and the moonlit ocean. Yes—definitely a person, someone getting to their feet now.

She gasped softly, knowing from the lean shape of his body and how he moved with a fluidity that seemed in kinship with the ocean that it was Pip. She wanted to jump over the balcony, as if she could sail five stories down and end up in his arms, that he would catch her.

Pip began signaling semaphore, shifting his arm positions slowly from letter to letter. R-U-O-K?

Megan stepped back from the railing just enough to give her arms room to sign a reply. Having spent plenty time interpreting flagged messages passed between the guards but not sending them herself, she needed to think about each letter. First making clear, YES. She was okay. Then: I-MISS-U. I-LOVE-U.

Pip replied: I-LUV-U. SO-MUCH. SO-MUCH. IM-OK. U-CAN-GO-HOME. C-U-IN-AM.

He remained still, looking up at her, not responding. Not moving. And she did the same. As if they were each searching for a way to reassure themselves that what seemed impossible might not be.

46.

Back in bed, Megan eventually drifted into that fluid phase between wakefulness and sleep where the mind charts its own course, breaking free of the willful intentions of its possessor. She experienced a confusing blend of memories and lingering emotions, thoughts of Stewart and Cassie like imprints of footsteps in the sand not yet washed away by the incoming tide, providing glimmers of hope that what had once been could be again. Only minutes later those feelings would drift and alter shape, becoming lies, at the very least burdens, the reality that life was never going to be as it had, that love could die the same way her father had—suddenly, unexpectedly, eternally.

When Stewart got up at 6:15, Megan listened as he made coffee and settled at the dining room table, his fingers tapping keys to his laptop. She fantasized he was writing her a note, saying he had to go back to Scottsdale or California, and that she'd pretend to remain asleep as he kissed her forehead and said goodbye.

But an hour later, Stewart was still there when she came out of the bedroom. Megan wore her bathing suit, not the blue one—that was at Pip's—but a ruched red one-piece that was more stylish than athletic, something she'd bought at Cassie's urging a few years ago to look less-mom-ish on vacation.

"Morning." Stewart looked up from his work, his laptop and an unrolled set of architectural drawings taking over the dining room table. His hair was uncombed, his t-shirt and pajama bottoms rumpled from sleep. "This your swim time?"

"Yes." She hoped sunlight spilling in from outside washed out any dark rings under her eyes.

She opened the cabinet—what usually would have been full of groceries but now was not—and pulled out the jar of peanut butter, getting a spoon from the drawer to collect a glob she ate as she cut an apple into quarters. Her breakfast. She asked if he wanted anything. "Eggs?" Half a dozen remained in the fridge.

"That's okay." He opened an email. "I might go out later and get something. Maybe do lunch?"

"Okay," Megan answered reflexively, then realized he was asking her to join him. "You mean me?"

"Yeah. Chowder House? I wouldn't mind one last trip there. If it's still decent." Stewart sounded as if already moved on, as if this would be his last time here.

She said, "I usually spend the day on the beach. Maybe dinner?" She looked for any delay.

"It'll be jam-packed. Assuming they still don't take reservations."

"I don't know." Chowder House was one of those overpriced places that up-charged for a view that wasn't nearly as nice as overlooking the bay from the Pip's cottage.

"Wherever you want to go," Stewart said, agreeable. "Lunch. Dinner. Both. I've got a video meeting at three but other than that, no commitments. Scott's in Montana on a hunting outing, which means as much bourbon as outdoors, so unless something unexpected comes up we should be good."

"Okay." Biting a crisp apple wedge, Megan tried to act as if life was normal, wanting to avoid any potential conflict with Stewart so she could get down to the beach and be with Pip— or at least be near him if not with him.

Ten minutes later, she crossed the dune line. The lack of sleep made her stride feel heavy and her stomach jittered with nerves. The morning sun was warm but failed to overcome the chill that braced her skin.

She was out earlier than usual, but not seeing Pip caused a quiver of panic—that he might not be there, might not be in love with her. A thought that was no sooner completed in her mind than he appeared just up the beach, trotting toward her with his buoy and carry bag slung over his shoulder.

As he approached, Megan whispered to herself, "Let's just go. Let's just leave." Not knowing what to say next, what they'd do, where they'd go. And by the time Pip was alongside her, she lacked the courage to repeat the words, reminding herself they needed a plan.

"You okay?" he asked, looking at her in a way that told Megan her lack of sleep surely showed.

She nodded and forced a smile. They stood with an unnatural distance between them, both more conscious than usual how they presented themselves in public, because today the roster of people able to watch them from their oceanfront balcony included Megan's husband. "I'm sorry again," she apologized. "About last night."

"It's okay."

"I don't want him here." She glanced toward her balcony, willing Stewart to stay inside. "I want to be with you."

"It's okay," he repeated.

But Megan sensed Pip was unsettled. His eyes were less clear, the suntanned skin beneath them shadowed and puffy. There was a slight slump to his shoulders as though he was weighed down, his natural buoyancy being pulled under.

"Can we start?" Megan asked, self-conscious being alone with Pip even though they stood four feet apart. She wanted to get into the water and swim away from where Stewart could see them.

Pip nodded toward the side street. "Will's coming."

The youngest of the guards sprinted carefree down the face of the dunes, bare feet kicking up sand. "Hey dudes," he greeted cheerfully, drawing to a stop and dropping his bag to the sand. "Beautiful day." Admiring the ocean, he bounced lightly in place and shook his slender arms.

Megan started some stretching.

"New suit," Will said. "Pretty cool."

It took Megan a moment to realize he was talking to her. She found herself struggling to offer an explanation to cover the incriminating truth of having needed to rush out of Pip's house last night without her blue one-piece—then decided just saying thanks was fine.

Minutes later, Adrian and Art arrived together. Art winced as he tugged off his sweatshirt. "Hungover. Sorry. Her fault." He pointed an elbow toward Adrian.

The dark-haired love of Art's life smiled. "All I said was, let's go dancing."

Art confessed, "I can't dance if I don't drink."

Adrian's smile faded as she looked between Megan and Pip, sensing tension. "Everybody okay?"

Pip replied, "Yep. Let's hit it." And started toward the ocean.

Adrian peered at Megan, who lacked the fortitude to lie. Jogging next to the young girl, trailing the boys into the water, Megan said, "My husband's here."

"Shit gets real," Adrian said, then dove into a wave.

47.

Megan couldn't get warm. Two blocks into their swim, the ocean still felt piercingly cold. Her shoulders ached and her leg kicks were sluggish. Even though Pip was setting a slower pace than usual, she fell behind and had to force herself to keep going, trying to will a burst of energy to kick in.

At the end of the third block, Pip had the others continue on and waited for her to catch up. "Are you all right?"

"No. No." She wrapped her arms around him, unsure they were far enough from her condo to be out of sight, and not caring. She buried her face against the side of Pip's neck and shivered.

He wrapped an arm around her and leaned back, both of them treading water to stay afloat. "I'll take you in."

"No. I'll be okay. Just give me a minute. I just need a minute." She drew a breath, settled against him. "And then we'll swim away. Okay? We'll just swim. And be gone. Far away. Far, far away."

"Okay."

She shivered again.

"Let's go in," he offered again.

"No." She shook her head, determined to steady herself. "I'm fine. I need to be ready."

"You're ready. You'll whip the guard test. You've been ready for days."

"Not that. For the day we swim away. I need to be ready for that." She gently eased from him and propelled herself after the other guards, following the quiet splash of their effortless paths through the ocean.

By the end of the next block, with Pip alongside her, Megan closed in on the trio, then angled to intercept them as Adrian shifted the group's course toward shore. The five of them came out of the water together and began a slow jog back up the beach, Adrian continuing to lead as Pip held back with Megan.

"An island then?" he asked.

She knew he was talking about where they would disappear to and liked the sound of that. "Yes."

"On the beach?" he wondered. "Or up in the hills?"

"Hills, I think… A little cottage with a porch."

"And a white picket fence," Pip said. "For the dog." A few strides later, Pip said, "And a baby."

The words filled Megan with such an unexpected warmth she closed her eyes for a moment.

Pip said, "I see us with a baby… Don't you?"

She looked at him and nodded and smiled.

Side by side, their strides became long and easy. They caught up to the others and Pip jostled briefly with young Will, passing him. Megan swatted Adrian's backside, challenging her to a final sprint to Pip's guard stand the younger girl won by just a few strides, a race that left them both breathless and bent over at the waist, as Adrian nudged Megan and asked, "This him?"

Megan looked up.

Stewart was coming toward them, aiming his phone and waving.

#

"Say hi to Cassie." Stewart seemed genuinely enthused, grinning as he offered his phone to Megan. "You have been underselling this! How far did you swim?"

From Stewart's phone, Cassie announced: "You look like my mother ... but you don't run like my mother! Nice going, M!"

Shading the screen with her hand, Megan greeted her daughter's image, "Hey, Cass."

Stewart introduced himself to the semi-circle of guards, starting with Pip, who happened to be closest. "Stewart Tyler. How are you?"

"Good. Thanks. Pip."

"Pip?" Stewart made sure he heard the name correctly.

Pip managed to smile, but Megan could feel his discomfort.

"All right," Stewart acknowledged. "I like it."

As the two shook hands, Megan experienced a strange unease, feeling untrue to both of them: cheating on Stewart and making Pip a necessary ally to her lies. In that instant, the differences between the pair became resounding and clear. Stewart would always have his agenda, his drive and ambition, measuring life by accomplishments. In the time Megan had been in the ocean that morning, her husband had showered, shaved, combed his hair, and dressed in one of his expensive new shirts that looked so out of place at this beach, projecting the image of a serious man coming outside with his trouser legs rolled up to say hello to children playing in a sandbox. While Pip stood lean and tanned in a skin-hugging bathing suit, very much in his element and not interested in leaving it.

Through the phone, Cassie continued to rave about Megan's sprint. "You never motored like that with us." Meaning when Megan used to run with Cassie and her lacrosse teammates.

Adrian leaned into Megan's frame, telling Cassie: "You should see her swim."

"Yeah—this guard test thing," Cassie said. "When is that? I might have to check it out. Come down and spectate."

Adrian stayed at Megan's shoulder: "You should try it, too. Your mom will kick ... your ... ass."

Cassie laughed, "I believe it."

"I'm Adrian," the girl said, then took hold of Megan's wrist to guide the phone's lens around the group. "This is Art. Say, hello, Arthur."

"Hey." Art waved.

"He's a little hungover. Big dancer last night."

Art defended, "I can't dance unless I drink."

Cassie laughed.

"And this is Will."

Will waved.

"Damn, he's cute, too. This is a ripped group."

"And that's Pip, next to your dad."

"Very hot."

"And here's mom." Having completed her video-guided introductions, Adrian released Megan's wrist, telling Cassie, "Now we all have to get to work." She motioned Art up the beach. "Let's go, Travolta." Her throwback reference was to Saturday Night Fever, which they'd streamed a few nights ago.

The group broke up, the guards heading to their stands. Stewart watched them briefly, standing within arm's reach of Megan, then checked his watch.

Megan looked at Cassie's digital image but didn't speak. How was she ever going to tell her about Pip? Cassie would be angry and bitter. All the years they'd spent happily together would be tainted.

Cassie asked, "So when is the guard test?" but Megan already sensed the girl's interest drifting and again reminded herself daughters were allowed to grow apart from their mothers, who were meant to stay close, ready, loyal, loving.

"It's soon," Megan answered, walking away from Pip's stand, self-conscious of him overhearing her conversation.

"Well let me know."

"I will."

Cassie looked to her side—at a screen Megan imagined—seated in a cubby at the office where she was interning. Someone crossed behind the divider that partitioned her workspace.

Coming alongside Megan, Stewart pointed toward the building and mouthed, "I'm going up."

She motioned for him to stay, telling Cassie, "Let me give dad his phone back."

"Keep it," Stewart said. "I've made my morning calls."

She shook her head. "I'm coming up to take a shower. I have a student in an hour." She spoke to Cassie: "I'll text you."

"Alright, M."

"Here's Dad." She handed Stewart his phone and continued walking with him.

He said to his daughter, "Good talking with you, Cass. That ten-sail project is amazing."

Megan had no idea what ten-sail was—or if she'd heard correctly. Maybe Stewart had said tent-sale. Or tensile.

Stewart ended the call and tucked his phone in his pants pocket. He smiled at Megan. "That was a long swim you all did. You really have been underselling that." He seemed less impressed than when he'd shared his observations with Cassie and now just seemed to be making conversation. "How far did you go?" he asked. "I looked out and didn't see until you were jogging back. Three blocks?"

"A little more than that." Halfway to the dunes, Megan wanted to look at Pip, thinking she should let him know she'd come back to the beach the way she always did.

"Pretty amazing," Stewart commented. "You are really in shape. Really into this."

So much needed to be said, Megan felt overwhelmed by where to start. Or when. They drifted into silence as families laden with beach gear eagerly made their way toward the shore, reminding Megan of when that used to be the three of them.

In the elevator, riding up to the fifth floor, Stewart asked, "What time's your student?"

"Ten."

He nodded as the elevator gears clinked at each floor. "You need the dining room table?"

"I can use the sofa. Put my iPad on the coffee table."

"I'll turn off my phone. Or take any calls back in the bedroom. Or just work back there."

"You don't have to do that. You're fine at the table."

"I'll type quietly," he promised with a smile.

She smiled back. "Okay."

"And then lunch?" he offered.

"I'll probably just get a sub from across the street. And eat down on the beach."

"All right. I can do that." He assumed she was inviting him to join her. But why shouldn't he? Why should he suspect the question she most wanted to ask was how long until he went back to California?

48.

Showered, her hair washed but not dried and pulled back into a ponytail, Megan sat on the sofa, iPad on her lap, waiting for her student to sign on. Liza was often late. She was one of Megan's more reluctant pupils, an easily distracted 13-year-old who favored wild earrings, streaked her long frizzy hair with bold primary colors, and talked eagerly about all the tattoos she was going to get once old enough to make that decision on her own. While most of the kids Megan tutored were Villa James students eagerly looking to get ahead in math, Liza attended public school and had been forced into these summer sessions by parents concerned she was falling behind.

With the sliding door open, Megan listened to the ocean while Stewart tapped rapidly on his laptop at the dining room table.

Five minutes passed ten, Liza appeared on Megan's screen with a dramatic "Boo," her face right up against her own screen as if emulating a ghost bursting out of a closet.

Megan smiled and responded, "Boo yourself." She tried to respond to Liza's often-juvenile antics in a way that didn't encourage more of the same but wouldn't seem "mean," an adjective Liza attributed to many people, including her parents. It was easy to imagine dinnertime at the girl's home including Liza making a dramatic departure from the table, leaving behind frustrated parents and a younger brother who, Megan gathered from discussions with Liza's mother, managed to shrug off his sister's somewhat chaotic personality. It took some maneuvering, but Megan could usually keep Liza on track for an hour at a time, twice a week, but appreciated it would be exhausting on a full-time basis. By contrast, Cassie had been so easy in her teens, like having a third, younger adult in the house.

"Did you swim this morning with the lifeguards?" Liza asked, always angling to postpone learning. "Pip and them." Liza knew the other guards' names, having shown greater interest in Megan's personal life than algebra.

"I did swim, yes."

"Thought so. Your hair's wet. Any big waves?"

"Not today."

"Can I see?"

"Sure." Usually Megan tried to get Liza "on lesson" before allowing a distraction break, but today she got up from the sofa with her iPad and went onto the balcony, standing with her back to the railing and aiming the lens over her shoulder to the crowded beach.

Liza smiled dreamily. "I can almost feel the breeze."

Megan expected the girl's next comment to refer to Hawaii, where Liza had never been but wanted to live in a hut with a Kanaka Maoli boy who would have even more tattoos than she did. But instead, she asked, "Where's Pip?"

Megan assumed she was holding her iPad in a way that blocked Liza's view of Pip's guard stand. But when she turned and looked, Megan saw Pip wasn't there.

\#

Forty minutes later, Megan couldn't concentrate on teaching. She kept waiting for Pip to return, thinking he'd gone in the ocean on a save, or was helping someone on the beach, looking for a child who'd wandered off perhaps. But while lots of people were in the ocean, there wasn't any sign of trouble. Most troubling, though, was how Art and Will had moved their own stands about thirty yards closer to Pip's beach, covering that area as well as their own.

The more time that passed without seeing Pip, the more Megan worried. She told Liza she was getting a headache and asked if they could cut their lesson short, adding, "Tell your mom she doesn't have to pay me for today at all, okay?"

"Oh, okay, Ms. Tyler. Feel better." The girl's concern was so sincere Megan felt guilty lying to her.

Megan went inside the condo, moving so quickly— hurriedly setting her iPad on an end table—that Stewart looked up from his work. "Something's going on down on the beach. I'm going to check it out." She didn't have the savvy to come up with another lie and didn't care.

Stewart stood. "Should I come?"

"No. It's just something with the guards. I'm trying to learn." That vague statement just came out—and maybe wasn't a bad lie after all. Megan went out the door and hurried for the stairwell, quickly descending concrete steps instead of waiting for the elevator.

She shoved open the door at ground level and ran into the path through the dunes, briefly slowing to squeeze around a line of teenagers. Reaching the beach, she sprinted toward Will.

The suntanned young guard sat forward on his stand, legs dangling, watching the ocean through cheap Wayfarers. Not showing any concern.

"Hey, Will," Megan called up to him, slightly out of breath.

He pivoted at the waist as Megan came alongside. "Hey." He smiled.

"Where's Pip?"

"He had to take off."

"Why?"

"Don't know," he shrugged. "He just said, cover for him…"

"Did he say when he'd be back?"

"Nope."

"Okay…" Megan ran a hand through her hair. "Damnit."

"Text him," Will suggested.

"Right. Yeah. Sure." The simplest course of action had eluded her. She felt her pocket—empty. "I don't have my phone. Can I use yours?"

"Sure." He reached into his bag, hanging on a peg alongside his stand.

"Is Pip on there? I don't know his number by heart."

"Yeah-yeah-yeah. I'll bring it up for you." Will worked his phone, then handed it down to Megan, the device sticky with dried sea air and sand.

"Can I call him instead of a text?"

"Sure."

She turned her back to Will and the ocean as her call began to ring. Pip's voice mail picked up. She said, "It's Megan. I'm using Will's phone. Where are you? Please call me. Anytime." She disconnected, said to Will, "No answer. I'm going to text him." She typed: *It's Megan. Using Will's phone. RU OK? Where RU? Call me. Text. Please.*

The message sent, she paced behind Will's stand, waiting for a response, then realized if Pip read her text or picked up her voice mail he'd probably respond to her phone, which was up in her condo—with Stewart. She gave Will his phone back and ran back to her building.

49.

By 2:30, Megan still hadn't heard from Pip. No one had. He hadn't answered any of her calls or texts.

Megan found it difficult to sit still, shifting positions in the shade of the beach umbrella Lulu had set up for her back near her "office" today instead of down by Pip's stand. Lulu had done that without asking, apparently knowing Mr. S was back in town—which meant Lulu knew about Megan and Pip, or at least had her suspicions. But of course she did—how could she not? Who were they fooling?

"I feel like I need to be doing something more than waiting," Megan said.

"I wouldn't worry." Lulu, in her bright green bikini, echoed similar assurances to those offered earlier by Will and Art.

Adrian had been less supportive—perhaps unsurprisingly—when Megan had jogged up to her stand. Adrian had that arrogance of youth, that certainty all decisions she would make in life would be right and the world would be a better place because of it. Adrian had shrugged when Megan asked if she had any idea why Pip left. And that shrug—in Megan's mind—implied what she already worried about: that something Megan had done was why Pip had gone.

"I can't just sit," Megan told Lulu.

"Mrs. M, I'm sure everything's okay." Lulu reached for Megan's hand, but Megan was up from her chair, ducking out from beneath the umbrella and starting toward the dunes at a fast walk that turned to a trot.

She went up the stairs, along the open hall. Going inside their condo, she heard Stewart talking loudly on the phone, the call on speaker. A woman on the other end Megan recognized as Stewart's long-time assistant efficiently recited a series of items as if confirming Stewart's instructions, Stewart acknowledging each item with a clear, "Yes" or "Good" then, interrupting, "Hang on a second." As Megan came down the hall, he asked, "How was the beach?"

"Good. Fine. I've got to get my keys and run down to the Surf Patrol office."

"Okay." There wasn't any suspicion in Stewart's voice, no questioning what Megan just said. "I'm on with Anna."

"Hello, Anna," Megan called, going into the bedroom.

Stewart spoke loudly enough for Megan to hear from the dining room. "I got a call from that real estate agent. She's got the listing agreement for us to sign and has comps she's emailing later today."

"Fine." Megan pulled a pair of shorts over her bathing suit as Stewart came into the bedroom. She tried to conceal the urgency coursing through her.

"I told her I could probably sign Sunday." Stewart leaned into the doorframe. "Turns out I'm going to need to be back in Scottsdale by Tuesday, so I've got Anna checking flights on Monday, but maybe Sunday. The agent said she'd meet me at the airport if need be. She's okay with digital signatures but would prefer to meet us. I didn't know how you'd feel about driving me up to BWI or National."

"Let's figure it out once you get your flight booked." She didn't care about any of that right now. Her shorts zipped and snapped, Megan pulled a t-shirt out of her drawer and put it on.

"We can do that."

Megan grabbed her car keys off the dresser.

"Did we decide on dinner tonight?" Stewart asked. Lunch had been tuna sandwiches and the remains of a bag of potato chips. He'd eaten at the dining room table while Megan took hers to the beach. Not that he was complaining, but he clearly wanted more out of his next meal.

"Anyplace you want," Megan offered. "I'll be back." Sandals in hand, she headed out the door, hustling down the stairs and across the garage without putting her shoes on, just tossing them onto the passenger seat.

#

"Pip?" Megan called his name as she opened the back door to the little bayside cottage and entered the kitchen. She didn't expect him to answer—didn't expect anyone to be home. There weren't any vehicles on the crushed-shell driveway and the front door had been locked when she tried that first. That the back door was unlocked wasn't a surprise because they weren't security conscious. Kelly doubted thieves would be interested in his cooper cookware, Ben kept his tools locked in his truck, and Pip's laptop was ancient.

"Pip?" Megan looked for any clue where Pip might be, then did the same upstairs in his bedroom, finding the space much as when she'd hurried out last night.

The bed was unmade. Her blue bathing suit hung on a bar in the bathroom. Pip didn't have that many clothes and what there was seemed to be in the closet and dresser. His laptop was on the rolltop desk.

Her fear—what she kept telling herself was a wholly irrational fear—that he'd packed up and run off, was calmed somewhat, but she remained worried. She sat on the end of Pip's bed and tried to calm down.

The realization that came forefront to her mind was that if Pip walked into the room and wanted her to decide then and there, she'd leave with him. She'd leave Stewart and worry about the consequences, the hurt feelings later, if it meant the difference between being with Pip or losing him.

Back downstairs, she searched the kitchen and living room for anything with Kelly or Ben's mobile numbers. Earlier, she'd tried the restaurant where Kelly worked and been told it was his day off. And the name Ben had painted on the side of his truck hadn't yielded any contact information on the Internet. Megan was about to open the doors to their separate bedrooms but decided that was too great a breach of privacy.

She considered driving to the Surf Patrol office to see if Pip was there but thought better of it. If his bosses didn't know he'd left his stand she might end up getting him trouble. But dammit, what was going on? Where was he?

Finally, on the end table, protruding as a bookmark from an old dogeared paperback of The Conte of Monte Cristo, Megan spotted a worn business card with Kelly's name, the designation, PRIVATE CHEF, and a number.

She called it. More voice mail. "Kelly, it's Megan. Do you know where Pip is? He left the beach this morning and I haven't seen him since. No one knows where he is and he's not answering his phone. Please call me." She texted a shorter version of the same message, then sat on the sofa. Waiting again.

Ten minutes. Then twenty. Nothing from Kelly. Had she done something to alienate all of them? Had she hurt Pip so badly to cause Kelly not to want to speak to her? She didn't want to think that was possible but lacked explanation to shake it.

Megan remained on the sofa, sitting forward, looking at her phone on the old wooden coffee table, willing it to bring her news. Nothing for almost an hour.

She jumped when a text came in. So wanting it to be Pip.

It was Stewart. *Barge @ 7?*

Megan dropped her head forward and exhaled. Stewart was making dinner plans. Barge was another of those bistro-come-lately restaurants that had opened in the past few years. Pricey and with a menu that looked as if every adjective having to do with taste or flavor had been penned by a marketing guru. All the chefs claimed wildly hyped credentials. Megan didn't want to eat there, but texted back, *Sounds good.* And in doing so, felt as if she'd just run across the dunes away from Pip as she'd done last night.

She sat back and shut her eyes, worrying she might not be brave enough to leave Stewart. And considering maybe Pip believed that, too, and that's why he'd gone off wherever he was.

50.

When they first came to the beach as a family, shortly after they were married, Stewart would drive up and down the big parking lot at the inlet at night, searching for a space. Cassie would eagerly peer out the window at all the neon lights of the boardwalk and all the people. For dinner, they'd eat slices of pizza while college boys behind the counter twirled massive circles of dough, tossing it so high it seemed about to brush the ceiling.

Now, a decade later, Stewart steered the Volvo into the valet lane of Barge, where a clean-cut young guy greeted, "Have a wonderful meal."

Over three hours had gone by since Megan called and texted Kelly. She'd continued calling Pip every hour since. And heard nothing from either of them. As worried as she'd been, she was now pushing back sadness, feeling the life she'd come to cherish over the last few weeks was over. As if it had all been just a summer vacation after all and she'd been foolish to expect more.

Yet, in her heart, she waited—hoped—she was wrong.

"The comps looked pretty good, I thought…" Stewart was picking up their conversation from the car, referring to the report emailed by the Realtor about their house in Hunt Valley. "What do you think?"

Megan had scanned the voluminous document on her iPad, too distracted to concentrate, her eyes glazing over endless lines of detail: square footage, lists of improvements, and actual sales figures adjusted up or down by differences in their home to suggest a listing price. "I'm going to go over it again later."

"Sure."

They were seated at a window table overlooking the ocean—a coveted view for Ocean City restaurants, where beachfront aspects were generally taken up by hotels and condos. The candle flickering on the table seemed out of place, as if all the noise and bustle of the busy place might blow it out.

Megan wore a pale-blue Banana Republic blouse with straight-leg pants, the first "dress-up" clothes she'd had on since California—a look she hadn't missed one bit.

Her phone rested on her handbag alongside her chair, so she'd see it light with any call or text, uncertain she'd hear incoming messages even with the volume all the way up.

Stewart talked more about selling their house. "The real estate agent says the sooner the listing goes live the better. That buyers are looking to get settled before school starts. How do you feel about that? There's a lot of stuff in the house you might not want left there with people coming through. Assuming you're okay to let her use a lock box and show the place while you're not there. I mean I assume you don't want to run up there every time someone wants to look at it. Or stay up there until it sells. And then getting stuff moved out to Newport Coast? Cassie says she can clear her stuff out in a weekend."

That this issue had already been resolved between father and daughter again made Megan feel like an outsider. But that had become as much a reflex as an emotion. That Stewart and Cassie had a closer bond was nothing new—and probably natural—although the hurt it triggered in Megan lingered, the memory of drunken Cassie telling her she wasn't her mother.

"I'll guess I'll have to start thinking about all that."

Stewart started to push for an answer but instead reached for his water glass. To Stewart, discussions like this didn't require rumination.

"What about your things?" Megan asked. "Your family heirlooms? And all the furniture? And everything in the

246

kitchen?" Her questions were delivered more aggressively than intended, but Stewart seemed not to notice.

He responded agreeably. "My family stuff isn't worth the cost of a shipping container. I'll let my brothers come get whatever they want. Otherwise ... Goodwill. Furniture's the same—it'll cost more to ship across country than it's worth and doesn't really go in the new house. But anything you want I'm fine keep, but feel free to buy new out in California. My clothes can be boxed up and shipped. The real estate agent said she has a service she uses for that and they're great. They come in and do it all. Sofa beds to thumb tacks. Pack it—ship it." Stewart made it sound simple.

Megan looked outside at the ocean through a light film of salt spray on the restaurant's big windows. Across the dunes, the top of a guard stand caught light from fixtures mounted in the restaurant's eaves. Maybe she was she being hypocritical to be hurt by how Stewart and Cassie seemed so willing to box up their old lives and give them away, when she was contemplating a similar but very different future for herself. She looked at Stewart. "Maybe that's the way to go then. Just pack it all up and go. Just like that." She snapped her fingers.

Stewart smiled. Simultaneously, Megan's phone alerted with a text, as if the crisp motion of her fingers had brought on both responses.

51.

The texts were from Kelly.

Pip is in Pittsburgh.

Aunt Nan in ICU. Bad stroke.

Pip is her medical agent?

Megan wasn't sure what the question mark meant. Maybe a typo. Or perhaps Kelly wasn't sure if Pip had Aunt Nan's medical power of attorney. Or wasn't sure what exactly it was called.

"That Jillian?" Stewart assumed of Megan reading on her phone.

She shook her head, a simultaneous wave of relief and sorrow sweeping over her. Pip hadn't left because of her. But Aunt Nan was sick. She started a reply when more came in from Kelly—a series of texts full of misspellings and auto-correct errors but Megan got the gist of it:

That morning, leaving the beach for Pittsburgh, Pip had stopped outside Ocean City for gas. He left his phone in the Jeep when he went inside to pay, and his phone was stolen. He didn't hang around to file a police report, just kept going to the hospital where Aunt Nan had been admitted—still seven hours away. He just got there a little while ago.

"Everything okay?" Stewart asked. Usually, he was the one reaching for his phone during meals.

Trying to sound nonchalant, Megan replied, "Lifeguard stuff."

Stewart opened his menu.

Megan scrolled through more texts:

Pip didn't have his contacts anywhere other than on his phone. Didn't have Megan's number. Didn't even have Kelly's number but got a message to him through the restaurant. Only Kelly had been out on a boat all day on a cooking gig and just got voice mails from Pip (and Megan) twenty minutes ago when he returned to the marina. Pip was trying to get a replacement phone.

Megan texted Kelly: *I wish I was with him. Please let him know he can call me anytime.*

Okay, from Kelly. Then: *He loves you girl.*

Those words sent a warmth through Megan that made her eyes well with tears she blinked back as she leaned over to set her phone back atop her handbag.

Stewart, reviewing specials listed on the menu's inset, said, "I wonder if the lobster thermidor's still good."

#

The lobster thermidor did prove as good as Stewart remembered. Megan had sesame-encrusted ahi tuna slices over black rice and arugula. She briefly felt pretentious as hell— almost embarrassed—when a food runner in a starched blouse placed the plate in front of her. Megan no longer felt she belonged in a place like this and wondered how she ever had.

Throughout dinner, Stewart was upbeat, buoyed that he'd finally smoothed down Megan's resistance to moving. Seeking to build upon that momentum, he offered eager comments about finding new restaurants like this in Newport Coast and again invited Megan to completely redecorate the new house— as if that would most tempt and interest her.

Waiting for her phone to deliver word from Pip, Megan's responses to her husband were falsely positive, their brevity and rhetoric more telling than their content: she said she was sure there would be plenty of excellent restaurants; that they'd wait and see how the furnishings that came with the new house felt to live with. Her conversation was on autopilot while her thoughts focused on Pip.

She pictured him alone, going through the awful hospital waiting game, watching doctors and nurses hurry about, hoping they'll bring good news and trying to remain positive, then overhearing them talk about how many hours (or minutes) until they can "get the hell out of here and go home." It was impossible to be passive in a hospital, as a patient or family member. You had to be an advocate, you had to push for answers. Megan hoped Pip knew that.

When their plates were cleared and the waiter asked if they'd like to see the dessert menu, Megan thanked him but said no. She was ready to leave, but Stewart wanted coffee. The meal, and their conversation, lingered. Stewart was in no hurry. Having been seated at that envied window table, he seemed reluctant to give it up.

Megan tried to remember what she and Stewart used to talk about. Before Stewart was approached almost two years ago about Dunlop Infrastructure buying his business. Before Cassie started receiving scholarship offers from colleges that set them off on dozens of family weekend trips, touring campuses along the east coast, some in the Midwest, one in Oregon. All that had happened while Cassie captained her high school lacrosse team through two undefeated seasons and got her driver's license but still preferred to have Megan chauffer her around.

For years, the Volvo had taken on the smell of Cassie and her sweaty teammates who Megan also gave rides to, often stopping for smoothies or burgers after games or practices— the odor settling into their family sedan like a kind of high school girl patchouli, a blend of exertion, fast food, and fruity shampoo (although one of Cassie's higher-maintenance friends favored a pleasant perfume Megan determined was the rather pricey Thierry Mugler Alien).

Megan and Stewart had always talked about Cassie. She'd been the primary source of their conversations when she and

Stewart met, and that continued once they started dating and even after they married.

Megan and Stewart had always taken great care to make sure their relationship didn't negatively affect Cassie. And as Cassie recovered from the loss of her mother, they'd felt a sense of accomplishment and wonder at her resilience, which Stewart often credited to Megan, saying she was why Cassie had become so confident and secure. "I can't imagine how she'd have grown up without you," Stewart often told Megan over the years—but hadn't said in a long time.

Once dinner was finally over and the check paid, Megan and Stewart left the restaurant and stood outside in the warm night, waiting for the valet to deliver their car. Stewart smiled at Megan and looked as if waiting for her to say something, so she complimented, "Nice meal."

He nodded agreement. For a moment, Megan thought he was going to put his arm around her, and she hoped he wouldn't, because she'd need to return the gesture and didn't want to push her lies that far. But how did you begin a conversation about ending a marriage?

That question entangled Megan during the drive back to their condo when Stewart, breaking a few minutes of quiet, said, "Tell me about Pip."

52.

Megan pretended not to have heard what Stewart just said, her nerve endings flaring with alarm as she braced for where this conversation might lead.

"That's his name, right?" Stewart asked. "Pip? The lifeguard in front of our building."

"Mm-hm." Megan looked straight ahead at summertime traffic, stopped at a signal on Coastal Highway.

"Do you know anything about him?"

"Like what?"

"How old he is."

Megan didn't respond at once, as if needing to recall. "Late twenties I think someone said."

"Seems old for that job."

After a few seconds, she replied, "I guess."

More silence.

Maybe that was all Stewart wanted to know. Idle curiosity. Or his attempt at conversation about her new swimming friends.

Ten minutes later, they were back at their building. Megan's phone alerted with a text as they rode up in the elevator. She resisted the urge to check it, keeping her phone in her bag.

At their condo, Stewart unlocked the door, which he held for Megan to enter ahead of him. She turned into the bedroom. He continued to the dining room where he switched on lights, calling back to her: "I'm going to do a little work. Won't bother you if I'm at the table here?"

"No…" Megan dug out her phone. The text was from Pip. She read it quickly, then spoke to Stewart's back, "I think I'll take a walk on the beach." She assumed he wouldn't want to go.

He replied, "Good for you."

#

"I feel like it's been a month since I was with you." Megan sat on a slope of dunes where graceful lengths of sea grass caught silvery light from the moon. Changed into shorts and a t-shirt, she held her phone against her bent knee and smiled warmly at Pip, hoping he could see her face.

"It has been a long day." He returned her smile but was clearly tired and worried, slumped in the driver's seat of his Jeep in the hospital parking lot. An ambulance siren wailed in the background.

"How's Aunt Nan?"

"No one's saying for sure one way or the other, but it seems really bad. She's completely out of it. Not exactly unconscious, but she's not there, either. Her eyes are open but it's like she can't focus. Like she's trying to wake up but can't. It's really sad. They're supposed to do more tests tomorrow."

"Kelly mentioned you have her medical power of attorney."

"I'm her health care agent—yeah. I thought she should have made it her sister, but she said her sister was too religious and wouldn't want to pull the plug."

"Don't talk like that. She'll get better."

"She always told me she didn't want to suffer or be a vegetable. And she wasn't afraid of dying. She used to have a notarized do-not-resuscitate order taped to the refrigerator door at the cottage. She had it stuck up there with little conch shell magnets."

"Very beachy." Megan tried to lift his spirits. "Where are you going to sleep tonight?"

"Don't know. Maybe here."

"The hospital?"

"The Jeep. It's a nice night. Wouldn't be the first time."

"Aren't there any hotels nearby?"

"See how it goes," he replied.

Maybe she shouldn't have mentioned that—maybe he didn't have money for a hotel. "How's Aunt Nan's sister?"

"Anxious. Scared. I'd forgotten how different she is— nothing like Nan. I don't think she's ever lived more than half an hour from this township. And she's got kids, but I don't know where they live. No one was with her when I got here. I drove her home about an hour ago when I went out to get this new phone." Pip had bought a pay-as-you-go to use temporarily, waiting for a replacement through the service plan on the one that had been stolen. "She's as worried about having to take care of Nan as she is her dying."

"Bring Aunt Nan back to the beach. We can take care of her in the cottage."

"I don't know. Maybe... You'd do that?"

"Sure. I mean unless she's got someone else."

"Not really." Pip seemed very tired.

"I'm sorry I'm not there."

"Me, too."

They looked at one another a few moments.

Megan said, "Stewart's leaving in a couple days. He asked me to drive him to the airport and I wasn't going to, but now I could. Then I could get a flight to Pittsburgh."

"How would you explain that?"

"I don't know," she replied frankly, hoping her smile was reassuring. "Figure out something. Maybe the truth. I don't know."

After a moment, Pip said, "He seems like a nice guy."

"He is." Megan considered adding how while Stewart was a very nice man, she didn't love him anymore, but worried that conversation wasn't for the phone. On one hand, the situation was very simple, but on the other very complex, and she didn't want Pip to think she randomly fell in and out of love—and one day she might stop loving him, too.

Pip shifted positions, trying to get more comfortable. "The waves sound nice." He could hear them through the phone.

"It's pretty calm. Can you see?" Megan switched her camera toward the shoreline, the small breakers rolling over, landing with a quiet thump, then sliding ashore.

"How can anyone not live near the ocean?" Pip wondered.

Megan couldn't imagine him anywhere else.

"Make sure you swim tomorrow," he encouraged. "Guard test's in ten days."

She switched her phone so Pip could see her face. "I thought you said I was ready."

"You are. But stay ready. I'll take care of Aunt Nan and be back before you know it."

Megan didn't want to end the call. "It's not the same without you here."

"I miss you, too."

"Love you," Megan whispered. "Take care of Aunt Nan."

"Love you so much. I'll be back soon."

53.

Early the next morning, Megan closed herself in the bathroom and ran water in the sink, making it seem she was washing her face when she checked her phone.

A few texts had come in from Pip overnight. Aunt Nan's condition hadn't changed. And he was told that while some tests would happen sometime today, there might not be a clear picture of her condition until Monday, because of the weekend.

In the next text, Pip said Megan should let Adrian run their morning swim—that Art or Will might be too soft on her.

As to that instruction, Megan texted back, Thanks a lot. Which got an immediate smiling-sunshine emoji from Pip.

What she'd really wanted to text him was that she looked forward to the day when he'd put her in charge of training someone new for the guard test. It was one of those times Megan realized she could be a little competitive after all, although nothing like Cassie.

Pip asked Megan to give the three guards his temporary mobile number and have them text him theirs. He was still without his contacts and wanted to be in touch.

Got it, boss, she sent back.

Still no tie, he responded, a reference to one of their first conversations.

Glad to hear that.

Have a great swim.

Megan changed into her red bathing suit—her blue one was still at Pip's. She opened the bathroom door and was surprised to find Stewart standing there. When she'd gotten out of bed, he'd shown all signs of being asleep.

"Hey." He was careful to direct his stale breath away from her.

"Hi." The phone felt obvious in her hand.

"Off for your swim?"

"Yeah."

"I'm going to meet Marcus Anderson for breakfast. He emailed me some updates last night and turns out he's down here with his family. I thought it'd be a good idea to get together with him—make sure he knows he's still an important part of the team no matter what goes on out west." Marcus was one of Stewart's longtime Maryland employees, a structural engineer.

"I'm sure he'll appreciate that."

Stewart peered through the living room at brilliant sunshine coming through the sliding glass door. "Looks like a beautiful day."

"It does." Megan eased out of the room around him. "High tide in two hours." She held up her phone, as if that's all she'd been checking, then headed to the beach even though the other guards wouldn't be there for an hour.

#

When Megan told Will about Pip, the young guard seemed relieved, as if not having been entirely confident of his own blanket assumptions why Pip had left so suddenly yesterday.

"Bad about his aunt, though," Will said. "How long's he going to be gone?"

"I think it depends on how she does."

"Bummer. I hope we don't get some jackass sub." Will began lifting on his toes, stretching his calves—or was it just nervous energy, Megan couldn't tell. "'Cause we can cover this," Will insisted, "Art, Adrian, and me—until he gets back. Just spread out stands a little. We don't take many days off anyway. And he's not back by the time you got the guard test, you can take his stand. When's that? Next week?"

"A little over a week."

"No problem. Everything'll be fine." He waved at Art and Adrian who jogged toward them. "Pip's okay. Just his aunt's sick."

Adrian waved back, then angled toward the shoreline and Art followed. They stopped to talk with a surf fisherman who'd cast a line beyond the breakers—Adrian no doubt reminding him he'd have to reel in soon. Adrian, Megan had noticed, was more of an enforcer than Pip, who tended to let deadlines slide depending upon circumstances. If no one was in the ocean late in the afternoon, Pip would let surfers go out before their designated time.

"Pip's okay," Will repeated when the lifeguard couple came alongside them.

"Good." Adrian pulled off her t-shirt and tied back her hair, handling that task in a matter of seconds like the girls Cassie played lacrosse with. "But what's going on with his aunt? Is this Nan?" She directed her question to Megan, who was surprised Adrian knew about Pip's family.

"She's had a stroke."

"That's bad. She dies, there goes the cottage." Adrian studied Megan for her reaction. "You know about the stepkids?"

"What stepkids?" Will asked.

Adrian explained, "Aunt Nan's husband had kids from another marriage. They're not kids now, though. Probably in their fifties. When Aunt Nan dies, those kids get Pip's cottage."

"How can that happen?" Will wanted to know. "That's Pip's place."

Adrian shook her head. "Aunt Nan's husband owned it. He died, Aunt Nan got it but only as long as she's alive. She dies, that's it. It goes to his kids."

"How can that be right?" Will shook his head.

Megan felt Adrian gauging her reaction, as if this circumstance might somehow change her feelings for Pip. She kept her tone matter of fact, telling Will, "It's just the way things get set up sometimes." But she had forgotten Pip explaining the arrangement with the cottage. Turning to Adrian, she said, "Pip wants you to lead today."

"All right. Then let's go."

The four of them strode into the water through small waves and swam out, turning south in deep water with Adrian setting a fast pace. Unlike yesterday when Megan struggled, she felt strong today. During a sleepless hour overnight, staring at the ceiling in the dark, thinking about Pip, and Stewart, and Cassie, she'd considered perhaps she'd been looking at this entire situation the wrong way.

#

Out of the ocean, Adrian had them run, not a straight line, but a weaving series of S's from packed wet sand at the ocean's edge, where the footing was firm and their bare soles barely left an imprint, up toward the dunes where each stride sunk into soft sand and required extra effort to push off.

"Don't worry," Will told Megan between deep breaths, "she's just trying to kill us."

Megan kept pace.

When they finally stopped at Will's stand, Adrian laid on her back, crossed her arms so each hand gripped her opposite shoulder, and told Megan, "Pull me."

Megan quickly got into position, not taking any opportunity to rest. She settled her grip in the girl's armpits, lifted her, then, bent forward, braced her legs and pulled, grunting from the effort. When Adrian dug her heels in, Megan leaned her face to the girl's ear and challenged, "Go ahead, try and make it harder. I'm moving you."

Bill Clary watched from his townhouse balcony. After Megan dragged Adrian beyond the required distance, Bill gave her a thumbs up.

Megan plopped down in the sand, exhausted.

Adrian got to her feet and stood over her. "You're ready." She gestured Will and Art to their stands. "Time to go to work boys."

Will took a few backward steps, smiling at Megan. "I told you everything'll be okay." He turned and trotted to his stand as Adrian and Art did the same.

Bill Clary called over to her. "That was at least seventy-five yards by my measure." He made a sweeping motion with his arm over the stretch of beach where Megan had dragged Adrian. "Requirement's only fifty. Not that you should ever actually use that technique to move someone injured other than as a last resort."

Megan got to her feet and walked to him.

Washington Nationals baseball cap tugged low over his eyes, Clary looked over his balcony railing. "Where's Pip this morning?"

"Family emergency." Megan brushed sand off her legs.

"Nothing serious I hope."

"His aunt's in the hospital."

"Bad place to be when you're sick—a doctor friend told me that once. Take my chances on a vet any day. Put this old dog down it gets bad. Don't keep me around miserable just to empty my wallet."

"What's Mary Jane think about that?" Megan asked of his wife.

He chuckled. "She'll be glad to be rid of me."

"I doubt that. Unless you give her an ironing board for your fiftieth next year."

Clary grinned. "That'd be justifiable homicide for sure."

Megan enjoyed the man's easy-going nature, how he gave all impressions of someone who had run their race and was satisfied with the outcome, although she imagined his air of content had its tipping points.

Clary gestured his coffee cup in the direction of her building. "This the husband?"

Megan turned and saw Stewart coming down the beach. Before she could ask Clary how he knew, the older man said, "Saw him with your group yesterday morning."

She said, "That's Stewart. I better go."

"Always a pleasure to see you, Megan. Be careful."

Megan did an easy run to Stewart, who carried his shoes and socks, his trouser legs turned up. "You have breakfast already?" she asked.

"Lucked out. Marcus knows the owner, so we didn't have to wait. And it's just a couple blocks up the road. Didn't even know the place was there." In contrast to Bill Clary's relaxed speech pattern, Stewart's sentences came close on the heels of one another. "Although I did end up cutting it a little short because Anna texted. She's got me on a flight tomorrow, but it's early. Six o'clock. I'm going to go up today and spend the night. And Georgianne Trimball—the real estate agent—is available today at two but only for an hour. So—"

Megan cut him off, expecting what he was leading to: "Let's go." She started toward their condo. "I'll take a shower, get dressed, be ready in forty-five minutes."

"Fantastic." He fell in stride beside her. "I could have Anna look for another seat on the plane."

"I want my summer here."

"Figured—but thought I'd ask."

Megan briefly wondered if their relationship would be different now if they'd been that direct in their discussions about her being in Scottsdale from the beginning. She didn't think so, although a month ago she may have felt differently. Because now she was also being more honest with herself.

Stewart asked, "Have you eaten?"

"I'll take something in the car. Maybe we'll get a quick lunch on the road." She stopped abruptly. "One second." She jogged to Will's stand.

He leaned over the side toward her. "What's up?"

"I'm taking my husband to the airport. But I'll be back. Maybe not tomorrow. But soon. Everything is going to be okay." With Pip gone, she sensed hints of insecurity in Will— that perhaps Pip was the older brother figure who smoothed over those moments of doubt. She said, "Make sure you text Pip so he has your number."

"I will."

"And remind Adrian and Art."

"Okay. She's not as mean as she seems, you know."

"Probably," Megan acknowledged, assuming Will was talking about Adrian. She jogged back to Stewart. Coming alongside him, for some reason, she challenged, "Race you to the dunes," and broke into a sprint, not expecting him to run with her, but he did.

#

There were moments, glimmers, when the past seemed more in rhythm with the present, blending what used to be wonderful with all that was new and different. Megan couldn't recall the last time she saw Stewart—the former high school football star—run. He stayed in shape in gyms that had the latest trending equipment, not outdoors.

Now, dashing 50 yards to the dune path, she had a head start and caught him by surprise, but he was closing on her as she reached her imaginary finish line.

"You're pretty fast," he appreciated, drawing full breaths that expanded his chest as he trailed her onto the path between protected areas of sea grass.

Megan glanced back over her shoulder. "You, too." She recognized too late that the way she looked at him and smiled sparked the impression of flirtation—that subtle playfulness that runs through marriages, even failing ones.

So, she wasn't surprised when, minutes later, Stewart came into the bathroom while she was in the shower and asked if he could join her.

From the shower, they moved to the bedroom, and it was the first time they had sex since California. It was as pleasant as it had been pretty much from when they'd first met. And it was familiar, which could be a pleasure in itself, reestablishing a connection. But in the end, beneath the afterglow of orgasm, Megan experienced the emptiness that, over the past year, had also become familiar, but in a different and disappointing way.

Last night, lying awake with Stewart asleep beside her, Megan had wondered if it was too great a burden to expect love to last eternally. And that if love didn't last, maybe it hadn't been love after all. Either way, when those feelings were exhausted, wasn't it better to move on than to live a lie? To accept the sadness but release the guilt and try to minimize the unloved partner's hurt feelings? Which had seemed possible— not a finagled justification—in the middle of the night with Stewart asleep, not holding her in his arms, not hard inside her the way he'd just been, and not getting out of bed now with any impression that their love was unbroken, when what Megan felt was further confirmation her love for Stewart was gone. An emotion she'd experienced before meeting Pip, only she hadn't wanted to believe it could be true.

54.

As Stewart steered the Volvo onto the bridge off the island, Megan remembered Pip telling her about the summer his uncle talked him into taking courses toward an MBA, and how he'd wanted to jump out of his Jeep and stay at the beach every time he had to leave. Megan's consolation was that she'd be back soon—hopefully with Pip returning from Pittsburgh if Aunt Nan was well enough, or maybe bringing Aunt Nan with him.

At the start of the three-hour drive to their home in Hunt Valley, Megan reviewed the documents sent by the Realtor, having only given the comparables a cursory review. She and Stewart discussed their equity after commissions and closing costs, and how that would impact purchasing the new house in Newport Coast.

"All do-able," Stewart affirmed with confidence.

Megan also made sure she had the correct figures for the mortgage on their condo, estimating she could cover that from whatever she'd earn teaching and with the surf patrol, planning to do both, but not mentioning any of that to Stewart. That discussion would come later.

For the time being, she tried to gauge what it would be like to be financially on her own again after more than a decade of marriage. Besides the money she had in her own investment account, she and Stewart had joint assets—much of that tied to Stewart's interest in Dunhill Infrastructure, obtained when his company merged with the much larger Scottsdale-based corporation—but Megan hoped they wouldn't have to get into that. If Stewart would sign over his interest in the condo and split their joint investment accounts, Megan figured she wouldn't have to draw that down too sharply while getting on her own two feet. Or maybe she was being optimistic.

Taking a mathematical approach to selling their home and separating from Stewart made it easier for Megan to think about. But then, driving into the small Eastern Shore town of Dalton, Stewart tempted, "Kicken Chicken?" And memories came back with waves of sentimentality.

#

"End times," Stewart kidded, pointing at the new menu board. "Kicken Chicken kale."

"Chopped kale," Megan read, "diced Vidalia onions, and shallots, stepped up with our special blend of Kicken Chicken spices. I think that sounds good."

Stewart didn't like kale, which Megan's grandmother used to eat cooked and dashed with vinegar. Not a childhood favorite, but Megan liked it now, just hold the vinegar.

The Kicken Chicken Shack had always been one of Cassie's favorite places—a required stop on their trips to the beach. Their specialty was Maryland-style fried chicken "boosted" with Louisiana heat. Originally located on an empty stretch of highway alongside a gas station, Kicken Chicken moved onto Dalton's Main Street during the small town's somewhat miraculous revitalization three years ago, when a Northern Virginia tech company made the surprise move of establishing a satellite office in an area that, at the time, barely had decent Internet.

No longer a shack, but a small storefront with a façade made to look like one, Kicken Chicken had a short line of customers at the window. The little waterman town of Dalton bustled as a day-trip destination.

Megan and Stewart each ordered a mini bucket: thigh and drumstick served in a small pail that used to be plastic and was now biodegradable (manufactured by a local box company that had been on the verge of bankruptcy before the town's rebirth). Stewart's chicken came with string fries. Megan got the kale.

"Wow." She blinked at the maligned vegetable's kick. "That is spicey."

"Kicken Chicken," Stewart reminded. "Look…" He pointed to an imprint on her napkin. "…they've even got a cartoon now. Has its own YouTube channel."

Sitting at one of seven fire-red metal tables, they were protected from the sun by a large shade sail strung between poles. Before taking another bite, Megan texted a picture to Cassie: *Remember this?*

Memories of how they used to laugh at eight-year-old Cassie swooning over bites of chicken interwove with images of having stopped for burgers in a different little town the night Pip picked her up at the airport—impressions from a past that was gone and the future Megan hoped for blended together like the unsettled change of the tide.

Stewart's thoughts were much different. Watching the order line grow longer, he said, "They should franchise this concept."

A little over two hours later, they were home in Hunt Valley.

#

When Stewart turned the car into the driveway, Megan already felt they no longer lived there. That the white Range Rover in the driveway belonged to the new owners, not the woman Megan assumed was the real estate agent, viewing their French colonial house from the stone walk.

"I guess this is her," Stewart said. He turned off the engine and exited the Volvo. "Ms. Trimball?"

"Georgianne," she replied, her tone friendly but businesslike. "Lovely home."

Megan got out and forced herself to smile.

"And Megan," the Realtor assumed.

"Yes. Hi."

They shook hands at the lamppost replaced a few years ago where the front walk met the driveway, a purchase Megan and Cassie spent hours shopping for online and in stores, once driving two hours to a custom metal shop—not because they were that demanding, but it had been fun.

"Wonderful neighborhood." Trimball admired the established street of well-built homes. With a large Tumi portfolio bag on her shoulder and a massive diamond in her wedding ring, the agent stood as tall as Megan but was twenty years older and broader. Smartly dressed in an expensive suit, her hair colored a rich blond and styled in a layered bob with side-swept bangs, she projected confidence that could go toe-to-toe with Martha Stewart.

Megan felt underdressed in her t-shirt and shorts.

"This house is going to sell very fast," Trimball assured.

Stewart appreciated that.

Megan thought their home seemed lonely despite the grass having been freshly mowed and the bushes kept trimmed by the grounds company, the weeds suppressed by the supposedly environmentally conscious spraying of another firm, and bills paid to keep the utilities on.

Trimball's praise continued once they went inside. Her compliments carried from room to room while Megan tended to the electric panel, switching on breakers and setting the air conditioning lower.

A knock on the front door preceded another hello, the arrival of Trimball's daughter, Margarette, somewhat breathless with apology for being late. Introduced as a part of Trimball's team, she delivered word to her mother of a three-million-dollar offer on one of their other listings, news Georgianne received without any fanfare.

In an hour, it was done. The home tour completed. An initial sales price determined. The lengthy listing agreement reviewed and signed. A timeline was established for installing a lockbox, having the home's rooms measured, and determining a deadline by which Megan and Stewart would coordinate with

Trimball's stager to get the house ready to show. Stewart remained hopeful that, pending a decision about staging, Trimball's offer to "hold the listing from going live," would find a buyer who would offer on the house as is—which would give them more time to pack. Although Stewart made clear he and Cassie could "clear out" in a weekend, Megan said she might need more time.

Trimball slid a brochure from her Tumi bag and handed it to Megan. "When we moved last year, I used this wonderful company. They packed everything very carefully into a few of those storage pods you see everywhere now. Even my mother's old antiques, which I'm keeping until this generation…" She nodded toward her daughter. "…learns to appreciate them. They store the pods in their warehouse and can deliver anywhere. They'll ship to Tahiti if you like."

Megan appreciated the information but felt slightly off-balance. Losing this house was going to be hard. What steadied her was thinking about Pip.

55.

Standing in the living room, Megan realized she'd made the decision to buy almost every piece of furniture not just in that room, but the entire house. She and elementary-school-aged Cassie had held hands going through furniture stores without any real design plan or particular taste, just plopping down on sofas, turning on lamps, looking at end tables and coffee tables. If Stewart had been along, he was in the background, usually on his phone, as that time period had been when his new company was starting to gain momentum (and clients) and whenever Megan and Cassie would ask his opinion he'd happily oblige, "Whatever you girls want."

Very few possessions had come from the house where Stewart lived with his late wife. And Cassie had been excited about having a new look for her room—wanting a big girl bed and dresser. Megan's own little one-bedroom condo had been sparsely furnished in little better than college-dorm quality, and what she didn't sell cheaply to her first tenant ended up going to charity.

In the kitchen, as Megan had become more interested in cooking, she'd picked out all the pots and pans and accessories, often again with Cassie. The two of them had spent hours in big box and department stores, occasionally pricier specialty shops like Williams and Sonoma or Sur Le Table. Megan had specific memories of Cassie—where they'd been, the time of year, even what Cassie had been wearing—as they'd chosen new sets of dishes, glasses, and stainless.

But what to do with it all now?

"You can take a picture."

Megan hadn't heard Stewart come back into the house. He stood at the threshold to the kitchen, catching her staring at the opened cabinet doors, everything stacked so orderly.

"It's what my mother told me when we moved from Rosemary Lane." Stewart's usual positivity was tempered with gentleness. "She said you don't sell the memories with the house." Rosemary Lane was where Stewart had lived with his first wife. "She also said staying in the same place won't bring anyone back. But if you're afraid you'll forget what it looks like, take a picture."

Megan wiped her eyes and nodded.

Stewart said, "I'm going upstairs to start organizing some of my stuff. Maybe pack some to take on the plane tomorrow."

"Okay." She nodded again.

Once Stewart left the room, Megan pulled her phone from her pocket, but the thought of taking pictures made her feel hollow, as if preparing an inventory to file an insurance claim. Instead, she sat for a while at the kitchen table and looked out the wide window onto the backyard.

The lawn was smooth and green, dappled with sunshine through leafed branches of oaks and maples that had grown and now covered more of their view of neighboring homes and the rolling hills beyond. They'd once considered having a pool put in, but then bought the condo at the beach. Until last summer, there had been a lacrosse goal in the yard and bare spots in the grass worn by Cassie practicing hard shots into the net, errant attempts slamming into a plywood backstop with such force it sounded like a gunshot until Megan had a contractor pad the splintering wood to muffle the violent sound.

She was yet to receive a response from Cassie about the pic of Kicken Chicken, and texted her again, this time letting her know they'd listed the house for sale. She asked if Cassie wanted anything for her apartment—any kitchen stuff or furniture—saying she could have "first dibs."

That text sent, she listened to make sure Stewart was still upstairs, then texted Pip. Any change with Aunt Nan? What did the neurosurgeon say?

Before leaving the beach, she'd texted with Pip, who mentioned a neurosurgeon consultation. And she'd let Pip know she and Stewart were meeting a real estate agent today to list their house, and she'd be in the car with Stewart for a few hours and might not be able to talk or text.

She'd also let Pip know that tomorrow she was dropping Stewart at the airport. And after that, she could be to Pittsburgh in four hours, figuring she could drive there about as fast as she could get on and off a plane, and maybe that would be simpler, having her own car instead of Pip needing to leave the hospital to pick her up or her getting an Uber once she landed in Pittsburgh. Included in those details had been what she cared about most: being with him.

Now, waiting for Pip to text back, Megan took a writing pad and pen from the built-in kitchen desk and started a list in two columns, one of items to take to the beach and another for what could go in storage. The K she notated by some items was not to designate kitchen (although that's what she'd tell Stewart if he asked) but to see if Kelly might want them.

Megan was halfway down the page when the doorbell rang. She leaned into the hall and saw their neighbor, Kathy Hillard, peeking through the glass inset beside the front door. Kathy waved when she saw Megan.

Megan waved back and started toward the door.

"I should have texted first…" Kathy talked through the window as Megan approached, finishing her sentence as the door opened. "…but my phone is D-E-A-D dead." The country-club tennis aficionado smiled dazzling whitened teeth, telling Megan, "You look beautiful. I would kill you for that tan."

"How've you been?"

"Good—the same." She held out a large, opened Amazon box and spoke a catchphrase modified from an old romcom: "You've got junk mail."

The box that once delivered something pricey and unnecessary to the Hillards now held all of Megan and Stewart's mail since three weeks ago when Kathy last FedEx'd the generally worthless fliers and advertising she collected for them.

"Thanks again for doing this," Megan appreciated. "Kids okay?"

"I think so, yeah. Who can tell. They don't really talk. Is Cassie with you?"

"No. In DC"

"That's right, the internship. Good for her. Work instead of the beach. God, I hope these kids of mine don't come home after college. That's hoping they get out of college. We should've just had one. Who knew what a fortune they'd eat up." As with most conversations, Kathy didn't take long to mention money—either how much someone had or made or how much something cost. "I can't believe you're moving."

"Me either. I'm trying to figure out how to pack all our stuff."

"Call an auctioneer. Sell it and buy new. You can afford it. Can't she, Stewart?" Hillard asked, peering around Megan at Stewart coming down the stairs.

"That's what I tell her," Stewart replied.

They chatted a few more minutes at the door, mostly neighborhood news, a little harmless gossip, and vague promises to get together. Kathy was envious when she found out Megan and Stewart were moving to Newport Coast, telling them, "And I thought Scottsdale would have been fabulous. But Southern California!"

As they continued chatting, Megan leafed through the mail, figuring most of it would end up in the recycle bin. Then, just as Kathy Hillard said goodbye and turned to leave, Megan found the official-looking envelope from Montgomery County District Court. It was addressed to Cassandra Tyler.

56.

"Any idea what this might be?"

When Megan showed Stewart the envelope from district court, he hesitated—that certain pause he acquired when faced with a question he would have preferred not to have been asked.

Almost apologetic, he said, "It's been taken care of."

"What's been taken care of?"

They remained in the foyer, the front door now closed as Kathy Hillard walked down their driveway to return home by the street instead of crossing the yard.

Stewart rubbed the back of his neck. He was not a liar, which Megan included among his many very positive qualities. At the same time, he might not volunteer a truth he wanted to remain unknown.

"Stewart—the longer you take to say something the worse I'm thinking this is." She gripped the envelope by its end. "A speeding ticket?" Her question was almost hopeful, as if a traffic infraction might not be so bad.

"No. But it's not serious," he tempered. "And, really, really, I promise, it's been taken care of. That's probably just a notice of the charge being dismissed."

"Charge? What charge?"

"I made that sound worse than it is—was," he corrected.

"What, Stewart? Worse than what was?"

He took a breath, then provided reluctant explanation: "Cassie was out with some friends from work…"

"Her internship?"

273

He nodded. "They were out after work ... at a restaurant ... that had a bar..."

Megan closed her eyes. "She got drunk," she guessed.

"No. No." He took offense at the suggestion. "She was not drunk. But she got served some wine and an off-duty cop happened to be there and saw and wrote her a citation for alcohol possession. It was a civil citation," Stewart was quick to add. "And it's done. It's over."

Megan crossed her arms, her head tilted downward.

Stewart said, "One of the lawyers in Lassiter's firm took care of it. Cassie went to some alcohol classes and once they were finished the citation was dismissed. An expungement's being filed. The whole thing will be like it never happened." Pointing to the envelope Megan held, he said, "That's probably the notice of the dismissal, or maybe the expungement. Go ahead and open it."

Whatever the contents, Megan set it on the hall table.

Stewart reached for it. "Here—I'll open it then."

"When did this happen?" Megan wasn't angry, but disappointed. And sad. Also embarrassed—not for herself, but for Cassie, although she doubted Cassie would feel that way. Cassie had probably felt inconvenienced and would now sigh with impatience if required to discuss the matter.

"A couple, few months ago. April, I guess."

"Not last November?" Megan asked, finding herself again reliving the painful memory of Cassie coming home drunk, telling Megan she wasn't her mother.

"Last November? No." Stewart was puzzled by that timeline. "April—maybe March. Why November?"

"Nothing."

"Something happened last November?"

Megan looked at him and bluntly asked, "Do you think she has an alcohol problem?"

"What? No." Stewart's shoulders pulled back and his tone sharpened. When Cassie was a little girl, Stewart used to worry how she was going to get over the death of her mother and looked for help to make the right decisions. Now, he defended her almost blindly and reacted to potential criticisms as if they were insults. "What makes you think she has an alcohol problem? One glass of wine?"

Megan wasn't as quick to respond as Stewart, nor was her tone as sharp. "She's underage. And it's against the law. Miranda Thompson got kicked off the lacrosse team for bringing beer on a team trip."

"Miranda Thompson? Your comparing Cassie to Miranda Thompson? First of all: that was three years ago and they were—what?—fifteen? Second: if Miranda Thompson wasn't voted most likely to become a meth head, I feel sorry for whoever came in first. And this is Cassie now. And one glass of wine." Stewart held up a single finger as if Megan needed help counting. "In Europe kids drink wine all the time."

Arms remaining crossed, Megan looked out the inset window. Kathy Hillard was no longer in view, their neighbor gone back to her own house, her own children, her own husband, her own problems. No one was immune.

She could feel Stewart waiting impatiently for what she was going to say next—his mind no doubt whirling with prospective responses. He once told her she was being passive aggressive when she fell silent like that, when what she was really doing was making sure she didn't say anything she might later regret.

When Megan remained quiet, Stewart said, "Cassie's always hung out with older people. When we had people over, she'd hang with us instead of her own friends. Remember?" He tried a smile, perhaps recognizing he'd become too aggressive—that she was his wife, not a structural inspector debating building codes. "She's out with people from work … they're older … she wants to feel like one of like them."

"Do you think she's ever been drunk?" Megan asked.

The question caught Stewart off balance. "Drunk?" He exhaled and pivoted uncomfortably in place. "I hope not. But is it possible? Is that what you're asking?"

"I'm asking if you think she's ever been drunk?"

"Is it possible?"

Megan waited.

"Yes. Okay. Yes," Stewart finally replied, a form of marital surrender. "Do I think it's possible? Yes. But do I hope she hasn't been? Yes—definitely."

"And how many times would she have had to be drunk before you'd consider maybe she has a problem with alcohol?"

Stewart exhaled more dramatically. "How many times?"

Megan gave a single nod.

He shrugged. "Ten?"

"Ten?" Megan was startled.

"I don't know. I picked a number and threw it out there. Because this doesn't make any sense. You're overreacting. How many times would someone have to be drunk before they might have a problem...?"

"Not anyone. I don't care about anyone. I care about Cassie," Megan stressed. "I always have. Since the first day she came in my class. The very first day. I loved that little girl the very first time I saw her."

Stewart briefly became speechless. In all the discussions they'd had about Cassie, while Megan's fondness for her had always been obvious, she'd never told him that.

Crossing the short distance that separated them, he hugged Megan. "And she loves you so much."

His words, intended reassure her, instead struck a cold, hard chord. Megan felt Stewart had just lied to her.

57.

"What's wrong?" Pip was concerned for Megan instead of responding to her questions about Aunt Nan.

She said, "It's been a rough day, but it's better now. Seeing your face." She wished she could touch him instead of merely looking at his image on her phone.

He asked where she was.

"The house. Stewart's getting carry-out for dinner. He'll be gone at least half an hour." She sounded relieved to be alone.

"What happened?"

She told him about Cassie's alcohol citation.

Pip was sympathetic, but said, "Just about every guard I ever worked with has gotten a fake ID—or tried to get one. Or got someone to buy them beer. Will's probably doing that right now. Art and Adrian used to. I used to."

Megan shrugged. "I guess I don't want to see Cassie that way."

"I get that."

"I also don't like they hid it from me. Like they didn't want to be bothered by my opinion."

"They probably didn't want to upset you," Pip suggested. "Didn't you and Cassie ever have secrets you kept from Stewart?"

"Some," Megan conceded. "Yes."

"Maybe this is no different."

"It feels like it is." She left out how she thought Stewart was lying when he told her Cassie loved her, because she didn't want to seem that needy. And she might be wrong about that. Made too sensitive by events of the past year.

Pip remained consoling. "She's not a kid anymore and that's gotta be hard."

Megan wondered if Stewart had responded to her concerns the way Pip did if their discussion would have gone more smoothly. Or was she giving Pip greater leeway? She returned to the purpose of her call: "How's Aunt Nan? How are you?"

"She's the same—no better, no worse. And I don't know if that's good or bad. I'm fine. Worried about her—and Aunt Betty. She's really struggling. I brought her here a couple hours ago, but she got too upset so I drove her back home—which is a bit of a haul. But I met with the neurosurgeon, who seems pretty sharp. She tried to be positive, and says that's what I need to be, but I get the feeling this is…" He hesitated, for a moment looking as if he might cry. "…bad. It feels bad."

"She'll get better."

Pip blinked and tried to bring back his smile. "The doctor said something about inducing a coma, which sounds scary as hell, but she says can be helpful—and sometimes it's necessary."

"Just hope for the best, okay. Know that I love you."

"I love you, too."

They looked at one another a few moments and Megan longed to be with him.

"Where are you sleeping?" she asked.

Pip managed to chuckle. "The backseat of a 1980 Chrysler LeBaron."

"What?"

"1980 Chrysler LeBaron," he repeated, mimicking the voice of a game show host. "With a mere 95,000 miles. It's Aunt Betty's."

"The Jeep too much for her?" Megan guessed, trying to picture an old woman holding onto the roll bar.

"The Jeep is dead," Pip reported.

"What? No."

"Yeah—it started making a really bad noise last night and crapped out."

"Oh, no."

"I had it towed to a place one of the orderlies recommended—guy's been really friendly. Hopefully they can look at it Monday. We'll see."

"I love the Jeep."

"Had it a long time."

"I'll come up tomorrow after I drop Stewart at the airport. We can sleep in the Volvo. Or get a hotel."

Pip shook his head. "I miss you like crazy, but you need to go back to the beach. I called Captain and told him I'm going to need more time off and he said he's losing two other guards in the next week, on top of two who already quit. Some always drop off during the summer, but me being gone and four more—that's a lot. So, he's moving the guard test up because there's a couple guards who want to come down from other beaches—New Jersey I think, and someone from Rehoboth, and you—four or five in all. You'll be getting an email."

"What's the new date?" Megan asked, excited by this news, but also a little anxious.

"Monday morning."

"This Monday? In two days?"

"Adrian says you're ready."

#

"I'm sorry about before," Stewart apologized. "I should have had Cassie tell you about that citation. But with everything else that was going on…" He left that thought unfinished. "Bad decision on my part. I'm sorry." At the kitchen banquette, sharing Thai food spooned from cardboard containers, he reached across the built-in table and touched Megan's arm.

They had spoken very little since he returned with their dinner. Their argument lingered like the swelling after a bad injury.

"I understand." Megan left it at that, seeing little sense getting deeper into her feelings of having become an outsider, how Stewart and Cassie—especially Cassie—were drifting away from her. That they were no longer the family they'd become. Besides, Stewart was leaving again tomorrow and discussions like that took time to resolve. And did it even matter anymore?

Megan steered her thoughts back to the guard test. Suddenly only 36 hours away.

They ate in near silence—polite comments about the food, a new restaurant Stewart noticed on his drive picking up dinner, and a for sale sign on a house half a mile away and what bearing that might have on their home going on the market. Then Stewart went into the den—the home office from which he'd tirelessly grown his business—and he returned to the task of deciding what he'd move to California.

As the summer sun set and light through the kitchen windows turned golden pink, Megan cleaned up, putting empty containers in a bag she'd seal tomorrow and take in the car to put down the trash chute once back at the beach, not wanting to leave garbage at the end of the driveway until pick-up day for racoons to claw through and make a mess.

She texted pictures of some kitchen items to Kelly to see if he wanted them. He enthusiastically texted back, *Yes, Love it, or Hell yes!* to nearly everything she offered—pots, pans, cookie trays, baking pans, muffin tins. She set those items in boxes and looked forward to seeing them in use at the cottage.

She packed some of her own clothes but didn't go into Cassie's room. When Cassie first left for college, Megan used to find comfort sitting in there, thinking back to when they first moved in, and a neighbor remarked how Megan and Cassie were like twins somehow born two decades apart. Not that they looked alike, but how they seemed so in unison with one another. How they did so much together. Now, Megan hadn't set foot inside Cassie's room for months, not since the last time Cassie came home for the weekend.

Shortly after ten, Megan went back downstairs and let Stewart know she was going to bed.

He considered her fondly from behind his desk. "I'm sorry again about before."

She nodded. "I'm not angry. And you're right, it's not just about a glass of wine. It's about the past year. Leaving here. Losing this."

"We're not losing it, though," he encouraged. "We're moving on. Getting better."

She nodded. And lied. "I know."

Seven hours later, it was still dark outside when they got out of bed to Stewart's alarm. They ate bagels Stewart had brought back last evening from a deli near the Thai place. Stewart had his with coffee. Megan drank tea.

Stewart squeezed a single suitcase of things to take to California in the Volvo's backseat, the trunk already filled with boxes of kitchen items and some of Megan's clothes. Stewart's mood was upbeat, telling Megan, "It's a start."

She closed up the house—turning off the proper circuit breakers, raising the thermostat, shutting off the water.

Driving to the airport, Stewart said, "I'm not sure when I'll be back. Whatever you decide about getting our stuff out of the house, I'm fine with." He paused in case Megan might respond. When she didn't, he said, "Use that company Georgianne recommended if you want. Ship stuff out to California. Sell it. Whatever. Take however much time you want. Maybe she sells the house without staging."

"Okay."

"And don't hesitate giving Cassie a hard deadline if she drags her feet getting her things cleared out."

"Okay," she repeated.

"And we'll keep an eye on her, okay. About any drinking," he specified. "If it looks like a problem, we'll deal with it."

She nodded.

In the BWI departure lane, they got out of the car and met by the trunk. Stewart set down his suitcase and they hugged. He said, "Everything's going to be great. Don't be sad about the house." He leaned back and looked at her. "Easy for me to say, right?"

She nodded and wiped her eyes. Not just about the house. But because her marriage was over.

By noon, she was back at the beach and in the ocean. Swimming. The guard test was tomorrow morning.

58.

Pip wanted to hear the ocean, so Megan took her phone down to the beach and sat by the water's edge, just far enough from where the waves' last push of momentum onto shore wouldn't reach her.

It was a warm, humid night.

Behind Megan, lights were on at most of the units in her building, people out on their balcony or inside their condo, talking, watching the ocean, some playing games. A few notes of music or pleasant laughter carried to Megan's ears between waves.

All Pip could hear was the ocean. "Sounds nice," he said. "Thanks." He was tired, but relaxed, that ever-present smile with him even folded into the backseat of his Aunt Betty's Chrysler, parked in the hospital lot where he planned to spend another night.

Pip asked if Cassie was coming to watch her do the guard test tomorrow.

"I haven't mentioned it to her."

"No…? How come? The other morning on the phone, she seemed pretty excited to watch."

"That may have been for her father's benefit."

"Seemed genuine to me."

"Maybe…"

Talking with Pip was so easy, so effortless. There was an honesty to him that felt innocent, a lack of agenda that didn't give rise to any motive for deception. He wasn't trying to make her believe or do anything.

"She's busy, though," Megan said of Cassie. "This internship is like her ocean."

"Hm…"

"And I guess," Megan admitted, "I don't want to get my feelings hurt by telling her about the guard test then she doesn't come. Yesterday, I texted her a picture—some place that reminded me of her—and she never sent anything back."

"Okay…"

"And more than that, I think she's probably done with me." Megan couldn't keep that thought inside, as deeply as it cut to say it. "There's no connection … because she's right: I'm not her mother."

"Come on, that's not true. There's no way that's true. I mean, okay, you're not her biological mother. But you're her mother just the same."

"I don't think she sees it that way."

"She's just growing up. She's feeling her independence. And that's a great asset for her. You should be proud of that. You've got to give her time."

"I always looked at her and thought with all my heart how I love this little girl like she's my own daughter. And she looks back at me and says I'm not her mother."

"She was drunk when she said that."

"That doesn't mean it wasn't a truth alcohol let out."

"You need to talk to her then. You can't keep letting it fester."

"I've invited her home over weekends. I asked if she wanted to go out for lunch or go shopping—that I'd drive down and pick her up from her apartment. I've let her know I'd love for her to spend time with me here this summer. There's always an excuse—school, her internship. She just doesn't want to do it—and the one thing you can depend on with Cassie is that if she wants to do something, she'll find a way to do it. The only time she came home was when her father was back in town, or something was happening with her high school friends—and even some of them call and say they don't hear from her anymore."

"It's going to be okay," Pip said. "You and Cassie. Something will happen, and it'll be like when the sun comes back out after its rained for days."

Megan held back tears and nodded. "Aunt Nan's going to be okay, too. She's going to get better."

"Yeah…" After a quiet moment, he said, "I could look at you and listen to the ocean for hours."

Which was what they did—not for hours, but a little longer—keeping the connection open, smiling fondly at one another as small waves rolled steadily on shore.

The guard test began in nine hours.

59.

A placard—SURF PATROL TEST—was hammered into the sand where the inlet parking lot met the wide beach, a large section of which had been roped off with orange caution tape.

At 7:45 Monday morning, Megan was the first applicant to arrive.

Under a hazy sky, she was greeted by the same Surf Patrol official to whom she'd delivered her written application days ago. His name was Ned Garrison and his rank—Captain—was stitched to a Surf Patrol t-shirt he wore along with red board shorts and deck shoes. "You're Pip's friend, right." Garrison, in his mid-40's, was officious, but pleasant, probably a good combination, Megan assessed, for handling a crew of young guards. He was also fit-looking, as if he could swim for miles.

They shook hands. Perhaps well-trained by the city's HR department, Garrison had not made any comments—shielded as levity or otherwise—about Megan's age nor had he posed any questions about her willingness to commit to a work schedule if hired.

"Shame about Pip's aunt." His eyes shielded from bright sunshine by aged aviators, Garrison shook his head mournfully. "My grandfather had a couple strokes … hopefully she recovers."

Behind Megan and Garrison, fishing cruisers and small boats eased through the inlet created decades ago when a hurricane plowed across the barrier island and formed the watery connection between the ocean and bay. Seagulls trailed the boats, squawking for hand-outs of bait fish.

Otherwise, the little beach town was quiet. The parking lot, which had been packed with vehicles last night and would soon be crowded again, was mostly empty. The boardwalk shops and amusements were yet to open. The rides, including Bonzai Bobsled where Megan found Pip weeks ago, calling out to riders if they wanted to go faster, sat still.

Garrison said, "We'll start at eight sharp. Expecting four others, but we might get a few walk-ups. Just posted the new date online two days ago, and sometimes we'll get people here on vacation want to see if they can do it. I'll weed out anyone not serious early on."

Doing some easy stretching, Megan said, "You're saying it starts out hard and gets easier?"

Garrison smiled. "You got the first part right."

Megan held onto her confidence. After talking with Pip last night, she'd ended up going to bed later than planned and awakened around 3:00 a.m., fully expecting a clutch of anxiety. But that didn't happen, and she'd fallen back to sleep. Now, she believed she realized why: Cassie. Despite all she'd said to Pip about losing touch with Cassie, after years watching her get ready for lacrosse games, all the team practices and drills done solo in the backyard, it was as if Megan had subconsciously stepped into that confident persona.

Bring it on.

#

It wasn't a competition against the other applicants. Everyone could pass or fail. Megan still wanted to win.

Chloe and Kem arrived together in an old Toyota compact with Jersey license plates that looked like it had been driven through a sandstorm. The car's black finish had been beaten to a dull grey and was further scarred with dings and scrapes.

Chloe was built like an MMA fighter: 19, 5-9, 160, with powerful legs and shoulders. She wore a one-piece black Speedo that wrapped her solid frame like a second layer of skin.

The same approximate age, Kem was short and lean, with black hair and almond eyes. His facial features suggested he might be Hawaiian, as did his t-shirt, screen-printed with a logo celebrating his participation in last fall's Ironman triathlon in Kailua-Kona.

Arriving moments later in a shiny Ford Mustang that came off the assembly line in the last year before the car went electric, was a cut physical specimen, 6-6 and agile-strong like a professional volleyball player. He had brilliant white teeth, a strong jaw, and razor-trimmed blond hair. He wore navy-blue running shorts, a close-fitting t-shirt, and beach shoes. Every part of his body that wasn't already perfect from genetics appeared refined by time in the gym.

"Hey, guys. How's everybody? I'm Mitch Cutler." He had the pleasant voice of a news broadcaster. Shaking hands all around, he just about swallowed smaller palms in his grip.

Behind Cutler's back, Chloe gave Kem a questioning look, like what the hell is this guy doing here? Megan knew what she meant. Cutler looked like he'd just stepped out of a fitness magazine, not like someone applying for a job that paid twice minimum wage.

Megan's confidence wavered briefly, but then recalled Cassie's team had beaten opponents that looked nastier than they played.

Garrison checked his watch, then announced, "Let's hit it."

#

On Garrison's whistle, Chloe sprinted to the ocean first and went in with the precision of a diver, barely making a splash as her powerful frame disappeared under a small wave. Heading into the ocean, she looked to have purposefully angled across Mitch Cutler's path, forcing him aside to keep from colliding with her.

Even though the 400-meter ocean swim wasn't a race, Chloe appeared determined to finish first, and looked to have sized up Cutler as her closest competitor.

Megan was the last one in but no sooner swam past the wave break than she felt her arm slap what she realized was a kicking foot.

She'd quickly caught up with Cutler, who, for his buff appearance was a sloppy swimmer. His line to the pontoon marker anchored 200 meters out was already off course.

Megan sprint swam around Cutler, which she realized was probably a bad decision—using up that much energy so quickly—but once past him, she found a good, steady rhythm.

She didn't look for Chloe or Kem until she reached the buoy. Taking a quick glance, she saw they were already a quarter of the way back to the beach.

Megan had no concept of how long she'd been in the water, but it could have been five minutes already. She kicked harder, not taking any chances of missing the ten-minute limit, and didn't look inland again until she reached the wave break. By that time, Chloe was already on the beach.

Moments later, Kem sprinted easily out of the water and made a line for Garrison.

When Megan saw the captain check his watch, a shot of adrenalin snapped through her. She swam fast into a building wave and rode it ashore.

Kem cupped his hands beside his mouth and called, "And she finishes with style!"

"Eight-ten..." Garrison counted. "...Eight-eleven."

Megan sprinted to Garrison's side, who announced: "Good time."

Kem held out his hand for her to smack. While he seemed genuinely happy for Megan, Chloe ignored her.

Cutler came out of the water and sprinted hard.

"Nine-twenty-seven," Garrison announced.

Breathing hard, the big guy exhaled, "That was close."

#

Garrison pointed down the beach. "The red rescue buoy. That's one-fifty meters. Down and back in sixty-five seconds. Go."

Kem darted off with an athletic lightness.

Chloe ran hard after him, strong legs pounding into soft sand. When Cutler passed her, Chloe looked agitated. For a big guy, Cutler was deft at sand sprinting.

Megan saw all this from the back of the pack, again reminding herself it wasn't a race against the others, but time. Still, she caught up to Chloe well before the buoy marker, and could have passed her, but chose to stay behind.

Kem made the turn sharply and was quickly back to top speed on the return to Garrison. Flashing past Chloe and Megan—who were yet to reach the turn—he cheered, "Go ladies, go!"

Chloe gave him the finger.

Cutler did a wind-sprint-style stop-and-pivot at the buoy marker seconds behind Kem. Exhaling a deep rush of air, he notched up his speed for the return leg.

At the turn, Chloe paused for a breath, and Megan had to stutter-step to keep from running up her heels. Megan went wide around the buoy, but still got Chloe's elbow into her side.

Megan dropped back a half step, letting Chloe move ahead. She stayed off her shoulder until they were a third of the way from Garrison, then put on a burst of speed and raced by.

Kem finished first. Cutler lunged past Garrison as though breaking an imaginary tape at a finish line.

Megan felt strong, taking long strides as Chloe tried to catch up. Megan could hear her breathing hard in pursuit, but she didn't have to glance back to know she was going to beat her.

"Forty-nine," Garrison counted off Megan's finish.

Chloe was five seconds behind her.

Megan peeled off to the side, keeping her back to everyone so as not to reveal her smile. That felt really, really good.

Chloe came toward her, winded, and slightly off stride. She reached her hand out at her side. "Good run." Saying it like she meant it.

Megan slapped her hand as they passed one another.

#

The pacing of Garrison's testing was unpredictable. Perhaps the idea was to simulate a lifeguard's potential day: periods of calm interspersed with intense physical demands.

After handing out bottles of water for them to drink, Garrison described, then demonstrated save and first-aid practices. He went through semaphore shorthand codes unique to his guards and confirmed that everyone could successfully send and receive the flagged signals.

CPR came next, and everyone breezed through it.

After that brief pause, they were back in the water for simulated saves that lasted an hour and kept everyone in near constant motion. Two applicants went out 50 meters as "victims" and had to tread deep water waiting for the other two "rescuers" to swim out and bring them ashore in separate saves.

Megan drew Kem as her first save, and he was encouraging, telling her to slow down a little when she started to swim him in. "Just be steady. It's still a long morning."

She followed that advice, and made a clean save, precisely timing the waves once they were inside the break line.

Twenty minutes later, Megan brought in Chloe, then Cutler, who hung onto the buoy, catching a rest.

The big guy's fatigue made Megan realize how tired she was getting. She tried to distract herself by thinking about swimming with Pip, or how Cassie had always been such a fierce competitor, never one to ease up, let alone quit.

Garrison showed the cross-chest carry and removal technique for unconscious victims. "Use the buoyancy of the water as long as possible bringing the victim out of the water."

Over the past hour, curious onlookers had gathered to watch, keeping a polite distance, and now numbered 50 or so. Megan heard a few of them comment how old she was.

Garrison started another round-robin of saves. This time the victim was closer to shore but floating as though unconscious or otherwise unable to hold onto the life buoy. The rescuer had to hold the victim alongside her body, which meant there was only one arm free to swim in, and attention had to be paid to keeping the victim's head out of the water.

The save required intimate physical contact between the victim and rescuer, but Kem was not self-conscious about that. With practiced technique, he looped his hold under Megan's arm and lightly pressed his hand near her clavicle. As Kem held her against his body and swam her in, Megan recognized the extra effort of his leg kicks.

Because the save was slower, getting ashore between breaking waves was more critical. Kem held Megan in place and let a series of breakers roll by, then got her in before the next set formed.

Once in waist-deep water, Kem adroitly maneuvered beneath Megan and pulled her arms over his shoulders, getting her on his back. Carrying her, his steps became shorter and somewhat staggered as more of Megan's weight came out of the water.

Beginning to sound more like a drill Sargent, Garrison barked, "Kem and Mitch in the water. Chloe, you take Kem. Megan, Cutler."

Cutler swam out, and as soon as he turned into a dead man's float, Megan ran into the ocean and dove into a wave.

She reached Cutler before Chloe got to Kem, but knew she wouldn't beat her back in. Buoyancy or not, Cutler had to weigh close to 190.

Megan wrapped her arm around his broad chest and began kicking.

"You know she called me 'pretty boy.'" Talking about Chloe, Cutler didn't sound as angry as he was amused. "Whatever her problem is."

Megan didn't respond. She was calculating how to get Cutler over her back. As soon as she could stand with her shoulders out of the water, she switched her hold on him, but lost her grip and he slid away.

Garrison shouted from shore when Cutler tried to right himself. "Don't help her!"

Cutler let himself go and sank in four feet of water.

Megan grabbed his arm and plunged down after him. Maneuvering beneath him, she got his weight on her back, and set her knees in the sand for support. Staying underwater, she gripped his wrists and pulled his arms around her shoulders.

Once she had his weight evenly balanced over her back, she stood upright. But as soon as she had him out of the water, a two-foot wave broke over them with enough force to twist Cutler away from her.

She drew a quick breath before being pulled underwater, and surfaced with her arms wrapped around him, grunting as she pulled his shoulders out of the water.

"Hang in there," he encouraged.

Another wave was forming. Breathing hard, Megan tugged him out toward it, and pulled him up and over the rising swell. Only now they were back in deeper water than where they'd begun. She had to start the save all over again.

Meanwhile, Chloe already had Kem ashore.

By the time Megan swam Cutler to shallow enough water to get him onto her back, her arms and legs were weary. It was all she could do to get him on the beach. Bent forward, she staggered forward, each step feeling as though it would be her last.

The number of spectators had grown to almost 100. Seeing Megan's exhaustion, many cheered her on.

She somehow got Cutler to Garrison, and eased him to the sand, then dropped to all fours beside him, no longer thinking about doing better than any of the others but worried she might not be able to go on.

#

"Cutler," Garrison directed, "you've got Kem. Chloe, you take Megan. Victims in the water."

Megan was surprised to find herself standing upright. She had no idea how. She'd never felt so exhausted. But she ran back into the ocean and dove under a wave.

She floated on her back with her eyes closed until Chloe expertly took her into a save hold and swam her toward shore.

Making steady progress inland, Chloe got Megan onto her back and carried her to the drop point beside Captain Garrison, making it seem easy.

Left lying on warm sand, Megan felt her thoughts drift away, but when Garrison called her name, she was up on her feet. It was a blur, going back out into the water, swimming to Chloe. Her arms felt rubbery and no longer obeyed signals from her brain. A rolling dizziness wobbled her head, followed by a spasm of nausea. She kept swimming.

She secured Chloe and turned toward shore, swimming more on her back than her side.

"You're going to make it. You're almost there."

Megan thought Chloe was talking to her. But it was Cassie's voice she heard. And Megan thought that maybe, at that very moment, maybe they were still part of one another after all.

#

"Try again next year." Garrison's words were encouraging in dismissal. "You only missed it by seventeen seconds. We do off-site tests in April. Then we're back here in May."

The final phase of the test had been a medley of running and swimming. 150 meters across the sand, 100 in the water, finishing with another 150 in the sand. It was the water that did in an already tired Mitch Cutler.

Chloe sat on the sand with her arms wrapped around her knees and her wet hair tangled around her face. Kem was sprawled across the beach beside her.

"Okay you three," Garrison said. "Let's go."

Megan remained standing. She'd done it.

#

In the small meeting room at the Surf Patrol's cottage office, Megan, Chloe, and Kem sat at student-style desks. There was paperwork to complete, and an extended orientation of practices and procedures including the review of an employee handbook. Pizzas were delivered and devoured.

As experienced lifeguards from other beaches, Chloe and Kem were each assigned to a senior surf patrol guard who would oversee their probation period. Being a new guard, Megan would typically have had to go through surf academy, but that didn't make logistical sense for a single hire, so Garrison said he was assigning Megan to work in tandem with Adrian until Pip got back. "That's what Pip suggested," Garrison said, "so that's what I'm going to do."

"Does he know I passed?"

"No—but he didn't have any doubt you would. When can you start?"

"Right now." She was exhausted but never felt stronger.

Garrison smiled. "How 'bout tomorrow? Your equipment's by the door. Glad to have you."

#

295

Megan took a selfie on the sidewalk outside the Surf Patrol office. She had on her newly issued red OCSP sweatshirt even though it was 85 degrees. Her rescue buoy was strapped over her shoulder. And in case all that wasn't evidence enough, her smile made clear she'd passed. She texted the picture to Pip along with three exclamation points. And waited for him to call.

60.

"I don't want a job. I just wanted to see if I could do it." Pip's face lit up Megan's phone. "That's what you told me two months ago."

"Did I?" Megan sat on the curb outside the surf patrol offices. Pip had called less than two minutes after getting her text. She told him all about the guard test, more excited than tired. "I couldn't have done it without all the swimming we did, though. Getting me in shape."

Pip asked if Cassie was there.

Megan shook her head.

"Didn't you tell her about it? Or didn't she show?"

"Didn't tell her."

"Okay." His response wasn't judgmental. "You going to tell her now?"

"I hadn't thought about it."

"Okay. Well, the crew'll be pumped. Will's been saying you'd make a great guard. And Kelly'll probably want to open a bottle of champagne. I'm sorry I'm not there."

"We'll celebrate when you get back. I think I'm going to sleep from now until tomorrow anyway. Although I need a new bathing suit. Captain Garrison—is that what you call him? Do you say his last name or just, Captain? Or is that only for old-timers."

"Old timers? Like me?"

"Guards who've been here longer than a couple hours."

"You say Captain, everyone knows who you mean. There's only one captain."

"Okay. He gave us a list of places that sell suits and give a surf patrol discount. I've also got to let my students know I'm going to have to switch their times around me being on a stand—I think they'll be okay with right after dinner. I'm also thinking about a haircut." She pulled back her hair, dried from the ocean. "Going shorter. What do you think about that?"

"Makes sense."

"But I want you to like it."

"I'll like it."

For a moment, it felt as though all decisions could be that easy, the way choices can be early in relationships unburdened by history.

Across the parking lot, tourists crowded the sidewalk, making the late afternoon trek back to hotel rooms and condos, sticky with sunscreen and seawater after a day on the beach, their skin redder than just hours ago.

Megan wanted to know about Aunt Nan and felt guilty for not asking sooner.

Pip kept his smile but said there wasn't any good news. The neurosurgeon had seen more test results and it looked like her stroke had been severe. It could be a long recovery. "I met with a social worker to figure out what kind of insurance Aunt Nan has and what it will cover and for how long."

"I can look into rehab places around here," Megan offered.

"I think I've got to figure out this insurance stuff first."

"Let me know what I can do to help."

"Okay."

"And the Jeep," Megan said. "What about the Jeep?"

"Still waiting to hear."

"And your replacement phone?"

"Tomorrow, they say." Pip managed a smile. "Glad we covered the good news first."

"It's all going to get better. I can feel it. Aunt Nan. The Jeep. Your phone."

"Okay … go get your bathing suit. And haircut. And have a good dinner."

"I'll call you tonight. I miss you. Love you."

"Love you and miss you, too…" He stayed connected, looking at her. "Text Cassie the picture, okay? Just the way you sent it to me. With the exclamation points."

#

Megan texted the picture to Cassie, but not until later—not until after stopping in a surf shop for two new red one-piece suits in beach-patrol-approved styles. And having her hair trimmed to shoulder length, just long enough to tie into a quick top knot. And eating dinner alone on her balcony, a tuna salad sandwich on grain bread, while watching the waves and the silhouette of Pip's stand, excited to soon have one of her own.

The sense of accomplishment, having passed the guard test, was powerful and made her feel independent, which she'd need to carry her through the next few months, to make her separation from Stewart final—to finish what he'd begun when he merged his company with Dunhill and went out to Scottsdale. She still had difficulty thinking about the word, divorce, but that would come, because it had to.

And once that process began, Cassie might never talk to her again. But hadn't that already started? Wouldn't that just be the completion of another separation already well under way? The little girl who'd lost her mother and captured Megan's heart had grown up and was starting out on her own, free of chains of sentimentality, perhaps never having felt that same emotional tether to begin with.

When Megan texted the selfie with her new surf patrol gear to Cassie, she felt as if saying goodbye.

When her phone alerted with a text five minutes later, she assumed it was Pip.

But it was Cassie: *OMG OMG OMG OMG OMG.* Followed by a line of celebration emojis: fireworks, a dancing Snoopy, a party hat.

More texts, one after the other: *I thought it was next week. I was going to watch.*

What did S say? Bet he flipped out.
Not sure he thought you could do it.
I knew you could.
You're a brute!
Texting your pic to everyone in the office.   #BADASSMOM.
#OCSPMOM
Say hi to all the cute lifeguards.
Send more pics!!!!!

Megan was momentarily overwhelmed by Cassie's reaction, and for a moment it was as if the two of them were knitted close together again, but then her phone fell quiet and there was only the sound of the ocean.

She texted Cassie back: *I love you.*   Because despite everything else, that was still true.

She was yet to let Stewart know about the guard test—that the date had been moved up or that she'd passed—and had only spoken briefly with him since he flew back to Newport Coast.   Their conversation last night had been short, their argument about Cassie's drinking still an emotional thorn.

Megan set her phone down.   It remained quiet until Pip called an hour later.

"Let's see the new hair," he asked right away.

She sat up on the chaise, angling her phone so it picked up enough ambient light on the balcony to show the inches she'd had trimmed.

"Looks great," he complimented.

"Thanks."   She ruffled her fingers through it, liking the feel.   It had been a long time since her hair was that short.

Pip said, "I can hear the waves."

"Bigger tonight."   Megan stood and aimed her phone toward the ocean, but the camera didn't pick up details in the dark.

He said, "I saw something today.   I'm texting you a picture."

Megan returned to the chaise.   "A house," she said when the image came through.   "How cute.   Where is this?"

It was a little blue cottage, its small yard and a line of azaleas along the front walk glowing in sunshine, the sturdy arms of an oak tree framing the right side of the picture.

"I took a different route from the hospital to Aunt Betty's—off the highways—and there it was. It reminds me some of where I grew up. You can't see in what I sent, but it's got a screened-in porch with two Adirondack chairs. And a brick fireplace. And there's a big back yard with a split-rail fence with wire inside it, like they might have a dog. There's also a garden out back—looks like some tomatoes and corn and beans and some low plants on a vine—cantaloupe maybe. And a separate garage, but it looks like it's used more as a workshop. Could be for woodworking because there's a homemade sign in the front yard—the outside of it is surrounded in this heavy rope, like from an old sailing ship and the sign says, 'A fisherman lives here with the catch of his life.'" Pip said, "I know how he feels."

Megan imagined the house in springtime with the azaleas in bloom. She saw it in the summertime with staked tomato plants and tasseled corn in the garden. She saw it in the fall with the leaves of the oak tree turned red. She saw it in the winter, blanketed in snow, with wisps of smoke rising from the chimney. And she saw herself bundled in a heavy coat on the front porch. And she saw Pip beside her.

61.

By the time Bill Clary stepped onto his balcony, the guards were already in the ocean, swimming south of his townhouse. He watched them through his binoculars, four of them this morning. Yesterday, they hadn't swum at all, and another guard he didn't recognize had been on Pip's stand.

Clary visually followed the guards until they came ashore two blocks south, bodysurfing good-sized waves onto the beach and jogging back at an easy pace. He didn't recognize Megan until they were closer. Her hair was shorter.

As she and the other three guards trotted nearer, Clary set down his binoculars. When Megan saw him, she waved.

He waved back, watching the group continue to Pip's stand, where they picked up their gear—rescue buoys and OCSP carry bags. They all picked up their gear, Megan included.

Grinning, Clary sent a text to Mary Jane, who was back in Charleston on that historic house remodeling project that seemed to keep getting bigger and bigger. Clary's text read: *Looks like our Megan's a lifeguard!* "Our Megan" was how he'd begun to refer to her when talking with Mary Jane, who at first had scowled at Bill using the same familiar reference he'd once attributed to their late daughter ("Our Penny") but she'd let it go—one of those marital compromises that made for a long and happy life.

#

Megan climbed atop Adrian's guard stand and stood, waiting. Hands on hips, holding semaphore flags. Lanyard around her neck, whistle held lightly in her teeth. With the warm morning sun and easy summer breeze on her face, she breathed the salty air.

At 9:00, the whistle signal that sounded the beginning of their workday made its way up the beach. Will flagged acknowledgement to a guard temporarily assigned to Pip's stand, a young kid named Bryan the others knew but Megan had just met—someone who'd grown up in town, volunteered nights and winters for the fire department, and was training to be a paramedic.

Bryan sent the signal to Art, who turned and relayed it to Megan, who pivoted north and whistled and snapped her flags to another guard, Taylor, who Adrian described as "decent" and said was a junior at Salisbury studying to be a teacher— something Megan figured they might have in common.

Lulu, the beach stand girl, captured the moment on her phone, having received an unexpected text from Cassie last night—the picture of Megan with her guard gear. "Woo-hoo," Lulu cheered. "Hashtag OCSP Mom."

"So far so good?" Adrian asked.

"Yeah." Megan buzzed with the excitement that had awakened her at 6:00.

"Okay—scooch over, I'm coming up."

Megan slid to the side to make room as Adrian ascended the wooden planks to join her.

Adrian was in one of her better moods, having smiled and hugged Megan when first seeing her that morning. Her congratulations had been sincere, although less constrained than Will, who'd thrown his arms around Megan, picked her up, and spun her around. She'd also gotten a hug from Art.

Aiming her phone at them, Lulu said, "Smile girls!"

When Adrian waved, Megan did likewise. Picture taken, Lulu headed back down the beach in a dayglo yellow bikini.

Hip to hip with Megan, Adrian put on mirrored Oakley sunglasses and gestured to two surfers lingering for a last wave of the morning. Surfers needed to be out of the water once the guards' day started at nine. Adrian said, "I'll give them a few minutes."

"Okay." Megan nodded.

Two minutes later, Adrian said, "This is the part no one says enough about: the boredom. My first couple days, I thought I was going to go crazy, waiting for something to happen. Pip laughed at me."

"I wish he was here." Megan said that without thinking, but now that the words were out figured there was no harm. She and Pip were no longer a secret with the other guards—maybe they never really had been,

"How's he doing?" Adrian asked.

"Worried about his aunt. Trying to figure how to help her."

"He texts me he's fine…"

"Oh…"

"Mostly he texts about you." Adrian patted Megan's thigh. "Make sure we keep you in shape. And that Captain assigns you up here."

"I appreciate that."

They looked out at the ocean, watching the surfers.

Adrian said, "He is crazy in love with you."

Hearing that made Megan's eyes tear with happiness. "I love him, too. So much I'm not even sure I realized what the feeling was at first. It scared me."

"I get that."

"Do you feel that way about Art?"

"Arthur?" She smiled easily. "We're just playing around."

"I think he's smitten."

"That's just his little puppy act—all playful and obedient. Summer'll end and we'll text and email and then it'll be over without either of us saying so. He'll be with someone new by Thanksgiving. Maybe the same for me." Adrian nudged Megan with her elbow and nodded at a surfer who caught a short wave and started back out for another. "You try to be nice…" she sighed, then instructed Megan: "Get him out of the water."

Megan stood and gave two short whistles, the way she would have called her class in from recess. When the surfers ignored her, she gave a sharper whistle and they both caught the next small wave to shallow water, one of them with his arms out to his sides, looking at her as if to say, Who me? before flopping backwards off his board.

Megan laughed and was still smiling as the pair in their late teens came ashore and trotted by, boards under their arms. One called out to her, "Hey, new girl. What's your name?" Flirting.

"Megan."

"All right, Megan. See you around."

"Welcome to the surf patrol," Adrian said.

#

Maybe boredom would come. It didn't that first day. Megan loved every minute, keeping watch on vacationers going in and out of the ocean, checking for rip currents, whistling warning to anyone floating out too far. Also minding activity on the beach. The town had ordinances against music being played too loudly, holes dug below ankle depth, or open containers of alcohol. No saves, though—not for her or any of the other guards for blocks.

During the morning, a handful of people took pictures of her and Adrian, which she'd seen happen with Pip—tourists capturing a vacation memory. She and Adrian smiled and waved, the way they'd done for Lulu.

Folks stopped to talk, some with questions about the ocean—little kids seemed especially concerned about sharks and jellyfish, and what were horseshoe crabs anyway? A few asked why Megan and Adrian were on the same stand. Guys flirted—some looked barely legal to drive while others could

PRESTON PAIRO

have been Adrian's father, and one bold fellow—with a choker of puka beads around his neck—was a couple decades older than Megan.

In the afternoon, the number of picture-takers steadily increased, which Megan didn't think about until a mother-daughter pair asked to make sure Megan was #OCSPMOM. The 13-year-old showed Megan her phone, on which was the selfie Megan had taken yesterday outside the surf patrol office and texted to Cassie, which Cassie, it seemed, had posted on Instagram with the hashtag, which, as of three hours ago, had made its way onto one of Ocean City's social media groups, where it leapfrogged to another, then another.

Megan was uncomfortable with the attention and hoped it didn't cause a problem.

"Don't worry about it," Adrian replied, still in one of her better moods.

By the time Megan whistled the end of the guards' day and tilted the stand on her back to drag it to the dunes, the extent of her sudden notoriety became more apparent. Since guards other than squad leaders weren't supposed to be on their phones while on duty, most kept theirs in their car. Megan had left her phone in the condo.

Now, checking for messages from Pip, she found dozens of texts, voice, and emails.

While not exactly the viral sensation a wannabe influencer's dreams were made of, #OCSPMOM was catching on.

306

62.

Pip looked worn down, slouched sideways in the driver's seat of Aunt Betty's Chrysler, the windows lowered, the remains of a carry-out sub that had been his lunch and dinner on deli wrap across the console.

While Megan had spent her day in sunshine, with pelicans swooping over the sea and single-engine planes pulling banners advertising sunscreen and restaurant specials, Pip had been in hospital rooms, windowless corridors, and offices—waiting. Waiting for doctors and technicians to bring better news. Waiting for social workers. Listening to bad music on hold, waiting for health insurance agents to pick up his call, only to tell him they needed to transfer him to a different department, where the waiting began again.

Aunt Nan's condition remain unchanged.

"I can be there in six hours," Megan said. That was an optimistic estimate of driving time, but she was ready to get in the car.

"I'm okay," he replied. "I'm getting some answers—or at least I know who to ask the next question."

"I miss you, though." As soon as Megan said that she wanted to make sure it didn't seem as if she wanted him to make decisions about Aunt Nan on her account. "But I understand. You do what you need to do. And however I can help, I will." She ached to be with him, picturing them in his cottage, but anywhere, really.

Five stories below, the beach was no longer crowded, just a few colorful towels spread across the sand. A circle of middle-aged friends sat in folding chairs, chatting as shade from Megan's building extended toward the ocean. A few surfers were out although the waves had diminished since morning.

Sitting forward on a balcony chair, Megan held her phone in both hands. Still in her bathing suit, she was sticky from perspiration and salt air. Her shoulders felt warm from hours in the sun, although she'd used plenty of sunscreen.

Pip wanted to hear about her first day.

She said, "It was amazing. I loved every minute. My semaphore's sad, but Art and Bryan were patient."

"You've gotta watch your overlap with Bryan," Pip advised. "He tends to look straight in front of him and miss stuff going on north or south. In the water, though, he could pull in a whale."

"Okay…"

"And you made sure to keep drinking?"

"Plenty of water—yep."

"Didn't hit ninety there today, did it?"

"Mid-eighties. And a breeze all day. Very pleasant."

"Nice." He closed his eyes, as if picturing it. Or maybe was just tired.

Megan knew the feeling. Her day was starting to catch up to her. And she had a student tonight at seven.

When her phone pinged with a text, she said, "There's another one," then explained: "I'm hearing from people I haven't seen or talked to in months. Years even. That picture you had me send Cassie…?"

"Yeah?"

"She posted it and now I've got voice mails and texts from Cassie's old lacrosse teammates—girls I used to drive home after practices and to games when she was in travel leagues. And some of the girls' moms I used to be friends with. And one of her old coaches and a teacher. A few neighbors. Thirty people must have taken my picture today. I kept waiting for Adrian to get pissed about it—thankfully she didn't."

Pip nodded, amused. "I saw."

"You saw?"

"Lulu posted the video she took of you, and it got reposted to the Surf Patrol Facebook page. OCSPMOM. I checked out that hashtag and all these other posts came up. The first was Cassandra Tyler on Instagram."

"Cassandra?"

"Yeah. What's wrong?"

"Something else I didn't know, I guess. She's going by Cassandra now. Not Cassie." Megan wasn't big on Instagram or Facebook or Twitter, especially Twitter, which had been savagely and anonymously used to harass a teacher in Cassie's middle school, to the point the woman took a leave of absence to seek mental health treatment. When Cassie played lacrosse, Megan had followed her and some of her teammates on Instagram but hadn't looked at that in over a year. And that Instagram account had been CassieTyler, not Cassandra.

"She's proud of you," Pip said warmly. "It's a good thing." His smile made everything seem better. "And the social media stuff will fade. It'll be like those old flash bulbs people used to take pictures with. A bright pop of light that leaves a spot in front of your eyes for a while, then goes away."

"Let's hope so," she said as another text hit her phone. And then there was another. Followed by an incoming call: Stewart, which Megan let go to voice mail as she and Pip talked more.

Pip had good news about his new phone, which he'd received and was charging. There were less positive developments about the Jeep, which had a transmission issue that needed further looking into.

"So, it's me and the LeBaron a while longer." Pip tried to keep a sense of humor about it.

Megan didn't want to hang up but needed to shower and have something to eat before her student logged on. They said goodbye and planned to talk again later.

Getting clean and eating dinner revived her enough to be sharp for tutoring and distracted her from thinking about returning Stewart's call. He'd sent a text after leaving voice mail. *Hope you had a terrific day. Talk tonight?*

She'd texted back: *9:30?* and he'd replied with a thumbs up.

Now, back on the balcony, with the ocean glimmering shades of silver under starlight and waves breaking on shore, Megan returned a few texts, including one from her friend Jillian, who she hadn't spoken to since coming back from Newport Coast.

Jillian had sent: *YOU'RE A BEACH PATROL GUARD!!!? What happened to California?*

Long story, Megan started to text back, but stopped, thinking that might seem mysterious and lead to questions she didn't want to answer. Instead, she sent a text suggesting they talk one night this weekend.

Jillian texted back: *You assume I don't have a date.* And included multiple laughing emojis.

Megan replied with a laughing emoji of her own—the accepted modern-day way to end a communication that seemed more juvenile than her youngest students.

She opened an email with the subject line, *Would Like to Schedule an Interview,* which came from an address of one of the beach's small newspapers. A reporter wanted to do "a short piece" on #OCSPMOM.

Megan replied she wasn't comfortable with that and really didn't want the attention.

Within minutes, the reporter replied: *Understand. But I think you're going to get that anyway. In case you didn't know, I think you're the most senior guard ever hired by OCSP.*

Megan emailed: *You mean oldest?*

Life experienced? the reporter offered.

Megan smiled at what she interpreted as a jab at political correctness.

The reporter asked if it would be okay for her to come by the beach tomorrow.

Megan sighed and replied, *Can I think about it?*

Sure. Let me know.

There were more unanswered texts and calls, but Megan set down her phone and watched the ocean and thought about Pip. She had 15 minutes until it was time to talk with Stewart.

63.

"I passed the lifeguard test," were the first words Megan said to Stewart after Hello.

"Congratulations. Very impressive."

"So, I'm a surf patrol guard now." Megan figured he already knew that, assuming he followed CassandraTyler on Instagram or Cassie had told him.

"Nothing short of amazing," Stewart said, but it was a distracted compliment, empty of joy, and made clear to Megan the distance between them was greater than the miles separating their respective coastlines. After a brief silence, Stewart gently moved to the purpose of his call: "I know you're angry with me about Cassie and that alcohol violation. And you're completely right to feel that way. I'm sorry how I handled it. And I haven't said anything to Cassie about it, but I will. But I wanted to talk with you about it first. I don't want to make matters worse by doing something without your input."

"Don't say anything to her," Megan replied. "It's over now. It's done. I would have liked to have known what was going on … but I get it."

He waited in case she wanted to say more, then asked, "Are you sure?"

"Yes." That was a lie, but it no longer mattered. "I guess it's something all kids do."

"I'm sorry I kept it from you. I won't make that mistake again." He sounded relieved. "I guess … you know … I also

312

guess I was embarrassed about it. What she'd done. I won't do it again," he repeated.

"Okay…" She didn't want to talk about it anymore because she didn't believe him. Not that he was lying, but that when the next situation arose that would make him feel as if he should put Cassie first, he would. Which Megan understood. What hurt was that he—and Cassie—had excluded her. Because she wasn't Cassie's mother. As much as she'd tried to be, as much as she'd wanted to be, as much as she loved her…

His voice soft, Stewart said, "I'm also thinking all this time apart—you and me—is maybe coming at a bad time … with Cassie being away…" He paused to see if Megan would reply.

She waited for what else he was going to say.

"I talked to Scott about blocking off some time I can take off. A month maybe. I'm thinking October into November. I know you want the rest of the summer at the beach, and how you like it there in September. And maybe we also put off dealing with the house if that helps. Maybe let that wait until after Christmas. We could take one of those trips we always talked about. A river cruise in Europe. Or a train across Canada."

Megan remembered those conversations—what felt like a long time ago. She also had a more recent memory of Holden Lassiter, Dunhill's attorney, talking to her on the patio of that restaurant in California last month, telling her Scott Dunhill didn't understand employees who gave their spouse priority over their job.

Megan closed her eyes. "Let's just keep going the way we're going, Stewart. Keep focusing on work. Don't miss out on this opportunity. You've worked too hard for it."

There was a heaviness to the silence.

"Really," Megan stressed quietly. "We'll deal with the changes…"

Stewart seemed unconvinced. "You're sure?"

"Yes."

"All right…" He remained uncertain. "Let me know if you change your mind."

"I won't."

He was asking about taking a long vacation together, but in Megan's mind she was answering another question: whether she still loved him. By the time they ended the call a few minutes later, she couldn't help crying—sad that she no longer loved him and mourning how all they'd had would forever be tainted by that loss.

#

Later that same night, a wave of Saharan air swirled off the west coast of Africa and headed for the Cape Verde Islands. It was not an unusual meteorological event, as such waves were typically produced every two or three days between April and November, and few ever formed hurricanes, especially early in the season.

64.

That it was the last day of July intensified Megan's feeling that summer was slipping away. In a few weeks, colleges would start up again. The students she'd said goodbye to at Villa James just weeks ago would return to their classrooms the week after Labor Day. Megan wondered if she might also be there again—if the new life she envisioned, separated from Stewart and in love with Pip—would find her back at Villa James. She needed to make a decision about that soon.

For the moment, though, glorious summer warmed her skin and made her smile. Seated hip to hip with Adrian on a guard stand, the pair watched the ocean, each immersed in their own thoughts, their silence broken every so often by a shared observation, idle bits of conversation, or chatting with tourists who strolled by.

"Cassandra was a lacrosse star, huh—in high school? Your daughter?" Adrian asked, ending another short period of quiet.

That Adrian referred to Cassie as Cassandra clued Megan that she'd seen Cassie's latest Instagram account, perhaps curious how many times she'd been included in pictures with Megan in #OCSPMOM posts—a hashtag that continued to trend upwards, with a dozen or so additional pics taken of them so far that morning.

"She's my step-daughter, actually," Megan replied.

"Oh." Adrian sounded as if having stumbled upon a sensitive subject, the way some people reacted when learning Megan wasn't Cassie's birth mother.

Megan had never wanted that to make a difference—and tried so hard to believe it didn't. "She was an excellent player. She set some school records—state records, too." Megan still felt proud saying that—having supported Cassie throughout those years in her life, all the hours driving her to and from practices and games, cooking meals recommended by a strengthening coach, washing uniforms, organizing fund raisers, watching her play from the time she began as a 9-year-old. Although it had quickly become less like play and more like competition for Cassie, who, by the time she was 10, was the youngest player on an advanced travel team. "Her school won back-to-back state championships."

Adrian pushed tinted sunglasses up the narrow bridge of her nose. "Weren't they undefeated too?"

"They lost two games in Cassie's sophomore year. None after that."

"Damn." Adrian was impressed.

Megan scanned the area behind them. The beach was crowded. The weather was perfect: sunny, clear, mid-80's, with a gentle breeze, and waves so small even more-timid kids didn't need much prodding from mom and dad to venture with them beyond water that reached their little knees.

Before work, Megan and the other three guards had swum farther than usual because there wasn't any current to challenge them. They'd jogged easily back on the beach, no longer getting Megan in shape for the guard test, but keeping themselves fit.

After a few minutes, Adrian asked if Megan had other kids.
"No."

"Did you want to?"

The question surprised Megan—not only its directness, but because, so far, her conversations with Adrian hadn't been very personal. "I thought about it, I guess, early on, but not for very long after Cassie came into my life. She was enough—I don't mean in terms of obligation or responsibility, but how much I loved her. Besides, Cassie was having a hard time after her mother died, and a new baby could have complicated things."

"Oh—your husband's first wife died?"

"She did."

"How old was Cassie?"

"When her mother died? She'd just turned eight."

"Oh, man…"

"It was fairly sudden. And I don't think she really understood what had happened … hadn't had time to process it—if that's even the right word at that age. Her father, Stewart, had thought about keeping her out of school. She was supposed to start third grade. But I think his mother was pretty instrumental in keeping him together … so Cassie started school on time and that's where I met her."

"In school?"

"I was her teacher."

"Really? You're a teacher?"

"Mm-hm."

"Elementary ed?"

"Yes."

"You still teach?"

"I started again last fall. And I tutor some kids online."

"That's cool. What subjects?"

"Math mostly."

"Not my strong subject," Adrian sighed.

"I think a lot of it has to do with how you're wired. Although it can be easier to learn than you think. There are different approaches and some work better than others. Cassie and I used to play a game at grocery store check-out. We'd add numbers in our head for the stuff we were buying as the cashier rang it up. Cassie was pretty good for about seven or eight items, then she'd lose count."

"You can do that in your head?"

"Yeah."

"Seventeen, a hundred-twenty-five, ninety-six."

"Two-hundred and thirty-eight," Megan answered almost instantly.

Adrian laughed. "I have no way to know if that's right."

Megan slowly added the numbers aloud to confirm the total.

Adrian squinted, following along, laughing again, "I feel so stupid. How do you do that?"

"I see the numbers."

"I don't know if that's cool or scary."

They drifted back to their own thoughts until Adrian said, "My father has a second family." The hurt in the girl's voice was unmistakable. "He got tempted away. His new wife's younger. And we could tell—my brothers and I—from day one, she was getting a baby. Now she has two." She sighed. "No way Pop's was getting away from that." She shook her head with disdain, looking at the ocean. "He's 55 and has a six- and a four-year-old. Both girls and both little shits."

"Sounds unpleasant."

"Oh, yeah."

"What about your mom? Did she remarry?"

Adrian shook her head. "I think she's still in love with my father ... in spite of everything. She's just depressed most of the time now."

"I'm sorry to hear that." Megan hoped Stewart would find someone else. That whatever pain she caused by ending their marriage would quickly fade and a new love would come into his life. "What about your brothers? How old are they?"

"Twenty-seven and thirty. I think I was a surprise," she added as to her age difference from her siblings.

"So, you're the baby," Megan imagined, at the same time thinking how that may have once been true but was no longer. Adrian's role had been supplanted by her father's new daughters, which probably stung quite sharply.

"How about you," Adrian wanted to know, "brothers or sisters?"

"Just me. I may have been a surprise myself. My parents were kind of old when I was born and my mom had had some medical issues in her twenties, and I don't think she thought her chances of getting pregnant were very good."

"She okay now—your mom?"

"She died six years ago. And my dad when I was in high school."

"That sucks."

Megan nodded. "I miss them a lot."

Adrian put her arm around Megan's waist and gave her a little hug, which Megan reciprocated, each consoling the other about parents they'd lost, although by different means.

They remained seated that way moments later when a young mother and her eleven-year-old daughter stopped in front of their stand, the little girl asking if they were OCSPMOM. Adrian pointed to Megan and pleasantly responded, "She is."

The little girl wanted to take their picture, so Megan and Adrian leaned even closer together and gave big smiles.

As mom and young daughter walked happily on, Adrian watched them, then sat forward, elbows on her knees, looking straight ahead. "You wonder what happens to people, don't you? How things change."

Megan didn't know if Adrian was talking about her own family or envisioning the future of the little girl who just took their picture. "It gets better," she consoled.

Adrian nodded, the way you do when making yourself believe the future will be kind.

They fell quiet again, watching the ocean until Adrian sat back and nudged Megan with her elbow. "You seeing this?"

"The woman on the surf mat."

Adrian nodded. "Let's go."

Megan got to her feet and whistled warning to Art and Bryan, then vaulted off the stand behind Adrian—not the method they were supposed to use, but because that's how Pip did it. Grabbing their rescue buoys, they sprinted into the ocean and swam hard.

A woman in her fifties hanging sideways across a canvas surf mat had drifted out in water over her head and started to panic when she couldn't get in. Megan and Adrian reached her

319

quickly and brought her to shore, by which time the woman gathered herself enough to joke about her exploit.

#OCSPMOM had her first official save—even if it was an easy one.

The event made it onto social media by the time Megan and Adrian returned to their stand, where two little kids offered them each a colorful necklace strung of Lifesavers and announced in sing-song unison, "We made this for you."

"Wow. Thanks," Megan smiled. "This is lovely. Do I wear it or eat it?"

"You wear it," the girl said, taking charge. "And eat it when you're hungry."

"Got it." Megan stretched the elastic around her head and put it on, feeling the candies sticking to her wet skin.

Less used to dealing with small children, Adrian awkwardly held her new "jewelry" and ended up roping it around her wrist, then took it off as soon as the kids walked away.

Megan was still wearing hers when the reporter showed up five hours later.

#

Janis Andersen was as young as Megan imagined from their brief email exchange last night. She had short dark hair, wore hiking shorts, a baggy t-shirt, hip sunglasses, and carried plenty self-assurance.

When she asked permission to take Megan's picture, Megan, as she'd been doing throughout the afternoon for all the other picture-takers, put her arm around Adrian's shoulders, and Adrian leaned close, arm around Megan's waist, their heads tilted toward one another as they smiled, making clear they were a team.

"I won't interrupt your work," Janis said, her friendly manner intended to get Megan to agree to be interviewed. "I'm going to sit back there..." She gestured toward the dunes. "...and if you feel like a little chat after you're done for the day that would be great. Nothing deep. Not looking to change the world. Just give people a reason to smile about something."

Andersen was still there when Megan flagged the end of the day and jumped off the stand with Adrian. "Walk you to your car?" the reporter proposed.

"I live down there. Ocean Vista."

"Really? Okay." She fell in stride alongside Megan. "So … what made you want to join the surf patrol?"

Megan thought about meeting Pip, and swimming the ocean, and the guards training her, but didn't want to share that so she made something up, saying it was always something she'd been interested in, and now with her daughter at college she had the time and thought, why not.

"Are you a single mom?"

"Nope. Married." Instinctively, she raised her left hand to show her wedding band only to realize she didn't have it on. She couldn't recall when she'd taken it off, but her hand was evenly suntanned, the paler circle where that ring used to be already gone.

#

The reporter was true to her word and kept her questions light and breezy, and thanked Megan for her time.

Once in her condo, Megan went directly for her phone, eager to check for messages from Pip. He'd texted a few times: he missed her, loved her, and was thinking about her. His last text, at 1:30, said he hoped she was having a great second day.

Megan rang him but he didn't answer. She was standing in the kitchen, still in her bathing suit, wondering what to make herself for dinner, when Pip returned her call fifteen minutes later. As soon as she saw his face, she knew. Aunt Nan had died.

65.

The sorrow showed most heavily on Pip's eyes, which were half closed and heavy and swollen from tears.

Just two hours ago. Pip had been sitting in Aunt Nan's hospital room, holding her hand, when her heart monitor suddenly went flat. Nurses ran in, then a doctor, everyone looking at Pip because of the DNR. Aunt Nan's do-not-resuscitate order was clear: she did not want to be revived; she was ready to go. But Pip, with authority as her health care agent, could overrule those directions.

"I did exactly what she told me not to do," Pip admitted to Megan. "I told them to save her. I said, Bring her back. But she was gone." He wiped his eyes with the sleeve of his sweatshirt.

"It's okay," Megan soothed, again wishing she was with him. "I would have done the same thing."

"It's so sad." He sat back and closed his eyes, his hold on his phone causing Megan's view of him to shift at an angle.

Sunlight coming into the car slanted across his face and he looked as tired as Megan had ever seen him. She wondered how long it had been since he'd slept in a bed.

"I can be there tonight," she offered.

"I'll be okay."

"Tomorrow then."

Eyes still closed, he sniffled and shook his head. "I'll be okay ... I miss you so much. But I'll be back soon. I just have to figure out some stuff ... what needs to be done here. They asked where her body goes and I'm not sure what to do. I have to talk to Aunt Betty. And Uncle Charles. Aunt Betty doesn't even know Nan is dead yet. I called Uncle Charles, but not her. I feel like I need to tell her face to face."

"Is there any way I can help? Whatever you need. Let me know."

He nodded.

"You have to get some sleep," she encouraged softly.

"I will." Opening his eyes to look at her, he took a few quieting breaths, then squinted slightly. "What's around your neck?"

Megan slipped two fingers inside her new necklace and gave it a little stretch. "Present from some kids."

He managed a smile. "Is that candy?"

"Lifesavers."

"That's sweet … if you get hungry you've got a snack."

"That's what they said."

He reclosed his eyes like he might drift off to sleep, then sat forward, shaking that urge. "I need to get to Aunt Betty. My cousin Matt's been by—one of her sons—but he's not really any help."

"Okay. Call me when you can. Or whenever you want."

"I want to hear about your second day."

"I'll tell you all about it."

"Call you back in a little bit."

"I'll be here," she promised.

"I love you."

"Love you, too."

Pip set his phone down but didn't end the call. Nor did Megan. They stayed connected while Pip drove to Aunt Betty's and Megan figured out dinner.

She told him about her first save—not as heroic as she might have imagined, but he said most saves were like that. She told him they were still swimming before work, and everyone missed him. He said his Jeep might be fixable, but the mechanic claimed it was getting to the point where repairs were going to cost more than the vehicle was worth.

Once Pip arrived at Aunt Betty's, he aimed his phone toward the house so Megan could see it: an old four-square in dire need of fresh paint and new windows. He said, "She convinced herself Nan wasn't going to ever get well enough to come home … and I guess maybe she'll be relieved she won't have to worry about getting her in some nursing home. But I think this is still going to be hard."

"I'm imagine so," Megan appreciated.

They shared I love you's and ended the call.

By the time they spoke again hours later, a few details had been worked out and even more were arranged over the next few days:

Pip's Uncle Charles flew up from Florida. Charles wasn't close with Aunt Betty—who was 9 years older—but they did keep in touch and Pip said he had a calming influence on her.

There was going to be a small memorial service for Aunt Nan, to be held at the cemetery where she'd be buried in a family plot alongside her parents. Megan wanted to go, but Pip said the surf patrol needed her more right now than his family, and besides it was going to be a very short service, more for Aunt Betty than anyone because so few of Nan's friends or family were still living or able to get out and about if they were.

One of Aunt Nan's stepdaughters came by Betty's house—Pip described her as the stepchild Nan had been most friendly with—and told Pip she'd talked to her brothers and while they were going to sell the cottage, Pip could stay through the summer. Pip tried to accept the news, having known "that day" would eventually come when he'd have to move out, but Megan could tell the actuality came as a blow. She thought about asking him to move in with her but was unsure how that might affect her getting a divorce, that her chances of Stewart accepting their marriage was over might be compromised if he knew Megan was with someone else. Instead she told Pip they'd figure out something.

She recounted more curious #OCSPMOM tourists stopping by to say hello or take pictures, including one of Megan's students from Villa James and his parents. They were amazed she was on the surf patrol, and when Ricky said, "See you in September," Megan had confirmed she'd be there. Because that was part of the plan she began to see taking shape. A new life. With Pip.

One night when Pip called, Megan was on her balcony, watching a storm out in the ocean. Pip wanted to see the lightning, so Megan aimed her phone toward the horizon.

"Amazing," he commented when a bolt struck the sea.

Quietly, Megan said, "I think if lightning had taken my father, I'd be angry every time I saw it. But you're not."

"My dad loved the power of nature. He was awestruck by it. Storms. Tides. The ocean. Whenever I went in the ocean—from the first time when I was a little kid—he used to tell me it's been here since before people came along and it'll be here long after we're gone…"

Megan loved the quiet calm of Pip's voice.

"…but storms—they were his thing. He loved working in them—especially thunderstorms. He'd say he was going to go ride the lightning bolts. He'd be on storm duty, and I'd lay there in the dark if the power was out. There wouldn't be any lights in the house. The storm would be raging. And after a couple hours, when the lights would flicker back on, I'd smile and picture my dad like he really was riding lightning bolts. And when he'd come home—which might not be for a day or two if it was really bad—I'd run over and tell him great job getting the lights back on. And he'd smile like he was in on a private joke and tell me, 'For now.' Because to my dad, it was just a matter of time before the lights went out again. And one day, he said, they'll go out forever, because nature always wins in the end."

"You still miss your dad," Megan said, able to tell from how Pip talked about him.

"Yeah. Don't you miss yours?"

"Yes … I do. And I hope he knew how much I loved him. Because he told me that all the time. But I don't remember telling him as much as I should have."

"I'll get my dad to make sure he knows."

Megan smiled at the kind thought. "And how will you do that?"

"I think I can see them out there."

Megan played along. "You do? Where?"

"Turn your phone back toward the storm."

Megan did so, holding it steady until a streak of lightning spread over the sky like a crack running through glass.

"There," Pip said. "See them?"

"Riding lightning bolts?"

"And waving to us," Pip said.

That image stayed with Megan throughout the night: her father and Pip's dad, two thunderbolt-riding cowboys harnessing lightning as it kicked hotly across the sky.

The next morning, the ocean was rough, stirred up by the storm Megan and Pip had watched. Adrian decided they wouldn't do their usual pre-work swim, figuring they'd be active throughout the day. And she was right. Adrian and Megan went out on a save as a team and Megan handled a second on her own, needing almost twenty minutes to bring a guy in out of a strong rip current who was not in bad shape but a terrible swimmer.

By the end of the day, Megan was tired but exhilarated. Upstairs in her condo, she went straight to her phone and checked for texts from Pip. It was the day of Aunt Nan's funeral and Megan hoped Pip had gotten through it okay. He'd been upbeat—or tried to be—but Megan could tell the loss was hard for him. And knowing his days at the cottage were coming to an end made the situation worse.

She tried not to worry when there weren't any texts or voice mails on her phone. But when she texted him and he didn't reply, those concerns deepened. All of a sudden, something felt very wrong. It was.

66.

"I can't break up your family." Those were the words that survived the shock and heartbreak. Everything else they said over a sorrowful half hour seemed to blur like grains of sand swirled off the beach and carried away in the wind.

"I fell in love with you the first day I saw you," Pip cried softly. "I don't even think you looked at me. You'd been out in the ocean and when you come back up the beach, I watched you the whole way ... and I knew. And it was so strong I didn't think about whether you were married or—or had a family. And by the time I found out, I was so far gone—so in love with you—I didn't let it matter... And that was wrong... It was so wrong. And then I met Stewart—your husband. And I saw how much he loves you... And you talked to Cassie on the phone... And she was so excited for you. And I tried to pretend—I tried to think about them like they weren't your family. But they are. And I can't take you away from them. I just can't."

Through her tears, Megan did her best to explain how her marriage had grown distant and her feelings for Stewart had changed but realized her actions didn't look that way. She'd flown to California without saying goodbye hours after Pip first kissed her. Then literally run out of Pip's cottage and gone to Stewart when he'd arrived unexpectedly at the beach. "It's not the way it seems," she pleaded. "When you come back, we can go over everything. And make a plan. I don't want Stewart to be hurt. But I don't love him anymore. And I never loved him like I love you. And Cassie—I don't know. I don't think she cares one way or the other—"

"She does."

"And if she does, I'll figure out how to explain it to her. We'll figure it out. When you get back, we can talk, and I can hold onto you, and you'll see..." She stopped and gasped, realizing from the way he was crying and shaking his head the decision he'd made. Feeling her world come apart, tears streaming down her cheeks, she could barely get out the words. "You're not coming back?" Pleading with him. "Oh, Pip, you're not coming back. No, no, you have to. You belong here."

He shook his head and said, "I can't. I can't come back."

#

Curled up on the sofa, Megan cried for a long time. Feelings of loss hollowed deeply inside her, leaving an emptiness she hadn't suffered since her father died.

At some point, she wasn't sure exactly when and had no specific recollection of doing it, she saw on her phone she'd sent Pip a text, *Please come back.*

He didn't answer. Maybe he was already on the plane, heading to Florida with his Uncle Charles. That's where Pip said he was going—because he couldn't keep living like a kid. He needed a career and Uncle Charles was offering him that: to work in his real estate company. And he needed to be able to afford a decent car and a place to live—not hope his Jeep lasted another year and rely upon a kindly aunt who charged cheap rent to let him stay in her little house on the bay.

Near midnight, her tears running dry, Megan pulled on jeans and a t-shirt over the bathing suit she'd never changed out of and left the condo. She didn't want to be there anymore. All the fond memories their place at the beach used to hold were suddenly why she'd lost Pip.

Megan went down the stairwell to her car. No shoes. No license. Just got in her car and drove to Pip's cottage, which sat dark and lonely at the end of the street.

Out of her car, she sat on the front steps in the warm night and listened to other people living their lives, their quiet conversations and laughter. A young couple held hands, walking their small dog.

Half an hour later, a car turned onto the side street, coming toward her. Megan shielded her eyes against its headlights as the vehicle's tires crunched onto the oyster shell driveway. The engine and lights went off and Kelly got out.

In his chef's jacket and checkered pants he came to Megan and offered his hand to help her up. "Sad day, my love," he said somberly.

They hugged and she nodded against his shoulder, beginning to cry again. "You talked to Pip?"

"Mm-hm."

"I don't understand."

"I know," Kelly sighed. They went inside and he switched on lights.

The door to the front downstairs bedroom was open, the furniture gone.

Megan sniffled. "Where's Ben?"

"Milford, Delaware."

"He moved out?"

"Two days ago." Kelly continued toward the kitchen. "He's been looking for a place for a while and a guy he does work for offered him a rent-to-buy deal. So he took it. We've known our days were numbered here before Nan got sick."

Megan sat with her elbows on the table, covering her face with her hands. "This is my fault."

"Nonsense." Kelly opened the refrigerator, and like every good cook asked if she had eaten.

"I'm not hungry."

"Not the question. Have you eaten?" He brought out a carton of eggs and checked his watch. "In eight hours you have to be at work. Hungry or not, you eat."

"I miss him so much. I just want him back."

"I know." Kelly cracked half a dozen eggs with one hand and whisked them in a large bowl. "Omelets for two." He turned on the range, added a hunk of butter to a pan and as that melted and began to sizzle, he expertly chopped mushrooms and green pepper, which he sauteed until soft, then slid them onto a plate and cooked the eggs, adding the vegetables back as he flipped and folded the eggs into a fluffy envelope and served. "I'd offer wine, but nights like this, the bottle tends not to have a bottom."

Hands still covering her face, Megan asked if he thought Pip might come back.

Kelly took a deep breath and exhaled slowly. "I don't know. Like I said, we knew this day was coming. Not you, of course. No one could have predicted you. But living here...? The thing about endless summers is ... they end. Of course," Kelly added in his philosophical tone, "this Florida..." He searched for the right word, finally deciding on: "...thing. I blame Uncle Charles."

Megan lowered her hands. "You know Pip's uncle?"

"Not to pick out in a line-up, but I know of him. About him." Kelly spoke with disdain. "He is very successful and very one-minded. A his-way-or-the-highway type. He's been after Pip to give up this—what did he call it?—little boy's beach life, I think he said, and get a real job—been after him to do that for years." Kelly nudged Megan's plate closer to her. "Before it gets cold."

Megan picked up her fork and sliced off a soft edge of omelet. "Thank you," she appreciated.

"Then again," Kelly appraised, "it could all have as much to do with me. I was married—did you know that?"

Eating slowly, Megan nodded.

"And she fell in love with someone else?"

She nodded again. "Pip told me."

"I've never gotten over it. Still have dark spells now and again. And Pip usually gets stuck having to pull me out through the other side—although I'm getting better bringing myself back to the surface. But what Pip probably doesn't know—because I've never told him, at least I don't think—is that I don't blame the guy my wife fell in love with. I blame love. Because while love is a wonderful and powerful force, it can also be brutally cold. Because it can turn off. And when it does, it's gone. And there's nothing you can do about that— try as you may. I also believe if you're in love—if you're truly in love—you're not going to fall in love with someone else. That only happens when love is gone." Kelly tried to smile. "The world according to me."

Megan fell into a stare. After a few minutes of quiet, she asked, "Can I stay here? I don't want to go back to my place."

"Certainly."

She ate some more, then closed her eyes. "I'm so tired. And I'm so sad." She began to cry. "I'm so sad."

"Okay. Come on." He took her fork when it seemed too heavy for her to hold any longer. "You're going to be okay."

"I want to sleep in Pip's bed. And snap my fingers and he'll come back, and we'll run off like we talked about."

"Okay."

"I'm going to go to bed now." She pushed back from the table and moved unsteadily for the stairs.

Kelly said, "Let me know if you need anything."

67.

Megan fell asleep in Pip's bed only to awaken after an hour. Immediately, she reached for her phone, hoping Pip had changed his mind and was coming back. Notifications of incoming texts proved no more than false hope. She scrolled quickly through a handful of messages, some from friends who'd just found out about #OCSPMOM, but nothing from Pip.

Megan laid back and stared into the dark angles of the peaked ceiling. She was confused and hurt how Pip could leave her like this.

When she'd gone off to California without saying goodbye it had been to avoid the temptation she hadn't realized was drawing her in until Pip kissed her—and even then she hadn't truly accepted it. She certainly hadn't appreciated she might be falling in love with him—or that he'd fallen in love with her. It had seemed like a fling—a beach romance maybe—because the truth seemed so unlikely.

So she'd fled to what she'd assumed was the safety of her marriage, only to be reminded how that union—that family— was no longer what it had once been. How Stewart and Cassie had eagerly started new lives that left her behind—although, in fairness to them both, the choices they made were natural progressions their lives had set years earlier. Stewart had worked hard to build his business while Cassie had studied as determinedly as she'd played lacrosse, always talking about going away to college.

But no amount of planning had prepared her for the loneliness of being by herself. Again, though, from Stewart's perspective, it had been her choice to stay in Maryland when he'd wanted—assumed even—she'd join him in Scottsdale. Even if he hadn't exactly been candid with her about moving, making it seem as though Arizona was temporary, because he'd known Megan hadn't wanted to leave their home in Hunt Valley.

Now, in Pip's bed, awake in the quiet after midnight, Megan considered maybe what she hadn't wanted to admit to herself over the past year was that she'd fallen out of love with Stewart before he ever mentioned moving to the desert southwest.

And she had been in love with Stewart—maybe not at first, not the way she'd instantly adored little Cassie—but she had loved him. A different kind of love—if that was possible—than what she felt for Pip. Because it had never been just her and Stewart. Cassie had always been a dominant presence in their relationship. They were always a trio—never a pair.

With Pip, when she was with him, it was as if there was no one else in the world. It was just them.

Eventually, she fell back to sleep, but again just for a little while, and again reached for her phone as soon as she reawakened—a pattern that continued until just after 7:00 when Kelly called up the stairs, making sure she was awake:

"Time to get ready for work, rosebud."

"I'm awake. Thanks." Out of bed, she quickly showered and put on the one-piece bathing suit that had dried on her yesterday.

Downstairs, Kelly sleepily offered coffee, which Megan politely declined. "I'm a tea person."

"Noted," he responded, looking as if this was well before his usual wake-up time, his eyes heavy, thick black hair uncombed, wearing a rumpled grey t-shirt and string-tie pajama bottoms. "Breakfast?"

She greatly appreciated his concern. "A little peanut butter."

"Joy..." he responded wryly.

She went into the pantry, which looked sparse. "I'll stop by the store and get us some stuff."

"You can leave a list and I'll shop. You live here, the kitchen is my domain, woman. You can pitch in some shekels."

Megan managed half a smile, digging a spoon into what was left of the peanut butter.

"At least you didn't use your fingers," Kelly commented watching her. "You going to be okay today?"

She nodded.

"I work dinner tonight, but I'll leave you something in the fridge with instructions."

"Thanks." She put her spoon in the dishwasher and headed out the door. Driving to her building with the car windows down, she noticed for the first time it was a beautiful, sunny morning.

She retrieved her life buoy and carry bag from the condo and went down the stairs and onto the beach. Adrian, Art, and Will were already there, looking uncertain and forlorn. Will, with his hood up and hands in his pockets, walked slowly in small circles, bare feet kicking at the sand. Art had his head down, rubbing the back of his neck. Adrian stared off toward the dunes.

Megan could tell they all knew Pip was gone and she was most concerned how Adrian would react—that she might blame her for Pip's decision. But the girl came to Megan with open arms and drew her into a warm embrace. "I was worried you might not come back either."

Holding onto Adrian, Megan felt her eyes begin to water. "I'm not going anywhere."

Arms around one another, leaning shoulder to shoulder, they walked slowly to Will and Art.

Will's eyes were red, looking beseechingly at Megan. "Why is he leaving? I don't understand."

Megan felt the age difference between them more than before. The three surf patrol guards were fit and better swimmers, which had made her feel as if she was aspiring to be more like them. Now, she sensed them looking to her, someone who could offer answers or at least guidance. Even Adrian, always so confident and self-assured in her view of the world, seemed shaken.

But before Megan could answer, Art, usually the quiet one, said, "I'm surprised he stayed this long, really. My first year, we were cutting back after Labor Day, moving stands farther apart, and he said he wouldn't be here next summer. Said he was going to work for his uncle." Art chuckled fondly. "Then he said the same thing again last year. I asked around and he'd been saying that for as long as anyone could remember."

Adrian said, "I thought he'd always be here. I've known him since I was fourteen. When he was down on fiftieth street, where we stayed every summer."

"What's his uncle do?" Will's question sounded like an accusation.

Adrian answered, "Develops real estate. Owns apartment buildings."

"What's so great about that?"

"It makes money."

Listening to them, Megan realized she didn't have answers they might be looking for. She might not have known Pip as well as they did—certainly hadn't known him nearly as long. She just loved him.

#

Bill Clary was watching the four lifeguards from his townhouse deck when Mary Jane joined him. "Something's wrong with our Megan's group out there," he said, coffee cup in hand.

Mary Jane still wasn't comfortable with her husband referring to a virtual stranger the way they used to talk about their daughter. But his grief fluctuated in waves, even all these years after Penny's death, and if this young woman offered some solace, Mary Jane wasn't going to scold him for it. Not this late in life.

"Looks like they're at a funeral," Bill commented. "And Pip's still not there. Something's going on."

"What'd you say she told you the other day, his aunt was sick?"

"This's more than that."

"Don't go butting in. It's not your business."

"Yep."

Mary Jane knew a rhetorical response when she heard one. "Well … you're going to stay out here, move back in the shade or you're going to need another Mohs procedure. Hat's not covering your nose."

#

It felt good to be back in the water. Swimming.

Megan thought the ocean would feel cold now that Pip wasn't coming back. The way she assumed it would be cloudy today, maybe raining. But the ocean temperature was mild. The waves were small. The current was calm. And sunlight sparkled across the surface.

Adrian led them on an easy pace and when she slowed and began to tread water, Megan thought she was taking them to shore already. Then she saw the fin. Then another. And another. More and more. Coming at them.

A pod of dolphins, sleek backs gently arching out of the water, swam so close Megan reached out in amazement and brushed her hand along one's dense flank, feeling the animal's strength when its tail slapped back into the ocean and splashed her.

"Wow," Will called. "Are you seeing this?"

Adrian swam around in place. "Incredible. You hear them squeaking?"

"Talking to us," Art said happily.

336

When the animals' long grey faces came out of the water, they looked to be smiling.

Megan touched another sleek fin and momentarily held onto it, feeling herself pulled along as if taking a ride before letting go.

As the last of the pod continued effortlessly by, the tinny echoes of their chatter began to fade.

"That," Will exclaimed, "was wild. I wonder if there's more." He craned his thin neck to peer in the direction from which they'd come.

Art said, "I lost count at twenty-six. I've never seen that many at one time."

Adrian said, "Let's do a hard sprint, see if we can catch them."

"Yeah, right," Art laughed.

But Adrian was already swimming.

They never got close. But that hadn't been the point. It was the joy of connecting to animals that didn't just visit the ocean for vacation but lived there.

In front of Megan's building, the four guards came out of the ocean, breathless but enlivened by the experience. Then they saw Pip's stand, back by the dunes, and were reminded he wasn't going to be there.

Pip's guard stand remained empty throughout the morning, and when no one came to substitute for him, Will and Art shifted their stands closer together to cover Pip's beach.

"At least it's quiet today," Adrian said to Megan.

An hour later, Captain Garrison arrived on a four-wheeler he dismounted in front of Adrian's stand. Businesslike, the head of the surf patrol pointed at Megan. "You ready be on your own?"

Before Megan could answer, Adrian said, "She's ready."

"Take Pippinger's stand," he instructed Megan. "That's your beach now."

Megan jumped off the stand, landing softly and reaching for her carry bag.

"Don't do that," Garrison barked. "You come down off there like that and blow out a knee, someone drowns 'cause you can't get to them and/or I'm down another guard."

"Sorry." Megan slung her bag strap over her shoulder.

"Copy Pippinger's good habits, not his bad ones."

"Sorry," Megan apologized again, grabbing her buoy.

"Adrian," Garrison continued, "you're a lieutenant. Don't thank me. The pay raise isn't commensurate with the added responsibility. You got from Will up to eighty-fifth. Here's a phone." He handed a mobile up to Adrian. "I'm going up to let the rest of your group know. Don't be too much of a hard ass. But anyone gives you trouble, tell me."

"Got it," Adrian acknowledged.

Megan set off at an easy run along the water's edge, feet pushing off firm sand, heading toward Pip's stand. Her stand. Her beach.

Art stood and flapped his semaphore flags at her, smiling as she trotted by, calling congratulations, "Shortest probationary period in surf patrol history. Go OCSP Mom."

A glimmer of pride rose through the heartache that wrapped around her like a shroud and with that came hope—that maybe Pip would come back. That he'd get to Florida and change his mind. Unless it had all been a lie ... unless he hadn't really loved her at all ... and it had just been something to tell her ... just a beach romance after all. A thought that hurt to her core and she tried to push away.

She trotted two blocks without breaking stride. By the dunes, she settled her back against Pip's guard stand and tipped it forward. Pip made it seem light. It wasn't. Her knees buckled as the hard planks dropped the stand's weight heavily on her shoulders. She heard herself grunt as she dug her feet in and tried to drag the stand on its two front legs, at first thinking she wasn't going to be able to do it, then it began to move. Only she wasn't navigating an empty beach but needed to weave through blankets and umbrellas and tourists working on their tans.

338

"Coming through, folks," she warned as she kicked up sand, starting to breath hard and not wanting to show it.

It took ten minutes to get the stand in position. Pip usually did it in less than one. She set her buoy and climbed to the top. Stood tall in the sunshine. Sweating, Megan whistled to Will, flagging the quick signal that let him know she was on duty. Once he acknowledged her, she turned north and sent the same message to Art.

She surveyed the ocean, checking who was in the water and how far out they were, making sure there were no surprise rip currents. Then she checked the beach around her. Her beach.

Lulu, out from beneath the shade of her rental umbrellas, smiled and waved, having captured it all on her phone, readying to post #OCSPMOM gets her own beach!

#

Megan didn't want the day to end. Work kept her thoughts from dwelling entirely on Pip.

But as shade cast by her building slid across the beach and Lulu began rounding up her umbrellas and chairs, Megan's thoughts turned darker. The rays of hope she'd been trying to find, envisioning being back together with Pip, seemed less possible.

Fifteen minutes before the end of her workday, a trio of surfers arrived and started their readying ritual, attaching leashes to their ankles and checking over boards already waxed and scuffed with age. They moved into ankle deep water, boards under their arms and when one gave Megan a glance, checking if she was going to make them wait until 5:00, she smiled and shook her head:

"Not on my first day solo, guys. Sorry. Maybe tomorrow." Deciding that even though few people remained on the beach, and no one was in the ocean. Pip would have let them in.

But Pip also jumped off his stand instead of climbing down the rungs. Which, contrary to Captain Garrison's order, Megan did again once Will flagged the day's-end signal. And while easily vaulting off her stand was technically an act of disobedience, it made her feel closer to Pip.

She dragged Pip's stand—her stand—back to the dunes, now fully in shade, already making quicker work of that than earlier.

Lulu, in a fire-engine red bikini, snapped shut the lock on the storage box where she kept her supplies and waved to Megan. "You good Mrs. M?"

"Have a nice night, Lulu."

"See you tomorrow."

Megan started toward her building but stopped hearing Adrian call her name. The surf patrol's newest lieutenant and Art were jogging toward her, so Megan met them halfway.

Adrian said, "We're thinking about going to Half Shell."

"Clams casino," Art smiled.

"Join us?"

"I'd like that, but I've got a student at seven. And Kelly said something about leaving me dinner."

"Kelly?" Adrian's dark eyebrows raised with surprise.

"I kind of moved into Pip's bedroom."

"Really?"

Megan shrugged a shoulder toward her building. "I didn't want to be here last night."

"But Kelly?—God, he's so weird. Always flirting. And talks like, I don't know what that is—like he's at some renaissance fare or something."

Art said, "I like him. And he makes this incredible crab imperial."

"He's different," Megan appreciated. "Could we do dinner tomorrow?"

"Yeah—sure. How would you feel about inviting some other people who knew Pip?"

"That would be nice."

Adrian hugged her. "Good first day on your own."

"Thanks," Megan appreciated. She went upstairs to check her phone, which had taken a lot of willpower not to sneak into her bag, knowing she'd have reached for it with every incoming text or call, wanting it to be Pip.

She was no sooner inside her condo than her phone chimed.

68.

"Swimming with dolphins," Stewart exclaimed. Someone had posted video of Megan and the other guards in the ocean that morning, capturing them in the middle of the dolphin pod. It hadn't taken long for someone else to tag that video #OCSPMOM. "Cassie just sent it to me." Half kidding, Stewart said, "I'm never going to get you away from that beach."

Megan wanted to tell him she wasn't going to California. And that she didn't love him anymore. But she couldn't make the words come out.

"You're becoming a celebrity," Stewart added. "Jackie Mack wants to brand you."

Megan thought both ideas were awful but didn't need to fashion a response.

Stewart moved on to the true purpose of his call, asking if she'd read Georgianne Trimball's email.

It took Megan a moment to recall who that was: the Realtor. "I don't have my phone with me on the beach. And I just came up." She checked her phone and saw dozens of unread texts and far more emails than the usual influx of junk. Also voice mails, including one from Jillian. And another from Alice at Villa James. Jillian would want to chat. Alice would want to know if Megan was coming back to teach—school started in six weeks. Nothing from Pip. "Do I need to read whatever it is now? I've got a student—"

"Save you the trouble. Georgianne's got a buyer for the house. First couple saw it has made a full-asking offer. As-is.

No inspections. No contingencies. Settle in thirty days. And any stuff we don't want to move out is fine for us to leave. Is that fantastic!"

"Yeah…" Instead of dealing with the truth, Megan forced enthusiasm, pulling out a dining room chair so she could sit down.

"Look—I'll call back tonight. I'm between meetings but wanted to make sure you knew the good news."

"Great." She made that sound as positive as she could. "Okay—thanks." She leaned her elbow on the table, supporting her arm as she rubbed her fingers across her forehead.

"Talk to you later."

"Okay…"

Megan set her phone down.

Certain changes made life seem unreal—as if it wasn't happening. Maybe it was a reaction to trauma. For days after her father died, she'd seemed to drift unconnected, the sounds of other peoples' voices echoing emptily in her head. Now, the actuality of selling their house, even when she'd known it would happen—they'd signed the listing contract just last weekend—the actual process moving forward was disorienting. It was sad. She knew that part of her life was over, but emotionally there was still a connection it was painful to lose, and every reminder triggered those feelings.

She got up from the table, showered and rinsed out her suit. In a clean t-shirt and shorts, she drove to Pip's cottage.

Kelly had left her pot roast for dinner, portioned in a Le Creuset cocotte, along with a small field green salad topped with blueberries and sunflower seeds and a side of basil vinaigrette. Kelly included written instructions for heating the pot roast on the stove that included a note of apology that managed to make her smile: These directions may be unnecessary for a woman of your caliber, but keep in mind I have been living with kitchen-impaired savages.

Normally, pot roast would have been too heavy for a summer meal, but Megan had eaten sparsely over the past 24 hours and used up a lot of calories. She ate on the back steps, a cloth napkin spread over her lap, and watched small boats skim along on the bay as the sun descended into distant trees on the mainland.

August sunsets were different than July, the horizon sometimes blanketed with clouds that erased color from the sky. Tonight, though, shades of purple and orange swirled in a bold and spectacular show.

After dinner, Megan remained on the porch to teach her online student and after that thirty-minute session she video-chatted with the girl's mother. News of Megan joining the surf patrol had continued making its way through Villa James. "What on earth made you think you could do that?" the girl's mother asked, a woman close to Megan's age who Megan—rightly or wrongly—associated with an older generation of less confident moms—nothing like she assumed Cassie and her friends would become. "Although I guess if anyone could do it, it would be you," her student's mom said. "You were always so fit. Taking the kids on all those hikes and skating."

As with the reporter the other day, Megan wanted to say her reason was, "Pip," but instead replied that it just seemed like it might be fun.

Setting aside her iPad after saying goodbye, Megan cleaned up from dinner, washing and drying everything by hand and trying to figure where Kelly kept things.

As the sky darkened, she unloaded boxes of kitchen wares from their house in Hunt Valley that had been in the Volvo's trunk since last Sunday and brought them inside along with some of her clothes. The kitchen stuff she left in boxes on the table for Kelly to go through. Her clothes she carried upstairs and put into Pip's closet and made room in dresser drawers, pushing aside hangers of his shirts and pants he'd left behind.

It struck her how few clothes he had. A handful of shirts that buttoned. Some jeans, chinos. Maybe a dozen t-shirts. A few sweatshirts and shorts. Bathing suits. A pair of hiking sandals. Canvas tennis shoes. Scuffed Nikes with laces turned brown, the way Cassie's used to get from the dirt of playing fields. At least a third of his wardrobe was imprinted with the OCSP logo, and some of that was worn to the point of being ragged. Only his underwear was new, some of that still in a bag that made her wonder if it had been a recent purchase for her benefit. There wasn't anything suitable for what her mother used to refer to as, "dressing up." All of which made her miss him even more—if that was possible.

She sat on his bed and took a selfie she texted him with a message: *Moving in. Hope you're okay. Love you.*

There was so much more she wanted to say, hoping to convince him to come back, but what could she add to all they'd talked about yesterday? And was it just yesterday? It felt like a month ago. If Pip was going to return, it would be because despite all the complications of their relationship that he couldn't live without her. Or so she told herself. So she hoped. Having no way of knowing about the proposition Pip's Uncle Charles had given him.

#

Megan spent most of the rest of the evening on her phone.

She replied to texts, sending more than generic snippets to people who'd gotten in touch because they'd heard about her joining the surf patrol.

She called Jillian, wondering how she was going to continue to avoid mentioning Pip to her best friend—a feat that being miles apart had made easier so far—only Jillian was working on a contract she wanted to present that night, and with apologies no longer necessary because they'd known one another so long said she'd call Megan back tomorrow or the next day.

When she phoned Alice, Villa James' director told Megan she looked splendid. They were on a voice call, but Alice was referring to a picture of Megan that Cassie had posted. "OCSP Mom. Good for you. Very impressive."

Megan felt comforted by Alice's voice. "Thanks. Are you still in New England?"

"No—back at school."

"Did you have a good time?"

"Very nice. A bit warmer than usual, but also drier. Now I'm back in the humidity. No more sleeping with opened windows." After a brief pause, Alice got to the business at hand: "I have to ask, of course, and you know this is coming…"

"Yes…" Megan sighed with regret.

"Oh, I was hoping not to hear that tone. But I'm not surprised. Are you sure? I can give you a few more days to think about it. The students will miss you. I'll miss you. Don't say no just yet."

"Okay…"

"Is this … does this have to do with your … new friend?"

"He's gone," Megan said. "To Florida, with his uncle. To work there. But that's also complicated."

"I see." After another pause, Alice surprised Megan, saying, "I suppose the sex was wonderful."

"Everything about him was wonderful. I want him back."

"Mm, my … you have really burned down the forest, haven't you?"

"I don't know what you mean."

"My mother used to tell me a story … about a little boy lost in the forest—she always used forest when it was going to be a scary story. Have you noticed how that happens? How woods are friendly and full of hopping bunnies and blue birds and deer, and forests are inhabited by goblins and witches and wolves. Anyway, this little boy, lost in the forest—it's a perfectly fine evening, the moon is full so he can see his way, but he's still alone and it's starting to feel a little cool—not cold, but the hint of a chill. And he decides it would be nice to have a fire to sit by. So he gathers some dry lengths of grass he puts in a pile, then collects some brittle twigs he sets on top of that, then finds two small branches that have fallen off a dead tree and rubs them together hard as he can, and pretty soon, because it's been so dry, the friction of the branches gets hot, and he sets fire to the bits of grass. And the grass catches the sticks on fire. And pretty soon, he's warm as toast. Only then he decides he's thirsty, so he goes off looking for some water, in a creek or stream maybe. And while he's away from the fire, because it's been so dry, the fire spreads and the entire forest burns." Alice paused, then appraised, "I thought that was a ridiculous story the first time I heard it—when I was ten, I believe. Because the boy was alone in the forest. He was lost. And he was cold. It doesn't matter he wasn't going to freeze to death, does it? What was he supposed to do? And he's young, he doesn't know about the dangers of fire. And I told my mother that, and you know what she said? She said, but the forest still burned down, didn't it?"

#

When Stewart called half an hour later, Megan was still on the back steps of Pip's cottage, watching the starlit bay. Since Stewart only made voice calls—not video chats—she didn't worry about what he might see in the background behind her.

She thought he did an admirable job concealing disappointment when she admitted not yet having gone over the contract for their house. "It's pretty straightforward," Stewart encouraged. "And I don't think we want to let these two get away."

"I'll do it as soon as we hang up."

"We can go over it page by page," he offered.

"I'll just sign it."

"You click the link in her email, and it opens the document and takes you to the first item to initial, then goes through the rest one at a time, and at the end you click submit and it's done."

"Okay."

"It's going to be great out here," he said, upbeat.

"I think so." She knew that was misleading, but meant that for his sake—that California, working for Dunhill, would be wonderful for him. She had no interest in being there with him, but still couldn't make those words come out.

"If you have any trouble with the electronic signing, call me back. I'm heading to dinner with one of the Talbot-Glen principals—one of the good guys—but we can talk if you need anything."

"I'm sure it'll be fine." She got up and opened the screen door and went inside. "I'll do it now."

"Fantastic. Talk to you soon. Love you."

"Love you, too," she made herself echo.

Megan made room on the kitchen table, moving one of the boxes from their house in Hunt Valley to the floor, and opened her iPad. Finding the real estate agent's email, she opened the link and scrolled quickly through the document, digitally initialing or signing when prompted, and hitting the submit button at the end. It was done in five minutes.

She went back outside with her phone and watched the bay. Hoping Pip would call.

She was still there an hour later when Kelly came home from the restaurant. When he found her outside, she thanked him for dinner and asked about his night.

"For being short one line cook and two wait staff, not disastrous. Typical August when the group who've just started to get broken in decide they're restless and don't want to work, just play until it's time to pack up and head back to school." He gestured to her phone. "Any word from Pip?"

She shook her head.

He patted her shoulder. "Well, tomorrow's another day."

As he retreated inside, Megan asked after him, through the screen. "Was it just a summer fling? Pip and me? What's the saying you all have," Megan asked, "until Sunday? Is that all we were?"

Kelly came back outside and sat beside her, his chef's jacket carrying aromas of garlic and spices. "Don't do that. Don't try to believe that to get over him."

Megan looked across tall cat tails waving lightly in the shallows, pushed by the flow of the tide. "I didn't give us a chance, did I? We didn't have enough time. I thought we'd have until the end of summer. Then Stewart came back, and Pip met him. And Aunt Nan got sick. We didn't have enough time," she repeated.

"Circumstances were not in your favor."

"It's like it was over before I knew what was happening. I didn't act fast enough."

"You fell in love."

"Is that my excuse?"

"I think so."

She tilted her eyes up toward the stars. "I don't want to be sad for the rest of my life, Kelly. I don't want to always wonder what could have been."

"That's the curse of the romantic," he pontificated. "Because there's always a life that could have been. What if you and Pip had run off and you woke up one morning and thought you'd made a mistake. Then you'd wonder how it would have been if you'd stayed with your husband."

"Are you saying it was a mistake?"

"Didn't you ever worry it might be?" he asked frankly. "Didn't you have that thought at least in the back of your head? Wondering? As intense as it may have felt, were you a hundred percent sure? Was it worth the gamble? Worth walking away from your marriage for some guy you'd only known, barely a month. Maybe a year from now you're in California or wherever your husband is, and you're thinking, phew, that was almost a really dumb thing I did."

"Is that what you think?"

"I'm asking if it's what you thought?"

"Was Pip was thinking that? Is that why he isn't coming back?"

"I doubt it, although I guess it's possible. I think you're being married was the big issue. Beyond that, who knows. He may have thought there was no way you could have the kind of life with him you have now. And I know you are not about material things, possessions, whatever you want to call them, but go upstairs and open his desk drawer and you will see, in a few sheets of paper, his net worth is so squeaky close to zero that net worth is hardly the appropriate term. We live paycheck to paycheck here. We pay rent that's dimes on the dollar what it should be. We drive old cars. We don't travel. We don't eat out much. We work side jobs. Ben kept this place running mechanically. And our prospects aren't lining up to make much of a change. Not to mention, we're getting older."

Megan countered with her own reality. "I don't love my husband anymore. I don't want to stay married to him. With or without Pip."

"Then I suggest you divorce well. Maybe you should go out to California and avail yourself of what I understand to be that state's very favorable community property laws. One of the restaurant owners used to live in Huntington Beach and curses the place every chance he gets."

"I don't want to go through that."

"Understood—you still need to talk to a lawyer. Take it from someone who's been through it."

Megan shook her head as Kelly went inside. There had to be another way.

#

For the second night in a row, Megan was tired but couldn't sleep more than an hour at a time before anxious thoughts brought her awake.

In the morning, she lacked energy, but managed to keep up with the other three guards in the ocean, and that exertion helped steady her thinking.

Work was further welcome distraction. The ocean remained calm and there weren't any calls for saves. Even more people stopped by her stand, at least a dozen from her building who'd just found out she was the new guard stationed on their beach. Some asked what happened to Pip.

Then, just after two in the afternoon, someone approached her guard stand from behind and happily called up to her, "Hey, M, don't you answer your phone anymore?"

Cassie.

69.

Megan still felt a swell of love whenever she saw Cassie or heard from her after they'd been apart for a while—even if that separation was only a few hours. She used to feel it every morning when Cassie was a little girl and Megan gently coaxed her awake, even when needing to jostle her out of bed in her early teenaged years, those efforts sometimes having turned into wrestling matches that made them both laugh and caused Stewart to tell them they were goofy. (He actually used to refer to them as "lunatics," as in "What are you two lunatics doing up there?" until Cassie scolded that wasn't an appropriate word).

In public, Megan had needed to tone down her displays of affection as Cassie had grown older. No more wrapping her up in hugs once Cassie turned ten and squirmed from that embrace, telling Megan she was embarrassing her in front of her friends. And no more holding hands when they walked through the mall. Over the years, as those layers of temperance piled one atop the other, Megan sometimes felt as if Cassie was pushing her away.

Now though, seeing Cassie for the first time since driving her to the airport in California weeks ago, Megan felt that same warm rush of love she experienced the first day she picked her up and held her in her arms, as if her feelings for Cassie were and always had been instinctual.

"Hey, Cass!" Megan leapt off the side of her perch, landed agilely in front of Cassie and gave her a hug.

Cassie hugged her back, laughing, "Oh, my God, you are so sticky!"

Megan started to draw back but Cassie held onto her.

"No, no. It's fine. It's cool actually. You look great. Look at this new haircut." Cassie leaned back just enough to survey Megan through stylish sunglasses. "I saw you'd gone short in the pics being posted, but it looks really good."

"Thanks. You look good, too."

"And this tan." Wearing a plain sea-blue t-shirt and Billabong shorts, Cassie compared arms side by side, briefly lifting her sunglasses to determine the actual differences in their skin tones. "I've got some serious catching up to do."

"It's so good to see you."

"I've been wanting to come down, but good stuff was going on at work, so it was like, do I stay, do I go? I think they might offer me a job."

"Really?"

"Not full-time. Nothing that would cut into school—which starts in three weeks, already, if you can believe that. It would be mostly remote stuff. Maybe an evening or weekend here and there. I don't know. We'll see. Nothing's definite." Cassie held her sandals by two fingers looped through the ankle strap. "It was just floated out there—a would-I-be-interested kind of thing. Of course, I am. But we'll see. Anyway…" Cassie waved her hand as if brushing those thoughts aside. "…this is kind of a semi-summer break week at work. And most of the team I'm with has scattered and are working remotely, so I ended up at the office pretty much by myself this morning, and Dorin said if I felt like taking off, I could. So … here I am. I texted you a few times…"

"Oh, sorry. We're not supposed to have personal phones while we're working."

"Okay—that's kind of old school. Is that even legal?" Cassie half joked.

A sing-song cheer sounded behind them. "Cassie Tyler!" It was Lulu, striding across hot sand, arms outstretched.

"Lulu! You're here!"

The two girls embraced, and Cassie laughed. "You're as gross as her. How much tanning oil have you got on, girl?"

Lulu kept hold of Cassie, bouncing her up and down and repeating her name: "Cassie Tyler. Cassie Tyler."

Megan loved seeing them together.

"Come back and sit with me," Lulu invited. "I haven't seen you in forever. I need to know everything that's going on."

"All right. Let me go upstairs and get a suit. Maybe throw this t-shirt away," Cassie teased, seeing her top blotted with suntan oil.

"Oh, here, have some more." Lulu hugged her again, purposefully rubbing against her.

Cassie reached playfully for Megan. "Guard! Help! Save me! I'm being attacked by a grease shark."

Lulu released her with a gentle shove. "Go get your suit on. Be quick."

Cassie started toward their building.

Megan called after her, "You have a key?"

"Yep."

"Have you had lunch?"

Cassie turned and walked backwards a few steps. "Kicken Chicken on the way down. Pics'll be on your phone once you're..." Cassie made air quotes. "...off duty."

Megan smiled and waved, then called a quiet, "Lu?" to the beachstand girl, who remained nearby.

"What's up?"

"Don't mention anything to Cassie about Pip, okay?"

Lulu scowled fondly. "As if..."

#

When fifteen minutes passed and Cassie hadn't returned to the beach, Megan experienced a swirl of panic. What if Cassie picked up her phone and saw her texts with Pip—a string Megan hadn't been deleting. Not that Cassie had a history of snooping, but it could be an innocent discovery, perhaps hearing Megan's phone ping and wanting to let her know she had a message. And her phone probably would be alerting to incoming texts and emails, given the recent influx of communications from people she hadn't heard from in months, or even years.

Megan also figured she needed to prepare excuses why the air-conditioning was set high, and the refrigerator was so empty.

It was almost 3:00 before Cassie reappeared, coming over the dunes in a swimsuit Megan recognized from two years ago, a pink floral print over a black background with boy short bottoms and a bandeau top. Cassie carried a towel and beach bag.

When Megan waved to her, Cassie waved back in what Megan optimistically took to be a cheerful manner, probably not the mood of someone who'd just discovered her mother had been with another man. Megan exhaled and sat down, facing the ocean, legs dangling over the edge of her stand. Checking behind her, she saw Cassie settle under an umbrella with Lulu.

Half an hour later, Cassie came alongside Megan's stand. Sunglasses off, shading her eyes as she looked up at her, she asked, "So how far is it you swim in the morning?"

"Depends. Two or three blocks."

Cassie looked at the ocean, the small blue waves breaking close to shore where little kids hopped in place or ran squealing as if the sea was chasing them. Beyond the breakers, vacationers lulled on plastic rafts or stood in chest-deep water, unbothered by riptides.

"Okay," Cassie estimated. "Here goes." She started toward the water with the determined stride Megan recognized from her lacrosse days.

"Go south, Cass," Megan called after her, pointing. "That way." Giving her the advantage of the tide moving gently in that direction.

Megan watched Cassie make her way into the ocean, doing the near universal lift up onto her toes, arms out of the water, when the first little swell broke across her midsection. The water wasn't cold—in the low 70's—but still felt chilly to sun-warmed skin.

After gliding over a few waves, Cassie went under one and surfaced, pulling back her dark hair. She swam out to deeper water—the point where guards kept closer watch and might warn people in—and started doing a freestyle stroke.

Megan flagged Will, letting him know a swimmer was coming his way. Adding: My daughter.

Will stood and surveyed Cassie's approach.

It wasn't long before Cassie needed to draw a breath on every pull of her right arm. The initial pace she set slowed. Not quite halfway to Will's stand, she stopped and tread water, looking as if checking her progress. Megan sensed her disappointment.

Not far beyond Will's stand, Cassie checked her location again, then re-started after a brief pause only to stop a couple minutes later and swim in. She started back up the beach on foot, hands on hips, wandering a bit side to side like someone catching their breath.

Will spoke to her as she walked by. She stopped and chatted with him a while, and Megan recognized their animated movements as flirtatious, with Will leaning far forward and Cassie shading her eyes with one hand, hip cocked.

When Cassie continued toward Megan, she was careful to walk around sandcastles and messages people had engraved in the sand with seashells.

"Pretty good," Megan complimented when Cassie was in earshot.

"That was shit," Cassie complained, then apologized to a little girl with a plastic shovel who'd heard that. "Sorry. Don't say that word."

"No," Megan said of Cassie's effort, "that's a decent distance."

"I was as good as done halfway before I stopped."

"Well, you are supposed to run back. At least jog."

Cassie groaned, then dropped to a sitting position alongside Megan's stand and leaned back on her elbows. After a moment, she smiled and looked up at Megan. "This is so wild."

"What?"

"You're a lifeguard." Cassie shook her head. "It's very cool. Kind of amazing, actually. But ... like ... out of nowhere."

"I started swimming again at Villa James over the winter. And kept that up once I got down here. And one thing kind of lead to another."

"There's swimming..." Cassie commented, then nodded toward the ocean. "...but that's swimming."

Lulu strutted by toting chairs she was collecting from folks finished for the day. "Want one?" she offered Cassie.

"I'm good—thanks."

"See you tomorrow?"

"Yep."

"Cool."

Megan asked, "How long are you down for?"

"Couple days, I guess," Cassie responded. "That okay?"

"Of course. The whole summer would have been fine. You know that." Megan wondered how different the past couple months would have been had Cassie been with her from the beginning.

Megan was happy she was here. But it felt strange, as if she was looking back in time at a life she used to have—then realized Cassie *was* still her life. Pip had come along, but Cassie—and Stewart—were her life. They were also choices she was going to have to make—planning to make—to leave. She suddenly felt as if there was no way she'd be able to do that.

Cassie said, "Mazzy Donruss invited me to her family's lake house, so I thought I'd go down there later this week, maybe into the weekend. But I don't know. This is so nice."

"You still in touch with Mazzy?"

"Yeah. She's playing midfield for William and Mary."

"How's her team?"

"Top twenty," Cassie knew.

It sounded as if Cassie missed lacrosse. Megan recalled her comment out in California about playing for Stanford as a part of changing schools—but imagined that comment had been more from being caught up in the moment than a real possibility. Stanford hadn't been mentioned since. Still, Megan asked if Cassie gave any thought to playing again.

"Sometimes. But it'll probably just stay club from now on. Not like there's a career in it. I'm not going to coach."

"You do love it."

"I thought you were glad I wasn't playing any more. You never liked it."

"Cass—that's not true."

"We were so aggressive you said. Remember?" Cassie's recollection wasn't damming, but amused. "You didn't think girls were supposed to play sports like that."

"I wasn't used to it. But I loved that you loved to play."

"I hit that girl in the head in the championship…"

"Cass, it knocked her out. She had a concussion." Megan could still picture the goalie collapsing on the field, her mother shrieking.

"I didn't try to do it. And I felt bad about it. But it happens."

"You're like your father," Megan appreciated.

"Am I?"

"It's not a bad thing."

Cassie looked back toward the ocean, then saw a woman angling toward them and warned Megan, "Here comes the comic book woman." Which was not reference to the woman being in the comic business but because Cassie always thought she looked like a comic book character.

Darlene—Megan couldn't remember her name at first—had a pile of orange-red hair and wore a leopard-print caftan and oversized sunglasses. Stopping in front of Megan's stand, her loud voice announced, "It is you! Harry Daniels in three-L

358

said it was and I told him he was having a spell. What happened to Pip?"

Megan kept it simple. "He moved to Florida."

"Did he? Well I guess that seems about right. How'd you get this job?"

Megan did her best to remain polite for what turned out to be ten minutes of fairly dreary conversation, throughout which Cassie rolled her eyes and tried to look around Darlene at the cute surfers who—like yesterday—arrived early in hope of being let in.

Just when Darlene seemed to be winding down, she recognized Cassie and dragged her into five minutes of Darlene bragging about her children.

When their boisterous fellow condo owner finally left, Cassie flung her head back and exhaled, "Well that was exhausting."

At fifteen minutes before the hour, Megan nodded the surfers into the ocean, seeing the nearest swimmers were down by Will's beach.

At five, the end-of-day signal came up from the south. Megan passed it along to Art and was about to hop down off her stand when Cassie asked, "Can I come up there with you?"

"Sure." Megan wanted to get upstairs and check her phone—maybe Pip had texted—but shifted to the side and made room as Cassie climbed the ladder rungs and sat alongside her.

"Definitely cool." Cassie watched the surfers.

Megan imagined the young boys were disappointed in the waves, which remained small and continued to break too close to shore to make for much of a ride.

"I can see you'd like this," Cassie said.

Megan didn't ask what she meant by that and took it as a positive comment. "What do you want to do tonight?"

"I don't know."

"Whatever you want is fine with me." Megan needed to text Kelly and let him know she wouldn't be there tonight. "And if you've got friends you want to hang out with…"

"No—I'd like to do something with you."

Megan felt a pleasant glow flow through her. "There's not much food in the place. I've been just buying what I need a little at a time." That felt like an awkward lie. "We can go anywhere you want. You want pizza on the boardwalk. Or go up to Turtle Bay Café."

"Do you like that place? Turtle Bay? I always thought of that more as a dad place."

"I guess it was."

"I don't know. We'll think of something." Cassie pointed north. "This your swim group?"

Adrian and Art came toward them, toting their buoys and carry bags. Megan tensed, concerned they'd say or do something that exposed her being with Pip.

"Seven o'clock," Adrian announced. "Half Shell," she reminded.

Megan had forgotten—the dinner with people who knew Pip. "Oh, guys, I don't think tonight works. This is my daughter. She just came down…"

Cassie leaned around Megan and waved hello.

"Cassandra, right?" Adrian greeted. "Recognize you from your Instagram. I'm Adrian. This's Art. How you doing?"

"Good."

"Bring her along," Adrian told Megan, then asked Cassie, "You like steamed clams?"

"Love steamed clams," Cassie replied.

"This place has the best."

"Half Shell." Cassie gripped Megan's arm. "That's the place S would never go because it looked like such a dump. And one time there were a bunch of bikers out front. We've got to do this."

"You'll love it," Adrian encouraged.

\#

Megan couldn't quiet her nerves. Getting ready to go out with Cassie, the two of them taking turns in the bathroom, deciding what to wear, Megan worried someone was going to say something tonight—do something—and Cassie would find out about her being with Pip.

Pip had said—hadn't he?— he wasn't telling anyone about them? But what if he had? Or what about Ben or Kelly? Just a comment here or there? Kelly with a couple drinks in him after work one night? And Adrian and Art and Will? Lulu? What were the odds none of them had mentioned anything to someone else—not being malicious, just tossing around opinions or observations, especially Adrian who'd been so negative when Megan first met her?

Applying a light lip gloss, Megan took a deep breath and decided if it came out tonight, then that would be that: she'd admit to Cassie she'd fallen in love with someone else. She'd try to explain it, not excuse it. And then it would be over, wouldn't it, her life with Cassie? Because Cassie would never understand. Never forgive her for cheating on her father. And then Cassie would be gone, just like Pip.

70.

The purposefully cockeyed letters over screened windows spelled out Half Shell, but the full name was actually David Jean's Half Shell on Caroline.

On a narrow side street a dozen strides off the boardwalk, Half Shell occupied the ground level of small wood-framed building originally built as a fifteen-unit hotel in an era when men wore striped onesie bathing suits and women carried parasols to the beach. The building was only historic in that it was old. There was nothing classical about it other than it had survived storms, fires, and periods of rampant real estate development that now found the structure jammed between a glass-and-steel hotel on one side and an unimaginative concrete box of condos on the other.

The interior wood slat floors were in dire need of repair. The air conditioning system groaned with age. A mismatched collection of picnic tables and benches supplied seating for no more than thirty. The kitchen footprint was smaller than some walk-in closets and at times produced more steam than the exhaust system could handle. But the food was fantastic.

While other seafood spots on the island wouldn't dare not offer steamed crabs, Half Shell proudly limited its menu to clams and oysters.

When Megan and Cassie arrived just after seven, the place was already packed and there was a line at the carry-out window that reached the boardwalk. A handwritten notice on the front door said PRIVATE PARTY ONLY.

Will saw them coming and waved them in. "I got door duty," he called.

Noisy conversation coming out through screened windows was amplified by low ceilings inside. So much for it just being a few people.

Will tapped the sign. "Captain pulled some strings with the owner. We got the place until nine." He smiled at Cassie, opening the door.

Megan didn't know most of the faces. As many people were standing as sitting. Buckets of steamed clams and plates of oysters were carried out of the kitchen and set on the tables.

Captain Garrison occupied a prominent position at the end of the largest table, seated with a group of men and women wearing some form of OCSP attire, most of it ragged, its decals peeling. Former guards, Megan guessed, some of whom still looked as if they could handle the job, while others had put on some weight, but, who knew, maybe could still swim.

Adrian and Art sat at a different table with a younger group, also guards Megan assumed from their tans and current OCSP t-shirts and caps. Adrian was laughing. Art dove into a bucket of clams as if he hadn't eaten in months, forking steamed clams from their shell and dipping them in melted butter. When Adrian spotted Megan and Cassie, she had Art slide down on the bench so they could squeeze in.

Adrian introduced the other guards, all of whom were now part of her crew, what had been Pip's crew. "Guys," Adrian told the table, "this's Megan in case you haven't met. She's on Pip's stand..."

"OCSP Mom," one of them called and waved.

"...and her daughter, Cassandra."

Cassie waved.

Megan didn't pick up on any odd looks, no scowls or resentment. The OCSP Mom reference had been friendly enough, no tone of mocking.

When she squeezed in alongside Art, one of the other guards—a girl named Kensey—passed Megan a bucket of clams and announced over the clamor, "They also have this

363

phenomenal noodle thing. Like the best pho, ramen, pasta mash-up you've ever had. They make their own noodles. It's phenomenal," she repeated.

Cassie joined in a conversation and, to Megan's relief, ordered iced tea to drink and made no effort to reach for the pitcher of beer. The food was amazing and kept coming.

Megan began to relax. The gathering wasn't at all what she'd expected. It wasn't like a memorial or a retirement dinner. She heard Pip's name mentioned in conversation, but not with any sadness or loss. Everyone seemed happy to have known him, from the older crew with Captain Garrison who'd worked with him when he was a kid starting out, to the younger ones, like Will, who looked up to him as a big brother. No one had heard from him since he'd left, even those who'd reached out—their texts or emails unanswered.

There were stories about saves—some having improved with age, the former guards laughing how they'd heard that one before and the details kept getting better. They compared places they'd stayed, cheap food they'd lived off, and remembered jelly fish infestations and shark sightings.

Adrian admitted taking a picture of Pip when she was 14 and having a poster made of it that she tacked on her bedroom wall and kept for almost two years. "Oh, yeah," she confessed, "mad puberty crush. Mad crush."

Some had pictures on their phone they passed around that were hard for Megan to look at. Every time she saw Pip smiling—and he was always smiling—she ached to be with him.

And then there was a group picture, taken at a beach party with a bonfire in the background, where Pip had his arm around a girl with short strawberry-blond hair.

"When was that?" someone asked. "I don't recognize any of those people. Oh, wait, is that Jerry Moss behind Pip, with the black hair?"

"Who's Jerry Moss?"

The phone made its way around the table and the random comments continued:

"This's gotta be, what, ten years ago?"

"Who's the chick with Pip? Was she SP?"

"She's got the suit."

"Where'd you get this picture? You would have been about ten when this was taken?"

"I was there, dude. Up in Fenwick. A bunch of OC guards came up to party with the guys in Fenwick."

"Boo—Fenwick," an Ocean City loyalist mocked the neighboring Delaware beach.

"Hey, my parents' choice. Not mine. My brother was friends with one of the Fenwick guys, so I tagged along. I think I had my first beer that night."

"Ask Captain. Text him the pic."

"Captain," one of the young guys shouted to their boss, "check your phone. Sending you a picture of Pip. Who's he with?"

In the picture, the girl was smiling at the camera, but Pip was looking at her, and it looked to Megan like he was in love.

Captain Garrison received the text and registered surprise, then started showing it around his table to nods and smiles of recognition. One of his table chums pointed, saying, "That's me," and laughed, "look at all that hair."

Garrison got up from the table, his broad frame seeming too large for the confined room. Ducking under low ceiling fans, he came to where Megan sat with the others. "Where'd you get this?" he asked of the photo.

The story was repeated by the young guard who'd been at the party as a kid.

"This is eight, nine years ago. End of Summer," Garrison said of the party that marked the close of the guards' season. "We had it in Fenwick because there was a bonfire ban that year down here. You were there, Rodriguez?"

"Yeah, Captain."

"Who's the girl?" Adrian asked. "With Pip."

Garrison squinted slightly, trying to remember. "Irish name…"

"Was she SP?" someone asked.

Garrison nodded, "Yeah. Bit of a hassle with her work visa. I think we called her Mair, but not short for Mary. Mairi, I think, with an I at the end. Went back to Ireland, pretty much broke Pip's heart."

#

Other pictures of Pip had been printed and pinned to an impromptu tribute wall. Someone stuck a post-it note to one of Pip on his stand: G-O-A-T. Greatest of all time.

As the evening wound down, Megan stole a look at the pictures while Cassie was the center of attention to a trio of guards, Will among them. Megan tried to seem as if just glancing at the pictures, not feeling as if each one dwelled in her heart.

Captain Garrison stood and offered the only formal words, keeping it short and sweet. "I'll miss you, Pip. Wish you were here for us to send you off in person, but I get it. Sometimes the only way to leave is just to go. Long time, my friend. Lot of waves. Lot of whistles. Lot of saves. In case you all don't know, we do keep track. And Pip holds the record for saves. Second place isn't even close. If one of you breaks that number, here's to you. In the meantime—to Pip: be well, old friend."

Everyone cheered.

"And, also," Garrison thought to add, waiting for the group to quiet, "also, special surprise: Mrs. Jean has picked up tonight's tab. So, many thanks, Mrs. Jean!"

Over wild applause, the owner announced, "Don't get used to it. I had some help."

No one knew what she meant, nor did they care. Free food was always a plus on surf patrol pay.

#

Megan and Cassie said their goodbyes and left Half Shell. For the moment, Megan's worries quieted about Cassie finding out about her time with Pip.

Cassie said, "That was really nice."

"It was."

"He was the guy on the beach that day, right?" Cassie believed. "When S did the video call for us. That was Pip?"

"That was Pip," Megan confirmed, starting down the side street toward their car, a block away.

"And he left to go to Florida? The comic book woman said that on the beach, and I heard other people mention it inside."

"Mm-hm. Seems so."

"His aunt died?"

"I think so. Yes."

As they approached the crosswalk, Megan saw a large BMW parked at a meter by the curb. The driver's window was down, and Megan recognized the man eating with chopsticks behind the wheel.

Bill Clary called over to her. "We're eating *al auto*."

Megan walked to the luxurious sedan and ducked to look inside, seeing Mary Jane in the passenger seat. "Hi, Ms. Clary. This is my daughter, Cassie."

"Nice to meet you, young lady," Bill Clary greeted. "And she's Mary Jane," he said of his wife. "Mrs. Clary was her mean old mother."

"He loved my mother," Mary Jane cut in.

"Had a right cross could deck a mule."

"Oh, stop," Mary Jane admonished.

Megan saw they were both eating carry-out from Half Shell. "You should have come in."

"Young fellah in front of our place—Will—he told me about it. Sounded like a young person's do."

"Hm. The owner picked up the tab for everyone."

"Good business practice," Bill commented.

"She said she had some help."

"Did she?"

"My guess is I should be thanking you for dinner."

Bill Clary smiled. "That's how rumor's get started." He expertly twirled noodles with his chopsticks. "Anyone hear from our boy?"

Megan shook her head, hoping Cassie didn't make anything of that personal reference.

"Damn shame," Bill said. "Well, he won't be the first person lost his mind and ran off to Florida. Paradise of fools. We had plenty friends do it. Most of 'em moved back, although some died before they realized it was a mistake. He'll realize that, too."

"Maybe. Thank you again for dinner."

Clary dodged Megan's appreciation, saying, "See you on the beach. Nice to meet you, Cassie. We're big fans of your mom. Brightens our day."

"Thanks," Cassie appreciated. "That's sweet." Then she surprised Megan, hugging her and telling the Clarys, "She brightens my days, too."

#

"You're asleep on your feet," Cassie laughed, standing alongside Megan in line for Dumser's ice cream. "You're doing that thing you do."

"What?" Megan was tired but didn't want this time with Cassie to end.

"You pull on your ear."

"I what?"

"You tilt your head to the side and do this." Cassie gently massaged Megan's earlobe between her thumb and forefinger.

Megan closed her eyes and sighed. "Mm, that does feel good."

"Come on, let's go. We'll get ice cream some other time."

"No. We're staying. I'll get a second wind. The sugar rush will bring me around." She put her arm around Cassie. "Just hold me up."

Cassie laughed again. "Fine."

They each got a cone—black raspberry for Megan, salted caramel for Cassie—and sat side by side on a bench outside. Cassie took a selfie of them she texted to Stewart. "I'm posting this, too," she told Megan, working her phone. "Dumser's with #OCSPMOM. You get enough followers you could be an influencer. The line'll be out into traffic."

Megan smiled, licking her ice cream. "I think Dumser's is doing just fine." She watched little kids with their parents, lots of questions about flavors and cone choices and add-ons. Decisions, decisions. Cassie had always known before they got out of the car what flavor she wanted—and just ice cream, no sprinkles or gummies, and always in a cake cone—Cassie liked how they got squishy at the bottom from melting ice cream and savored that final bite.

When Cassie's phone pinged, she showed Megan Stewart's text. Having seen Cassie's picture of them together, he wrote: *Love my girls.* "He can be a softy sometimes," Cassie said of her father.

Megan suppressed a shudder when the feeling ran through her that it had been a mistake to be with Pip. Only moments later the thought of never being with him again made her want to cry. She pushed back those emotions and focused on Cassie.

On the drive back to the condo, Megan felt her eyes getting heavy—that second wind not materializing—and concentrated more on staying awake than what else to talk about.

Riding up in the elevator, when Cassie laughed, Megan realized she was giving her ear a pull. "Sorry," she apologized. "I think it's bed for me."

"You think?" Cassie teased. "That's okay. I'm probably not far behind you."

"I like you being here."

"I like it, too." Cassie surprised Megan again, reaching over to take her hand and keeping hold of it as the elevator doors opened and they walked to their condo.

Maybe if Megan hadn't been so tired, she'd have picked up that Cassie was worried about something, and that's why Cassie felt the need to hold her hand in a way she hadn't done in years.

It wasn't until an hour later, after they'd gotten sheets out of the linen closet and made up the sofa bed and washed their faces and brushed their teeth and gotten into bed that Megan found herself looking up at the dark ceiling, not falling asleep after all. Only instead of thinking about Pip, she was thinking about Cassie.

Megan got out of bed and walked softly to the living room.

Cassie was sitting up in bed in the dark, arms wrapped around knees drawn up to her chest, looking out at the ocean.

"Cass…?" Megan asked quietly. "…you okay?"

As Megan settled onto the pull-out bed and put her arm around her, Cassie leaned against her and very softly asked, "Do you still love dad?"

71.

The question caught Megan so by surprise she couldn't speak. The tenderness in Cassie's voice was heartbreaking and she suddenly seemed younger and vulnerable, referring to her father as "dad" and not "S" for the first time in years.

Megan clutched hold of Cassie, who hugged her in return and whispered, "If you don't love dad anymore, I kind of understand. He's older—he seems older now. I mean, he's always been older, but when you got married, you seemed more the same age. Maybe because I was little. Now it seems more like your worlds have kind of gone apart. And I know he's not very romantic, he's all about work. And half the time he's talking with you he cuts you off or answers something for you—not that it's mean or demeaning, he's just so inside his own head, I think. He does it to me, too. Like he's always got to be the leader."

It saddened Megan to hear Cassie talk like this, having no idea she'd been holding back those thoughts.

"And last summer," Cassie said softly, "when dad sold his company and you didn't go with him to Arizona, I told myself it was because you wanted to be near me, starting school, so I tried to show I didn't need you to stay, but you still didn't go. And then in California last month, I thought maybe things would be different, like they used to be, and for a while it seemed good—when we looked at all those houses—but then I could tell you didn't really want to be there. And then you came back here. And now you've got a job here and seem like you fit in with this group—like tonight at dinner, it felt like you

371

so belonged. And what worries me the most, really, is, and, I don't know, but I understand if you don't want to be with dad anymore, it makes me sad, but I do kind of get it. But I'm really afraid … I don't want you to stop loving me. I mean, I think you do—love me—I hope so. Because you're my mom, you know, you've always been my mom."

Megan held Cassie tightly, as if to let her know her love for her would never let go. "I have always loved you. I've loved you from the first day you walked into my classroom. I love you so much. And it's been so hard since that night you told me I wasn't your mother."

Cassie stiffened upright. "What? Oh my God, no. I've never said that. I would never say that."

"You did. That night last fall when you'd been drinking."

"Oh my God, I said that? Mom, I am so sorry. I am so, so sorry. I never think that. I am so sorry. Last fall, I don't know, I felt like everything was changing, being away from home, and you and dad, and I think part of me was bracing for you leaving, because I used to worry, when you and dad got married, that you were going to have a baby and you'd love that baby more than me because I wasn't yours."

"Cass—you never had to worry about that. The whole reason I didn't have a baby was because I wanted you to be mine."

"Did you want a baby?"

"Your dad and I talked about it, but not for long."

"You mean adopting."

"No…"

"Because Dad told me you couldn't have a baby."

"I assume I can—could. I don't have any medical issues."

"I always thought you couldn't. Why would he say that?"

"It's fine. It doesn't matter. Maybe because dad had a vasectomy not long after you were born and would have had to have that reversed—maybe I shouldn't have said that. But he was probably just trying to make it simpler for you, so you wouldn't worry. We didn't want you to worry."

"That was so unfair … for you."

"Cass, I made my decision—my decision—that it would just be you. And I will always love you, Cassie. Always."

#

Megan and Cassie sat side by side on the sofa bed, facing the sliding glass door with a view of the moonlit ocean. Each with an arm around the other. Cassie's head was on Megan's shoulder as Megan stroked her back.

Quietly, Cassie said, "I don't even think about my mother anymore. I don't remember her that much. Sometimes—although not as often as he used to—dad will say something to me about her and ask if I remember, and I'll say I do. But I really don't. When I was going through stuff to take to school last year, I came across some pictures of her dad printed and put in my dresser drawer after she died and told me she'd always be there for me to look at. And it felt strange seeing them, because what she looked like in the picture wasn't how I remembered her. It was like I was looking at a stranger."

"You were little when she died."

"I have no memory of her touching me. Not a single one. And in the pictures, we might be together in some of them—there was one where we're standing close together, and I've got on some frilly pink dress—but she's not touching me. Not really."

"It's hard when you lose somebody and they're not here to talk to anymore."

Cassie said, "I remember the first time you touched me. I fell in the hall at school, and I think I was about to cry, and you came running over. And all of a sudden, I was off the floor, and you had me in your arms, and I remember I clung onto you like a koala bear," Cassie sniffled happily, leaning hard against Megan. "And you felt so warm and smelled so good, and you said to me, 'I've got you little girl. I've got you. You're fine. Everything's all right. Everything's going to be all right.'"

373

Tears falling across her cheeks, Megan put both arms around Cassie and whispered, "I've got you little girl. Everything's all right. Everything's going to be all right."

#

Megan and Cassie fell asleep together on the sofa bed and awakened with the sunrise to a renewed connection, both smiling as Megan made toasted English muffins with peanut butter and jelly.

"This is some training breakfast," Cassie teased, seated at the peninsula. "Tasty, though."

Already in her bathing suit, Megan carried her plate to the balcony and checked the ocean.

Sunlight glistened off the smooth sea. No white caps. Small waves.

"The weather's been amazing."

Cassie asked, "Remember that summer it seemed like it rained every weekend?"

"We must've played a thousand games of Pictionary. You and every friend you had come down with us. Remember we bought that game at a flea market?" Megan licked a bead of jelly off her fingers. "We got a lot of mileage out of that for probably five dollars."

"It was two. The guy wanted five and dad offered two. He said it was late in the day and the guy could have two bucks or take the thing home and bring it back to try to sell another day."

In the quiet that followed, Megan wondered if Cassie was still waiting for an answer whether she still loved Stewart. Megan had an answer prepared but wasn't entirely convinced— or that Cassie would be convinced—it was the truth.

Finishing her breakfast, Megan put her plate in the dishwasher. "All right, Cass. I'm off to work."

"Swim first?"

"Yep." Her carry bag and buoy were in the front hall.

"Can I come with?" Cassie asked.

"Sure."

Cassie took two big bites, chewing as she went into bedroom, leaving her dish on the counter, which Megan cleaned up after her.

Minutes later, mother and daughter crossed the dunes side by side. Cassie in a black one-piece. Megan in her red suit, carry bag slung over her shoulder, buoy in the opposite hand.

Will waved, "Hey, Cassie!" Happy to see her. "Coming with us?"

"Going to try. Don't let me drown."

"You got this."

Megan stuck her buoy nose first into the sand.

Adrian and Art were on their way. And Bill Clary was standing on his balcony with a coffee cup. Megan waved to him.

It was a beautiful morning.

Then she experienced a whisper of heartache. Missing Pip. But when they all dove into the ocean, those thoughts were pushed away by Cassie swimming with her.

Megan stayed alongside her daughter. After a block, Cassie stopped and tread water, taking deep breaths and checking how far they'd gone and how far ahead the others had swum. "I'm holding you back," she told Megan.

"It's fine."

"No—you go. I'll swim in and wait for you. Let's see if you can catch them," Cassie challenged.

Megan nodded. "Let's see if I can." She sprint-swam until her arms and legs ached, coming up on Will, who Megan thought was waiting for her, but as she came alongside him realized he was watching Cassie swim to shore.

"I'm going in," he told Megan, not waiting for her response before swimming hard for the beach.

Megan kept going, closing on Adrian and Art, and easing her pace to match theirs for the final hundred yards.

As Adrian turned them toward the beach, she paused and looked around, realizing their numbers had diminished, then she spotted Will and Cassie on the beach. "There they are. Cassie okay?" she asked Megan.

"Fine."

"Will is in love with her," Adrian smiled. "She's all he talked about last night after you guys left."

Megan considered mentioning that Bill Clary had been the one to pick up their bill at Half Shell, but he didn't seem as if he wanted that known.

Adrian asked, "Hear anything from Pip?"

Megan shook her head.

72.

It became the week Megan had dreamed of back in May, being with Cassie at the beach—their beach, where they'd spent so many summers together. Never envisioning she'd be seated atop a guard stand, working for the surf patrol, while Cassie split her time between a blanket spread alongside Megan's post, sunning with Lulu back by the dunes, or sitting next to Will's stand. Cassie spent more time with Will as the week progressed, and went out with him Thursday night—and, no, it wasn't a date, just dinner then a free concert.

Cassie had returned to the condo just after midnight, and in a very good mood, laughing with Will outside the front door, then a bit of quiet—five, ten minutes—followed by some hushed conversation Megan tried not to listen to just outside her bedroom window before Cassie came in.

"Have fun?" Megan asked from her darkened bedroom as her daughter passed by her door.

"I did," Cassie replied happily. She sat on the side of Megan's bed, thankfully no smell of alcohol on her breath. "He is so goofy," Cassie laughed about Will. "Not in a bad way. He's fun."

"And cute."

"He is cute. But seventeen." Cassie covered her face. "Oh my God, I went out with a kid."

"You're just a kid."

"Not like that." Cassie smoothed her hair back. "How was Maths tonight?" Asking about Megan's young student who referred to calculus that way.

"He was good." Megan touched Cassie's arm. "I love you being here. I love you."

"I love you, too."

Cassie was yet to repeat her question whether Megan still loved her father, nor had Megan volunteered a response.

Their days on the beach had been—and continued to be— idle pleasure. Their conversations mostly about friends and memories and what to do for dinner.

They had a long video chat with Jillian—Megan and Cassie both sitting atop the guard stand at the end of the day while surfers waited for waves that never came.

They played putt-putt. They had pizza and Fisher's popcorn on the boardwalk and enjoyed hotly contested games of skeeball. They drove up to Rehoboth one evening and shopped the outlets. Another night, they brought back a bag of steamed crabs they ate on the balcony.

Cassie swam with Megan and the other guards every morning and increased her distance each day but never made it the entire way. When she tired and got out of the ocean, Will went in with her.

It wasn't until Friday night that they talked about California, a return to reality prompted by an email sent by Stewart. Closing on the sale of their home in Hunt Valley had been scheduled. The date was 30 days away and they had to pack.

Sitting on the balcony on a mild night, the moon over the ocean, Cassie said, "I don't need to go back to the house."

Megan thought that sounded cold until Cassie added: "I took a lot of pictures last fall before I left. I saw online about doing that as a way to deal with being homesick. And that it might seem like looking at pictures would make it worse, but it actually made it better. Sometimes it did. I think now, though, if I went back, I'd get sad. S sent me intel on that company the real estate agent lady said packs your stuff up. I think I'm just going to do that. And maybe put it in storage or—I don't know—send some out to California. But if you want to go back to the house, I'll go with you if you want."

Megan exhaled softly. "I'm going to miss that house."

"Yeah…" Cassie understood.

"I knew you'd go away to college one day. I hated to think about it, but I knew you'd go. But I always thought you'd come back to that house. That we'd be there. And here."

Cassie moved behind Megan's chair and hugged her. "It's okay, Mom. It'll all be okay. Like you told me when you picked me up that time I fell."

They had one more day together, Saturday, but like all vacations, each hour that drifted by was hard to enjoy for thoughts of Cassie leaving. And that they may never be like this again.

If Megan and Stewart ended up apart—she still found it hard to use the word, "divorce," which seemed so ugly—how would she remain a part of Cassie's life? Would Stewart stand for it? Or would he be so hurt he'd force Cassie to make a choice? And if he did, how could Cassie turn her back on her father?

After Megan relayed the end-of-the-day signal north to Art, Cassie climbed up on the stand and they sat together one more time.

A block south, Will remained atop his own stand and began flagging a message.

"What's he saying, mom?" Cassie asked.

Megan recited the words as Will signaled them. "I … will … miss … you."

Cassie stood and waved her arm, not needing semaphore to beckon Will to join them.

He hopped off his stand and trotted to them.

Cassie leaned over the side, reaching a hand toward him. "I'll miss you, too."

He stood close enough so she could touch his hair, then he climbed the side rungs of the stand when Cassie gestured him closer so she could give him a kiss goodbye. "Bye, Cass." And then he dropped back to the beach, picked up his buoy and bag and set off down the beach, waving to Bill Clary out on his deck.

Cassie watched him go, then turned toward the ocean.

There were no surfers today because there were no waves. A fisherman stood in knee-deep water and cast his line.

Thinking about Will, Cassie said, "He starts school in three weeks. High school. High school," she laughed.

Megan patted Cassie's knee. After Cassie left tomorrow, the others would begin to follow. By the end of the month, they'd all be gone—Will, Lulu, Art, and Adrian.

The shadow of her building would reach farther over the beach every afternoon. And while the days would remain warm, the shade would feel cooler. The end of summer was in the air.

#

Megan and Cassie planned to stay in Friday night, but in the elevator going upstairs after work, Megan changed plans. "Let's do this right."

They took showers and debated what to wear, deciding to keep it beach simple with t-shirts and shorts, but how about just a little make-up. They set out in the Volvo with the windows down, letting in the sticky evening air.

At a restaurant overlooking the bay, they shared a seafood broil—clams, crab legs, mussels, flounder, and shrimp, spiced with Old Bay and served with silver queen corn and an Eastern Shore staple: lima beans and dumplings.

They had Dumser's ice cream again—not at the place on the highway, but the original stand at the end of the boardwalk, amidst the bustle of all the rides, amusements, and arcades.

They rolled a skeeball rematch. Then took a ride on the Ferris wheel, where, at the top, Megan heard the DJ operating Buckaroo Bonzai calling out if everyone wanted to go faster. They shot water into a fiberglass clown's mouth—a contest against ten other people to see who could make the balloon growing out of the clown's head pop first. And a horse racing game where balls were rolled into cut-out holes, moving their horse along a track—another competition among other happy people on vacation—and Cassie won a stuffed bear she gave to a little boy who'd been less lucky.

They walked out on the pier and looked back at the boardwalk, lit up like a Christmas garden in summer. Cassie bought boxes of saltwater taffy to take back to fellow staffers at her internship.

Driving back to the condo—a slow trip in traffic—they kept the windows down and Cassie got a playlist going through the car speakers, songs she said reminded her of summers here. Megan recognized some but imagined now she'd never forget any of them.

Once back at their place, they sat on the balcony and talked about dolphins, and all Cassie's friends they used to bring down with them, and where those girls were now. After a short while, they fell quiet, sitting side by side, holding hands.

Cassie still had not asked for Megan's answer: whether she still loved Stewart. Maybe, Megan believed, Cassie knew.

In the morning, after another round of English muffin PB&J's, and with Adrian, Art, and Will waiting for Megan on the beach, mother and daughter hugged. Each held back tears—which was the first time that had happened with Cassie, saying goodbye.

And Cassie whispered to Megan, "Like Captain Garrison said the other night … sometimes the only way to leave is just to go."

73.

Sunday was Megan's first long day. Time passed slowly and with a certain dullness. The weather was hot and dry, with an inland breeze that brought in a persistent string of annoying and biting flies.

Adrian supplied Megan with a can of insect repellent she squirted on over her usual sunscreen. "First time we've had to deal with these all summer," the girl commented.

The ocean remained calm, which allowed even the most-timid swimmers to seek relief from the temperature and the flies.

Throughout the morning, Megan thought about Cassie—where she would be on her drive and if she might stop at Kicken Chicken on the way. And she wondered about Pip—trying to picture where he might be living, what kind of work he would be doing with his uncle. Would he wear a tie? She hoped not.

She also thought about Stewart—imagining him in meetings. No longer as directly involved in projects as when he had his own company, but supervising others. Working even longer hours but relishing his success while eager to achieve more. More contracts. More prestige. More money. Coming home at the end of the day to a big house overlooking the Pacific Ocean. That life awaited her in Southern California. All she had to do was get on a plane—tomorrow, possibly tonight. It would be that easy. All she had to do was go.

Instead, at sundown, she returned to Pip's cottage.

#

It was too lonely in the condo with Cassie gone, so Megan texted Kelly, asking if she could come back. His reply had come quickly: *Of course.*

So that's where she was, sitting on the back steps, watching the sun set across the bay, the August sky alite with brilliant swirls of color.

Kelly texted from work that she could help herself to leftovers in the fridge if she wanted dinner. But Megan wasn't hungry.

She was still getting texts and emails and a few calls from friends just finding out about her being on the surf patrol. She'd fallen behind on her replies while Cassie was in town, so she did some catching up.

Then she texted Pip for the first time in almost a week—sending him a picture of her with Cassie eating ice cream. She thanked him for telling her that Cassie still loved her because he was right. She let him know they'd had a few wonderful days together. *Not exactly as it used to be*, she wrote, *because we've both changed. I thought it was just her changing but it's me too.* She hoped he was well and enjoying work, adding, *But I hope you don't have to wear a tie.*

She sent that, then, moments later, another: *I still miss you every minute. And hope you'll come back. Love, Megan.*

The sun fell behind the horizon without any response from Pip and it made her sad to think she might never hear from him again.

She went inside and although still not hungry knew she needed to eat something. There was some fancy cheese in the refrigerator she had with crackers, then went upstairs where Pip's bedroom was warm and empty.

Switching on the ductless system that only cooled the converted attic, she made a mental note to give Kelly some money toward the utility bill. She took a quick shower, brushed her teeth, and got into bed with echoes of loneliness that had become all too familiar since last fall—so many nights spent by herself. Only now the emptiness wasn't just from being alone but carried shadows of loss. As enjoyable as it had been to spend time with Cassie, it made clear that although their feelings for one another remained strong, their lives were unlikely to ever intersect as they used to. Cassie might still want Megan in her life, but it would be more at a distance.

When Megan had come to Maryland to teach after graduating from Bridgewater, she'd been concerned about leaving her mother, but her mom had a strong support system of family and friends. And Megan and her mother had not been close. They loved one another but had never been as entwined in one another's day-to-day lives as she'd been with Cassie.

Megan was still awake with these thoughts when Kelly came home. She called to him from bed: "How was your night?"

"Organized chaos," his baritone voice called from the bottom of the stairs. "How are you? How was Cassie?"

"Really good. I miss her. And I miss Pip. Have you heard from him?"

"Not a word. You?"

"No. I sent him some texts tonight. I didn't while Cassie was here—well, once, to let him know she was here. Maybe I should have."

"I don't know what to tell you, love. I wish I did."

Megan got out of bed and padded barefoot to the top of the steps. "Have you been okay?" She looked down at him in the dark.

"I only got drunk one night—so, if that's any measure, yes. Thank you for all the kitchen goodies by the way. I imagine wherever I live next is going to be smaller, so I hope to have room for them all."

"Have you started looking for a new place?"

"Some."

"And...?"

"A discouraging start."

"I'm sorry. You'll find something." She tried to sound positive.

Kelly said, "I'm giving thought to going back to Cleveland."

"Really? Is that something you want to do?"

"Not tops on my list of options. But it may be a practical solution, cost of living wise."

"Not very romantic."

"No ... although there's always sitting by a fire while lake effect snow piles up outside. Has less charm if you're alone, though."

Megan thought back to her own winter nights by herself in the big house with Cassie and Stewart gone. "I'm going to try to sleep, although I'm not sure how that's going to go."

"Sweet dreams."

"I ate some of your cheese by the way. It was very good. I'll pay you for it."

He waved away the offer. "*Mi queso es tu queso.*"

#

Monday was another scorcher. Temperatures climbed into the mid-90's and the air remained still and heavy with humidity. The flies were back, and beachgoers crowded into the calm ocean looking to get away from them.

"Worse than Saigon," Bill Clary pronounced, having walked over from his townhouse, braced against insect onslaught in a long-sleeve shirt and chinos. "You getting eaten alive up there?"

Megan showed him her can of bug spray. She also wore a long sleeve tee, which stuck to her skin with sweat, and an OCSP cap.

Bill pointed toward Will, down the beach. "Boy said your girl's gone back to Rome—what's she do there?"

"Goes to college and has a summer internship with an analytics firm."

"Speaks the devil's language, does she?" Bill chuckled. "Where's she go to school?"

"GW"

"Good school. Good for her. Seems like a nice girl. You're lucky to have her."

"I am."

"Treasure that. Every minute."

"I try."

"All right, darling. Well you take care of yourself out here. Just wanted to see how you were holding up."

"Thanks. Say hi to Mary Jane."

"She's fixing hot dogs for lunch today. I have to be on my best behavior, remember to pretend they're not made from chicken. Mention going across the street for a cold cut sub to her's like suggesting we try a few rounds of Russian Roulette."

As he turned to leave, Megan said, "Mr. Clary...?"

"It's Bill," he reminded, facing her again, and asked, "What do you need, darling?"

She leaned over the side of her stand, keeping their conversation as private as possible. "Was there ever a time you worried or thought you might not love your wife anymore?"

Stepping closer, he pulled off his cap and ran his hand over his thinning hair, thinking before replacing the hat and looking up at her. "Love is an investment. You might think it's an emotion, and it is. It's wonderful and passionate and exciting. But it's really an investment. And investments are best handled in one or two ways, neither of which is jumping in and out. Buy-sell-buy-sell. I've got a friend, every time the stock market does one of those dipsy doodles, he panics, calls his broker, Sell, Sell, Sell, then when the market starts to come back and gets frothy, he's Buy, Buy, Buy. He's probably a million dollars to the worse than if he'd just stuck with it or gotten out and stayed out. Because what you do with an investment, is you either stay for the long run—ride the ups and downs, and in the end, if you've got a good investment, you come out ahead. Or, you've got a bad investment, you get the hell out. Cut your losses and don't look back. Move on to something else. Or nothing else."

"But how do you know which to do?"

"You take a hard, honest look at what you've got. Then take a hard, honest look at yourself. And you'll know. And if you don't, give it a harder more honest look." As Megan considered that, Bill grinned seriously. "And here you were expecting a yes or a no."

#

Monday after work, Megan went back to the cottage. As a perfect filet of flounder Kelly had prepped for her broiled in the oven, Megan texted Pip: *It's been so hot. And the flies. Ugh. And then late this afternoon all of a sudden: jellyfish. Out of nowhere. Like a plague. People were getting stung like crazy. One group of little boys—I guess they were 10—tried to figure out how to pick them up without getting stung. Some of the small ones—jellyfish not boys—had really long tentacles. Kind of creepy. Adrian said to smear petroleum jelly on our legs and arms in case we had to go in on any saves. Did you ever do that? Love, Megan.*

She sent that text, then another after dinner, sitting on the back steps as the sun set: *Cassie called today and said she missed me. A call, not a text, which was nice. I told her she could always come back, and she said maybe right before Labor Day. But I don't think she will, because she started talking about something at work she was excited about. A project she's hoping will finish before she starts back to school. BTW: they've offered her a part-time job, which she's even more excited about. They gave her a proposed contract today she's having a lawyer she knows look over. I hope you're okay. Love, M.*

Her phone rang as she was getting ready to take a shower. Always hopeful it would be Pip, she hurried to pick up. But it was Stewart, asking what she wanted to do about packing up their house. Closing was in four weeks. Megan said she'd take care of it.

#

Tuesday, Megan went up to the condo for her lunch break instead of eating on her stand. She called the packing company the Realtor had recommended and scheduled a video conference with one of their agents. Turns out, the entire process could all be handled remotely. The company's rep would go through the Hunt Valley house room by room and get the family's instructions: what to pack, where to ship it, what to give to charity or arrange to have sold at auction. And yes, they could ship anywhere, and they could hold items in storage.

"I guess that'll be easy enough," Cassie said that evening on the phone, then asked Megan, "You sure you're okay doing that?"

Megan said she was, then told Cassie how the jellyfish had disappeared as fast as they'd come. And that the temperature had improved a little, and there were fewer flies.

Cassie said she'd texted a few times with Will, and he'd told her it had been brutal. She said it had been really hot in the city.

#

Wednesday, Megan crossed Coastal Highway on foot to get lunch at Greenie's. Ever since Bill Clary mentioned cold cut subs the other day, she'd been thinking about that.

As she waited at the crowded counter, the deli guy fixing her sub noticed her surf patrol t-shirt, pulled on over her red suit. "You SP?" he asked.

"Mm-hm."

"Really?" About her same age, he sounded surprised. "I thought maybe you put on the shirt for the discount."

"There's a discount?"

"Ten percent." He shrugged, as if admitting that wasn't much of a savings. "But if you saw eighty cents on the ground, you'd pick it up, wouldn't you?"

"I suppose I would."

"Where's your beach?"

"Across there." She pointed through the window, half covered with soft drink and beer posters. "In front of Ocean Vista."

"Pip's beach?"

Hearing his name excited Megan as if Pip had been spotted walking into the store, then made her sad because he wasn't there.

"He's in Florida?" the friendly guy asked.

Megan nodded again. "Mm-hm."

"With Rich Uncle Pennybags I bet—that's what we used to call him. Like the character on the Monopoly box?" He began wrapping Megan's sub in deli paper. "You know, everyone pictures Uncle Pennybags has a monocle, but he doesn't. Just a big bushy moustache. You think he has a monocle, that's the Mandela effect of false memories."

"You know Pip's uncle?" Megan asked.

"Stories about him—how way back he offered Pip a lump of cash to get his MBA." The guy laughed. "Pip took him up on it—lasted about a month." He handed Megan's sub across the counter. "This one's on me."

"I'll pay. You can give someone else a sub for me."

"You got it, SP."

#

Thursday evening, Megan texted Pip a selfie taken on the back steps of the cottage with the beautiful sunset behind her. She did her best to smile. *In case you forget what it looks like. Me or the bay.*

Then she sent another text—a longer one, because the thoughts just kept coming: *Ben has moved out. Maybe you already know that although I don't know how. No one says they've heard from you. Kelly said Ben found a house somewhere in Delaware. Kelly is talking about going back to Ohio, but I don't think he wants to. I hope he finds some way to stay. Or maybe it's time for him to go. And if not Ohio then somewhere else. To start again. Maybe that's what he's thinking. I guess maybe that's what you're doing. I didn't understand at first. Maybe I still don't. Why you aren't in touch with any of us. Even to let us know you're okay. But maybe it's the only way you feel like you can do what you need to do. Maybe you have to make a clean break I guess you could call it. Maybe you don't even read these texts. Maybe you hope I'll stop sending them. If you want me to stop, I will. Just text me a single word. STOP or something like that. And I'll stop. Stop sending texts, anyway. I'll never stop missing you or loving you. M.*

\#

Friday evening, after a quiet day on the beach, Megan logged into the video conference with the house-packing company. The firm's agent, Doreen Marley, was a professionally dressed woman about Megan's age, with brunette hair styled in a wavy bob.

At exactly the scheduled time of 7:00 p.m., Doreen connected the Tyler family from their respective locales: Cassie in her off-campus studio apartment, Megan at the dining room table of the Ocean City condo, and Stewart in his large corner office in Scottsdale. Doreen was the only one in the family's Hunt Valley home. She stood in the foyer, lit by slanting light from the setting sun glowing along the hallway from the kitchen. Megan, Stewart, and Cassie each appeared on Megan's iPad in separate small insets along the edge of her screen, with Doreen taking up the bulk of the image.

Doreen asked, "How is everyone?"

Her manner was friendly but serious, which Megan appreciated. She'd hoped this wasn't going to be a one of those rah-rah experiences, where they were all prompted to be having a wonderful time. Perhaps Doreen could shift into that mode if so called upon, but she didn't look as if she intended to lead the charge.

Stewart replied, "We're all good. Thank you. Looking forward to your assistance." He was strong and positive.

Cassie waved. "Hi everyone."

Megan added her own, "Hi." Sitting forward, elbows on her thighs, she had her iPad propped up on the table the way she positioned it for her tutoring sessions.

Doreen explained the process and didn't give the slightest sign of being in a hurry to wrap this up and get on with her Friday night. To the contrary, she secured the impression she would go until dawn if they asked—which Megan interpreted as the demeanor of the well-compensated. Megan had never asked what any of this would cost because Stewart told her not to worry about that.

Doreen had already "toured the entire property" and suggested they start in the "shared living spaces" so that's what they did. She went into the kitchen first, followed, Megan now realized, by a videographer. While Megan was on her iPad, Cassie on her phone, and Stewart on the same desktop with the mammoth screen he used for technical drawings, Doreen Marley had a cameraman.

"We can do this item by item or in lots," Doreen advised.

"Whatever the girls want," Stewart replied. Sitting back, elbows on his chair arms, he made a tepee of his fingers on which he rested his chin.

The kitchen took 20 minutes, with all the choices given to Megan. Each item or group of items was electronically tagged and assigned a specific color code that digitally "attached" to the item on the screen and indicated where the item would be shipped, or if it was to be stored, consigned to an auctioneer, given to charity, or disposed of.

One of the last items was the Kitchen Aid blender, the first solid appliance Megan bought after of college.

As Megan fell into a stare, Cassie said, "It's a workhorse." As if Megan might be thinking about getting rid of it. "All the cookies we made in that," Cassie celebrated.

But that wasn't what Megan was thinking—not at all. And after a moment, she simply said, "California."

#

It was after eleven by the time Megan steered the Volvo onto the cottage's crushed shell driveway.

Inside the small house, a beautiful opera aria played on the sound system and a hand mixer whirled in the kitchen.

Megan set her surf patrol bag at the foot of the stairs and found Kelly alone in the kitchen, still in his checkered chef's pants from work.

"Greetings, love," he announced over the mixer and music. "Immaculate timing. Whatever is ailing you, this will fix it. Anti-depression stew. AKA, chocolate mousse." Picking up a rubber spatula, he deftly spooned heavy cream, whipped to stiff peaks, into a ceramic bowl of cooked and chilled semisweet chocolate, vanilla, and cream.

Megan sat and rested her head on her arms on the kitchen table. She was tired and sad.

"You'll need to sit up, though." Kelly gently blended in the cream, then tapped the spatula on the edge of the bowl. "I don't have an IV drip for this. Although what a breakthrough that would be. Call George Foreman. Maybe he can hook me up with those invention people he advertises for on TV."

Megan spoke in a quiet voice. "I spent three hours tonight on a videoconference with my husband and Cassie, going through our house back home, telling a woman how to pack for us."

Kelly said, "I didn't know there was such a thing. But I'm not surprised." He got two old-fashioned ice-cream-sundae glasses from the cabinet.

"I don't know how this all happened. It's never felt like a conscious choice—a decision." Megan sat up as Kelly placed his freshly made sweet in front of her along with a spoon. "It just seemed to come out of ... I don't know where. The house

392

in California—that I don't really like or want to live in—the house or the place—the area. But all of a sudden tonight, I started seeing our belongings from the house we have now going out there and filling up that place. All our furniture and clothes. All our things. And me," she added sorrowfully, then repeated, "and me. I started to see me out there, too. Because I'm not sure I've got the courage not to go."

She looked at Kelly with pleading eyes, feeling as if being carried off by a current that had started to flow last fall and turned into a riptide. "I had my chance." Her words were soft with regret. "I had my chance and I let him get away. I let Pip get away."

#

An hour later, Megan texted Pip: *Here I am again. Because you haven't told me not to. I'm in your bedroom in the cottage. I like it best here. It would be better if you were here. But I think that goes without saying. It was quiet at work today. But it wasn't boring. No saves but a lot of people. I liked watching them. Mostly parents with little kids. The real little kids. I missed that age with Cassie because she was already in school when I met her. I really feel summer slipping away though. Did you used to feel that? I know on the calendar summer lasts until the third week of September, but it really doesn't. Lulu leaves in two weeks to go back to college. Captain sent us all emails, wanting to know how long everyone can stay. I told him I'd be here as long as he needs me. Maybe you'll be back by then. Or maybe I shouldn't keep saying that. I'll try to stop. I'll try to just be a friend who loves you. Is that okay?*

#

Over the weekend, the beach was as crowded as it had been all summer. Megan heard someone refer to it as the last hurrah. Even though Labor Day was two weeks away, for a lot of people the sun was setting on vacation season. It was time to start "getting back in the swing" of the coming school year.

Megan picked up two new online students, both Villa James fourth-graders who wanted refresher sessions after a couple months away from the classroom.

Cassie called Sunday evening and said she thought the house packing call went well, then there was a long pause, waiting for Megan to respond, which eventually took the form of agreement, Megan saying, "It did."

Cassie picked up that those two words were joyless syllables of resignation. "What's wrong?" she asked.

"I'm a little sad. But that will pass. It will all take some getting used to, maybe. California. It's going to be different."

"When are you thinking about going out? Maybe I'll go with. Like the beginning of October? Gives you every last day of summer at the beach," Cassie offered positively. "And I'll have a short break from school that week."

"Well, we can shoot for that." Megan tried to sound upbeat. She appreciated Cassie's concern. "I told the surf patrol I'd stay for the season, which ends the last weekend of September. No guards are on duty from that point on, so…"

"Okay. Cool." After a pause, Cassie said, "California … here we come."

"Here we come," Megan echoed.

Three days later, unable to shake the foreboding weight of becoming trapped in a life she didn't want, Megan met with a divorce lawyer.

74.

"So at this point it would come as a surprise to your husband," the lawyer asked. "Your interest in a divorce?"

Megan thought that was an odd way to phrase it: an interest in a divorce. "We haven't discussed it, no. I mean, it's not my first choice, either. What I really want is our old life back."

"Do you though?" Jodie Lawson, the lawyer, raised her hands off the keyboard of her laptop, having been quietly taking notes for half an hour as what Megan thought would be a simple few-paragraph summary of her marriage turned into a monologue. "You said you met someone else," Lawson recounted without judgment. "Someone you thought about 'running off with' you called it. And you say he's gone now, but…" She made an open gesture with her hands. "…if I had a magic wand—which I don't, of course. But if I did, and I could wave it to create your perfect world, would you be back in your old life or in a new life with whoever it was you met?"

Megan had not mentioned Pip by name. "I guess, if there was a way to do it without anyone being hurt—my husband or Cassie—I would have the new life. Because it would be holding my husband back to stay the way we were. And I wouldn't want to do that."

"Forget your husband a moment. Tell me about you. This is your fantasy perfect world we're imagining," Lawson said, her voice taking on a serious animation Megan imagined could enthrall a jury. She guessed the woman's age in her late 40's, an impression formed by the family photographs on her credenza—the happy vacation smiles of Lawson and an intelligent-looking husband and two teenaged daughters who shared their mother's thick, dark hair—and the date on Lawson's framed diploma from American University Washington College of Law. "What if you could have your old life back and Stewart would be as thrilled with that life as you. And Cassie would never age."

"But that's not possible…"

"Of course not." Lawson had a warm, comforting smile for a lawyer, but behind that friendly veneer, Megan detected the firmness of a litigator willing to do legal battle. "What I'm really asking," Lawson proposed, "is who you love more."

"That really doesn't matter, does it?" Megan shifted in the padded armchair.

"Humor me," Lawson asked.

Megan looked off to the side, toward the wall of floor-to-ceiling windows with blinds slanted most of the way closed, blocking the sunset. Megan had driven by Millhouse-Tawes' modern two-level building hundreds of times over the years, thinking the serious business looked so out of place in a vacation town and never imagining there would be a reason for her to set foot inside. "Cassie," she answered after a moment.

"Oh, what a good answer," Lawson appreciated as if having been tricked by a worthy foe. "But a safe answer. Stewart or the new man? Who do you love more? Pick one?"

Megan thought a moment. "I love Stewart for what we've had. I love—" She stopped, starting to say Pip by name, and reminding herself not to involve him in these discussions, regardless of Lawson's pledge that whatever Megan said to her was forever bound to confidentiality. "I love the new guy for what I think we could have in the future."

"Okay…" Lawson sat back in her swivel chair, no longer adding notes on her laptop. "Here's the issue with divorces. They are nasty, brutal, emotionally upheaving beasts. And those are the uncontested ones. Here's my fantasy world—the divorces where no one shouts or cries or calls one another nasty names. The divorces where you and I sit down with

Stewart and his lawyer and we calmly mediate a split of all your assets, and everyone has a sense of fair play and equity."

"I've been thinking about that. And what if I decide I don't want any assets—except the condo here. And could work out a way to buy out my husband's half…"

"Let me stop you there." When Lawson sat forward, Megan thought the lawyer was going to tell her their time was up—that she'd already gone beyond the point of what Lawson's paralegal had said would be a free consultation—but the lawyer looked Megan in the eye and made a firm declaration. "You need to think hard about a divorce. You even start the process, the word so much as whispers out of your mouth to Stewart and it's like jumping out of a plane. There's no getting back in. Ever. Ever. You become forever in a marriage where, at any point in the future, you will look back and know that you thought about getting a divorce. And that's a scar—and even if it's not a big one, it's always going to be there.

Lawson continued patiently, "You are in a very complicated situation. And I think you appreciate at least part of it. It's almost as if your husband has cheated on you, but not with another woman, but another life. He sells his company and in essence gets a new job and is ready to move household and finances to Arizona, now California, and what that says to you—in your heart—is he didn't like your life together enough to keep it the way it was. He wanted more. And he took it without asking you if it was okay, because—and I'm going to guess here—but I imagine he thought you would be as happy about the change as he was. Like you said," Lawson gestured to the notes on her screen, "the two of you were always pretty much in agreement about everything. So this was new—you not seeing eye to eye. He didn't expect it. Now, to his discredit, he should have been more forthright about what was happening. At the same time, possibly you could been more assertive and said at some point, I really don't want to do this. But be all that as it may. You two end up in this—maybe it's overstatement—but let's call it a quiet war.

Happens all the time in marriages—the good ones and bad ones. He's in Arizona. You stay in Maryland, not just to be near Cassie but because you don't want to leave. And you're each waiting for the other to give. You're waiting for some change of events that will bring Stewart back to Maryland with his job. And he's waiting for you to move west. And when the end of the school year doesn't bring an answer, you make plans to spend the summer apart. And low and behold ... another man. And he sounds pretty terrific from what you've said. Except for the now-he's-gone part. And whether you were just a fling, or he really does feel guilty about possibly breaking up your marriage, who knows."

Lawson paused briefly before continuing. "That's the part I think you probably get, right? Maybe? Close? Maybe you don't agree with everything I've said. Probably I wouldn't say no surprise about you having an affair if I had to say it over again ... so sorry about that if I offended you. What I meant was I understand the temptation. You'd been alone for months. A judge might not agree with that, but, again, who knows."

Megan nodded.

"Here's the part I don't think that you..." Lawson searched for the correct term. "...fully appreciate. You've got a hint of it." She scrolled through her notes. "You mentioned a lawyer named Lassiter, Holden Lassiter. And how he said something to you when you were in California about Stewart's new boss, Scott Dunhill, having concerns about whether they needed to 'worry about you,' you said. And you are now wanting to make sure that if you and Stewart separate, if you divorce, you don't want that to effect Stewart's job. His possibly taking over Dunhill's position in the company."

"Right," Megan agreed.

"Okay—so, as you were talking, and I was listening, I assure you, I did a search for Holden Lassiter, and Scott Dunhill, and I also searched Stewart Tyler. And you know how sometimes you do a search and all you get are ads or suggestions you may have misspelled something? Not the case here." Lawson turned her screen toward Megan. "I'm surprised Google's servers didn't crash. There are hundreds of links. Not just Lassiter and Dunhill, but your husband. Have you ever Googled him? Especially in the past year? This is from a Dunhill Infrastructure press release." Lawson tapped a search result, and a picture of Stewart appeared.

He was standing on a steel girder, hundreds of feet above ground, wearing a hardhat and overlooking downtown Phoenix.

Lawson said, "Now I have no way of knowing exactly what Holden Lassiter was referring to when he spoke to you in California, but there is a reference in one of the first business journal articles that came up after Stewart merged his company with Dunhill about Stewart being considered as Dunhill's successor. And if Stewart already has or is in line for any equity interest in Dunhill's company, you could be entitled to a share of that in a divorce—especially under California law, which I would need to discuss with a lawyer who practices family law out there, and where it might be better for you to file if you do go forward. And that very well could complicate matters for Stewart with Dunhill."

"Like I said," Megan defended, "I don't want any of that. Can't I just waive that, any right I have to it?"

"You could—but I would strongly advise against it. Even so, those types of negotiations take time and perhaps Dunhill finds out about it and gets uneasy."

"But how would he find out if it's just Stewart and his lawyer and you and me?"

"He might not until a divorce case was filed, which would then be a matter of public record and come up in any routine credit check Dunhill's company does on your husband—which I'll assume is happening. But if your husband is in a position of confidence with Dunhill and doesn't tell him about his divorce until months after it's a done deal, Dunhill could wonder what else your husband might be keeping from him. He could lose Dunhill's trust."

Lawson proceeded to counsel about an additional unpleasant reality: "And remember what I said about my fantasy divorce world? Where everyone gets along and is fair and equitable? At the other end of the spectrum is shouting and screaming and name calling and ten-hour depositions and document productions that fill a flash drive. Lassiter's law firm is huge. It is international. These are very heavy hitters and I'm going to admit, I'm a little intimidated, and I don't usually say that. In fact, I'm not sure I've ever said that, even when I was starting out and didn't know any better and looked at lawyers from big law firms as a challenge. Now I appreciate how much more complicated they can make life for you. And this is about you, not me. If it turns nasty, they will try to turn you inside out. And I understand you don't want to tell me the name of the man you were seeing, but that won't remain a secret for two seconds if this turns ugly. They will get records of your texts and phone calls and unless you've been using a honeyline—that's what some of us in the divorce business refer to as a burner—they won't even need subpoenas if the phone accounts are in Stewart's name. And they will drag your friend into it, whether he's in your past or not…" Lawson was about to say more but stopped when Megan closed her eyes and began rubbing her temples.

75.

Bill Clary watched the rain from beneath the overhang of his front deck. It had been pouring from the bleak grey sky for three days now, the remains of a tropical storm that had stalled off the coast, churning wind and waves and rain. And more rain.

The summer drought that had lowered the water table and threatened farm crops now seemed like a distant memory. But also erased were the happy times of sunny vacations, because when it rained incessantly like this at the beach, it could seem like it might never stop.

The island couldn't shed the water as fast as it fell and numerous side streets became ankle-deep canals.

The ocean roared like a monster. Waves rose out of the dark ocean, the wind blowing white foam off their crests as they rolled and crashed like buildings being demolished.

The surf patrol guards hadn't swum for three mornings now. Throughout the day, they sat atop their stands zipped into bright yellow rain gear, hoods pulled over their heads, making sure no one got in the ocean. "Their Megan" as Bill continued to think of her, held her post even when the others occasionally sought cover. Sometimes she stood and looked out at the ocean, then turned in place to scan the beach through the driving rain. Bill would set down his binoculars and wave whenever she looked his way. Sometimes she saw him and waved back. Other times, the rain was too heavy.

"Why doesn't she go inside?" Mary Jane asked yesterday, standing alongside Bill, both of them focusing binoculars on Megan.

"Sometimes," Bill responded, "you want to prove how tough you are to everyone else. Other times you want to prove it to yourself." But that had just been one of his theories ... until now.

With the rain streaking down, Bill saw young Will, stationed in front of his townhouse, suddenly get to his feet and start snapping off semaphore. He abruptly stopped and leapt down to the beach, grabbed his buoy and took off sprinting.

Bill felt his pulse speed up as he focused his binoculars on Megan and saw her going into the ocean—quickly in up to her waist where the strong current pulled her sideways and seconds later swept her off her feet.

She tried to reel her buoy closer as a crashing wave delivered a churning wall of water that left her completely submerged.

Ten seconds. Fifteen.

"Where are you girl? What're you doing?"

Twenty seconds.

The red buoy popped to the surface behind the white-water of the wave that put Megan under. Her head and shoulders appeared a moment later. She was being pulled up and away from the beach as another wave rolled and crashed.

Both arms around her buoy, she turned her back to the surge of water and braced for it to hit her, already half a block north of where she'd entered the ocean.

Bill saw Will running hard up the beach. The other fellow from the next block up was readying to go in the water after Megan but as she came out of that second wave, she waved him off.

With the rip current pulling Megan farther from shore, Bill Clary jerked open his door and started outside. He stopped when rain slashed his face. Swearing under his breath, he felt helpless from the passage of time—that he was no longer young and heroic as he'd once been. All the medals they'd been so nice to frame for him didn't mean a damn.

76.

It's me, Megan began, texting Pip for the first time since meeting with the lawyer. She'd erased all their old texts on her phone, even though the lawyer said that wouldn't get rid of them, because her mobile carrier kept records. And she'd thought about a burner phone—a honeyline the lawyer called it—but decided against that. Another option would have been to use an app from a company that didn't store texts, but Pip would have to use the same app and that would just emphasize they were sneaking around.

She texted: *It's been raining since Wednesday. Really raining hard. And no sun at all. It's from Tropical Storm Bernice. I've never seen the ocean this wild. Did you have any of that weather in Florida?*

Megan set down her phone, but after just a few seconds picked it up again and got her thumbs going: *Today I got my first reprimand. Not sure it was official. Adrian was really angry because I went out in the ocean. I don't think she told Captain though. Art wasn't happy about it. Will was okay. When it was just the two of us, he said it was pretty steel.*

She sent that, then added*: It was scary. But only before I got in and now thinking about it. While I was in there it was almost peaceful. Which sounds strange. The rip was intense. I ended up four blocks north before I could start getting in. And I got pulled way out. But I'd looked at the ocean for three days wondering if I could do it. Because the only time I've been in a hard rip was with you. Remember? You held me and told me what to do.*

For three days I psyched myself up. Today I got out there and let the riptide pull me and I waited and waited and waited and then it broke.

And when it did, I swam in. It took a while, but I got in. I'm still exhausted. A little keyed up too. I guess that's why this text is so long.

She sent that and started another: *I'm in your bed BTW.* And sent more after that:

I haven't texted in a while because I've been doing a lot of thinking. The rain is good for that.

I called Villa James yesterday and let Alice know I won't be coming back to teach. That was a sad conversation. And I let some of my students and their parents know. That was also hard to do.

I love you. And I miss you. But maybe you're tired of me saying that.

I guess that's enough for now. This is a lot more than I thought it would be. I hope you read this. I hope it's okay I keep sending these. It's my happiest time of day and feels good even if you don't text back.

One more thing. Ben came back yesterday and fixed a leak in the roof. I can't imagine him out there in that wind and rain and I'm sorry I wasn't here to thank him. But the drip I'd been using one of Kelly's soup pots to catch has stopped. Although there's a big wet stain in the ceiling.

And Lulu left. The weather report was pretty bad so she figured she wouldn't have much business and her parents came up with the idea to take a trip to Nashville and Lulu decided to go with them.

Summer is ending, she texted, then ended with: *Love, always, Megan.*

She set her phone on Pip's nightstand and the room fell dark along with her screen. If at some point in the future, a lawyer got hold of her wireless carrier's records and Stewart saw this text, Megan would deal with that. But she doubted that would ever happen, because one of the other realizations she'd come to, thinking in the rain, was that in a few more weeks she'd be in California. And that would be that. She'd been hoping against having to move for almost a year, but some currents were stronger than others. Inevitable even. She didn't see any other choice.

But she didn't tell Pip about that—not yet. Instead, she closed her eyes and snapped her fingers, still hoping he'd reappear.

#

Overnight, the weather finally broke, and by mid-afternoon the clouds had gone and carried away the humidity with them. But that change was too late to save the weekend and there was a slight chill in the breeze, especially in the shadows, that made it feel more like fall than summer and found Megan pulling on her hoodie.

By 4:00, only a handful of people remained on the beach, and no one was in the ocean. While the riptides had abated, the waves remained too big for casual swimmers, so Megan let a dozen eager surfers go out ahead of the usual permitted time. She confirmed her decision with Adrian, not wanting to find herself in the doghouse two days in a row, especially after Adrian had sternly reminded Megan that morning: "No crazy crap today, right?" And Megan had apologized again.

After all the dreary rain, the surfers provided welcomed entertainment, getting long rides on waves that formed distinct barrels and provided good angles. There was quite the range of ages on those boards. A few younger teenagers. Two girls Megan guessed to be Cassie's age. A handful of guys in their twenties and thirties Megan imagined might have snuck out of work early. And one man on a longboard who looked at least 50.

She couldn't hear their conversations, but from their body language the group seemed to share a friendly comradery, unlike the surfers out in California she'd seen shout aggressively at one another as if defending territory.

Once the end-of-the-day signal came up from Will and she relayed it to Art, Megan stayed on her stand, sitting on the front edge, idly kicking her legs back and forth, knocking sand off the top of one foot with the heel of the other as she watched the surfers.

A week from tomorrow was Labor Day. After that, Adrian, Art, and Will would only be back to work for two weekends. And while they were sentimental about summer ending, they looked forward to being back in school—even Will, which surprised Megan until she realized he was going to be a high school senior this year and he mentioned playing varsity basketball and soccer.

After fifteen minutes or so, she jumped off her stand and went upstairs, going directly for her phone, scrolling through texts and emails, always hopeful to hear from Pip even though it had been three weeks since their last phone call. His telling her he wasn't coming back to the beach remained a painful echo.

There was nothing from Pip. Stewart had texted as had Jackie Mack, the California real estate agent with the healthy cleavage. Stewart let Megan know Jackie would be getting in touch, and she'd done just that, advising Megan she'd communicated with the logistics company transporting their household items and confirmed arrival not just for Thursday—three days from now—but at 3:00 p.m., what would be 6:00 on the east coast, when Megan would be "off duty."

Jackie assured she'd be at the house to supervise delivery and looked forward to helping Megan in directing where everything should go. We'll get the house settled so all you'll need to do when you get here next month is come inside and have a glass of wine! I'll pour!!

Megan put her phone in her hoodie pocket and drove to Pip's cottage, where Kelly once again had left dinner for her, complete with instructions.

#

On the cottage back steps—what had become her favorite place to watch the sunset—Megan began a new text to Pip as the sky turned dark.

No rain! Finally. I guess three days wasn't that long, but it felt like it. Cassie called while I was having dinner. She's been in touch more often since our week together. Which is nice. She's not coming down for Labor Day, though. She starts school tomorrow and signed the contract to start work where she's been interning. I'm not sure which she's more excited about.

I was going to stay in tonight. Kelly left me another amazing dinner. Shrimp and pasta in vodka sauce. But I cleaned that up and I'm going to out. I'll text you when I get there. Love, Megan.

#

Framing the skeeball lane to include her 310 score and a length of prize coupons from earlier games spooling onto the floor, Megan sent the picture to Pip. *Wish you were here.*

The arcade was bright with lights and electronic noise, but few people were inside. The beach town was hungover from all the bad weather, with countless puddles serving as reminder of the rain. Only a smattering of tourists strolled the boardwalk, the most telltale sign being the lack of a line for French fries at Thrasher's—which Megan also took a picture of and sent to Pip, asking: *When's the last time you saw this?*

In her surf patrol sweatshirt, jeans, and sandals, Megan walked to the end of the boardwalk, passed beneath the little amusement park's arched entranceway, and made her way to Buckaroo Bonzai. The ride she'd operated with Pip sat quiet, lit but without riders. She took a picture and texted Pip: *Doesn't look like anyone wants to go faster.*

As she walked back to her car, Stewart called. He was in California, having flown in from Scottsdale with Dunhill on a private plane. Calling from "their house," Stewart said, "Really looking forward to you being out here. It's been a long year."

When Megan replied, "Looking forward to it, too," she did her best to make it sound as if it was true. Because sometimes lying to yourself was easier.

#

Fifteen minutes later, Megan sat in her car with the glow of the boardwalk's neon lights reflecting on her windshield. Waves rolling into the inlet crashed against the rock groin that separated the empty parking lot from the water.

The town always felt so lonely at the end of the season. Like a big house after the holidays when all the family had dispersed.

Megan took out her phone, but instead of texting Pip, she called him. Hearing his voice made her gasp, even though it was a recording: "Hey, it's Pip. Leave me a message."

"Hi…" she began in a quiet voice, her eyes becoming moist with tears. "…I thought maybe if I called you might see it was me and pick up… Anyway … something I didn't mention before, but the other week when Cassie was here, she asked me if I still loved her father. I never answered her, and she hasn't asked me again. I don't think I love Stewart anymore …. but I don't know. And even if I don't, I guess maybe I might again … sometime. Anyway, what I'm getting to is I understand if I wasn't right for you. I had my chance, didn't I?"

Megan wiped her sleeve across her face. "The first time you kissed me, I ran away the next day and didn't even say goodbye. And the night Stewart came back, I had you drive me to the beach so I could pretend I was taking a walk instead of admitting to him I'd fallen in love with you. I never thought we were an affair. I never thought I was just there until Sunday, or for the summer, or whatever the saying is you guys have—you and Kelly and Ben. My feelings for you surprised me. If I got to do it over again—and I've thought about this a few hundred times—I'd have snapped my fingers that night, remember when you said that, I should just snap my fingers and we'd go. I'm sorry I didn't do that. I'll always be sorry. Because I still miss you every minute of every day."

She blinked her teary eyes. "Sorry…" She tried to clear her voice. "Anyway … I saw on the weather report about two hurricanes around Florida. I don't know where you are, but one's in the gulf and the bigger one's in the Caribbean and the

409

forecaster said landfall might be in West Palm Beach in a couple days. So I hope you're safe. And I love you." She started to end the call, but instead, snapped her fingers. "In case that might work," she said. And snapped them again.

\#

In Naples, Florida, a man listened to Megan's voice mail message on Pip's mobile phone. And re-read the countless texts she'd sent, starting with the very first one he'd read weeks ago and ending with the series that came in earlier that evening. And the man began to think perhaps he'd made a mistake.

77.

As Labor Day weekend approached, the crowds returned to the beach, but the temperature fell into the 70's and seemed chilly when clouds blocked the sun. As kids and adults romped in the ocean and banner planes flew countless advertising sorties, there was an urgency to the change of seasons. What now? What next? What tonight? It all had to be squeezed in because summer was drawing to an end.

Megan and the other guards were kept busy, mostly handling the "policing" tasks sometimes met with snarky responses by offenders—people drinking alcohol on the beach, digging deep holes in the sand, letting dogs run loose, throwing footballs and frisbees where they might hit someone, or playing music too loudly.

There were two separate lost children alarms, but both kids turned up safely within half an hour. Megan found one little boy in a shallow furrow he'd scooped out and pulled a beach blanket over himself to hide. The small guy was quite pleased with his efforts and said he was playing spy. Megan told him next time he might want to choose a hiding place where someone might not unwittingly lie down on top of him.

Megan had one save, a borderline false alarm, swimming out to a pale-skinned man who'd floated on his back beyond the waves and panicked when realizing was out over his head. In the short time it took Megan to swim to him, the man made his way to shallower water.

Lulu sent a selfie from the Grand Ole Opry, saying she was having a great time but missed everyone. *See you next summer?* she asked. To which Megan replied, *Most def.* Because it was easy to feel hopeful in the middle of it all, as if how could she ever spend summer anywhere else?

The nights were more troubling.

#

One night, Kelly heard her crying and came up the stairs to knock lightly on her opened bedroom door. "What's wrong, hon?"

She told him Pip not responding to her voice mail felt more like rejection than having three weeks of texts go unanswered. It seemed more final—that he was over her—and with that her last twinkle of hope had begun to dim.

"He's not being himself," Kelly appreciated. "And I don't know what's going on with him. He's not answering my texts either. But hang in there."

Megan sat up and asked Kelly if he'd found a new place to live.

"Going back to Cleveland, my love. I reconnected with an old boss who turns out is starting his own place and asked if I wanted to run his kitchen."

"That sounds good."

"It sounds like cold winters. But I will manage. And you?" he inquired. "California-bound?"

She shrugged with regret.

He crossed his arms. "Not our first choices, hm? Well … try to sleep. And don't give up on our boy just yet."

As Kelly descended the stairs, Megan got out of bed and stood at the window. The bay was quiet and still, the white caps of last week having smoothed like glass.

She started to send Pip a text but for the second night in a row called instead. When voice mail again picked up, her words remained choked by spent tears. "I just need to know you're okay. And if you don't love me any more … just let me know. I don't know that I'll ever get over that. But it might help me start to try if that's the way you feel."

Sunrise came without a response.

#

With the ocean having calmed, Megan and her fellow guards were back in the routine of their morning swim. Bill Clary waved from his balcony as they jogged by on their way back up the beach.

At noon, a young family of five introduced themselves to Megan, saying they'd been there all week and had felt safe going in the ocean with Megan watching over them. They brought her lunch, sliced chicken breast on grain bread with cheese and mayo, and a small container of macaroni salad. Written along the edge of the paper plate mom handed up to Megan was: *Thanks from John, Chris, Amy, Todd, and Kurt.*

When the family's 8-year-old asked if he could see what the ocean looked like from Megan's stand, his mom said she was sure that wasn't allowed.

Megan said, "Well how about just sneak up here for a minute."

Todd was athletic and made quick work of the sandy ladder steps. Megan slid over so he could sit beside her. His short hair was blond from summer sun.

Taking in the view, he said, "Cool," and sat with her for 15 minutes. When it was time to go, he surprised Megan and gave her a hug. And it reminded her of when she first picked Cassie up into her arms. She didn't want to let him go.

That night, when Megan's friend Jillian called, they talked for half an hour. Megan mentioned Kelly—referring to him only as someone she happened to talk to who mentioned moving to Ohio—and that he might be someone Jillian would look up one day. "He's a pretty fabulous chef, so I'm sure the food will be great."

As when they last spoke, Jillian apologized for not calling more often. "We said when I moved, we wouldn't let that happen." After bringing Megan up to date on her own busy summer, Jillian said, "Enough about me, what all's been going on with you? How's the lifeguard life?"

"Well," Megan began, "today was pretty interesting..."

"Were you a hero?"

"No. I ... um ... I started to think I want to have a baby."

Silence from Jillian, who was happily childless. Then: "You're kidding..."

"Biological clock, I guess," Megan lied, because she didn't want to tell Jillian the truth. Their friendship that had shared many private thoughts no longer held the capacity for Megan to divulge her feelings about Pip, who she called again later.

Her voice mail message to him that night began: "I never told you, but when I was out in California, I saw these little houses right on the beach. They were built in the sixties and looked like they were made of driftwood and mismatched boards and all these other mixes of shingles and other materials. And I went inside one and wondered what it would have been like to live there back then. And I imagined you there. And I imagined a little girl with long blond hair. And that she was our daughter. And then today, a little boy came up onto my stand and sat with me for a little while. And he had blond hair like you, and I thought if we had a boy, he might look like that... That's all. That was today." She ended the call and gently placed her phone on Pip's nightstand.

78.

It was "moving day." That was how Stewart enthusiastically referred to it in a series of texts Megan didn't open until back upstairs in the condo after finished work for the day. By then, Stewart had sent five texts, counting down the hours as though it was New Year's Eve until their furniture was scheduled to arrive at their Newport Coast house. Each text included a link to a live map that showed the three delivery trucks' current location. Stewart's most recent text: *ETA one hour!*

Jackie Mack had also been texting. She was already at the house with her own movers, those she trusted when staging her multi-million-dollar listings. She sent a picture of five serious-looking men standing ready in the foyer, all outfitted in black like special ops forces. The logistics employees coming on the moving trucks would unload the Tylers' belongings, but Jackie's group would bring everything inside and place it at the family's directions. Jackie also introduced "her star decorator," a striking blond named Olivia who "had some ideas."

Megan showered and ordered a pizza, bracing herself for a long night. Already maudlin over the end of summer, the thought of their Hunt Valley home now sitting empty was disorienting and sad—the realization she would never set foot inside there again. Maybe she should have gone back and taken a few days to pack, perhaps that would have been a more proper farewell, but that would have also meant leaving the beach, because the house had sold quickly, and the new owners were eager to take occupancy. Her life seemed to keep moving on someone else's schedule.

Megan showered and her pizza arrived by the time Jackie Mack texted that the moving trucks were delayed by "freeway traffic." Something to get used to, Jackie advised.

Fifteen minutes later, their communications switched to video conference, joined by Stewart and Cassie.

Jackie wore another expensive-looking ensemble that straddled a fine line between professional and tawdry. Her blouse's top-most buttons were strategically undone just enough to celebrate her ample cleavage. Her slacks were tight at the waist and hips with wide legs. Her heels would have caused a less-practiced fashionista to stumble.

Cassie, seated at the desk in her studio apartment, rubbed her hands together and said, "So exciting! Mom this is so great!"

Cassie was still calling her mom and had gone back to Stewart being "dad." The simple words provided Megan with a joy that had fallen dormant, like seeing a spring flower appear through frost-coated grass.

Cassie's enthusiasm wasn't limited to the move. She was excited about her first week back at GW and having begun her paid position at the analytics firm. She was in the midst of describing being assigned her own cubicle at work when Jackie broke in, "They're coming folks!"

Megan's iPad cut to an aerial view. A drone over San Joaquin Hills picked up a trio of large trucks exiting the freeway onto Newport Coast Drive, beginning down the verdant hillside. All the large homes with red-tiled rooves looked like Monopoly pieces from the sky, built into the rock hills and ravines. Megan had no idea which house—which neighborhood—was theirs.

"Fabulous day out here," Stewart said, seeing the coastal cliffs bathed in sunlight.

The ocean sparkled, vibrant and crystal blue.

Jackie strode onto the front landing as the moving trucks came down the street. She directed the order in which the trucks would back into the driveway to be unloaded.

As the rear doors of the first truck opened, Megan wanted to tell everyone to stop. To not take anything off the trucks but turn around and head back east. She wanted to "unsell" their house in Hunt Valley. Wanted Stewart to "unsell" his company to Dunhill. Wanted Cassie back home, back in high school, or even better, back in elementary school. It wasn't the first time she'd felt that way. But, at that moment, she decided it needed to be the last. Because it could not be undone. And while she'd always known that, she'd never accepted it.

She looked at Stewart's image, appearing in a small square inset on her screen. He was at his desk in his sunny corner office, with a view she had not yet seen in person of a city she did not know. He peered intently at his monitor as the first boxes came off the truck, wheeled down the ramp on a series of hand carts. She felt an undeniable fondness for him, but it was no longer love. Perhaps that could return.

Over the next five hours, their lives from Maryland were unpacked in Newport Coast. Furniture was unbound from protective padding and positioned in the proper room, with most of the staging furniture taken out, although some pieces remained. The larger furnishings—sofas, chairs, tables, lamps, beds, dressers—went into place first and at Megan's direction, but soon Jackie and Olivia's "suggestions" turned to directives. By that time, Megan was doing her best to conceal growing weary of the process and was happy to merely give approval, which Cassie joined in. By the end, most of the rooms had been rearranged, with a third of their furniture going back on the truck—not to be returned to Maryland—but to go into storage, replaced by new items, including an oversized leather Chesterfield sofa that Olivia "virtually" situated in the living room and Stewart and Cassie agreed was a show piece.

"I'll put the orders in first thing in the morning," Olivia assured Megan of the new furniture. "It will all be here by your arrival date." Olivia treated Megan as if she was a top-tier celebrity—maybe that was her usual clientele.

The trucks unpacked, the niceties spoken, it was almost midnight by the time Megan got back to Pip's cottage.

Kelly was in the kitchen, leafing through an old *Good Housekeeping* recipe book Megan had found in their Hunt Valley kitchen, left forgotten in the back of a cabinet. "How did it go?" he asked, aware of Megan's moving business scheduled for that night.

She pulled out a wooden chair and sat. Setting her iPad on the table alongside the opened cookbook, she started the slideshow of photographs Jackie Mack had already put together: all of their furniture (and virtual furniture) professionally arranged around the house; clothes hung or folded in custom dressers in massive walk-in closets; art pieces and mirrors and photographs on the walls; kitchen wares arranged as if opening a new Williams and Sonoma location.

Kelly marveled, "Good Lord, girl, look at the size of this place. This is your new house?"

Megan stared across the kitchen without focusing. "It all feels like a lie. Like I'm trying to make my marriage work, but I'm really waiting—hoping—for Pip to come back. Which means I'm not really trying to make my marriage work at all doesn't it?" She considered Kelly, his chef's coat loosened at the collar.

He asked, "Do you want your marriage to work?"

She thought a moment, how to make sense of her feelings. "I did before I met Pip."

"Then that's a no," Kelly determined. "Being second place in love is much closer to being last than first. Nobody's marriage should be the consolation prize."

"I don't want to hurt him."

"Your husband?"

Megan nodded. "I'm not sure the love is going to come back. On one hand, I think I should try ... on the other..."

"Do you want the love to come back?"

Megan lifted her hand from the table, then dropped it. "Is that really a question? How does that work? You say to someone, I want to love you ... can you make that happen? No, it just happens. You fall in love."

"Was it love at first sight with your husband?"

"No."

"All right. So something happened, over time. Events took place and you fell in love because of them."

She considered that. "My feelings were never as strong for him as they are for Pip. With Pip, I think it happened so powerfully and so fast I didn't even realize what it was at first. I never tried to love him. I just did." Megan idly smoothed her palm over the tabletop. "Maybe this is what lost love feels like."

"Which one? The love you lost for your husband? Or Pip being gone?"

79.

The following morning, Friday, Megan missed her morning swim to attend a meeting at the surf patrol office. In the same florescent-lit room where she'd gone through orientation, she introduced herself to the handful of guards who'd arrived ahead of her—none of whom she recognized.

Captain Garrison strode into the room, clipboard in hand, at 7:45. By that time, Megan was surprised to count only 31 guards, half of whom, including Megan, took a seat at schoolroom-style desk-chairs. The rest stood or leaned against the wall.

It was like being in a classroom of athletes, all tanned and in shape from a summer on a stand. There was an even mix guys to girls. Some looked like surf rats. Others could have been marines. Megan figured she was the oldest by at least a decade. She got a few inquisitive looks and heard at least one whisper of, "OCSP Mom." Her social media tag had begun to fade, though still accounted for a few greetings and well-wishes most days.

Garrison didn't small talk, making clear he wouldn't keep them long. The meeting was to outline changes being put into place now that the number of guards was going to drop from the full summertime roster of 150 to about a fifth of that next week.

Garrison rattled off assignments. Megan's current stand was among many being de-activated. She was being shifted a block north to take Art's stand and would now be responsible to cover four total blocks. The stretch of ocean she'd covered with Will, Art, and Adriane was now hers alone.

"Next issue," Garrison continued. "We've got a hurricane coming. Noah," he pronounced, meaning NOAA, "has updated models with landfall anywhere from Wilmington, North Carolina to Westerly, Rhode Island. But last week they said it was going to hit West Palm Beach, so who knows. They clearly don't. It comes here, it's not until after Labor Day. Just in case, go through your handbooks—yeah, you know those things you claim you read but didn't—remind yourself what we do to assist emergency responders. If it's going to hit us, we'll meet again and go over it." He checked the diver's watch on his thick wrist. "Questions?"

There were none. Megan imagined that, except for her, they were a seasoned bunch.

"Okay. That's it."

As the group amiably filed out of the room, Garrison got Megan's attention, saying, "Tyler—with me." And had her follow him to his cramped office of wood-paneled walls.

Once there, he closed the door and dropped his clipboard on a metal file cabinet. "This is informal," he said, firm but reassuring. "But it's a little more than a wink and nod."

"Okay…" Megan anticipated what was coming.

And Garrison looked as if he knew that she knew. "The other day … you don't go in the ocean when it's like that on your own. We have controlled training sessions for that. You go out there and get in trouble, you put other guards at risk. Because they're not going to let you drown—even though they might drown coming in after you. I told you the other week, follow Pippinger's good habits. Not his bad ones. Being confident is one thing. Thinking you're invincible's just plain stupid. And dangerous."

She nodded with contrition. "I understand. I'm sorry. I apologized to Adrian and Art."

"All right. There's that then," Garrison sighed, scratching grey hairs at his temple as he moved behind his desk. "Every time I had this discussion with Pippinger, him swimming out there when he shouldn't or doing something else, he just smiled at me. Same thing every year, telling me, oh, come on, how the riptide always breaks. And I told him, no, sometimes it doesn't. Not soon enough anyway."

Megan nodded. "I understand," she repeated.

Garrison waved her toward the door. "Okay—that's it. Go to work."

"Yes, sir."

"You hear anything from him, by the way? Pip?"

"No, sir."

"I called him a few times, see how he's doing. Just got voice mail. Guess he's all right."

"I hope so." Megan reached to open the door.

"End of season party tomorrow night," he reminded. "You going?"

She turned to face him. "I wasn't here the whole summer." She shrugged. "Doesn't seem right."

"That's crap—you should come," he invited. "Fall-timers have a special place in my heart."

#

Fall-timers was what the surf patrol called guards who stayed beyond Labor Day to work out the entire season.

Saturday night, with a bright moon shining through thin clouds and a bonfire crackling sparks into the sky above an open stretch of Assateague Island beach, Captain Garrison gave special praise to his latest crew of Fall-timers. "To hell with education or careers or families," he offered with an uncharacteristic smile, raising his third bottle of Yuengling Amber in toast. "Just stay on your stand as autumn winds sweep in and the crazy tourists go home, and you've got the beach all to yourself." He took a swig of beer as his Fall-timers, including Megan, cheered, then he wiped his mouth and added, "Not that we don't love the rest of you."

The remaining guards and their plus-ones joined the chorus of self-applause.

"You all had a good season." Garrison unfolded a page and cited impressive statistics, ranking this year's crew against those from years past, a history that extended over 80 years. "And most importantly," he finished, "no fatalities."

Everyone cheered.

"Now let's line it up," Garrison directed. "Guards in front of the dunes between those two markers."

The nearly 100 guards in attendance, having already been happily fed barbeque, arranged themselves in three rows—kneeling in the front, leaning forward in the middle, standing in the rear—for a series of photographs, some taken by the local papers, others by their dates or friends. Garrison stood in the center. Megan knelt toward one end, with Adrian on her left and Art next to Adrian, the three of them close together, arms around one another.

Will wasn't there. He'd hugged Megan goodbye after the end-of-day signal yesterday, telling her, "Great summer. Cassie was great. But you hear from Pip, tell him I'm still ticked he left."

"See you next summer...?" Megan had asked, not sure if she was asking him or herself.

"Who knows," Will shrugged. "Hope so." And then he'd trotted off down the beach one last time.

Now, as professional cameras cast fill-in flash to evenly light what the bonfire put in shadow and mobile phones were focused, picture after picture was taken. The group held still for a minute before becoming playfully restless, then stayed mostly in position as they jostled and laughed, only settling again when Garrison barked for everyone's attention. He counted down for a final shot that was captured to video. And on three, everyone called out loudly: "Where are you Pip!"

#

"Where are you, brother? We miss you." One of the older guards cocked his head to the side, peering into the camera. Megan recognized him from the dinner at Half Shell.

"Miss you Pip," another guard said somberly.

"Never met you," a young guy said, "but heard the stories. Cool stuff, dude. Be well."

"Hey good-looking, where'd you run off to?" a girl in her twenties asked.

"Time marches on, old friend," one of the Fall-timers toasted with his beer.

There were a lot of hang-loose hand gestures, smiles, a few blown kisses.

Art tried to smile, but ended up shaking his head, "I don't get it, but wherever you are, I hope it's good. I miss you."

"Me, too," Adrian said, putting both arms around Arthur as she moved in to share the frame. "Thanks for everything, big brother. Making me the guard I am."

Captain Garrison waited until everyone else had their chance, then stood in front of the camera. He started to say something but ended up looking off to the side as if holding back tears, then walked away.

When no one else stepped into position, the cameraman turned toward Megan, sitting on the sand off his shoulder. He focused his viewfinder on her. "Anything to add?" he asked.

She smiled fondly. "He knows how I feel."

Two hours later, she texted Pip the link to the tribute, now posted on the surf patrol website along with the still photo from the End of Season party that would soon hang in the paneled hall of the surf patrol office. The first picture in over a decade without Pip in it.

Three days later, the season was over.

80.

It was the third of September, and the beach was empty. The kids were back in school.

Megan dove into the ocean, which felt warm compared to the air. Alone, she swam south for three blocks, then started back up the beach at an easy jog.

Summer's end seemed so sudden, even though she'd felt it coming for weeks. The start of September was always bittersweet. While it marked the end of her favorite season, the new school year had always promised adventures and opportunities, new friendships, new subjects to learn— experiences she'd first enjoyed as a student, then a teacher, and finally as a mom to Cassie. She didn't feel that same way now, when all that waited for her was California, with Stewart.

To avoid looking forward, she looked back, and thought about the first time she'd gone out in the ocean to swim back in May—how when Pip had talked to her, she hadn't even been able to see his face for the bright sky behind him. But there had been something immediate in that moment—she realized that now—an undefinable spark that ignited feelings she couldn't ignore.

From his deck, Bill Clary cupped his hands around his mouth and called out, "And then there was one!"

Megan detoured from her direct course up to Art's stand—what was now her stand—to say hello.

Clary gestured with open arms as if welcoming the empty beach. "The barbarians have receded," he grinned. "At long last. Only now we've got a hurricane coming."

"I saw the forecast this morning," Megan acknowledged. "Kind of puts us in the middle of things."

"Let's hope not. It's been unpredictable so far. I'm hoping it wobbles and stays out there." He waved toward the horizon. "The missus is talking about bugging out, though. We stayed through one a few years back—she said never again."

"Where will you go?"

"House in Annapolis. Our main place."

"I like Annapolis. It's very pretty there."

"Except for all the politicians," Clary sneered, then, more hospitably, said, "Talked to the boy before he left last week." Referring to Will. "Said no one's still heard boo from Pip."

Megan shook her head. "No."

"They'll be an explanation. Got all the markings of an intervening hand. A meddler," Clary winked, always expressive with he spoke.

"Maybe."

"How long you staying?" he asked.

"Through the month."

"Good. Glad to hear that."

"How about you?"

"Probably about the same. But I do what the missus tells me—she says that's good for me. Might go with her down to Charleston she heads that way in October. Sneak off and have some shrimp and grits while she's working."

"I guess I'll be in California by then."

"With the husband?" Clary asked, then winked again. "I wouldn't be so sure."

She tried not to feel hopeful. "You know something I don't?"

His voice deepened to accentuate his single word response: "Intuition."

#

The start-of-the-day signal was feint and distant, relayed by the guard almost three blocks away. The breeze nearly carried the sound of his whistle out to sea.

After relaying the signal north, Megan settled onto her stand, sweats pulled on over her wet bathing suit.

No banner planes flew all morning. When a lone seagull passed overhead, its squawk echoed hollowly, a sound looking for a friend.

By noon, only a few families arrived to enjoy the sunshine, their blankets, playpens, and umbrellas brought from home since Lulu and her competitors had closed for the season. Happy grandparents doted on toddlers, who squealed getting their feet wet when the salty ocean rolled ashore. Moms and dads took pictures and videos of kids too little to be in school. A few folks went into the ocean, but everyone stayed within the wave break, which was relatively tame. Usually there would have been more people, but the threat of a hurricane kept tourists out of town. No sense renting a condo for a week if half that time was going to be washed out by rain and wind.

Megan felt the first change in the weather when the tide came in later that afternoon. The sky remained clear, but there was an uneasy shift in the wind and the ocean turned choppy. Waves, which had been small, grew larger—three-foot breakers that brought smiles to a handful of surfers who Megan let in the ocean ahead of the permitted time. Two of the surf riders laughed about having skipped out of school early. The one saying, "Picking up right where we left off."

By the time she dragged her stand back to the dunes at the end of the day, the waves were even larger, and the breeze picked up. There was a heaviness to the air. And for the second time in a week, the guards were called into the surf patrol office.

#

"Dominic," Captain Garrison warned his Fall-timers, "is currently Cat-four, likely to make five unless it hits the Outer Banks, and they take some of the force out of it. Best case scenario: we're looking at high winds and surf, lots of beach erosion. Twenty years ago, we had a hurricane lay off the coast for days and got such massive rips you couldn't let anyone in the water even to their knees. You didn't have to look for the rips, you could see them dredging out gulfs in the sand two feet deep. Worst case: the town's talking about an evacuation order if there's a chance of a direct hit.

"Everyone's getting a mobile phone," he continued. "We're still on flags but in case something breaks fast use the phone. We've got three mobile units who can get to you if you need help." Garrison named the guards assigned to those patrols, who would no longer be on stands but would ride up and down the beach or highway on a pair of four-wheelers and a Jeep. As one of the least experienced guards, Megan was not assigned to any of those units.

"Keep in mind, these phones you're getting are surf patrol property. Only for work business. No personal calls or texts. None. Downtown will be able to see whatever you do on these phones. Needless to say, but I'm saying it anyway: no porn, no online poker, no YouTube, no sports bets, not even any pizza deliveries."

Each separate admonition caused a chuckle or wry comment which Garrison ignored.

"If we get an evacuation order, you keep check on your beach and your beachfront block. Sand to highway. Let people know about the order. Let them know whether it's mandatory or not. Make sure they know, either way, emergency responders will not come if they call. Fire, police, ambulance. They need 911 they're out of luck. Which of course is not necessarily true but make them believe it is."

#

"Maybe I should be scared. I'm not, though. Not yet anyway." That evening, Megan left another voice mail message for Pip. She stood on the steps of the cottage with the breeze at her back as nightfall washed fading colors of dusk from the sky and tall cattails swayed in the shallows.

"I went up on the boardwalk after the meeting and it was like a ghost town. There were only a handful of cars on the road. I stopped by Dockside Annie's to see Kelly and they were empty—only some guys at the bar. Kelly fixed fish and chips and ate with me. He'll probably be home soon. He's started packing … which is sad. But he seems to be looking forward to working for his old boss. I think he was going to be lonely here by himself this winter."

She pushed hair from her face. "The wind's picking up. Maybe you can hear. And there're white caps on the bay. If this keeps up, I probably won't swim tomorrow morning. I would have if you were here, though."

She stepped onto the yard for a wider view of the sky, looking for stars between clouds that had rolled in. "I miss you even more without everyone here. Actually … no … that's not true. It's not possible to miss you any more than I already did." She paused, then added softly, "Love you. I'll call again tomorrow."

#

Overnight, the wind increased, whistling beneath the aged cottage's roof eaves and seeking ingress around its windows and doors.

Hurricane Dominic was coming.

429

81.

Wednesday morning, Megan needed to force her car door open against the wind to get out. Starting toward the dunes, she leaned into the steady gusts to stride forward, her sweats whipping against her arms and legs. She tilted her head to the side and held her wrist taught to prevent her buoy from twisting in her grip. Her free hand shielded her eyes against the sting of blown sand.

She heard the waves, crashing like thunder, but was still surprised by the sheer size of them. The swells were powerful and huge, rising and breaking one after the other, throwing the tide onto the beach almost to her stand, pulled back to the dunes.

Buffeted by the wind, she kept her stand where it was and climbed to the top, bracing herself so as not to be blown off. Her nearest fellow guard—three blocks south—was barely visible through swirling sand and salt spray.

Not fifteen minutes later, her cellphone lit with a text. The beaches were being closed.

Megan spent the morning on foot, patrolling along the dune line as the tide continued to rise, the surge of churning surf pushing closer. Her carry bag and buoy, slung over her shoulder, constantly wanted to twist in the wind.

She turned a dozen people away from the beach. Most were teenagers, two of whom came with surfboards they could barely manage to hold under their arms, and even they thought better of their chances in the ocean after Megan let them get a glimpse of it.

By mid-afternoon, the sky was blanketed by clouds sweeping northward as if trying to outrace Dominic's cyclonic grasp. The sound of the wind and waves was joined by hammers and nail guns as homeowners boarded up windows.

It turned out to be a long and tedious day. Watching and waiting to see what the storm would bring. Megan's face burned from the wind.

Late in the afternoon, Bill Clary trudged over the dunes to intercept her. Holding his Washington Nationals' cap in place on his head, he talked loudly over the thump of the waves. "Misses says we're bugging out. We're going to get up the road before dark. Talked to a friend and he's pretty sure the town's going under an evacuation order. They're hoping against hope but looks like we're in for a hit."

"I've heard the same," Megan replied, setting down her buoy and bag, glad to have the weight off her shoulder.

"You be careful in this mess."

"I will be."

"And you don't mind…" He pulled his phone from his pocket. "…I give you my contact information, will you call us? Let us know you're okay?"

"Sure—happy to." She knelt into her bag for her personal phone—which she now carried along with the mobile issued by the surf patrol—and exchanged texts with the older man. "You be careful too," Megan said. "I'll miss you being here."

"We'll miss you, too. You made our summer. Gave us some joy. Maybe we have a chance to have some more once this blows through." He smiled fondly. "I hope you hear from your boy."

"Me, too."

"Love can be hard sometimes. Always worth it, though."

She nodded, then gave him a hug.

He patted her back, his eyes becoming moist looking at Megan once she eased away. He hesitated a moment before telling her: "We had a daughter. Name was Penny. And she died—sudden. And you remind us of her—what she would have looked like come to your age. Maybe remind me more than Mary Jane—she has a harder time thinking about her. Cause we only had the one. And once she was gone … well, it was too late for having more. Not sure we would have anyway."

Megan could tell his pain lingered from that loss. "I'm so sorry. I can't imagine how awful that must have been."

"No one should have to go through that."

"No, they shouldn't." Megan hugged him again, then saw Mary Jane up on their deck, binoculars hanging around her neck, waving both arms to get their attention and calling something they couldn't hear.

Bill turned and hollered to his wife, "Can't hear you, darling."

Mary Jane shouted back and pointed toward the ocean.

Megan turned and saw the wave, rising like a shimmering monolith. She tensed with fear as the swell slowly rolled over and crashed, spraying white water and pushing a surge of seawater toward the shore.

But it wasn't the wave Mary Jane had been pointing to. Visible once the ocean momentarily lost some of its height, a pair of dolphins coursed through the churning surf, seemingly unaffected by the strong pull of a receding wave. With a flex of sleek bodies, they eased through whatever the ocean brought to bear. Over and over, their smiling faces, then fins, then tails appeared, like riders on a watery merry-go-round, positioned side by side, gliding along as if the white caps were a mere resource for their merriment.

As Megan and Clary watched them, Megan's surf patrol phone sounded an alarm. She dug into her bag and read the message aloud: "Mandatory evacuation tomorrow at noon."

Clary smiled grimly. "Here we go then. You take care of yourself. Be careful."

#

As Megan pulled up to the cottage in her Volvo, Kelly came out carrying a full moving box and was pushed sideways by the wind.

"All good things have to end sometimes," he called as she got out of her sedan.

She slung her carry bag over her shoulder but kept her buoy in the car, needing to push hard on the door to close it. "You heard about the evacuation order?"

"I did." He fit the box into his trunk, already packed with cartons of various sizes, pieced into place like a 3D jigsaw puzzle. Shutting the lid, he smiled at Megan as if a happy expression might make it better.

Inside the cottage, Megan's relief to be out of the wind was short-lived. She was surprised to see more packed boxes and a suitcase lined alongside the stairs. Kelly looked to have spent the day packing and it didn't seem like the effort of someone temporarily fleeing a storm. "You're leaving-leaving?" she guessed, not wanting that to be true.

Alongside her, Kelly said, "Surprising how little there is to move in a life in ruins."

Some of the boxes were marked KITCHEN in black marker.

He said, "Turns out my most treasured possessions are stuff you gave me. Not just what it is, but that it's from you."

Megan thought she might cry. She didn't want him to go. Didn't want to lose another connection to what, for such a very short time, had been the perfect summer. In love with Pip. Moving into this cottage. Meeting Ben and Kelly. Swimming with Adrian and Art and Will.

Kelly hugged her. "Don't cry, darling. There are fewer reasons for me to stay than to go. You are probably the only reason to stay. But maybe the storm is a sign. I came here a few years ago to get over my wife leaving me, and I think I finally may have done that. You helped more than you'll ever know. But what I need now I don't think I'll find here. This place—the beach—is where people come to escape and dream. I've done that. I think I'm ready to face reality."

She nodded against his shoulder. Because she did understand. "I'll help you with the rest of the boxes."

"It can wait until morning." He turned for the kitchen. "I've got dinner starting."

She asked if he'd put on the opera music that had been playing the first evening Pip brought her there, and while he didn't remember the aria, he started a favored opera playlist and turned it up loudly enough to be heard over the howling wind that pushed against the little house.

Megan settled on the sofa, closed her eyes, and listened to the music. It had been a tiring day. Tomorrow promised more of the same. There would not be any start-of-the-day signal, but at 9:00 a.m. she was to start going door-to-door, notifying anyone still in town of the requirement to evacuate. Just days ago, some prediction models had Hurricane Dominic going out to sea—now it was expected to make landfall as early as tomorrow night.

After a few minutes, the smell of steak made Megan realize how hungry she was. She pulled herself off the sofa and went into the kitchen to help Kelly with dinner. Usually, he would have banished any would-be assistants from doing more than setting the table, but tonight they worked as a team.

"You missed your calling, love," Kelly said as she prepared salad dressing. "We could have used you at the restaurant."

For an hour, they ate and talked as if no storm was coming, and no loves had been lost. By the end of the meal, the aria that greeted Megan's arrival to the cottage began to play. She said, "This is the one," and closed her eyes and listened, and pictured Pip in a collage of memories: that first day they'd spoken, him telling her about the guard test, him getting his crew to become a part of her morning swims, which turned into training, then that day in the lightning storm, Pip running for cover, then going up to her condo, kissing her, then weeks later meeting her at the airport, the drive to the beach in the Jeep with the top down, in bed with him that first time, and all the times after, until that night when Stewart surprised her, coming to town without notice, and Pip had hurriedly driven her to the beach, and she'd run out onto the dunes, leaving Pip behind when what she should have done was snapped her fingers and said, "Let's go."

That had been one of the last times she'd seen him in person. After that, it had been mostly video chats while he waited for doctors to update him about Aunt Nan, and when she'd died it was as if Pip had died along with her.

Megan took a deep breath and opened her eyes, surprised to find Kelly had cleared the plates from dinner, leaving her to her thoughts.

An hour later, the first band of rain from Hurricane Dominic slashed against the cottage windows, and the lights began to flicker.

#

Cassie texted. Having heard about the evacuation order, Cassie asked where Megan was going to go and was surprised by Megan's response: *I'm staying here. Working.*

After a few back-and-forth's that explained the change in Megan's surf patrol duties, Cassie expressed concern: *They say it could be really bad. Historic bad!*

Megan suppressed fear that had been rising with the wind speed and assured Cassie she'd be fine.

Not ten minutes later, Stewart called for the first time in three days. "I'm just seeing about this hurricane. I'm sorry. I feel ridiculous not knowing, but it hasn't really made the news out here. I mean, I've been seeing about it for a while, when it was down by Florida, but I thought it was going out to sea. And we've got all these wildfires in the news out here. But this looks bad. They've evacuated the town?"

"Tomorrow at noon." Megan had gone upstairs to Pip's bedroom to take the call, closing the door even though Kelly turned down the music.

The windows rattled in their frame, beaten by wind and another band of rain.

"You're really going to stay? You think that's a good idea?"

"It's fine. I'll be fine. I'm not out on the beach." She offered the same explanation of her shift in responsibilities she'd given Cassie.

"I don't know ... this seems really dangerous. Hunkering down in our condo is one thing—the building's sound." Stewart had been on the condo board three years ago when the Ocean Vista underwent an intensive structural inspection. "But outside? All those old places? I'm looking at your wind forecasts. Roof shingles are not going to stay on. They'll start sailing around like knives."

"I'll be careful. If it gets bad, I'll stay in. I'll hunker down," she assured, using his phrase.

"I'd feel better if you'd get out of there. Go stay with Cassie. She'd love to have you for a few days. Then go back after it's over. Or better yet just come out here. The house is just waiting for you."

"I'll be fine. Really. I'll be careful."

The wind roared and the cottage's lights flickered again. Went out. Came back on. And went out.

#

An hour later, the power remained out and it began to get warm in the cottage. The wind was loud and seemed as if throwing itself against the outside walls.

Megan called Pip and left another voice mail, wondering, as she always did, if he got her messages and what he thought when he listened to them. And why he didn't call back. She wasn't ready to believe he didn't love her anymore. She couldn't let that go.

She told him about the waves and the wind, that it had been raining off and on. "It's scary, but when I think about you it makes it better."

In the dark, with wind gusts causing the old house to creak and moan, Megan sat on the edge of Pip's bed and looked toward the window. She couldn't see the bay, but imagined it covered with white caps, pushing in through the cattails toward the back lawn.

She told Pip's voice mail: "Kelly's going back to Cleveland tomorrow. He's pretty much all packed. And he seems like he's ready. I think I'm going to stay here, though, even after he's gone. I don't know..." She laid back. "...after the past year, I guess I've gotten used to being lonely. Everybody goes and it's just me. Anyway..." She didn't want it to seem as if she was trying to make him feel sorry for her. "...Cassie called tonight. Then Stewart. Then both want me to leave before the hurricane, but I said no. And I think tonight Stewart realized what I was saying was I'd rather be here in a hurricane than out there with him ... in a million-dollar house overlooking the Pacific. I should have told him that the night he came back, and I'll forever regret not doing that. Not snapping my fingers and letting you know we should leave. I'm going to try to do that now, though. Even if it's too late." She reached her arm above her, her hand barely visible in the dark, and snapped her fingers. "Let's go. Just you and me."

82.

Pippinger Real Estate Holdings, LLC occupied the top floor of a classic Spanish-style building overlooking shimmering Naples Bay. The office structure had been designed and built by the company's eponymous founder, Charles Pippinger, who ignored the warnings of consultants that Spanish architecture was overdone in South Florida and tenants wanted glass and steel, black and grey. Then those tenants could go somewhere else, Charles told the consultants, and went ahead to do the project the way he wanted, as he typically did. And the building had been fully occupied since day one.

Charles Pippinger was usually right. But not always.

Early Thursday morning, a Maserati Ghibli Trofeo in metallic *blu emozione* turned into the office parking lot, which was mostly empty that early in the day. The sleek sedan was steered to its reserved covered space beneath a second-floor terrace.

57-year-old Charles Pippinger got out from behind the wheel and firmly shut the door. Charles was six-two, handsome, lean, although not as slender as when he used to play tennis before his right knee started barking at him. He wore a custom-tailored dress shirt and slacks with a one-inch cuff. It was his look, and he wasn't going to change, any more than he was going to style his hair other than combing it straight back. And maybe his hair was a little longer than it should be, maybe it blew a little in the Florida breeze sometimes. Ask him if he cared what anyone else thought.

Charles was not married and never had been. He dated—and still called it that—and always women who were age appropriate and liked to read. He had not been in love romantically since high school. He was 17 when Marci moved away with her family. After a few months she told him she was seeing someone else, which broke his heart so hard he promised himself he'd never fall in love again.

Not that he was incapable of love. He had always dearly loved his family—his parents, siblings, nieces, and nephews—but that was different. That love was innate and as much about loyalty as emotion.

He was especially fond of his late brother's boy, Blake, who in truth was his favorite. He'd tried numerous times since his brother's sudden death to take Blake under his wing, build him into a success, but the boy couldn't let go of living a life at the beach. Of being a boy. No matter how enticing a carrot Charles had dangled at the end of the stick, Blake couldn't be convinced. Until now…

Charles finally felt like he had Blake focused. Trouble was, now he wasn't so sure it was the right track after all.

Riding the elevator to the fifth floor, Charles scrolled through the text messages on Blake's phone. Charles had read the texts dozens of times already—Pip had not, because that was part of their deal. Now, Charles read them again. Entering his office's reception area, he spoke over Marta's friendly, "Good morning," and asked, "Blake in his office?"

"Pip left about ten minutes ago."

Charles insisted on introducing his nephew as Blake, but everyone always ended up calling him Pip.

Marta said, "I thought you might have passed him coming in. He's going to Sapphire Bay. The tenants really seem to have taken to him. Everything all right?" The long-time staffer read her employer's concern.

Charles sat in one of the room's matching chairs and ran a hand back through his hair.

The reception area was a modest size. All the bragging was done by a wall of framed photographs: two decades of successful projects. Through up cycles and down, Charles Pippinger never had a loser. Not a single one. It had been close once or twice, but he'd bailed them out. Then again, success was not easy.

"Sir…?" Marta questioned.

Looking out the window at the sparking bay, Charles admitted, "I may have done the boy a disservice."

#

"Be safe." Megan raised her voice over the wind for Kelly to hear.

"You, too."

Beneath a low sky of fast-moving clouds, they hugged on the oyster-shell driveway. The air was heavy with humidity and the morning light cast an eerie pale green as though carrying ocean water soon to be delivered in torrents. The latest band of heavy rain had stopped two hours ago, but random drops continued to fall, plopping into puddles the already-saturated ground couldn't absorb.

Kelly was ready to go. Megan had helped him carry out the last boxes, cramming them into the backseats once the trunk was full.

They had tried to be jolly over a breakfast of cold cereal, finishing a half gallon of milk which otherwise would probably spoil in the fridge with the power out. They'd ignored the real possibility they may never see one another again—that they would each become a pleasant memory of an unforgettable summer. Then again, who knew life's path.

Before either of their watery eyes shed tears, Kelly got in his car and drove off. Megan waved as he turned onto the highway and felt echoes of loneliness in the pit of her stomach once he was out of sight.

Already in her red one-piece and sweats, Megan went back inside the cottage for her carry bag, which today included a rain slicker, two peanut butter sandwiches that would be lunch, and a jug of water.

Time to go to work.

Hurricane Dominic was predicted to make landfall in twelve hours.

#

Pip sat in the passenger seat of his uncle's Maserati, reading text messages on the cellphone he hadn't held in his hand since boarding a flight from Pittsburgh a month ago.

The car's windows were down, a gentle breeze blowing through. Uncle Charles rested his elbow on the sill and looked out onto the Gulf of Mexico. This had been the first waterfront property he'd developed. Sapphire Bay. He'd paid a premium for the land because of the view and been rewarded for his efforts. Pip had been seven years old back then. And when Charles had emailed him a picture of the gulf, Pip had replied, Where are the waves? Their priorities had always been different, even though they looked more alike than Pip and his father, Charles' brother.

People still commented about their resemblance. "He smiles, though," one of the long-time Sapphire Bay tenants told Charles, adding, "You should try it sometime."

As Pip read Megan's texts, Charles watched pelicans skim across the blue water and told his nephew, "Whatever you want to do."

#

The little beach town was clearing out. The evacuation order— still a couple hours away—may have been made unnecessary by the weather forecast.

On Coastal Highway, traffic lights gone blank without electricity swayed in the wind. Cars lined up to take the bridge off the island. An empty soup can spun across the street like a dervish.

A few businesses Megan drove by had boarded over their plate glass windows, but some of those efforts were incomplete, made impossible by wind gusts twisting large sheets of plywood from workers' grip.

This stretch of coastline, rarely in a hurricane's path, wasn't used to dealing with such storms, the general belief being that disaster would choose another path.

When Megan drove beneath the Ocean Vista and pulled into their condo's assigned spot, hers was the only car in the garage.

Sand blew around the building's concrete pilings and mounded against the lobby door.

As the boom of the waves thundered through the whipping wind, Megan leaned hard to stride toward the beach, clutching her bag and buoy against her body with both arms.

There wouldn't be a start-of-the-day signal today. Overnight, town maintenance crews had removed all the guard stands from the beach. But she needed to report the tide level.

Her head turned from blowing sand, she fought her way to the top of the dune path. Ocean water sprayed her eyes, its taste salty on her mouth.

She was awed and scared by waves powering up onto the beach, white water rolling ahead of waist deep surges that reached the face of the dunes then swept back, beginning to uproot clumps of planted grass and drag it out to sea.

The horizon was obscured by the unsettled ocean and galloping clouds, as if the sea and sky were being made one by the approaching storm.

Megan retreated to her building's stairwell, where intruding threads of wind whistled inside the concrete-block shaft. She texted her observations of the ocean to the surf patrol office, then started going door-to-door through her building, making sure no one had remained.

Inside her own unit, it was warm and dark, the stale smell from her absence accentuated by the electricity having gone off.

The view through the glass balcony door—the vantage point from which Cassie had spotted dolphins their first time here—was now terrifying. The ocean rose as if driven by demons, coming to get them.

The building may have been structurally sound, as Stewart said last night, but Megan didn't feel as safe here as in Pip's cottage. She closed the blinds and locked the door on her way out.

Going down the stairs, her neighbor-check complete, she turned her shoulder into the wind and started across the side street toward the row of townhouses where the Clarys had their place. She worried how close the ocean might get to their decks.

That was when she saw the dog.

#

Charles Pippinger was going to get out of his car to give Pip privacy, but Pip pushed out ahead of him, leaving the door open as he headed for the beach, making a call on his phone. Pip was probably angry with him. And maybe had a right to be.

Charles had always wondered about his friends who had children. Most of them did. He'd wondered, but never asked, how do you get them to make the right choices? But as time had gone on, and those friends' children—quite a few anyway—turned into one form of disaster or another, Charles decided his friends obviously had no idea how to help their children. And he'd thought less of them for it. Perhaps it was more complicated than it seemed.

#

The little Highland terrier Bill Clary called Houdini dashed into the dunes, looking as if he was barking, only Megan couldn't hear for the wind and the waves.

She dropped her bag and kicked off her trainers, sprinted barefoot onto a parallel dune path, feet kicking up sand, hoping to get down the beach to intercept the dog before he ended up in the ocean.

As she reached the crest of the dunes, a wave receded, its foamy water sliding back into the sea. She figured that was enough of a break.

She raced onto the wet beach, expecting the dog to dash from the sea grass at any moment. But then another wave came, a crash that shook the shore, and the water rushed hard and fast across the sand, only thigh-deep but powerful enough to knock Megan off her feet. And before that wave pulled back another came in behind it, and perhaps if she'd found her footing, she could have held her place. But then another wave broke, and the ocean took her, a powerful riptide that swept her from shore.

Megan held her breath, tumbled by waves crashing on top of her. Salt water went up her nose. Her buoy line jerked her wrist.

She became disoriented and couldn't tell which way was up. A lack of oxygen began to burn her chest as she felt blindly for the buoy line through swirling water. Her fingers caught the line and she tried to use it as a compass to the surface. Only the buoy was being kept submerged by the weight of the waves.

#

"Talk to me." Charles Pippinger found Pip at the southern end of the Sapphire Bay property, not far from the cabanas that provided welcome shade on hot days.

Pip's jaw was set. His ever-present smile—that Uncle Charles had tested a few times over the past month—was gone.

Pip clutched his phone. No matter how many times he'd called Megan over the past 15 minutes, she hadn't answered. "I need to be there."

"Okay."

"Now," Pip emphasized. "I need to be up there now."

"All right…" Charles wasn't going to debate the point. Because the way to resolve a mistake was to get on top of it fast. He gestured toward his car. "Let's go then."

"Driving's not fast enough."

"Who said anything about a car?"

#

Held underwater by wave after wave, the ache in Megan's chest expanded as her air ran out. She struggled to keep her mouth pressed shut as desperate gasps coughed out. Eyes open, she hoped the brighter color of the sky would show through the ocean and guide her, but the light and the dark seemed like one.

She thought about Cassie. And Pip. And braced for the water to rush into her lungs.

#

The drive to Page Field took 45 minutes.

Pip kept trying to reach Megan, hanging up when his calls went to voice mail.

Uncle Charles suggested he leave a message.

Pip exhaled regret and frustration. "I need to hear her voice when I explain what I've done."

"You can blame me," Charles suggested. "Tell her it was my idea."

"That I agreed with."

An hour later, Pip was ascending into the clear-blue sky, strapped into the passenger seat of a twin-engine Cessna 310 with a veteran pilot who knew how to get down in storms.

445

But unlike in his air force career, and later doing security and private charter work, the pilot needed an airport, and all the small airports along the mid-Atlantic seaboard were already closed because of Hurricane Dominic. Over engine noise, the pilot informed Pip, "And they're talking about closing BWI and National and Philly. Maybe we get up there soon enough. Maybe Dulles stays open. Or I can offer you a parachute."

"I'll do it."

The pilot shook his head. "I'm joking. Wind like they're getting, you'd drop like a spear."

"Get me over water. I'll dive in."

The pilot chucked, then asked, "What's her name?" Assuming all this had to do with love.

"Megan."

"All right. Let's get you to Megan in one piece." He banked the plane hard, heading north.

83.

The pouring rain had guided her, pelting the ocean like small stones that oriented Megan to the surface. She kicked hard and broke the stormy waterline, gasping for air, coughing out seawater that splashed into her mouth. She drew her buoy against her and clutched both arms around it, hanging on as the ocean rose and fell.

Wiping water that splashed her eyes, she swiveled in place searching for shore, but there was no land. Just the rolling ocean and near-blinding rain streaking from clouds that tumbled so fast across the sky Megan couldn't gauge if she was being swept farther out to sea or staying in place.

She tested for the ocean floor, stretching her legs and briefly daring to put her head back underwater. Her toes never touched bottom.

She repositioned herself on her buoy, holding it against her chest as she peered through the rain, desperate to find the shoreline. And told herself she wasn't afraid.

That was an hour ago.

#

The rain didn't let up. The ocean swells continued to lift and drop her, causing bouts of nausea Megan fought to suppress. The weight of her water-logged sweatshirt and pants felt as if pulling her under. She was also getting cold, her body temperature dropping in the ocean water, while being unable to see more than twenty feet in any direction induced a compressing claustrophobia.

But mostly, it was the relentless pounding of the rain, striking her head and shoulders and sounding like tiny panes of glass breaking against the sea.

Pip had told her riptides always fade, so she held on to that hope. If that's even what had drawn her out to sea. It happened so fast it didn't seem real.

Her fear became constant, a mantra she tried to accept and channel aside. But it worsened like the nausea and became harder to ignore.

To fight the cold, she kicked her legs, mindful to conserve strength she'd need to get to shore. To escape the nausea, she took deep breaths and swallowed. To combat the fear, she closed her eyes, hopeful when she opened them the rain would have subsided enough to reveal which way she needed to swim.

She also thought about the white dog, Houdini. And hoped he was safe.

She thought of Cassie, always remembering that first day she'd picked her up and held her in her arms.

She thought about her father, and that if she drowned maybe she'd see him and her mother. She wondered what they'd look like.

She thought about Stewart, and realized how over the years, when she pictured him, it was always in his office or on a construction site. That she didn't picture them together.

And she thought about Pip. How she had never felt about anyone the way she felt about him and how it had taken too long for her to recognize how much she loved him—as if her emotions had been a foreign language she'd been unable to interpret. So simple and yet so complex. A deep intensity behind the pleasure of being with him.

After another thirty minutes, nausea overcame her. She clutched hard onto her buoy and vomited into the ocean. The pressure of being in water made it hard to clear the ropy liquid from her throat and left an acidic residue that burned down into her chest. She kicked her legs but still shivered from the cold and twinges of muscle cramps tightened her calves. Her neck began to stiffen.

When she cried for help it was a feral sound smothered by the wind. Then something bumped against her, and she kicked hard and wildly flailed one arm, splashing at whatever it was, yelling at it. Readying to use her buoy as a weapon when she saw the fin. Then another. She kicked and splashed harder. Yelled, "No, no! No!"

#

As the Cessna flew over South Carolina, Pip tried to reach Megan—again. This time, when his call went to voice mail, he tried Kelly instead.

Kelly, taking his time on the long drive to Cleveland, answered on the third ring, not with hello, but: "You're a jackass you know."

It took Pip fifteen minutes to explain why he'd stayed out of touch. Kelly sighed and muttered, "Friggin' Uncle Charles. But you're still a jackass. And she loves you in spite of that."

"Then why isn't she answering her phone?"

The next time he tried to call Megan, the line didn't ring. Instead, there was a mechanical message that the network was down. He tried to reach Captain Garrison—same result.

#

Megan heard the metallic chirp. And saw more fins. And cheerful long faces and smiling eyes.

She was in a pod of dolphins. They glided through the rollicking sea, bumping against her. She touched their smooth, hard flanks. Grasped the stiff cartilage of a fin and briefly held on as if to take a ride before the dolphin slid away.

And then they were gone. And her fear that abated for seconds returned. As though their presence had somehow been an opportunity she'd missed.

But then she remembered: anytime she'd seen dolphins in the ocean, their course had been parallel to the shore.

She swam for an hour with faith she was keeping a steady direction—hoping she'd aimed herself toward shore and wasn't swimming farther out to sea.

Land refused to appear. The rain and wind remained intense. Swells rose on the ocean, sometimes feeling as if about to lift her from the sea.

She kept swimming. Ignoring she was getting colder. Scissor-kicking through leg cramps until her calf tightened so hard it felt as if the tendons might snap and she had to stop. Wrapping one arm around her buoy, she massaged her leg until the pain abated. Yet as soon as she started to swim again, that muscle tensed unless she kept her ankle bent to stretch her calf. She stopped again to rub her leg. And heard the crash of waves.

Through the rain, the shore appeared in grey silhouette that was blocked from Megan's view whenever a wave crested and rolled over, slamming onto the beach.

Seeing the low buildings, she controlled the urge to swim harder. She wasn't in a riptide, but the storm-driven ocean simultaneously pushed and pulled her. She needed to time her efforts to take advantage of how the sea moved around her. Needed to get through the waves without their force breaking on top of her.

She paddled into a rising swell and was lifted seven or eight feet that caused her stomach to drop as the wave swept past and tumbled onto the beach. When she started forward again, the withdrawing rush from a spent wave drew her back toward deeper water.

She swam harder against the outgoing tide, her arms tiring. Her leg wanted to cramp again. She glanced over her shoulder and saw the next wave rise to a frightening height. She didn't want to get pulled back out. She needed to take this chance.

She sprint-swam until the wave lifted her up, and kept swimming into its face, feeling as if briefly airborne as the wave curled, its bottom dropping out beneath her. She held her breath, being taken down in a heavy crush of white water, her wrist jerked by the hard tug of her buoy's leash as the wave's weight slammed her to the sea floor.

The water rolled her over until she managed to get onto all fours, gasping for breath when another wave crash behind her and knocked her face down.

She clawed wet sand, fingers digging through tiny shells, desperate to cling onto the land.

#

She didn't cry until she was out of the water. Her legs shook and she fell three times, crawling onto the dunes, her sopping-wet sweatshirt and pants becoming coated with sand. She didn't know exactly where she was. Didn't recognize the block where she collapsed beneath the deck of a beach house.

Out of the rain, the panic she'd managed to control while in the ocean seized hold. She wrapped her arms across her chest but couldn't stop shaking, cold, exhausted, and numbed by the realization she could have drowned. Having lost all concept of time—that she'd been in the ocean for almost three hours.

Across the dunes, waves continued to slam onto the beach. The wind howled mercilessly and blew wet bits of sand that stung her face.

She thought again about her father and mother. And cried for Cassie, who she loved as if she was her own daughter. She cried for Stewart, who she had once loved. She cried for Pip, for letting him get away. And she cried for the end of summer.

Until a wave came over the dunes.

84.

Megan struggled to her feet as the breakwater rushed onto the beach—the surge not deep or forceful, but a warning that the ocean was coming. She needed to move.

Coming out from beneath the deck, she was blown sideways and staggered to a signpost where she hung on, her face angled from slanting rain.

Aiming herself toward the highway, she needed to test each forward step with her bare feet, the side street covered above its curbs with water. She saw from the street sign she was eleven blocks north of her building—having been carried so far by the sea she'd come out of the ocean closer to Pip's cottage than her own condo.

There were no cars. No traffic. No people. Only rain and wind.

A row of roof shingles peeled off a small apartment building and sailed into the dark-grey sky like a flock of birds.

Megan ducked low, moving toward a fire hydrant. She was pushed off course by a gust of wind but grasped the hydrant's top just as her toes jammed a submerged curb. From there she sought brief refuge against the side wall of a motel, partially shielded from wind and rain by four levels of concrete block.

She looked at her foot and saw blood oozing around her middle toenail. She took a deep breath and pushed on.

Point by point, she sloshed to the deserted highway. Holding onto the stanchion of a powerless traffic light, she hoped for a vehicle to appear through the rain, someone who might help her. But there was nothing. Signs rocked as pieces of flying debris splashed down onto the street.

She was halfway across the road when the wind knocked her to her hands and knees. In inches of rainwater, she alternated between crawling and walking, the palms of her hands, knees, and feet scraped by loose chunks of macadam. She just kept going. Kept going. But was so tired. So weak.

On all fours in the road, she paused and closed her eyes. Just to rest for a minute.

#

The Cessna 310 set down in Frederick, Maryland. The twin-engine craft no sooner stopped on the runway than Pip shook the pilot's hand and ran through blowing rain toward the small terminal building. The flight had taken six hours, the last sixty minutes of which had been a harrowing battle against violent turbulence the pilot seemed to have enjoyed.

As they'd made their way up the east coast, airports had closed in front of them. Frederick Municipal, at the eastern end of the Blue Ridge Mountains, was as close as they could get to Ocean City, still 180 miles away by road. And that was assuming the Bay Bridges remained open.

Inside the terminal, a representative from a concierge service that Pip's Uncle Charles used handed Pip the keys to an SUV. The paperwork had already been taken care of.

Ten minutes after landing, he was on the road, windshield wipers slapping at the rain. He tried to phone Megan—again. The call still wouldn't go through. The storm had taken out cell service.

Pip drove fast through the weather. Over an hour later, when he got to the Bay Bridge, there was a high wind warning, but the spans were still open.

Across the Chesapeake and on the Eastern Shore, the rain intensified. Visibility became a challenge. And darkness was setting in.

Pip kept calling Megan, then tried Garrison, but the connections wouldn't go through.

Once he reached Easton, it rained even harder. Wind buffeted the heavy vehicle. But Pip knew these roads. Had driven them since he was 16. And going in this direction had always been the best—going to the beach. Not away from it. Damned Uncle Charles. And damned himself for listening to him.

Half an hour later, where Route 50 made a bend through Cambridge, Pip could barely see two car lengths in front of him. Flashing taillights warned of two other cars inching their way forward through standing water in both lanes.

Pip checked the latest weather updates on his phone. Hurricane Dominic had category 4 wind speed of 140 miles per hour and was predicted to make landfall in four hours. In Ocean City.

85.

The storm disoriented Megan to all sense of time. She had no idea how long she'd been out of the ocean but could finally see Pip's cottage. Through driving rain and the onset of nightfall, the little house appeared at the end of the street.

She leaned forward at the waist, using her arms for balance like wings against the wind. Each stride sloshed through ankle deep water and the soles of her feet, even though calloused by a barefoot summer, became raw from loose bits of road detritus. The oyster shell driveway was especially torturous, each step shooting pain.

She again ended up on her hands and knees to close the final distance to the front door, then realized she didn't have a key to get inside. She hung her head, her wet hair falling around her face, rain pelting her back. Thinking she needed to find a way to break in, she remembered Kelly saying something about jiggling the doorknob. So she tried that, turning it back and forth, slowly at first, then rapidly, until the knob twisted freely, the door opened, and she was inside.

She put her back against the door and shoved it closed, then slid down to the floor, dripping wet, a puddle forming around her as she closed her eyes.

It was warm in the house. And dark—the power still out. It seemed quiet because the walls partially muffled the storm's screams that had been driving straight into her ears for hours.

She wiped a hand across her face, pushing water from her eyes, and swept back her hair. She was relieved, but so tired. And scared.

She felt the cottage being moved by the wind, rocking on its foundation.

Was this the hurricane? Was it here? Or was it going to get worse? There was no one to ask. Her phones were back on the beach, possibly out in the ocean now, left in the carry bag she'd dropped in the dunes when she'd gone running for the dog. There was no landline in the cottage. No power to supply the wi-fi router or TV.

She pulled herself to her feet and made her way shakily to the downstairs bathroom. Without hot water to take a shower, she peeled out of wet clothes and wrapped herself in a towel. It felt good to be dry. The toe she'd stubbed had a split nail but was no longer bleeding. The bottoms of her feet were scraped, but not cut.

In the kitchen, windows let in what remained of the sky's dark-grey light. Megan looked outside. The bay had risen through the cattails and submerged the yard, pushing small waves against the cottage's back wall.

Please let the storm stop. But she imagined there were hours yet to go.

Eyes growing accustomed to the darkness, she filled half a dozen glasses with water from the tap and drank one, gulping back an initial swell of nausea it brought on. She opened the jar of peanut butter and slowly ate a few spoonsful sitting at the table, keeping her eyes closed most of the time, trying to block back the fear.

She couldn't seem to stop shaking. Her entire body trembled. Anxiety she guessed. Exhaustion. Hunger?

An especially intense band of rain beat hard against the old windows, a rapid succession of marble-sized droplets smacking the glass.

Moments later, Megan noticed a wet spot on the floor. Bay water was finding its way inside along the door sill.

She went upstairs to Pip's bedroom, where it was warmer than downstairs and much louder from rain pounding the roof and wind trying to pull it apart. She put on shorts and a t-shirt and crawled into bed, folding a pillow around her head to try to block out the noise.

The bed felt good and after a few minutes with her eyes closed, she drifted into a strange sleep that was more like exhaustion and began to dream of the people she'd thought about while caught in the ocean.

She imagined her father and mother as they looked when she was a little girl, the way she remembered them the best. The happy family they'd been before her father died and her mother never truly smiled afterwards—as if the sole source of her happiness had been taken away.

She saw Cassie as that little girl the first day she picked her up into her arms. But then also as the young adult who drunkenly told her she wasn't her mother.

And then there was Stewart, who she'd found attractive and caring that evening they met, and later began to feel she was trying to make whole again after the death of his wife—someone who had lost their beloved spouse, as had her mother. And while she had loved and cared for Stewart, what she was most drawn to about him was that he was Cassie's father. In Megan's dream—or was she awake?—she wondered if she would have fallen in love with Stewart if he'd simply been an unmarried man without such a precious child? There was no way to know.

And then there was Pip. Picturing him, she heard her father's voice, telling her how no one loved her as much as he did, but he hoped one day someone would. And how for the sweetest of moments this summer, it had seemed as if her father's wish for her had come true. But then summer ended.

Megan wasn't sure if she was awake or still dreaming as she thought of Pip and snapped her fingers and whispered, "Let's go. You and me. Let's just go." Moments before the water came.

The tidal wave, driven by the hurricane, started off the coast and rose high and strong and merciless. It crested, turned over, and slammed onto shore, driving a wall of water through the dunes and across the highway, shoving small buildings off their pilings, throwing aside cars, taking down powerlines, smashing windows, and was still five feet deep as it charged across the narrowest point of the island toward the bay and broke down the cottage front door without needing to jiggle the lock.

Megan heard the water coming, but also a voice. And felt arms lift her. Pip's voice. Pip's arms. He said, "Let's go."

86.

The storm damage could have been much worse.

Bill Clary scoffed at that sentence in the newspaper—the print version he picked up from the small grocery store he walked to from his house in Annapolis. It could have been worse—someone always said that after a bad storm, no matter how horrible it had been, as though it was supposed to make people feel better. Scare them to death beforehand, then show a silver lining after it's over. That's what journalism had become. Sensationalism to sell papers, or hold eyeballs, or whatever they called it online.

Five days after Hurricane Dominic's wind and rain slammed Ocean City, the sun shone and the sky was clear and blue, as if Mother Nature would never cast bad fate upon anyone.

The Clary's beachfront townhouse had suffered minor damage, or so the group that managed their oceanfront complex reported: minimal water intrusion around the ocean-facing storm doors Bill had been telling the condo board needed to be replaced for years. Bill would see for himself in a few days. He and Mary Jane had planned to return to the beach tomorrow, but something had come up.

Bill read the rest of the front-page article in a small coffee shop around the corner from the Naval Academy gates. The most severe damage from the storm had been caused by the tidal wave that surged across the town's narrowest stretch, completely taking down some of the older wood-framed houses and condo buildings and so severely damaging a handful of concrete buildings that they'd been condemned. Powerlines had been toppled and sections of road washed away, including portions of Coastal Highway, which was no longer passable. Aerial images of that two-block span of bomb-like devastation had appeared in news articles worldwide. Damages sustained by the rest of the town, while into the hundreds of millions of dollars, seemed minor by comparison.

There were seven reported deaths, which made the storm the island's deadliest in history. That number was expected to rise as a dozen people remained hospitalized, and, at last count, 11 others remained missing. Among the missing was Megan Tyler.

Rescue workers found Megan's surf patrol bag, soaking wet and half covered with sand, its carry strap caught around a broken signpost at the head of the side street just south of the Ocean Vista. Speculation was that she'd gone in the ocean on a save.

Social media, as it was want to do, swarmed back to #OCSPMOM. Bill Clary did not understand the psychology that drove Twitter and the like and was unsure why people were compelled to publish their feelings and condolences, as if trying to use a tragedy to steal attention for themselves. He found it vulture-like, but recognized he was from a different generation. His time, his era was over.

Although, now and again, he was still called on to rise to the occasion.

Finished his coffee—all while resisting a doughnut—he set his Washington Nationals' cap on his head and walked back to his house along tree-lined streets. Stepping inside, he announced, "I'm back," to Mary Jane, saying that loudly enough to project through the entire 2,800-square-foot home. "You ready?"

His wife appeared at the top of the stairs, tastefully dressed in a blouse and slacks as if meeting a design client.

Bill rested his sun-spotted hand on the heavy newel post that was original to the 90-year-old house.

Mary Jane hesitated. "It doesn't feel right."

460

Bill nodded. "I understand, darling." It had taken him a while to come around to the idea himself.

"But you want to go," Mary Jane advised, "you go ahead."

"All right."

"Drive safely."

"You know I will."

Bill blew her a kiss, then continued along the hallway, the walls painted a rich caramel above white wainscoting. Car keys already in his pocket, he went out the side door to the attached garage, got into his BMW and turned onto the cobblestone street, making his way out of town. Merging onto Route 50, he normally would head east—toward the beach. Today, he turned to the west and *Rome, DC.*

#

The concierge in the small apartment house off Dupont Circle, near Ambassador's Row, delivered the letter-sized envelope to Cassie Tyler's studio on the second floor, reporting that it had been dropped off by an older gentleman who had a very nice Rolex watch and a wore a baseball cap of some sort.

Cassie assumed it was another condolence, although no one who'd called or texted or stopped by so far had wanted to suggest or imply what Cassie believed was true—and was the reason Cassie had cried for days and not been to school or work: that her mother—that Megan—was dead.

Her father wanted Cassie to come to California. But Cassie was determined to remain until she knew for sure what had happened to her mom.

The envelope did not have a return address, only Cassie's name penned on the outside, in a handwriting she didn't recognize.

But the writing on the letter inside she knew at once.

#

461

Cass—I'm alive and I love you. I need to say that first. Next is to apologize for not saying all this in person or at least on the phone. But I hope you will read all this before you do anything or tell anyone, including your dad.

When we were last together at the beach, I told you how I have loved you since the first day I saw you when you'd fallen and were crying, and I picked you up. I can still feel what it was like to hold you in my arms. I still love you. I will always love you.

During that same visit, you asked me if I still loved your dad. I didn't answer because I was struggling with that. I knew I felt differently about him, but I couldn't figure out if it was just the way love changes over time for husband and wife, or if that love had gone away.

On the day of the storm, I was on the beach and saw a little dog I thought was going to get swept away in the ocean. I was trying to stop him from getting near the water when a wave came and I can't remember exactly how it happened, but it pulled me in. I ended up being taken out in the ocean and it was incredibly rough for what I guess was a couple hours before I managed to swim in.

And now I realize I did think I was going to drown, but that thought didn't stay in my mind while I was actually out there. And I think the reason I managed not to panic or give up was from watching you—how you played sports. That determination you got from your dad, and probably your mom. You gave that to me, and it saved my life.

While I was out in the ocean, I thought about people I loved, and I thought about you, and my mom and dad. And I thought about your dad, and how he has always been such a wonderful parent, how protective he is of you, how much he loves you, and how generous and smart he is. What a wonderful businessman he is. All such wonderful qualities, which makes me sad to realize I don't love him anymore. I wish I did. But he and I have become so different. The world is full of women who would love to love him. I'm just not one of them anymore. I'm so sorry.

I will leave it entirely to you whether to tell your dad about this letter. Or to tell him that I'm alive. Maybe it's best for him to believe I'm dead.

When we were in California, the lawyer, Lassiter, told me your dad was being considered to take over the new company he's with. Maybe you know this. Lassiter told me my role as your dad's wife was critical to his

DREAMS FOR THE END OF SUMMER

success. That Mr. Dunhill wouldn't want to think I was any sort of distraction for your dad. And I think us getting a divorce might cause a problem for your dad with Mr. Dunhill. Maybe I have that wrong, but I talked with a lawyer a week before the hurricane, and it seems like maybe it's simpler for me to be dead, at least as most of the world is concerned.

I didn't plan this. To disappear. But when the storm hit, I wasn't in our place. I was somewhere else, and it was right where the tidal wave came through. It was harrowing but I got out. And when it happened, all I wanted was to go. To leave. To disappear. It was like what Captain Garrison said that night we had dinner with the surf patrol guards. Sometimes you just have to go. That's exactly what it felt like. And that's what I've done.

I'm a long way away now. Farther away than I've ever been.

Your dad may not understand how I can do this. You may not understand. But I'll leave it to you whether to try to explain it, or whether you think he may be better off, less hurt, thinking I'm dead. However you believe it's best for the two of you, I will do. And if you want to believe I'm dead, if you're angry or hurt, I understand. If you never want to have anything more to do with me, I'll need to accept that. Or maybe we can find some way to stay in touch. Because the chance of losing you is the hardest part of all of this. But you will be strong because that's just the way you are. And you will be determined. And you will do what's right, even if I haven't.

Please be assured that I'm safe now, and healthy, and, most of all, I am loved.

The letter was signed simply, *Mom.*

87.

19 months later.

For their 50th wedding anniversary, Bill and Mary Jane Clary flew first class from Dulles to Juan Santamaria, the flight from suburban Virginia to San Jose, Costa Rica taking just over five hours. Another two-plus hours from the airport by Jeep, crossing lush mountains and descending toward the coast, the roads no longer paved but turned to gravel then dirt, and they arrived in a beach village usually identified by its proximity to populated towns.

Although unnamed on maps, locals had begun to refer to the secluded spot as *Playa de los Sueños*—the beach of dreams—as the stretch of crystal sand was now called by the couple who had built a small bungalow and trio of colorful two-room cottages they rented out by the week.

Online, the property was marketed as a resort, but made clear it was more like stepping back in time than being emersed in indulgences. Yes, there was air-conditioning, and electric, and filtered running water, and a reasonable cell signal and satellite wifi, but beyond that there was only the silver beach and turquoise ocean. The nearest town with shops and restaurants was a 45-minute drive away. At night, the only sounds came from insects trilling in the nearby jungle and waves gliding onto the sand.

As the driver set the Clarys' luggage on the crushed shell driveway and thanked Bill for a generous tip, Megan came out of the house, waving happily as she stepped off the front porch.

Mary Jane whispered gladly to her husband with a sense of relief: "She looks wonderful."

"Love what you've done to the place," Bill called as Megan came toward them along the walkway.

She'd let her hair grow and it fell over her bare shoulders. She wore a strapless sundress of a bold tropical print, orange and red flowers against a background of palm fronds. Her skin was deeply tanned. She was six-months pregnant.

Bill hugged her, mindful of her belly. "Bambino still doing good?"

"Fantastic." Megan held onto him and patted his back. "It's so nice to see you."

"You too, honey."

"He been behaving?" Megan asked Mary Jane, giving the shorter woman a hug.

"Mostly. When I'm watching."

"Happy Anniversary," Megan congratulated.

"Thank you," Mary Jane appreciated.

Bill pointed beyond the sway of palm trees toward the beach and chuckled. "Love that touch."

The familiar outline of a lifeguard stand made for a striking silhouette against the ocean.

"That our boy out there?" Bill squinted into late afternoon sun.

Megan shaded her eyes and spotted Pip swimming beyond the waves.

"Never gets old, does it?" Bill asked, sensing Megan's contentment as they stood in the breeze.

They watched Pip angle toward shore and catch a wave he bodysurfed to the beach. Seeing their guests, he came trotting across the soft sand. "You made it! Happy Anniversary!"

"Here's our boy!" Bill greeted as Mary Jane stepped forward for a hug.

"I'm all wet," Pip warned with a smile.

Mary Jane didn't care.

Like Megan, Pip's hair was longer than when he worked for the surf patrol and during that brief stint for Uncle Charles, but it was still blond. And while he remained dark-tanned from days in the sun, he was slightly thicker in the arms and shoulders, because hours once spent in the ocean now involved swinging a hammer and hauling lumber.

"Looking good, son," Bill said as their handshake turned into a hug.

"You, too. Let's get you settled." Pip reached for their suitcases.

Bill said, "We packed light. One of us, anyway."

They strolled to the cottage closest to the main house, the one painted bright blue with yellow shutters, inspired by the little beach houses Megan had seen in Newport Coast two years ago.

"You're making good progress here," Bill congratulated.

Behind the three oceanfront guest houses, land had been hand-cleared for two more and small marker-flags noted the proposed corners of the next foundation.

"It's been good," Pip replied. "But no guests this week. Just the four of us."

"Four and a half," Bill said, smiling at Megan.

"Four and two-thirds," Pip calculated based on Megan's due date.

Inside the blue guest cottage, sunlight shone through ocean-facing windows. The ceilings were open to the rafters, which made the small space feel larger. The living area was open to a compact kitchen and included a table that seated four. The bedroom felt a little snug with a king bed, but there was a small walk-in closet and an ample bathroom with a tub/shower combination. The interior walls were a colorful mix of painted drywall and paneling and some tile, a design element suggested by Mary Jane to give the feeling the construction had been from salvaged materials. The floors were painted wood.

Mary Jane and Bill had been involved in the project from its inception—the idea of it, not the financing. Funding came from Uncle Charles, who had "restructured" the deal he'd offered Pip after Aunt Nan's death. That original proposal from Uncle Charles had been that Pip not return to Ocean City but work for him in Naples.

If Pip worked for 90 days, during which he would completely break all contact with his "beach life" including the "married woman" he'd gotten involved with, Uncle Charles would pay Pip $50,000 in addition to his salary. And after 90 days, Pip would get his money and could stay on in Naples with Uncle Charles or go back to Maryland or do whatever he wanted to do. And if the married woman Pip was involved with really loved him, she'd wait for him. That's what Uncle Charles had told Pip. And Pip, backed into a financial corner—his Jeep beyond repair and his cottage on the bay soon to go to Aunt Nan's stepchildren—not to mention the guilt he felt for having fallen in love with another man's wife, had agreed.

Part of that deal had included Pip giving his cellphone to Uncle Charles—not that Uncle Charles didn't trust him to abide by the terms of their arrangement, but to eliminate the temptation.

"The pictures don't do it justice," Mary Jane said once inside the blue cottage. "This is so lovely. Or maybe it's just seeing the two of you."

Megan put her arm around the shorter woman. "We love you, too."

"Good job here," Bill said of the construction. "You're a quick learner."

"Hope so," Pip appreciated. "I'm doing the next two on my own. Marco's gone back to Florida."

Marco had been a dispatch from Uncle Charles as part of his investment, a construction manager who guided Pip through the development so far.

Uncle Charles, though, had yet to set foot on the property, part as a means of showing Pip he believed in him but also in apology to Megan for interfering with their lives and wanting to make clear he would keep his distance and not repeat that mistake. Although Megan had forgiven him, understanding decisions made out of love were not always logical.

Megan and Pip assumed the Clarys would want to rest up after their trip, but Bill and Mary Jane were both eager to catch up. It had been a long time since they'd been together in person—a tense visit in Mexico City over a year ago when the logistics of Megan's continued disappearance had been arranged.

After the hurricane, Megan and Pip had gone south, not to Naples but New Orleans where one of Pip's former surf patrol guards managed a small hotel. It was there that Megan wrote the letter to Cassie that Bill delivered.

Mary Jane had been unsettled by Megan's decision to "stay missing," and hadn't wanted Bill to become involved. She kept telling him Megan was none of their business. But at the same time, Mary Jane felt it too, deep inside, the connection to their late daughter that Megan awakened in both of them. Still, Mary Jane had been uncomfortable about the plan, always having been the black-or-white thinker of their marriage while Bill's career had navigated a much greyer world. But she'd come around.

Three months after Hurricane Dominic, Mary Jane flew to Mexico City with Bill, a place they'd lived for a year when it had been one of Bill's first posts after Vietnam, a location where he still had friends. Megan and Pip had entered the country by boat, because while Pip had a passport and other papers, Megan had none, which made their arrival and travel in a foreign country nerve wracking. But they'd followed Bill's directions and met the Maryland couple in Mexico City, where Bill arranged for Megan to get a Canadian passport, her name now Megan Kelly.

They stayed in Mexico City for a couple months, both getting jobs at an international school. Every morning and night, Pip asked Megan if she wanted to go back to the states, if living what felt like "on the run" was too much for her. And her answer was always the same, that she loved him more now than ever and had no urge to go back. He said he felt the same.

Less than two years after not wanting to move to Scottsdale with Stewart, Megan found herself traveling happily across Central America with Pip—but that's the way love was.

It wasn't long after arriving in Costa Rica that they'd decided it would be home. And when first visiting the beach where they were now, Megan had been reminded of the old cottages she'd seen being restored on the beach in Newport Coast, and they came up with the idea of building a small resort.

Pip had arranged meetings with a local real estate agent and banker and was trying to develop a plan to attract investors when Uncle Charles stepped in and said he'd put up the cash.

That good news had arrived the same day that Megan received a text from Cassie. Their communication had become strained since Megan's letter, but Cassie had kept Megan's secret, ultimately not out of love or loyalty to Megan, but because she thought her father would be devastated to know Megan had left him for someone else. Not knowing details of Megan's new life, including who she was with or where, Cassie thought it would be easier for Stewart to believe Megan was dead.

Stewart had moved forward on that assumption. Less than five months after Megan was reported missing, Stewart filed legal proceedings through Lassister's law firm that resulted in Megan being declared dead. Months later, just as Megan and Pip were finishing construction on their new beach house and first cottage, Stewart was named CEO of Dunhill Infrastructure and married Jackie Mack, the real estate agent who'd shown them the house in Newport Beach. Stewart and Jackie Mack-Tyler had since moved into a larger house closer to the beach and were now considered one of Orange County's new power couples.

As for the Clarys, their involvement with Megan and Pip over the past year-plus had awakened their wanderlust.

During dinner on the Clarys first night in Costa Rica, the four of them eating grilled fish at a table on the beach as the last of sunset glowed along the horizon, Bill said that after their planned week at *La Playa de los Sueños*, they were going on a month-long tour of South America. And from there, who knew. They were getting tired of the cold and the crowds—not just at the beach, but in Annapolis. "Sure see the appeal of a place like this," he remarked. "The quiet."

"Far from Rome, DC," Pip said.

"Yes, it is," Bill chuckled.

When Megan asked Mary Jane if that meant she was retiring, the older woman said she'd already cut back and had only been doing small jobs close to home. "No more traveling. No more days at a time apart."

"Misses me," Bill grinned.

"Imagine that." Mary Jane shook her head.

Bill said, "And we got an offer to sell Ocean City—the townhouse. Might as well take it. Town's not the same. I picture going there, I'm seeing the way it was years ago. Not how it is anymore. Your boy Will was there again last summer. And the girl runs the beach stand, rents the umbrellas—she was back."

"Lulu," Megan said fondly.

"Yep. Never saw the other two."

Pip set down his fork, finished the fish he'd cooked. "Art started working with his dad in an elevator company. And Adrian's with a guy who goes to medical school up north, Tufts. Boston? And she's thinking about medical school herself. Or being a physician's assistant."

Megan missed them whenever she heard their names. The hardest part about what she'd done, apart from Cassie, was no longer being in touch with the people she'd grown so close to the summer she met Pip.

She and Pip had taken a few chances. When they were in New Orleans, Pip had called the three other guards and Lulu and told them not to be sad about Megan, without divulging she was still alive. Only Adrian had guessed, "She's with you, isn't she?" And Pip hadn't denied it.

The only person Megan had reached out to, other than Cassie, was Kelly. She'd called him in the middle of the night, and when he'd groggily answered his phone, she said, "Kell, you need to pretend this is a dream. This is Megan. I've run away with Pip. We're alive and we're fine. Hiding from the world." After taking a moment to digest that, Kelly had responded, "Hide well, my loves."

Megan often thought about Alice and the students she used to teach at Villa James and online. She hoped they had the imagination to think she'd disappeared, not died. She had not been in contact with Jillian, who not that long ago she'd considered her best friend, but from whom, like Stewart, she'd grown apart. She didn't trust Jillian to keep secret that she was alive, much as she'd never confided in her about Pip.

After dinner, the two couples carried their empty plates into the main house, where Bill and Pip handled clean-up. Megan and Mary Jane sat in the living room, the windows open and a gentle breeze coming through the screens.

When Bill made noise about expatriating and moving to Costa Rica and not paying any more taxes, Mary Jane warned him not to tempt her.

Bill laughed, "Never thought she'd agree with that."

Over the next few days, that idle fantasy started to take shape. Bill joined Pip and an architect at a meeting at the municipal permits office, where applications were filed for the next two cottages. Mary Jane accompanied Megan to her obstetrician's appointment, an hour's drive away. They all went into town, where Megan and Pip introduced them to some of the people and places they'd been telling them about during phone calls that had become more frequent over the last months.

Their time together was easy and warm, as though they'd all known one another for years.

Two nights before the Clarys were scheduled to leave, Megan rolled over in bed and touched Pip's chest. "I like having them here."

He nodded. "I know."

The next evening, as the four of them enjoyed another barefoot dinner on the beach, their conversation ebbed into a thoughtful moment of quiet—an easy silence that Bill broke, his voice quieter than usual as he reached for Mary Jane's hand and gave a gentle squeeze, as if seeking her permission. After she nodded, Bill said, "We been talking—the two of us. About maybe building a little house like this ... maybe not too far away ... be nice to watch a young one grow up."

Megan stood from the table and went around to Mary Jane, hugging her from behind. "We don't want you to go."

Pip told Bill, "We started talking about it last night. We can have the architect redraw one of the next cottages—make it bigger. However you want it. Stay as long as you like."

And with that, plans were changed—both on paper and in life. The Clarys' South American tour was cancelled. Airline tickets were refunded. Their house in Annapolis was listed for sale.

The only sad times were when Megan thought about Cassie.

"You haven't mentioned her all week," Bill said, finding Megan alone on the beach one morning. Pip had gone into town and Mary Jane had ridden shotgun, eager to start setting up their bank accounts. "You hear from her?" Bill asked about Cassie.

"Not for a few months now—no." Megan looked out at the calm sea, so much different from the raging ocean that had carried her from shore during the hurricane. "I see online she seems to be doing well. She's still at GW. And working for the same company part-time—and that company's growing."

Bill exhaled sympathetically. "I know that hurts. But not everyone stays close to their children no matter what. I have friends whose kids live halfway around the world. Hardly ever call."

"I knew it was a lot to ask her to keep my secret from her father. As far as I know, though, she never told him I'm still alive. But I think for her to stay in touch with me, I think that was too much. I don't blame her if she's angry."

"Don't blame yourself, either. The bigger lie's pretending something's there when it's not."

"I just never thought it was possible to be this in love with someone."

"And one day, your Cassie will know that, too. And she'll find someone to love, who loves her back as much as you love Pip."

"I hope so."

"Dreams do come true."

THE END

The author hopes you enjoyed this book and welcomes your comments, which may be emailed to: pres@prestonpairo.com.

Your rating or review at Amazon.com or Goodreads would be appreciated.

—

Preston Pairo is the author of 15 novels, including the thrillers *The Pretty Woman Who Lived Next Door, Her Honor, City Lies,* and *Razor Moon Antigua;* the Ocean City Mysteries, *Big Blow* and *One Dead Judge;* and *The Builder,* a modern romance.

For more information, please visit:
www.prestonpairo.com
or follow Pres at:
www.facebook.com/prestonpairo/

To receive email updates about Pres' books
and other writing, including free offers please visit:
https://prestonpairo.substack.com/

(6/12/24)

474

Made in the USA
Middletown, DE
02 August 2024

58408808R00286